The Collected
Supernatural and Weird
Fiction of
Sabine Baring-Gould

The Collected Supernatural and Weird Fiction of Sabine Baring-Gould

Including Three Novelettes
'Margery of Quether,' 'Mustapha' and 'A Profes-sional Secret' and Twenty-Two Short Stories
of the Strange and Unusual

Sabine Baring-Gould

LEONAUR

The Collected
Supernatural and Weird
Fiction of
Sabine Baring-Gould
Including Three Novelettes 'Margery of Quether,' 'Mustapha' and 'A Professional Secret'
and Twenty-Two Short Stories of the Strange and Unusual
by Sabine Baring-Gould

FIRST EDITION

Leonaur is an imprint
of Oakpast Ltd

ISBN: 978-0-85706-876-7 (hardcover)
ISBN: 978-0-85706-877-4 (softcover)

http://www.leonaur.com

Publisher's Notes

The views expressed in this book are not necessarily
those of the publisher.

Contents

Margery of Quether

(A tale from *Margery of Quether and Other Stories*)

This is written by my own hand, entirely unassisted. I am George Rosedhu, of Foggaton, in the parish of Lamerton, and in the county of Devon—whether to write myself Mister or Esquire, I do not know. My father was a yeoman, so was my grandfather, idem my great-grandfather. But I notice that when anyone asks of me a favour, or writes me a begging letter, he addresses me as Esquire, whereas he who has no expectation of getting anything out of me invariably styles me Mister. I have held my acres for five hundred years—that is, my family the Rosedhus have, in direct lineal descent, always in the male line, and I intend, in like manner, to hand it on, neither impaired nor enlarged, to my own son, when I get one, which I am sure of, as the Rosedhus always have had male issue. But what with Nihilism, and Communism, and Tenant-right, and Agricultural Holdings legislation, threatened by Radicals and Socialists, there is no knowing where a man with ancestral acres stand, and, in the general topsy-turvyism into which we are plunging—God bless me!—I may be driven, heaven preserve me, to have only female issue. There is no knowing to what we landed proprietors are coming.

Before I proceed with my story, I must apologise for anything that smacks of rudeness in my style. I do not mean to say that there is anything intrinsically rude in my literary productions, but that the present taste is so vitiated by slipshod English and effeminacy of writing, that the modern reader of periodicals may not appreciate my composition as it deserves. Roast beef does not taste its best after Indian curry.

My education has been thorough, not superficial. I was reared in none of your "Academies for Young Gentlemen," but brought up on the Eton Latin Grammar and cane at the Tavistock Free Grammar School. The consequence is that what I pretend to know, I know. I am a practical man with a place in the world, and when I leave it, there will be a hole which will be felt, just as when a molar is removed from the jaw.

There is no exaggeration in saying that my family is as old as the hills, for a part of my estate covers a side of that great hog's-back now called Black Down, which lies right before my window; and anyone who knows anything about the old British tongue will tell you that Rosedhu is the Cornish for Black Down. Well, that proves that we held land here before ever the Saxons came and drove the British language across the Tamar. My title-deeds don't go back so far as that, but there are some of them which, though they be in Latin, I cannot decipher. The hills may change their names, but the Rosedhus never. My house is nothing to boast of. We have been yeomen, not squires, and we have never aimed at living like gentry. Perhaps that is why the Rosedhus are here still, and the other yeomen families round have gone scatt (I mean, gone to pieces). If the sons won't look to the farm and the girls mind the dairy, the family cannot thrive.

Foggaton is an ordinary farmhouse substantially built of volcanic stone, black, partly with age, and partly because of the burnt nature of the stone. The windows are wide, of wood, and always kept painted white. The roof is of slate, and grows some clumps of stone-crop, yellow as gold.

Foggaton lies in a combe, that is, a hollow lap, in Yaffell—or as the maps call it, Heathfield. Yaffell is a huge elevated bank of moor to the north-west and west, and what is very singular about it is, that at the very highest point of the moor an extinct volcanic cone protrudes, and rises to the height of about twelve hundred feet. This is called Brentor, and it is crowned with a church, the very tiniest in the world I should suppose, but tiny as it is it has chancel, nave, porch, and west tower like any Christian parish church. There is also a graveyard round the church. This occupies a little platform on the top of the mountain, and there is absolutely no room there for anything else. To the west, the rocks are quite precipitous, but the peak can be ascended from the east up a steep grass slope strewn with pumice.

The church is dedicated to St. Michael, and the story goes that, whilst it was being built, every night the devil removed as many stones as had been set on the foundations during the day. But the archangel was too much for him. He waited behind Cox Tor, and one night threw a great rock across and hit the Evil One between the horns, and gave him such a headache that he desisted from interference thenceforth. The rock is there, and the marks of the horns are distinctly traceable on it. I have seen them scores of times myself. I do not say that the story is true; but I do say that the marks of the horns are on the stone. It is said also that there is a depression caused by the thumb of St. Michael. I have looked at it carefully, but I express no opinion thereon—that may have been caused by the weather.

Looking up Foggaton Coombe, clothed in oak coppice and with a brawling stream dancing down its furrow, Brentor has a striking effect, soaring above it high into the blue air, with its little church and tower topping the peak.

I am many miles from Lamerton, which is my parish church, and all Heathfield lies between, so, as divine service is performed every Sunday in the church of St. Michael de Rupe, I ascend the rocky pinnacle to worship there.

You must understand that there is no road, not even a path to the top; one scrambles up over the turf, in windy weather cling-ing to the heather bushes. It is a famous place for courting, that is why the lads and lasses are such church-going folk hereabout. The boys help the girls up, and after service hold their hands to help them down. Then, sometimes a maiden lays hold of a gorse bush in mistake for a bunch of heath, and gets her pretty hand full of prickles. When that happens, her young man makes her sit down beside him under a rock away from the wind, that is, from the descending congregation, and he pricks the prickles out of her rosy palm with a pin. As there are thousands of prickles on a gorse bush, this sometimes takes a long time, and as the pin sometimes hurts, and the maid winces, the lad has to squeeze her hand very tight to hold it steady. I've known thorns drawn out with kisses.

I always do say that parsons make a mistake when they build churches in the midst of the population. Dear, simple, conceited souls, do they really suppose that folks go to church to hear them preach? No such things—that is the excuse; they go for a romp. Parsons should think of that, and make provision accordingly, and set the sacred edifice on the top of moor or down, or in shady corners where there are long lanes well wooded. Church paths are always lovers' lanes.

When a woman gets too old for sweethearting—if that time ever arrives, in her own opinion—she goes to church for scandalmongery, and, of course, the farther she has to go, the more time she has for talk and the outpour of gossip. I know the butcher at Lydford kills once a week. Sunday is the character-killing day with us, and all our womankind are the butchers.

Well!—this is all neither here nor there. I was writing about my house, and I have been led into a digression on church-going. However, it is not a digression either; it may seem so to my readers, but I know what I am about, and as my troubles came of church-going, what I have said is not so much out of the way as some superficial and inconsiderate readers may have supposed. I return, for a bit to the description of my farmhouse. As I have said once, and I insist on it again, Foggaton makes no pretensions to be other than a substantial yeoman's residence. You can smell the pigs' houses as you come near, and I don't pretend that the scent arises from clematis or wisteria.

The cowyard is at the back, and there is plenty of mud in the lane, and streams of water running down the cart ruts, and skeins of oats and barley straw hanging to the hollies in the hedge.

There is no gravel drive up to the front door, but there is a little patch of turf before it walled off from the lane, with crystals of white spar ornamenting the top of the wall. In the wall is a gate, and an ascent by four granite steps to a path sanded with mundic gravel that leads just twelve feet six inches across the grass plot to the front door. This door is bolted above and below, and chained and doubled-locked, but the back door that leads from the yard into the kitchen is always open, and I go in and out by that. The front door is for ornament, not use, except on grand occasions.

The rooms of Foggaton are low, and I can touch the ceiling easily in each with my hand; I can touch that in the bedrooms with my head. Low rooms are warmer and more homelike than the tall rooms of Queen Ann's and King George's reigns.

On the other side of Heathfield is Quether, a farm that has belonged to the Palmers pretty nigh as long as Foggaton has belonged to the Rosedhus. Farmer John Palmer is a man of some substance, one of the old sort of yeomen, fresh in colour, with light blue eyes and fair hair; he is big-made and stout. He is a man who knows the world and can make money. He has a lime-kiln as well as a farm, but the lime-kiln is not his own; he rents it. His daughter Margaret is a very pretty girl. He has several sons, and a swarm of small children of no particular sex. They are all in petticoats. So Margaret can't take much with her when she marries. Margaret used to go to chapel, but her religious views underwent a change since one Sunday afternoon she visited Brentor church. This change in her was not produced by anything in the parson's sermon, but by the fact that I was there, aged three and twenty, was good-looking, and the sole owner of Foggaton.

I accompanied her back to Quether. Since that Sunday she has been very regular in her devotions at St. Michael de Rupe; she has, I understand, returned her missionary box to the minister of the chapel, and no longer collects for the conversion of the heathen. As for me, I became a much more regular attendant at church after that Sunday afternoon than I had been before. When the day was windy, I helped Margaret up the rock, and

held her hand very tightly in mine, for had she missed her foot-
ing she might have perished. When the day was rainy, we shared
one gig umbrella. When the day was windy *and* rainy, it was better still; for the gig umbrella could not be unfurled, so I folded
my wide waterproof over us both. When the day was foggy, that
was best of all, for then we lost our way in the fog, and could not
find the church door till service was ended. On sunshiny days
we were merry; in rain and fog, sentimental.

One Sunday she and I had gone round to the west end of
the church after service. I told her that I wanted to show her
Kit Hill, where the Britons made their last stand against King
Athelstan and the Saxons; the real reason was that there is only
a narrow ledge between the tower and the precipice, on which
two cannot walk abreast, but on which two can stand very well
with their backs to the wall, and no one else can come within
eye and ear-shot of them. Whilst we stood there, a sudden cloud
rolled by beneath our feet, completely obliterating the landscape,
but we were left above the vapor, in sunlight, looking down, as
it were, on a rushing, eddying sea of white foam. The effect was
strange; it was as though we were insulated on a little rock in a
vast ocean that had no bounds. Margaret pressed my arm and
said, "We two seem to be alone in a little world to ourselves."

I answered, looking at the fog, "And a preciously dull world
and dreary outlook."

I have not much imagination, and I did not at the moment
take her words as an appeal for a pretty and lover-like reply. I
missed the opportunity and it was gone past recall. She let go of
my arm in dudgeon, and when I turned my head Margaret had
disappeared. With a step she had left the ledge, and a few paces
had taken her to her father. The fog at the same time rose and
enveloped the top of the Tor and the church, so that I could no
longer see Margaret, and the possibility of overtaking her and
apologising was lost.

Next Sunday she did not come to church. This made me
very uncomfortable. I like to have the even tenor of neither
my agricultural nor my matrimonial pursuits disturbed. I had

been keeping company with Margaret Palmer for seven or eight months, and I had begun to hope that in the course of a twelvemonth, if things progressed, I might make a declaration of my sentiments, and that after the lapse of some three or four years more we might begin to think of getting married. This little outburst of temper was distasteful to me; I knew exactly what it meant. It showed an undue precipitancy, an eagerness to drive matters to a conclusion, which repelled me.

My sentiments are my own, drawn from my own heart, as my cider is from my own apples. I will not allow anyone to go to the tap of the latter and draw off what he likes; and I will not allow anyone to turn the key of my bosom and draw off the sentiments that are therein. On the third Sunday, I did not go to church, but I sent my hind, and he reported to me that Margaret Palmer had been there. I knew she would be there, expecting to find me ripe and soft to the pitch of a declaration. By my absence I showed her that I could be offended as well as she.

That next week there came a revivalist preacher to the chapel; he was a black man, and went by the name of "Go-on-all-fours-to-glory Jumbo." I heard that Margaret Palmer had been converted by him. The week after there came a quack female dentist to Tavistock, and I went to her and had one of my back teeth out. Margaret Palmer learned a lesson by that. I let her understand that if she chose to be revived by Methodies, I'd have my teeth drawn by quacks. I'd stand none of her nonsense. My plan answered. Margaret Palmer came round, and was as meek as a sheep, and as mild as buttermilk after that. Next Sunday I went as near a declaration as ever a man did without actually falling over the edge into matrimony.

Foggaton is a property of 356 acres 2 roods 3 poles, and it won't allow a proprietor to marry much under fifty; my father did not marry till he was fifty-three, and my grandfather not till he was sixty. Young wives are expensive luxuries, and long families ruin a small property. One son to inherit the estate, and a daughter to keep house for him till he marries, then to be pensioned off on £80 a year, that is the Rosedhu system. Now you can understand why I object to being hurried. Foggaton will not allow me to marry for twenty-seven years to come. But women are impatient cattle. They are like Dartmoor sheep; where you don't want them to go, there they go; and when you set up hurdles to keep them in, they take them at a leap. I've known these Dartmoors climb a pile of rocks on the top of which is nothing to be got, and from which it is impossible to descend, just because the Almighty set up those rocks for the sheep not to climb.

To my mind, courting is the happiest time of life, for then the maiden is on her best behaviour. She knows that there is *many a slip between the cup and the lip,* and she regulates her conduct accordingly. I've heard that in Turkey females are real angels; they never nag, they never peck, they never give themselves airs. And the reason is that a Turkish husband can always turn his wife out of the house and sell her in the slave market. With us it is otherwise; when a woman is a wife she has her husband at her feet in chains to trample on as she pleases. He cannot break away. He cannot send her off. She knows that, and it is more than a woman can bear to be placed in a position of unassailable security. As long as a man is courting, he holds the rod, and the woman is the fish hooked at the end; but when they are married the positions are reversed.

Well, to turn to my story. We made up our quarrel and were like two doves. Then came the event I am about to relate, which disturbed our relations.

It had been the custom on Christmas Eve from time immemorial for the sexton and two others to climb Brentor, and ring a peal on the three bells in the church tower at midnight. On a still Christmas night the sound of these bells is carried to a great distance over the moors. I daresay in ancient times there may have been service in the church at midnight, but there has been none for time out of mind, and the custom being unmeaning would have fallen into disuse were it not that a benefaction is connected with it—a field is held by feoffees in trust to pay the rent to the sexton and the ringers, on condition that the bells are rung at midnight on Christmas Eve.

Of late years there has been some difficulty in getting men together for the job. Wages are so high that labouring men will not turn out of a winter's night to climb a tor to earn a few shillings. Besides the sexton has been accused of disseminating a preposterous, idle tale of hobgoblins and bogies to frighten others from assisting him, so that he may pocket the entire sum himself.

Be this as it may, it is certain that on the Christmas Eve that followed the quarrel I have spoken of, no additional ringers were forthcoming. The sexton, who was also clerk, Solomon Davy, worked for me and occupied one of my cottages. I beg, parenthetically, to observe that the cottages that belonged to me would do credit to any owner. My maxim is, look to your men and horses and cows that they be well fed and well, housed, and they are worth the money. Solomon Davy was an old man. His work was not worth his wages, but I kept him on because he had been on the farm all his life, and had married late in life. During the afternoon of Christmas Eve, Solomon Davy sent for me. He was taken ill with rheumatism and could not leave his cottage.

"I've ventured on the liberty of asking you to step in, sir," said he, when I entered his door, "because I've been took across the back cruel bad, and I can't crawl across the room."

"Sorry to hear it, Solomon. Who will do the clerking for you tomorrow?"

"I'm not troubled about that, master, as Farmer Palmer do the responses in a big voice. That which vexes me is about the ringing the bells this night."

"It can't be done," said I.

"But, sir, meaning no offence, it must be done or I don't get the money. The feoffees won't pay a farthing unless Christmas be rung in."

"You must send somebody else to do it."

Solomon shook his head. "Then that person pockets the money, and I get naught." He remained silent awhile, and then added, "Besides, who'd go?"

"Make it worth a man's while, and he'll do anything," said I.

Again he shook his head, and this time he said,

"There's Margery of Quether."

"What do you mean?" I asked, flushing. "What has Miss Palmer to do with the bells? Oh, I understand; she likes to hear the peal, and you would not disappoint her."

Solomon looked up at me slyly. "I didn't mean she."

"Then who the deuce do you mean?"

"Her as never dies."

"Solomon, the lumbago has got into your brains. I'll tell you what I'll do. I will ring the bells for you, and you shall draw the fee for having done it. That, I hope, will content you, my good man."

"Now that be like you, master, the best and kindest of your good old stock," exclaimed Solomon. "I never heard of a master as was of such right good stuff as you. You don't turn off an old man because he is past work, nor grudge him a bit of best garden ground, took out of one of your fields, nor deny him skimmed milk because you want it for the pigs and calves, nor refuse him turnips and pertatees out of the fields as many as he can eat." So he went on. I do not hesitate to repeat what he said, because he confined himself strictly within the bounds of truth. I flatter myself I always have been a good master, and just, even generous, to my men. I have been more, I have been considerate and kind. Lights were not made to be put under bushels, and I am not one of those who would distort or suppress the truth, even when it concerns myself. I know my own merits, and as for my faults, if I light on any at any time, I shall not scruple to publish them."

The old sexton jumped at my offer—I mean metaphorically, for his lumbago would not allow him to jump literally. I had made the offer out of consideration for him, but without considering myself, and I repented having made it almost as soon as the words had left my lips. However, I am a man of my word, and when I say a thing I stick to it.

"Where is the key?" I asked.

"Her be hanging upon thicky (that) nail behind the door," answered the old man.

As I took down the great church key, Solomon said, in a hesitating, timid voice. "If you should chance to meet wi' Margery o' Quether, you won't mind."

"I do not in the least expect to see her," I said, getting red, and hot, and annoyed.

"No—meb-be not, but her has been seen afore on Christmas Eve."

"Margaret on the tor at midnight!" I exclaimed; then, highly incensed at the idea of the old man poking fun at me, and even alluding to my weakness for Margaret Palmer—love is a weakness—I said testily, as I walked out swinging the key on my forefinger, "Solomon, I object to Miss Palmer's name being brought in in this flippant and impertinent manner. What with the Gladstone-Chamberlain general topsy-turvyism of the government, the working classes are forgetting the respect due to their superiors, and allow themselves liberties of speech which their forefathers would have turned green to think of."

If I was regular in my devotions every Lord's Day, a labouring man in one's employ earning thirteen shillings a week had no right to suppose that I did not ascend Brentor from the purest motives of personal piety. It is the duty of one in his position to think so. His insolence jarred my feelings, and I already regretted the offer I had made. It is a mistake to be good-natured. It is lowering in the eyes of inferiors; it is taken for weakness. The man who is universally respected, and obtains ready attention and exact obedience, is he who cares for nobody but himself; is loud, exacting, and self-asserting.

To be goodnatured involves a man in endless troubles. I had undertaken to ring the bells at midnight in midwinter in the windiest, most elevated steeple in England; I had to ascend a giddy peak on which one false step would precipitate me over the rocks, and dash every bone in my body to pieces. I am not one to shrink from danger, or to shirk a responsibility, freely, if inconsiderately undertaken. I have already said that I would frankly admit my faults when I noticed them; and now the opportunity arises. I admit without scruple that I am too prone to do kind acts. This is a fault. A man ought to consider himself. Charity begins at home. In this instance I did not think of myself, of the discomfort and danger involved in ascending Brentor at midnight.

I took a stiff glass of hot rum and water about half-past ten or a quarter to eleven, and then turned out.

There was no snow on the ground; we are not likely to have seasonable weather so long as this Gladstone-Chamberlain-Radical topsy-turvy Government remain in power. Our sheep get cawed with the wet, the potatoes get the disease, the bullocks get foot-and-mouth complaint, and the rain won't let us farmers get in our harvest. If only we had Beaconsfield back! But there, politics have nothing to do with my story.

The evening was not cold, it was raw, and the night was black as pitch. I had a lanthorn with me (I spell the substantive advisedly in the old way, lanthorn and not lantern, for mine had horn, not glass, sides). I knew my road perfectly. The lane is stony, wet, and overhung. Stony it must be, for it is worn down to the rock, and the rock breaks up as it likes and stones itself, just as the coats of the stomach renew themselves. Wet it is, because it serves as main drain to the fields on either side. Overhung it is, because trees grow on either side. If the trees were not there, it would not be overhung. You understand me. I like to be explicit. Some intelligences are not satisfied with a hint, everything must be described and explained to them to the minutest particular.

By the lanthorn light I could see the beautiful ferns and mosses in the hedge, and the water oozing out of the sides, and the dribble that ran down the centre of the lane and then spread all over it, then accumulated on one side, and then took a fancy to run over to the other side. I notice that a stream in going down the hill zigzags just as a horse does in ascending a hill, and as a woman does in aiming at anything. The road rises steeply from my backyard gate to the church porch. When I say road,

I mean way. For after one comes out on the moor, there is not even a track.

I knew my direction well enough, so I went straight over the heath to the old volcano, and as I ascended the peak I thought to myself, if any traveller were on Heathfield tonight, what a tale he would make up of the Jack-o'-lanthorn seen dancing in and out among the rocks, and winding its way up the height, till at last it hopped in at the church door of St. Michael on the rock, and then a faint glimmer was visible issuing from all its windows. Probably he would suspect some witches' frolic was going on there such as Tam o' Shanter saw on All Hallowe'en, when—

Kirk Alloway seem'd in ableeze,

though the "bleeze" could not be bright that issued from my tallow candle in a lanthorn.

The sky was overcast. Not a star was visible; only in the S.W. was a little faint light, and a thread of it ran round the horizon. The simile is not poetical, but it is to the purpose, when I say that the earth seemed under a dish-cover which didn't quite fit.

I reached the church in safety, dark as the night was; the few gravestones lit up with a ghastly smile as the lanthorn and I went by them in the little yard. I set down the dickering article on the stone seat in the porch, turned the key, resumed my lanthorn and went into the tower.

The church was not in first-rate repair. I believe the Duke of Bedford, who owns all Heathfield, did intend to do something to the church. He brought an architect there, and the architect said he must pull down the old church that dates from the thirteenth century, and build a sort of Norman Gothic cathedral in its place. You see the architect thought only of the duke's pocket from which to draw; he gets five *per cent* on the outlay. But when the parson heard that, and I too, being churchwarden, we put our foot down and said, No! We loved the little old church; it was seen by Drake and Raleigh as they sailed into Plymouth Sound, just the same as we see it today, and we would not have a stone changed of the carcase. They might do what they liked with the vitals inside, that we conceded. Since that day we have heard nothing more of the restoration of Brentor church. Consequently, the sacred edifice has been getting more and more out of repair.

The rain had driven for centuries through the joints of the masonry, even through the stone itself, and had streamed down inside, rotting the joists of the bell-chamber where they rested in the wall. I don't blame the builders, they did their best. The walls are thick, but there is no stone in the country that is impervious to a south-western wind charged with rain. Granite is worst of all. You might as well build of sponge. Brentor Church is built of the stone of the hill on which it stands, a sort of pumice, full of holes, and therefore by nature spongy. It holds the wet, and weeps it out at every change of weather. Now the belfry joists had given way, rotted right off, and had brought the planking down with them, and lay a wreck at the bottom of the tower.

By day, I have no doubt, anyone looking up would see the three bells, and the holes in the lead roof above them. It was difficult for me to get at the ropes, so encumbered was the floor with fallen beams and boards that smelt of mildew and death. I fancy the floor had given way since last Sunday, and that was why the litter lay there. Some of the sexton's tools had been knocked over by the fallen beams. He wants strong tools, for the graves have to be hewn in the rock.

After I had removed some of the rotten timber, I made myself space, and stood in a pool of coffee-coloured water that had leaked from the roof, and drained from the sodden joists, and then I began to ring the bells. As I rang I looked round now and then. It was, of course, possible, though hardly probable, that the blacksmith or Luke Petherick might come up and take a turn at the ropes. I did not expect anyone, but I thought one *might* come; and I almost wished I had knocked the blacksmith up on my way, and asked him as a personal favour to join me. He couldn't have refused, for he does all my blacksmithing for me. But it might have seemed as if I were afraid to go alone, and it would have deprived Solomon of half the ringer's fee. Looked at in another light, it would not have done, for one in my position is hardly the person to be seen ringing a church bell, and to be known to have done it out of good-nature.

I soon found that, for one unaccustomed to bell-ringing, the exertion was great; it brought into play muscles not usually exercised, and I began to feel the strain. I paused and wiped my forehead. My hands were getting galled. I did not moisten them in the customary way, which is vulgar; but I dipped my palms in the coffee-coloured solution on the pavement at my feet. I had hitherto rung the "cock," as Solomon designates one old heavy bell that has a curious Latin inscription on it, which begins, "*Gallus vocor.*" Now, as I rose from moistening my palms, I looked at the rope of the tenor bell, intending to pull that next.

As I did so, I noticed something dark, like a ball of dirty cobwebs, hanging to the cord, rather high up. I elevated my lanthorn to see what it was, but the light afforded by the tallow dip was not sufficient to enable me to distinguish the outline of the object. I supposed it might be a great mass of filthy-cobweb, or perhaps a piece of broken flooring which had remained attached to the rope, caught when the rest fell away. I considered that if I pulled the rope, I should probably bring the thing—whatever it was—down on my head. You will understand that my desisting from touching that cord was prompted by the wisest discretion, not by inane fear. So I rang the treble bell, and ever and *anon* cast up my eye at the remarkable mass above.

Presently, I desisted from ringing altogether. I thought that the object was descending the rope slowly. I say I *thought* so, I did think so at first, but very soon I was certain of it. So certain was I, that I stepped back, and in so doing fell over a balk. When I had picked myself up the thing had reached the bottom. I should have liked to leave the church, but to do this I must step past this creature; I must do more; it was in the only clear space between me and the tower arch, so that to get out I must lift it from its place to make a passage for myself, and this I did not feel inclined to do. I never have believed in the supernatural. I do not believe in it now. Ghosts, goblins, and pixies are the creations of fevered imaginations and illiterate ignorance. It puts me out of patience to hear people, who ought to know better, speak of such things. I did not for a moment, therefore, suppose that the object before me was a denizen of another world.

As far as I can recollect and analyse my sensations at the time, I should say that blank amazement prevailed, attended by a dominating desire to be outside the church and careering down the flank of the hill in the direction of Foggaton. I had no theory as to what the thing was; indeed the inclination to theorise was far from me. The creature I could now see had a human form. It was of the size of a three months old baby. I have had no experience in babies myself, and am no judge of ages, so that when I say three months I do not wish to be tied down to that period exactly. In colour the object was brown, as if it had been steeped in peat water for a century, and in texture leathery.

It scrambled, much as I have seen a bat scramble, out of the puddle on the pavement to the heap of broken timber, and worked its way with its little brown hands and long claws up a rafter, and seated itself thereon, holding fast by a hand on each side of what I suppose was the body, and then blinked, much in the same way as a monkey blinks, drawing a skin over the eyes different in colour from the skin of the face.

"I be Margery Palmer of Quether," it said in strange, far-off, mumbling words. "I couldn't bide up yonder no longer; the wood be that rotten, it is all giving away, and I be afeared I may fall and break my bones. That 'ud be a gashly state o' things, my dear, to hev' to bide up there year after year with a body o' bones all scattered abroad (broken to pieces), and never no chance of the bones healing."

"Who are you?" I asked, perhaps not as loudly or with as firm a voice as that in which I usually accost a stranger. The creature did not hear me. It went on, however, in its mumbling voice, and with a querulous intonation.

"I be Margery Palmer of Quether. I reckon there be some-one before me, but, my dear, I cannot see you, and if you speak I cannot hear you. I be deaf as a post, and I've the eyes white wi' caterick."

"Are you a spirit?" I inquired. She did not hear me; so, waxing bolder, I put my hands to my mouth and shouted, as through a speaking trumpet, "Are you a spirit?"

"Spirit—spirit?" she echoed. "Laukamussy! I wish I was! Spirit! No such luck comed to me yet. If I was I'd be thankful! Ah! Wishes don't fulfil themselves like as prayers do."

"How came you here?" I called.

"Hear!" she repeated. "I can't hear. I be got too old for that, I reckon. I be Margery Palmer o' Quether."

"Impossible," I said. Were my senses taking leave of me? "This is a sheer impossibility."

She did not hear my protest, but went mumbling on. "I lives up yonder among the bells. I've lived there these hundreds of years. I reckoned it were the safest place I could be in. I'd not ha' come down now, but that I were fear'd the bells would give way and all fall together, and my bones would ha' broke. It 'ud be a gashly thing to live on for hundreds o' years wi' broked arms and legs, and mebbe also a broked neck, so that the head hung down behind, and with no power to move it, not a bit and crumb. There ain't no healing power in my bones now: they be as ancient as they in the graves, and no more power of joining in them than the dead and mouldering bones hev."

I held up the lanthorn to inspect this curious creature squatted before me on a beam. It was, as I said, of the size of a baby; but otherwise it was a grown woman very aged and withered. The face was not merely wizen: it was dried up to leather, quite tanned brown, the colour of the oak beams; the hands and arms were shrivelled and like those of a bat. There was actually no flesh on them, they were simply dry tanned skin about bone. The garments seemed to have been tanned like the hide by the liquor distilling from the oak. The eyes were blear.

"I can't see, and I can't hear," she went on, "except just a little scrap o' light which I take to be a link. I gets blinder and ever blinder, till in time I shall look into the sun and see only blackness and darkness forever. I gets deafer and deafer, but I can hear

23

the bells still. I can also feel a little with my skin, but not much. I've one tooth remains in my head, and I hang on by that. I drive it into the oak beam, and cling around the beam wi' my arms, and strike my nails in too, and so I hold fast. But I knowed very well that the wood were rotten; I knowed it by a sort of instink, and so I've a-comed down today. I reckon my hair be all failed off now: I can't tell by the feel, my hands be that numb wi' cling-ing that the feeling be most gone from them. But you can see for yourself."

She put her hand to her head and thrust back a leathery hood that had covered it. The little skull was bald. I opened the door of my lanthorn and took out the candle to inspect her better. The head was as if cut out of a thornstick. Only at the back at the junction with the neck was a little frizzle of ragged white hair. I observed as she moved that her neck creased like old hide that threatened to crack at the creases. The flexibility was gone from it. "Hold the candle before my eyes," she said; "I like the light. I can feel it shining through my dull eyes down into my stomick. What be your name, now?"

"George Rosedhu." I yelled my name into her ear,

"Ah, George! George!" exclaimed old Margery, "you put off and off too long. You should have married when the fancy first took you. Now it be too late; we be shrumped up (dried up) like old apples."

What could this extraordinary creature mean?

"Ah, George! George" she went on, "that were a cruel, un-kind act of yours, keeping company with me so long, and then giving me the slip after all. Do you mind how we used to meet here of Sundays, and how on the windy days you helped me up the rock, and on windy and rainy days you wrapped your cloak round the both of us, and how, when the days were foggy, we used to lose our way in the mist, and never were able to find the church door till the service were over? And do you recall how one day you took me round to the west end of the church, after service, where we could stand at the edge of the rock, wi' our backs to the tower, and you said you wanted to point out Kit

Hill to me—"

I sprang forward and put my hand over her mouth.

"Good heavens!" I exclaimed. "Will you drive me mad? What do you mean? Who are you?"

She went on, when I withdrew my hand. "Ah, George, George, you knew there was not much to be got with me. There were my brothers and a swarm of little ones coming on, and so you left me out in the cold, and took up with Mary Cake, of Wring-worthy, who was twenty years older than me. You said I were too young; and now Mary Cake, that became Mary Rosedhu be dead and mouldered these hundreds of years, and I—I be alive and old enough even for a Rosedhu."

Then the old creature began to laugh, but stopped with a short scream. "I must not do it. I dare not laugh. I be too old, and I shall crack my sides and tear my skin. Then what is cracked bides cracked, and what is tore bides tore."

What did the creature mean by her allusion to Mary Cake? That was my great, great—I'm afraid to say how many times removed—grandmother. She died about two hundred years ago. She brought an addition to the property of fifty-three acres, which I now possess. I have the marriage settlements in the iron deeds-chest under my bed, the date 1605.

"Well, well," the little old woman went on, "we all make mistakes. Life is but a string of them. Coming into the world is the first; courting, marrying, everything in succession is a mistake. You, George, made a mistake in taking Mary Cake instead of me. Her led you a cruel, sour life to my thinking. Her had a vixenish temper as would worry any man, out of conceit with life. I, on the other hand, was all lightsomeness and fun. You knew that; but what cared you for a pretty face and a sunny temper alongside of a few acres of moorland? You Rosedhus are a calkelating family, and you reckon up everything wi' a bit o' chalk on the table.

"I hadn't the land that Mary brought, but I'd youth and energy and a cheerful disposition. But, Rosedhus, you are all afraid of long families, and are a grasping and a keeping set. You always marry late in life, and oldish women, lest a lot of children should eat the property as mice eat cheese. It be a mistake, a gashly error. But there, now, I won't aggravate you. Now tell me this: How come you alive at this time? I thought you'd been dead these two hundred and fifty years. Can't you find your rest no more nor I? Did you also pray that you might never die?"

I could not answer. I have no imagination, and I was unable to follow her, mixing up the past and the present in such an unaccountable manner. As far as I could understand, she confused me with a remote ancestor of the same name who died in 1623. That was the George Rosedhu who married Mary Cake, of Wringworthy, in 1605.

"I made my mistake when I prayed for life," said the old woman. "I was so joyous and fond of life and full of giddiness that I used to pray every Sunday when I came to church, and every evening when I said my Matthew, Mark, Luke, and John, that I might never die. I were also mortal afraid of death. The graves here be digged out of the living stone, and be full of water afore the coffins be splashed into them, and the corpses don't moulder; they sop away and go off the bones just as if they was boiled to rags. That terrified me, so I always prayed for one only thing, that I might never die, and my prayer hev been heard and answered. I cannot die, but I can grow older and more decrepit and dried, for I never considered to pray that I might always bide young.

"So you see, even when we pray, we make mistakes. Now I cannot die. I get older and older, and shrump (wither) up more and more, and get drier, and blinder, and deafer. I can no longer taste, and I cannot smell, and I can hardly feel. I have no pleasure in life at all now, and the only feeling in me is fear—fear lest I should get broke or tore, for I be past mending; if I be broke or tore I must so bide to the end of time. On a very hot day, when the sun shines, I seem to have a sort o' a sense of warmth, and the frost must cake me up in ice before I knows I'm cold. I reckon in another hundred years my tongue will have dried up, and then I sha'n't be able to talk no more; but that is the last organ to go in a woman, as her temper is the first; her mind may go, her teeth may go, her sight may go, her hearing may go—but her tongue dies hard.

"In another hundred years I shall not be able to feel the streak of midsummer sun that falls on my back, nor the winter icicle that hangs from my nose. I sit bunched up on a beam above the bells, and hold on with a tooth drove fast into the wood right home to the gum, and my nails hev grown till they go round the beam I clutch. The dry rot has got into the wood, and it be turned to powder, so that the crust has given way and I've sunk into the dust and mildew.

"You must put me away where I can be safe for another two or three hundred years, out o' the way of dogs, and rats, and boys. Dogs would tear my skin, and rats gnaw holes in me, and boys pelt me wi' stones and break my bones. What is broke is broke, and what is tore is tore—I be past all healing. I were put up in the belfry above the bells as the place where I might be safest, but now that the rafters and joists be rotten and falling about me, it b'aint safe no more."

She ceased, and sat blinking at me. The skin of her eyelids was the only part of her that retained any flexibility, and any likeness to human skin in colour and texture. The eyelashes were white like frost needles. I was touched with compassion. As I have already said, I have no intention of disguising or hiding my faults, and I frankly confess that a too great readiness to be moved by a tale or stirred by a spectacle appealing to human sympathy is one of my worst faults. I fear it is ineradicably ingrained in my constitution; I was born with this just as some unfortunates come into the world with the germs of scrofula in their blood and tubercles in their lungs.

I remembered now to have heard, when a boy, of a certain girl who was said to have been so much in love with life that she had prayed she might never die, and who, accordingly, was doomed to live forever; but I thought that she raced on stormy nights with a white owl hooting before her over the moors in the train of the Black Hunter and the Wisht Hounds. I know my

27

old nurse had told me some such a tale to draw a moral from it of content with what Providence disposes; but it was news to me that this Undying One had been put away to wither up among the bells of Brentor Church. What a wretched existence this poor creature had dragged on!

My ancestor, who had flirted with her, and then jilted her, had lived over two hundred years ago, and she would be alive, drier and more wretched two hundred years hence, when Margaret and I are fallen to dust, and our lineal descendant in the male line is reigning at Foggaton. My kindly disposition was touched—my heart softened. In a sudden access of pity, I put my arms round the poor old creature, she was as light as a doll, and crooking my finger through the ring of the lanthorn, I said, "I will carry you home, old Margery! You shall feel a Christmas fire, and taste Christmas beef and plum-pudding."

She did not understand. I do not think she heard me, but she laid hold of me tenaciously, as she had laid hold of the beam on which she had crouched for two centuries: she drove her single tooth through my coat and waistcoat, even cutting my skin, and her bat-like hands and claws clutched me, the nails going into me like knife-blades, I left the church with her, and carried her home; that is to say, she adhered to me so tenaciously—I might say voraciously—that I had no occasion to use my arms for her support; she was like a knapsack slung on the wrong way, and quite as securely fastened—faster, for a knapsack will oscillate, but old Margery stuck to me as tight as a tick on a dog.

When I got home I said, "Now, old Margery, shake yourself off and sit by the brave big fire, and I'll give you something warm to drink that will cheer the cockles of your leathery heart." But not a bit would she budge. I shouted into her ear, but she could or would not hear. Her tooth, which was driven into my chest like the proboscis of a mosquito, held her fast, and her hands were no more to be unlocked from my arms than the laces of old ivy from an oak. There was nothing for it but for me to sit down in my armchair nursing her.

The situation was almost grotesque; it was altogether undignified. So I sat on, occasionally expostulating, and always in vain: and I thought I should have next morning to get a man with a knife to slit up my coat and waistcoat behind so as to let the old creature slip off with the garments. But I was saved this annoyance by her tooth gradually being withdrawn and her fingers relaxing. She fell off, and dropped on my knees, and lay there like a sleeping infant after its meal.

I threw a bunch of gorse on the fire, and it roared up the chimney in a sheet of golden flame, filling the little parlour with light. I was able now to study the face of the little creature on my lap, entirely at my ease. It struck me now that old Margery looked younger than I had taken her to be when I saw her in the belfry. She was a very old woman, indeed, still, but there was a human-like moisture on the leathery skin, which also looked less liable to part at the folds, and there was even a rosy tinge on the lips. I suppose that from holding her so long I was somewhat more able to appreciate her weight. It was not that of a doll stuffed with bran, but of a baby with milk and flesh and blood in it adapted to its age. I thought her also rather larger than I had at first supposed, but that may be because she was now asleep on my knees, and there is a gain of an inch or two in repose, owing to muscular relaxation.

I put her down very gently on my sofa, and set a chair against the side, lest she should roll off on the floor; then I went in quest of a clothes basket, which I filled with soft pillows. This I set in the ingle nook, and laid old Margery in the maund. I covered her over with an eider-down quilt taken from my own bed, and she seemed very cosy in the extemporised cradle. I did more. I got a Florence flask that had contained sweet oil, and rinsed it well out with a strong solution of soda. When it was quite clean, I filled it with hot strong rum and sugar and water. I wished I could find a flexible india-rubber tube, but I was unprovided with such things. There had been no call for them hitherto, in my house—Hold! there was, though! I recollected that one of the cows after calving had died of milk-fever, and the calf had been brought up by hand.

I remembered a vulcanised india-rubber contrivance that had been tried but had not answered, as the calf disliked the taste of the sulphur; I now found this, and with some little ingenuity adapted it to the Florence flask, and then put into the basket beside Margery. I put my finger into her mouth first to encourage her, but she only played with it, and then I inserted between her almost tooth- less gums the vulcanised india-rubber contrivance—I forget its proper name. I thought it would keep her quiet, but she dragged so hard at it that the tube came out, and all the rum and water ran among the pillows. So I had to take her out again, and dry the cushions before the fire, and make up the bassinet, with fresh pillows. Poor little thing, she slept through it all like an angel.

All this took me a long time, and gave me great exertion: it called into requisition faculties of the mind and heart that had not been previously exercised. I was very tired; I sat back in my chair and fell asleep. I did not dare to go to bed lest old Margery should wake and want me. When I opened my eyes it was Christmas Day. The clerk was ill, I was churchwarden, and must be at St. Michael de Rupe on that sacred festival to give the good day and the best wishes of the season to all my neighbours—sweet, blooming Margaret Palmer of Quether included. I went upstairs and dressed myself in my Sunday suit, and a blue neckcloth, and I put on my cairngorm pin with a terrier's head in it, put some pomatum on my hair—that I always do on Sunday the last thing before going to church—and before I left I drew down the coverlets and looked at old Margery.

She was sleeping still—bless her!—with her old brown thumb in her mouth. I was uneasy because the nail was so long, I thought it might scratch her palate or irritate the uvula, so I got a pair of scissors and cut it. I felt strangely moved with pity, and with that pity there awoke in me a sort of sense of personal property in old Margery. Also, I presume, because of that, I was aware of some pride in her. I knew that she was wizen and old and hideous, and I knew also, that if any woman had come into my house with her baby in her arms and had asked me to ad-mire it, and then had looked disparagingly at Margery, I should have hated that woman ever after. As it was, that day a child was christened in the church. I looked at its soft pink skin, and went away from the sacred edifice with envy and anger rankling in my heart.

CHAPTER 2

I left Foggaton that morning with great reluctance, and all the time of divine service I was thinking far more of old Margery than of young Margaret, as I ought—and I do not mind confessing my fault openly. My seat is a little forward of the Quether pew on the other side. Usually, when standing for the psalms and hymns, I stand sideways, that the light may fall on my book, and I may look over the top at Margaret, who does the same; but as she is on the other side and the window opposite mine, she turns towards me that she may get the light on her print, and so our eyes are always meeting. When the parson is praying to us, I lean forward with my head on the book-board, and let my eyes go diagonally backward; Margaret leans her head in an opposite fashion, and so her eyes go diagonally forward, and our eyes are always meeting in the prayers, as in the psalms.

During the sermon I am obliged to turn round on my seat, as I am hard of hearing in my right ear, owing to a cricket ball having hit it when I was at Tavistock Grammar School. Margaret always somehow has her bonnet string over her left ear, so she is forced to sit roundabout on her seat and expose the hearing ear to the preacher, and so it always comes about that during the sermon, our eyes are meeting. This Christmas Day it was other with me; I could think of nothing but my poor little old Margery in her bassinet by the fire, and I kept on wondering whether she would wake up in my absence and fret for want of me. Then I had all through the sermon a pricking feeling in my chest—I suppose where her teeth and nails had held so tight—and I was restless and uncomfortable to be back at Foggaton.

After service, as I was shaking hands all round, feeling eager to get it over and be off, Farmer Palmer said to me, "Come home to Quether with us, Rosedhu, and eat your Christmas dinner there. We are old friends and hope to be closer friends in time than we are now. I don't like, nor does Margaret here, to think of you sitting lonely down to your meal on Christmas Day. There is a knife and fork laid ready for you, and I will take no refusal."

I made a lame sort of excuse. I said I was unwell.

"That is true enough," said Palmer; "you don't look yourself at all today, and Margaret is uneasy about you. Your face is white, your hand shakes, and you look older by some years than when I last saw you. When was that?"

"Sunday, father," said Margaret with a sigh.

I assured them that I was too indisposed to accept their kind invitation, and I saw that they believed me. Margaret's brown eyes were fixed anxiously and intently on me. I had been up all night, and much worried, that was why I looked older and unwell, but I only said by way of explanation to Palmer, that I had something "on the nerve," which covers all kinds of ailments.

As I walked home every person I passed and spoke to said, "How oldened you are!" or "How ill you look!" or "Why, surely that baint you, Mr. George, looking nigher forty than twenty."

I wish Mr. Palmer would not try to thrust Margaret on me. Margaret invites me to dinner. Margaret is concerned at my looks. Margaret remembers when last we met. That is all hyperbole and figure and flower of speech, and means in plain English, I want you to take my eldest daughter off my hands, but I am not going to give more than a trifle with her.

I never was more pleased than on this occasion when I got home again. I unlocked my parlour door, and ran in and up to the clothes' basket, and cried in a sort of fond foolish rapture, "Bless it! bless it! O my Beauty!"

The little old woman opened her eyes—they were not clouded with cataract; that must have been a fancy of mine before: she saw me and smiled, and made a sort of crowing noise in her throat. I stooped over to kiss her, when—click! in an instant she had fastened herself on me, and driven her tooth into my chest, and grabbed me with her hands, so that I was held as in a vice. To wrench her off would have been impossible. I believe if torn away the hands would have held to me still, and the arms come off at the wrists. I know that when a ferret fastens on a rabbit you may kill the beast before he will let go, unless you nip his hind foot; then he opens his mouth to squeal, and loosens his grip to defend himself I did not think of this at the time, or I might have called in someone to pinch Margery's foot; but I doubt, even if I had remembered this, whether I should have had recourse to this expedient.

I did not care to have my situation discussed; moreover, I was conscious of a soothing sensation all the time Margery was fast. Besides, I knew by this time that when the little old woman had had enough she would drop off, just as a leech does when full. I would not have you suppose that Margery was sucking my blood. Nothing of the sort; that is, not grossly in the manner of a leech. But she really did, in some marvellous manner, to me quite inexplicable, extract life and health, the blood from my veins and the marrow from my bones, and assimilate them herself.

Presently she fell off, as I knew she would when satisfied, and lay in my lap, across my knees. She looked up at me with a smile that had something really pleasant in it. She was positively taller, her skin fresher, her eye clearer than before; her eyelashes were grey, not snowy; and there was actually a down of grey hairs covering her poll, like the feathers on a cockatoo. I wrapped a blanket round her, and was about to replace her in the basket, when I found, to my surprise, that it would cramp her limbs; she could not kick out in it. So I got a drawer out of my bureau, fitted it up with pillows, and laid her in that.

I really do think there is something taking about her expression. When you consider her age, she gave wonderfully little trouble. At first it was strange to me to have to do with this sort of little creature—it was my first and only—but I saw that I should soon get used to it. In the afternoon I employed myself in making a pair of rockers, which I adjusted to the drawer, and by this means converted it into a very tolerable cradle. I am handy at carpentering.

Indeed there are not many things which I cannot do when put to it. When the emergency arose, as the reader will see, I became really a superior nurse, without any training or experience. Indeed, I feel confident that in the event of this Radical Gladstone-Chamberlain Government altering the land laws, and robbing me of Foggaton, I could always earn my living as a nurse; I could take a baby from the month, if not earlier, or a person of advanced age lapsed into second childhood. Never before have I taken in hand the tools of literature, and yet, I venture to say that—well! there are idiots in the world who don't know the qualities of a cow, and to whom a sample of wheat is submitted in vain.

Such persons are welcome to form what opinion they like of my literary style. Their opinion is of no value whatever to me. There is no veneer in my work, it is sterling. There is no padding, as it is called; my literary execution is substantial and thorough as were the rockers I put on thicky (I mean, that there) cradle. The rockers were not put on many days before they were needed. Old Margery became very restless at night, and she would not let me be long out of the house by day. She was cutting her teeth. The back teeth are terribly trying to babies—they have fits sometimes and big heads and water on the brain, all through the molars.

If it be so with an infant of a few months, just consider what it must be with an old woman in her three-hundreth year, or thereabouts! I bore with her very patiently, but broken rest is trying to a man. Besides, about the same time I suffered badly in my jaws, for my teeth, which were formerly perfectly sound, began to decay, break off, and fall out. I may say, approximately, that as Margery cut a tooth I lost one; also that, as her hair grew and darkened, mine came out or turned grey. Moreover, as her eye cleared, mine became dim, and as her spirits rose, mine became despondent.

In this way, weeks, and even months passed. It really was a

pretty sight to see the havoc of ages repaired in the person of Margery; the sight would have been one of unalloyed delight, had not the recovery been effected at my expense. The colour came back into her cheek as it left my once so florid complexion; she filled out as I shrivelled up, she grew tall as I collapsed; the drawer would now no longer contain her, and a bed was made for her by the fire in the parlour. I noticed a gradual change in the tenor of her talk, as she grew younger.

At first she could think and speak of nothing but her ailings, but after, she took to talking scandal, bitter and venomous, of neighbours, that is, of neighbours dead and dropped to dust, whose very tombstones are weathered so as to be illegible. Little by little her talk became less virulent, and softened into harmless prattle, and was all about the things of the farm and house. She was a first-rate worker. I was glad she took such an interest in the farm; she brisked about and saw to everything. I was not able now to get about as much as I might have liked, as I suffered much from rheumatism and bronchitis.

Neighbours came to see me, and all were in the same tale, that I was becoming an old man before my time, that the change in me was something unprecedented and unaccountable. I could not walk without a stick. I stooped. My hair was thin and grey, my limbs so shrunken that my clothes hung on me as on a scarecrow. I was advised to see a doctor: that is—everyone had a special doctor who was sure to cure me; one said I must go to Dr. Budd at North Tawton, and another to Dr. Kingston at Plymouth, and one to this and one to that; they would have sent me flying over the country consulting doctors, and varying them every week. Some said—and I soon found that was the prevailing opinion—that I was bewitched, and advised me strongly to consult the white witch either in Exeter or Plymouth. I turned a deaf ear to them all. I wanted no doctors. I needed no white witch. I knew well enough what ailed me.

I never now went up Brentor to church. Dear life! I could not have climbed such a height if I had wished it! My poor old bones ached at the very thought, and my back was nigh broken when I walked through the shippen one day to the linney (cattle shed.) Besides, I had grown terribly short of wind, and I had such a rattling in my chest. I almost choked of a night. That was the bronchitis, and when I coughed it shook me pretty well to pieces.

So time passed, and I knew that I was sinking slowly and surely into my grave; there was no real complaint on me to kill me. I was breaking up of old age, and yet was no more than three and twenty. Everyone said I looked as if I was over ninety years. If I could see the hundred, it would be something to be proud of before I was four and twenty. One thought troubled me sorely. Whatever would become of Foggaton without a Rosedhu in it? I should die without leaving a lineal descendant in the male line. It would go out of the family. I had not a relation in the world. We Rosedhus always marry late in life, and never have large families. I was the single thread on which the possible Rosedhu posterity depended.

I believe that an aunt had once married, and had a lot of children, but she was never named in the family. It was tantamount to a loss of character in Rosedhu eyes. I did not even know her married name. She was dead; but her issue no doubt remained, though I knew nothing of them. They, I suppose, would inherit. I found as I grew older that this fretted me more and more. I would soon pass beyond the grave into the world of spirits, and I knew, the moment I turned up there, that all the Rosedhus would be down on me for not having left male issue to inherit Foggaton, each, with intolerable self-assurance, setting himself up before me as an example I ought to have copied. As if, under my peculiar circumstances, I could help myself. The only one of my ancestors with whom I would be able to exchange words would be the George Rosedhu who had married Mary Cake. I could cast it in his teeth that had he been faithful to his first love, this disastrous contingency would not have occurred.

"Ah!" said I, in a fit of spleen, "it is all very well of you, Margery, to go about the house singing. What is to become of the Rosedhus? To whom will Foggaton fall? You have drawn all the flush and health out of me and made yourself young at my charge—but I get nothing thereby."

"I will nurse you in your decrepitude, dearest George," she answered, and a dimple came in her rosy cheek, the prettiest twinkle in her laughing blue eye. Upon my word she was a bonny buxom wench, and it would have been a delight to be in the house with her, had I been younger.. Now I could only gaze on her charms despairingly from afar off, as Moses looked on the Promised Land from Pisgah. What a worker she was, moreover! What a manager! What an organiser! What a housekeeper, cook, dairy-woman, rolled into one! Never was the house so neat, the linen so cared for, the brass pans so scoured, the butter so sweet, the dairy so clean. She had been brought up in the old-fashioned, hard-working, sensible ways of a farm in the reign of Good Queen Bess.

In our days the women are all infected with your Gladstone-Chamberlain topsy-turveyism, and farmers' daughters play the piano and murder French, and farmers' wives read Miss Braddon and Ouida and neglect the cows. Her ways were a surprise to all on the estate. The men and the maids had never seen anything like it. Folks could not make Margery out, who she was, and where I had picked her up. Nobody seemed to belong to her; she had never been seen before, and yet she knew the names of every tor, and hamlet, and coombe, and moor, as if she had been reared there. But though she knew the places, she did not know the people. She spoke of the Tremaines of Cullacombe, whereas the family had left that house two hundred years ago, and were settled at Sydenham.

She talked of the Doidges of Hurlditch, a family that had been gone at least a hundred years. Kilworthy, she supposed, was still tenanted by the Glanvilles, whereas that race is extinct, and the place belongs to the Duke of Bedford, who has turned it into a farm. On the other hand, what was curious was, that Margery hit right now and then on the names of some of the labouring poor; she would salute a man by his right Christian and surname, because he was exactly like an ancestor some two hundred and fifty years ago. Though the great families have migrated or disappeared, the poor have stuck to their native villages, and reproduce from century to century the same faces, the same prejudices, the same characteristics. They are almost as unchangeable as the hills.

As I have said, Margery was a puzzle to everyone, and because a puzzle, the workmen and girls looked on her with suspicion. They resented the close way in which they were kept to their work and the rigid supervision exercised over them. Solomon Davy, the clerk, alone suspected who she was. He called several times to see me, and looked hard at me, with an uneasy manner, and seemed as though he wanted to ask me something, but lacked the courage to do so. Margery is always pleasant to Solomon, she knew the Davys that went before him, but he gives her a wide berth; he never lets her come within arm's reach of him. She feels it, I am sure, by her manner; but she is too good-hearted to remark on it.

I cannot deny that she was goodness and attention itself to me, and that I was fond of her. Just as a mother idolises her baby that draws all its life and growth from her, so was it with me. I begrudged her none of her youth and beauty; I took a sort of motherly pride in her growth and the development of her charms, and for precisely the same reasons—they were all drawn out of me.

One day Margery announced that she intended to marry me, and told me I must be prepared to stir my old stumps and go to church with her. She explained her reason candidly to me. She knew that I had a clear business head, and so she consulted me on the subject, which was flattering, and I should have felt more grateful had I not almost reached a condition past acute feeling. She told me that she would nurse me till I expired in her arms, and then, as my widow, would have Foggaton. This would secure her future, for with her renewed youth and with her handsome estate she could always command suitors and secure a second husband, from whom she could extract sufficient life and health to maintain her in the bloom of youth.

When he was exhausted and withered up and dead, she could obtain a third, and so on *ad infinitum*. She objected to being again consigned to mummification in the tower of Brentor Church, and this was the simplest and most straightforward solution to her peculiar difficulties. The plan suggested was feasible, and, from her point of view, admirable. I was now so shattered mentally and physically that I was in no condition to raise an objection.

Indeed, I had no objection to raise. I freely, willingly submitted to her proposal. She exercised no undue compulsion on me; she appealed to my reason, and my reason, as far as it remained, told me that her plan was sensible, and in every way worthy of her. She was a handsome woman, with a fine head of brown hair, and the brightest, wickedest, merriest pair of blue eyes. As for her cheeks—quarantines were nothing to them. A man in the prime of life would be proud to have such a woman as his wife, and her selection of me was, in its way, complimentary, even though I knew that I was taken for the sake of Foggaton.

So I consented, and she herself took the banns to the clerk. Solomon opened his eyes when she told him her purpose, moved uneasily on his seat, and scratched his head. He hardly knew what to make of it. He came to see me, and looked inquiringly at me, but I had one of my fits of coughing on me. When I was sufficiently recovered to speak, I told Solomon how impatient I was for my wedding day to arrive, and how kind and excellent a nurse Margery was to me. He went away puzzled and rubbing his forehead. I made but one stipulation with respect to my wedding, that was, that I should be conveyed to the foot of Brentor in a spring-cart, laid on straw, and thence be conveyed up the hill to the altar by four strong men, in a litter, laid upon a feather-bed, and with hot bottles at my feet and sides. I was entirely incapable of walking.

This was at the beginning of November. Consequently ten months had clasped since that fatal Christmas Eve on which I had made the acquaintance of Margery of Quether. So the banns were read on the first Sunday in the month at the afternoon service, there being no service that day in the morning in the little church. The banns were published between George Rosedhu, of Foggaton, bachelor, and Margaret Palmer, of Quether, spinster. If anyone knew any just cause or impediment why these two should not be joined together in holy matrimony, they were now to declare it. That was the first time of asking.

A pretty sensation the reading of these banns caused. Farmer Palmer's face turned as mottled as brawn, and Miss Palmer blushed as red as a rose and buried her face in her hymn-book. My old Margery had overshot her mark, as the sequel proved. She had not reckoned with young Margaret her great, great, great, great, grand-niece.

When public worship was concluded, Mr. Palmer and his daughter, instead of directing their steps homeward towards Quether, where tea was awaiting them, walked in the opposite direction, and descended on Foggaton, to know of me what was meant by the banns—sober earnest or silly joke.

Margery was not at home. She always frequented St. Mary Tavy Church, because she had a dislike to Brentor; it was associated in her mind with two centuries of chilling and repellent associations. Margery was a regular church-goer. That was part of her bringing up. In her young days, if anyone missed church, he was fined a shilling, and if he did not take the sacrament, was whipped at the cart-tail. These penalties are no longer exacted; nevertheless, Margery is punctual in her attendance. Such is the force of a habit early acquired.

Thus it came about that Farmer Palmer and his daughter arrived at Foggaton before Margery had returned from church. I am sorry that my hand is not expert at describing things which I neither saw nor heard accurately. I have no imagination, which is a delusive faculty leading to serious error. Palmer and his daughter were attended by Solomon Davy, who I believe endeavoured to explain the situation to them and told them who Margery really was. I had become so dull of hearing, and so cataracted in eye, that I was unable to understand all that went on, and to follow and take part in the somewhat heated and animated conversation.

If, like a modern writer of fiction, I were to give the whole of what was said, with description of the attitudes assumed, the inflections of the voices, and the degrees of colour that mantled the several cheeks, I might make my narrative more acceptable, no doubt, to the vulgar many, but it would lose its value to the appreciative few, who asked for a true record of what I observed.

I believe that Solomon in time made it clear to the dull intellects of the Palmers that the banns were for my marriage with the great, great, great, great-aunt of Margaret, and not with herself. What he said of poor Margery I don't know. I strained my ears to catch what he said, but heard only a buzzing as of bees. I doubt not that he spiced the truth with plenty of falsehood.

Farmer Palmer has a loud voice. I heard him say to his daughter, "Wait here a bit, Margaret, along with George Rosedhu, and bide till t'other Margery arrives; I back one woman against another."

"Oh, father!" exclaimed the pretty creature, "where be you a-going to?"

"My dear, I shall be back directly. This be Fifth o' November, and bonfire night. The lads will be all collecting faggots for a blaze on the moor. I'll fetch 'em here, and they can have the pleasure o' burning the old witch instead of a man o' straw."

I held out my hands in terror and deprecation. "You durstn't do it!"

"Why not?" asked the farmer composedly. "Her's a witch and no mistake. Her have sucked you dry of life as an urchin (hedgehog) sucks a cow of milk."

"But," protested Solomon, "though that be true enough, what about the laws? I won't say but that it be right and scriptural to burn a witch; for it is written, '*Thou shalt not suffer a witch to live*,' but I reckon it be against the laws."

"Not at all," said Palmer. "No man can be had up for burning a person who has no existence."

"But she has existence," I remonstrated. "That is the prime

cause of her trouble; she has too much of it; she can't die."

"There is no evidence of her existence," argued Palmer. "You, Solomon, tell me how far back your registers go in Brentor Church."

"Back, I reckon, to about 1680."

"Very well, then they contain no record of her birth and baptism. Now you cannot be hung for killing a person of whose existence there is absolutely no legal evidence. The law won't touch us if we do burn her."

"But—but," I said, crying and snuffling, "she is your own flesh and blood."

"That may be, but that is no reason against her cremation. My own Margaret stands infinitely nearer to me, and her interests closer to my heart, than the person and welfare of a remote ancestress. As the banns have been called, Foggaton shall go to my daughter and to no one else. In three weeks' time Margaret shall be Mrs. Rosedhu." He spoke very firmly.

"Father, dear father, how can you be so cruel to me?" cried Margaret. "Do y' look what an atomy Mr. Rosedhu be come to?"

The burly yeoman paid no heed to his daughter's protest, knowing, no doubt, its unreality. He said to me, "Look y' here, George Rosedhu, you've had my daughter's name coupled wi' yourn in the church today, and read out before the whole congregation, without axing my leave or hers. I won't have her made game of even by a man o' substance like you, so her shall marry you before December comes, whether you like it or not."

"Oh, Mr. Palmer, sir," I pleaded, "how can you think to force your daughter into nuptials which must he distasteful to her?"

"Don't you trouble your head about that. Margaret knows which side her bread is buttered. She can distinguish between clotted cream and skim milk."

"Besides," I argued, "I am bound by the most solemn engagements to my Margery. I have promised to settle Foggaton on her."

"You cannot," shouted the farmer of Quether. "The thing is

impossible. You cannot marry a woman who has no existence in the eye of the law. The only Margaret Palmer of Quether of whom the law has cognizance is she who now stands before you. She has been baptized, vaccinated, and confirmed. What more do you want to establish her existence? Whereas, what documentary proof can the other Margery produce that she exists? There is but one Margaret Palmer of Quether in this nineteenth century; that's flat." He slapped the table, and then, with the air of one administering a crushing argument, he added, "Now, tell me, is it possible for a man to marry a woman from whom he is removed by from two to three centuries? Answer me that."

"Put in that bald way," I said, "it does seem unreasonable; but in these Radical-Gladstone-Chamberlain times one does not know where one stands. All the lines of demarcation between the possible and the impossible are wiped out, reason and fact do not jump together."

"I leave you to digest that question," answered Palmer triumphantly. He saw I was pushed into a corner. Then he went out, along with Solomon Davy.

I do not think that Margaret objected to be left to meet Margery. I noticed her pluming and bridling like a game-cock before an encounter, She stroked down the folds of her gown, and pursed up her lips, and now and then shot out her tongue from between her lips, as I have seen a wasp test his sting before stabbing me. I was getting uneasy for Margery and was myself uncomfortable. I said, "Miss Margaret, will you be so good as to pick me up my handkercher; it is lying there on the floor, and I be so cruel bad took with the lumbagie that I can't bend to take it myself."

She complied with my request somewhat surlily. Then I said, "Would you mind, now, just uncorking that bottle there on the shelf, and putting a drop or two on a lump of sugar, and giving it me. My hands be that shaky I cannot put it in my mouth myself, and I've no teeth to hold it by. The drops be *ipecacuanha*, and be good for bronchitis."

"No, I won't do it, you nasty old man."

43

"Then, miss, will you rub my spine with hartshorn and oil? You'll find a bottle of the mixture on the sideboard, and a bit of flannel in the cupboard."

"I will do nothing of the sort," she said, testily.

"You won't, miss? Then please to take me up in your arms and carry me to bed. Margery does it. She is very kind and considerate; she begrudges me no trouble, and feeds me out of a spoon."

"I will do nothing of the sort," she said again, in short, angry tones, and with an air of supreme disgust.

"I am sorry for it," said I. That was Gospel truth. I knew that when the two women met such a storm of words would rage as would wreck my poor nerves, and I wanted to be in bed and out of it, before the hurricane broke loose.

"You'll have to do all this for me," I said, "when you become Mrs. Rosedhu. A very old person needs just as much attention as a baby. I know that, for I've gone through it myself; I've done the nursing. Why will you not leave me alone, and allow Margery to marry me? She will take care of me; she kisses and fondles me. Will you?"

"You disgusting old scarecrow and atomy, certainly not."

"An atomy—scarecrow and atomy—what next will you call me? Yet you want to marry me!"

"You fool!" said Margaret, shortly. "I put up with you for the sake of Foggaton."

"It's the same with Margery," I said; "but she put it more pleasantly. Her manners are better than yours; but then she belongs to the old school—the good old school!" I sighed.

What I said made her angry. She did not like to have comparisons drawn between herself and her remote great aunt, to her own disadvantage.

"I suppose I am to have a voice in the matter," I went on; "and though I have liked you very much, Margaret, yet I like the other Margery better. One thing in her favour is—she is older than you."

"You are not going to have her—who has drained life and

spirit out of you. Do you think I will allow it.? Don't you see I bear her a grudge? She has turned the fresh and hale George who courted me into a shrivelled old man. It would have been a pleasure to have young George, it is a penance to have the old one. I owe her that, and I shall scratch her eyes out when we meet."

"Whatever you do," I pleaded, "do not hurt her. Your father has made a dreadful threat. I hope he will not execute it."

"There she comes!" exclaimed Margaret Palmer, starting to her feet in a tremor of delight. "I hear her step on the walk."

"Throw the hearthrug over me," I entreated, "I cannot bear to be agitated. Toss the table-cover above the hearthrug, all helps to deaden the sound." Margaret complied with my request. Here again my narrative must present an appearance of incompleteness. I cannot describe what I neither saw nor heard during the interview between Margaret and Margery, because I was buried under a heavy sheepskin rug and a thick, coloured, damask table-cover on the top of that. I have no imagination, and I only relate what I actually saw and heard. I saw nothing, and what I heard resembled the jangling of pots and pans when a host of maids are going after a swarm of bees. Of words I could distinguish none, till after awhile the hearthrug and table-cover slipped off, owing to my coughing a great deal, the dust out of the hearthrug having got into my bronchial tubes. Then I saw a sight which filled me with dismay.

My room was full of men and boys, with their caps and hats on. Their faces were flushed and eager; savage delight danced in their eyes. One had a pitch-fork, several had sticks, one was armed with a flail. Head and shoulders above the rest stood Farmer Palmer, keeping back the mob that crowded In at the door. In the front of all, as if in a cockpit, opposite each other, stood the two Margarets, red in face, blazing in temper, their tongues going, their eyes sparkling, their hands extended. I will say that poor Margery acted solely on the defensive. She held up her arms in self-protection. Margaret had driven her nails into her cheek and a red streak down the side showed that she had drawn blood.

"See, see!" exclaimed the younger Margaret, "the witch! her power is broken. The blood is running."

This is a popular belief. If you can draw blood from a witch, her power—at least over you—is at an end.

My poor Margery gazed with alarm at the crowd of red, threatening faces that looked at her. She shrank from the sticks, the clubs, the pitchfork and flail. She drew behind me, as if I, broken down into premature old age, could defend and assist her. I raised my shrill pipe in entreaty, but my words were without effect. Those horrible faces glowered at Margery with the savagery of dogs surrounding a hare they are about to tear to pieces. The fear of witchcraft blotted all human compassion out of their hearts.

Suddenly a red light blazed in at the window. The evening had fallen fast and it was now dark.

"Look! look there!" shouted Farmer Palmer. "Look there, you witch, at the bed made for you. There are plenty of faggots to heap over you should you complain of the cold,"

Margery uttered a scream of terror and clutched my chair, whilst she cowered on the floor behind it.

"Oh, George!" she cried in her agony of dread, "save me! save me! They cannot kill me but they can fry and burn me! Then I shall live on—on—on, a scorched morsel, not like a human being."

"My darling," I answered, "I can do nothing against all these men." I, however, made a desperate attempt. "I am master in this house," I cried in my shrill old tones; "no one has any right within the doors without my permission, and I order you all to go away peaceably and to leave me alone."

The men and boys, led by Palmer, laughed and did not budge an inch. There came a shout from outside.

"Bring out the witch, and let her burn!"

There is an innate cruelty in human nature which neither Christianity, nor education, nor teetotalism will eradicate. I always thought the peasantry of the West of England wonderfully

46

gentle, kindly, and free from brutality, and yet—scratch the man and the beast appears—here were my peaceable, tender- hearted countrymen ravening for the life of a poor woman, really pretty, and as good-dispositioned and without malice as an angel. I knew that they would gloat over her anguish in the fire, that they would poke up the fuel to make her burn more thorough-ly—they would do so without compassion; not really because they thought her a witch, but because Farmer Palmer had told them they might burn her without fear of the law.

A fresh heap of fuel had been tossed upon the pyre, and the flame spouted up to heaven. A roar from the boys without. "Bring her out! Let her burn!"

Poor Margery covered her eyes with her hands to shut out the terrible light.

"Oh, George, George!" she cried, "save me, and I will give you back some of your youth and strength again."

"Stand back," thundered Palmer, as the circle of men con-tracted about her, and hands were thrust forth to grasp and tear her from my chair. "Do you hear me? She has offered to recover our friend Rosedhu."

"You cannot do it, my poor darling," I said.

"Oh, save me, George, and I will indeed."

"You hear her," shouted Palmer. "Stand back, and let her fulfil what she has undertaken."

Then Margaret put in her voice. She was afraid that her rival would escape. "No, father, do not trust her. She can do nothing. She is a witch, and wants to cast spells over you all. Take her away, boys, and pitch her Into the fire. Don't listen to a word she says, however hard she prays to be let go."

"Into the flames with her!" shouted the men, and stepped forward. "That is the place for such as she."

"Fair play, my lads," said Palmer, and with his strong arm he drove the rabble back. "As for you, Margaret, don't you interfere. Now then, you—Margery—or whatever you call yourself, stand up and come forward. None shall hurt you if you really recover Rosedhu of his age and incapicity. But, mind you, if you fail, I swear that with this cudgel I will break every bone in your body, and then throw you into the fire with my own arms."

Margery quivered and cried out at the threat.

"Are you going to do it or not?" asked Palmer.

Poor Margery, feeling the necessity for prompt action, if she would save herself from terrible torture, rose from her crouching posture and stole tremblingly forward.

"Stand out o' the road, boys," shouted Palmer; "clear away with you," and with his stick he swept a circle round Margery and me.

"Oh, George," she said, with tears of mortification in her blue eyes, "I am sorry to do it. I wouldn't if I could; I really wouldn't. But I cannot help myself. These cruel men do so scare me. We might have been so comfortable together; I'd have nursed you into your grave quite beautiful and convenient like, and then I'd have had Foggaton to myself, and it would have gone so well for all parties. But now, you see, that blessed arrangement you managed so nicely for me won't come to nothing because of the wickedness of evil men, who walk about like unto roaming and roaring lions seeking whom they may devour. I cannot help myself, George. You'll do me the justice to say it were against my will and under compulsion. There, give me your two hands into mine."

She took my hands and stood opposite me, holding them at arms' length, and looking into my eyes. Poor thing! her lips trembled, and the tears stood on the lids and overflowed and trickled down her soft red cheeks. It was a sore trial and disappointment to her, but she bore it like a Christian, and never cast a word of bitterness at those who forced her to it. And to think what a sacrifice she was making! Those rude creatures knew nothing of that, and could not appreciate the greatness of her self-sacrifice. I submitted, because I saw that in this way only had I the means of rescuing her.

As she held my hands, I felt as if streams of vital force were flowing from her up my arms into my body. The aching in my bones ceased. My legs became stronger, my head lighter and more erect; I could see better, and hear better. I began to smell the peat burning on the hearth, I felt an inclination to draw Margery on to my knees and kiss her; but when I looked at her, the desire passed, she was waning as I waxed. She grew older, the colour left her cheek, her eyes became dim; then, all at once I sprang to my feet and shook off her hands. "Enough Margery, enough," I said. "You have restored to me sufficient of my strength and health, the rest I freely make over to you. Now for the rest of you."

My voice was full and loud as that of Palmer himself. "Every one of you listen to me. This is my house, and an Englishman's house is his castle. Leave this room, leave my land at once, or I prosecute every man jack of you for burglary and trespass. Good Lord! Do you know where you are? Do you know who I am? This is Foggaton, and I am a Rosedhu. Gladstone and Chamberlain and that Harcourt fellow haven't brought matters quite so far yet that every dirty radical may come inside a landed proprietor's doors and snap his finger under his nose." I snatched the stick out of Palmer's hand and went at the men with it. Not one ventured to show me his face. I saw a sudden change of posture, and a crush and rush out of my door and down my little passage. "You bide here, Palmer," I said: "and Margaret also. But as for all this ragtag and bob-tail that you have brought in, I'll make a clean sweep of them in a jiffy."

"It is all very well, Rosedhu," said Palmer, folding his arms, and setting his legs wide apart. "You have got rid of the rabble, and you are right to do so if you choose. But you do not get rid of me and Margaret so fast. The banns have been called between my daughter and you; I take no account of the other, she has no legal existence."

I was silent, and looked from Margery to Margaret.

"Besides," Palmer went on, "you may not think so much of her now. In appearance she is old enough to be your grandmother."

Certainly Margery looked aged, a hale woman, but still old—too old to be thought of as a bride at the hymeneal altar. Margaret was young and pretty; I wish she had not been quite so young and opened such an alarming *vista* of possibilities. But then I looked at myself in a glass opposite, and saw that I was gray-headed and on the turn down the hill of life. That was an advantage. "There is one thing," I said musingly; "in the matter of amiability there is no comparison. Margery is as good—"

"We will have no comparisons drawn," interrupted Palmer, as the girl darted a look at me that plainly said, "You shall suffer for this someday." "Hold out your fist like a man and say you will take my daughter for better, for worse, and make her Mistress of Foggaton within the month. The first time of asking took place today."

"Let us say in another couple or three years," said I, with the principle of the family at heart.

"No," answered Palmer curtly. "Within the month. Unless you consent to that—into the fire the old hag goes."

"Oh, Palmer!" I exclaimed, "you passed your word to her that she should be spared."

"No, no. I said that unless she restored you I would break every bone of her body and throw her into the flames myself. I will certainly not touch her with my stick, nor commit her myself to the flames, but I will let the men outside deal with her as they like. I see what it is, there is no security for you from the witchcrafts of that old hag till there is another woman in this house. That woman must be my daughter, and when she is here I defy all the witches that dance on Cox Tor, and all the pretty wenches of Devonshire to get so much as one foot inside the door."

"Father!" protested Margaret.

"My dear, I know it."

"Well, you need not say it."

"Give me a twelvemonth's grace," I entreated.

"No, not above twenty days."

A howl from without—a fresh faggot was cast on the fire. The pyre was not on my ground but on a bit of waste adjoining the lane, and as I am not lord of the manor I have no rights over it. That the rascals knew.

Poor Margery laid hold of my arm. Margaret at once intervened and thrust her aside. "You do not touch him again."

"You see," laughed the father, "it is as I said. Come, your hand."

I gave it with a sigh.

I have written these few pages to let people know that Margery of Quether is about somewhere—where, I do not know for certain, but I believe she has gone off into the remotest parts of Dartmoor, where, probably, she will seek herself a cave among the granite tors, in which to conceal herself, where no boys will be likely to find her and throw stones at her. I am uneasy now that there is such a rush of visitors to Dartmoor to enjoy the wonderful air and scenery, lest they should come across her, and in thoughtlessness or ignorance do her an injury. Now that they know her story, I trust they will give her a wide berth.

I think that what I have gone through has taught me a lesson, but it is not one much to be recommended, though it is one largely followed: Never succour those who solicit succour, or they will suck you dry.

Colonel Halifax's Ghost Story
(A tale from *A Book of Ghosts*)

I had just come back to England, after having been some years in India, and was looking forward to meet my friends, among whom there was none I was more anxious to see than Sir Francis Lynton. We had been at Eton together, and for the short time I had been at Oxford before entering the army we had been at the same college. Then we had been parted. He came into the title and estates of the family in Yorkshire on the death of his grandfather—his father had predeceased—and I had been over a good part of the world. One visit, indeed, I had made him in his Yorkshire home, before leaving for India, of but a few days.

It will easily be imagined how pleasant it was, two or three days after my arrival in London, to receive a letter from Lynton saying he had just seen in the papers that I had arrived, and begging me to come down at once to Byfield, his place in Yorkshire.

"You are not to tell me," he said, "that you cannot come. I allow you a week in which to order and try on your clothes, to report yourself at the War Office, to pay your respects to the duke, and to see your sister at Hampton Court; but after that I shall expect you. In fact, you are to come on Monday. I have a couple of horses which will just suit you; the carriage shall meet you at Packham, and all you have got to do is to put yourself in the train which leaves King's Cross at twelve o'clock."

Accordingly, on the day appointed I started; in due time

reached Packham, losing much time on a detestable branch line, and there found the dogcart of Sir Francis awaiting me. I drove at once to Byfield.

The house I remembered. It was a low, gabled structure of no great size, with old-fashioned lattice windows, separated from the park, where were deer, by a charming terraced garden.

No sooner did the wheels crunch the gravel by the principal entrance, than, almost before the bell was rung, the porch door opened, and there stood Lynton himself, whom I had not seen for so many years, hardly altered, and with all the joy of welcome beaming in his face. Taking me by both hands, he drew me into the house, got rid of my hat and wraps, looked me all over, and then, in a breath, began to say how glad he was to see me, what a real delight it was to have got me at last under his roof, and what a good time we would have together, like the old days over again.

He had sent my luggage up to my room, which was ready for me, and he bade me make haste and dress for dinner.

So saying, he took me through a panelled hall up an oak staircase, and showed me my room, which, hurried as I was, I observed was hung with tapestry, and had a large fourpost bed, with velvet curtains, opposite the window.

They had gone into dinner when I came down, despite all the haste I made in dressing; but a place had been kept for me next Lady Lynton.

Besides my hosts, there were their two daughters, Colonel Lynton, a brother of Sir Francis, the chaplain, and some others whom I do not remember distinctly.

After dinner there was some music in the hall, and a game of whist in the drawing-room, and after the ladies had gone upstairs, Lynton and I retired to the smoking-room, where we sat up talking the best part of the night. I think it must have been near three when I retired. Once in bed, I slept so soundly that my servant's entrance the next morning failed to arouse me, and it was past nine when I awoke.

After breakfast and the disposal of the newspapers, Lynton

retired to his letters, and I asked Lady Lynton if one of her daughters might show me the house. Elizabeth, the eldest, was summoned, and seemed in no way to dislike the task.

The house was, as already intimated, by no means large; it occupied three sides of a square, the entrance and one end of the stables making the fourth side. The interior was full of interest—passages, rooms, galleries, as well as hall, were panelled in dark wood and hung with pictures. I was shown everything on the ground floor, and then on the first floor. Then my guide proposed that we should ascend a narrow twisting staircase that led to a gallery. We did as proposed, and entered a handsome long room or passage, leading to a small chamber at one end, in which my guide told me her father kept books and papers.

I asked if anyone slept in this gallery, as I noticed a bed, and fireplace, and rods, by means of which curtains might be drawn, enclosing one portion where were bed and fireplace, so as to convert it into a very cosy chamber.

She answered "No," the place was not really used except as a playroom, though sometimes, if the house happened to be very full, in her great-grandfather's time, she had heard that it had been occupied.

By the time we had been over the house, and I had also been shown the garden and the stables, and introduced to the dogs, it was nearly one o'clock. We were to have an early luncheon, and to drive afterwards to see the ruins of one of the grand old Yorkshire abbeys.

This was a pleasant expedition, and we got back just in time for tea, after which there was some reading aloud. The evening passed much in the same way as the preceding one, except that Lynton, who had some business, did not go down to the smoking-room, and I took the opportunity of retiring early in order to write a letter for the Indian mail, something having been said as to the prospect of hunting the next day.

I had finished my letter, which was a long one, together with two or three others, and had just got into bed when I heard a step overhead as of someone walking along the gallery, which I now knew ran immediately above my room. It was a slow, heavy, measured tread which I could hear getting gradually louder and nearer, and then as gradually fading away as it retreated into the distance.

I was startled for a moment, having been informed that the gallery was unused; but the next instant it occurred to me that I had been told it communicated with a chamber where Sir Francis kept books and papers. I knew he had some writing to do, and I thought no more on the matter.

I was down the next morning at breakfast in good time. "How late you were last night!" I said to Lynton, in the middle of breakfast. "I heard you overhead after one o'clock."

Lynton replied rather shortly, "Indeed you did not, for I was in bed last night before twelve."

"There was someone certainly moving overhead last night," I answered, "for I heard his steps as distinctly as I ever heard anything in my life, going down the gallery."

Upon which Colonel Lynton remarked that he had often fancied he had heard steps on his staircase, when he knew that no one was about. He was apparently disposed to say more, when his brother interrupted him somewhat curtly, as I fancied, and asked me if I should feel inclined after breakfast to have a horse and go out and look for the hounds. They met a considerable way off, but if they did not find in the coverts they should first draw, a thing not improbable, they would come our way, and we might fall in with them about one o'clock and have a run. I said there was nothing I should like better. Lynton mounted me on a very nice chestnut, and the rest of the party having gone out shooting, and the young ladies being otherwise engaged, he and I started about eleven o'clock for our ride.

The day was beautiful, soft, with a bright sun, one of those delightful days which so frequently occur in the early part of November.

On reaching the hilltop where Lynton had expected to meet the hounds no trace of them was to be discovered. They must have found at once, and run in a different direction. At three o'clock, after we had eaten our sandwiches, Lynton reluctantly abandoned all hopes of falling in with the hounds, and said we would return home by a slightly different route.

We had not descended the hill before we came on an old chalk quarry and the remains of a disused kiln.

I recollected the spot at once. I had been here with Sir Francis on my former visit, many years ago. "Why—bless me!" said I. "Do you remember, Lynton, what happened here when I was with you before? There had been men engaged removing chalk, and they came on a skeleton under some depth of rubble. We went together to see it removed, and you said you would have it preserved till it could be examined by some ethnologist or anthropologist, one or other of those dry-as-dusts, to decide whether the remains are *dolichocephalous* or *brachycephalous*, whether British, Danish, or—modern. What was the result?"

Sir Francis hesitated for a moment, and then answered: "It is true, I had the remains removed."

"Was there an inquest?"

"No. I had been opening some of the tumuli on the Wolds. I had sent a crouched skeleton and some skulls to the Scarborough Museum. This I was doubtful about, whether it was a prehistoric interment—in fact, to what date it belonged. No one thought of an inquest."

On reaching the house, one of the grooms who took the horses, in answer to a question from Lynton, said that Colonel and Mrs. Hampshire had arrived about an hour ago, and that, one of the horses being lame, the carriage in which they had driven over from Castle Frampton was to put up for the night. In the drawing-room we found Lady Lynton pouring out tea for her husband's youngest sister and her husband, who, as we came in, exclaimed: "We have come to beg a night's lodging."

It appeared that they had been on a visit in the neighbourhood, and had been obliged to leave at a moment's notice in consequence of a sudden death in the house where they were staying, and that, in the impossibility of getting a fly, their hosts had sent them over to Byfield.

"We thought," Mrs. Hampshire went on to say, "that as we were coming here the end of next week, you would not mind having us a little sooner; or that, if the house were quite full, you would be willing to put us up anywhere till Monday, and let us come back later."

Lady Lynton interposed with the remark that it was all settled; and then, turning to her husband, added: "But I want to speak to you for a moment."

They both left the room together.

Lynton came back almost immediately, and, making an excuse to show me on a map in the hall the point to which we had ridden, said as soon as we were alone, with a look of considerable annoyance: "I am afraid we must ask you to change your room. Shall you mind very much? I think we can make you quite comfortable upstairs in the gallery, which is the only room available. Lady Lynton has had a good fire lit; the place is really not cold, and it will be for only a night or two. Your servant has been told to put your things together, but Lady Lynton did not like to give orders to have them actually moved before my speaking to you."

I assured him that I did not mind in the very least, that I should be quite as comfortable upstairs, but that I did mind very much their making such a fuss about a matter of that sort with an old friend like myself.

Certainly nothing could look more comfortable than my new lodging when I went upstairs to dress. There was a bright fire in the large grate, an armchair had been drawn up beside it, and all my books and writing things had been put in, with a reading-lamp in the central position, and the heavy tapestry curtains were drawn, converting this part of the gallery into a room to itself. Indeed, I felt somewhat inclined to congratulate myself on the change. The spiral staircase had been one reason against this place having been given to the Hampshires. No lady's long dress trunk could have mounted it.

Sir Francis was necessarily a good deal occupied in the evening with his sister and her husband, whom he had not seen for some time. Colonel Hampshire had also just heard that he was likely to be ordered to Egypt, and when Lynton and he retired to the smoking-room, instead of going there I went upstairs to my own room to finish a book in which I was interested. I did not, however, sit up long, and very soon went to bed.

Before doing so, I drew back the curtains on the rod, partly because I like plenty of air where I sleep, and partly also because I thought I might like to see the play of the moonlight on the floor in the portion of the gallery beyond where I lay, and where the blinds had not been drawn.

I must have been asleep for some time, for the fire, which I had left in full blaze, was gone to a few sparks wandering among the ashes, when I suddenly awoke with the impression of having heard a latch click at the further extremity of the gallery, where was the chamber containing books and papers.

I had always been a light sleeper, but on the present occasion I woke at once to complete and acute consciousness, and with a sense of stretched attention which seemed to intensify all my faculties. The wind had risen, and was blowing in fitful gusts round the house.

A minute or two passed, and I began almost to fancy I must have been mistaken, when I distinctly heard the creak of the door, and then the click of the latch falling back into its place. Then I heard a sound on the boards as of one moving in the gallery. I sat up to listen, and as I did so I distinctly heard steps coming down the gallery. I heard them approach and pass my bed. I could see nothing, all was dark; but I heard the tread pro-ceeding towards the further portion of the gallery where were the uncurtained and unshuttered windows, two in number; but the moon shone through only one of these, the nearer; the other was dark, shadowed by the chapel or some other building at right angles. The tread seemed to me to pause now and again, and then continue as before.

I now fixed my eyes intently on the one illumined window, and it appeared to me as if some dark body passed across it: but what? I listened intently, and heard the step proceed to the end of the gallery and then return.

I again watched the lighted window, and immediately that the sound reached that portion of the long passage it ceased momentarily, and I saw, as distinctly as I ever saw anything in my life, by moonlight, a figure of a man with marked features, in what appeared to be a fur cap drawn over the brows.

It stood in the embrasure of the window, and the outline of the face was in silhouette; then it moved on, and as it moved I again heard the tread. I was as certain as I could be that the thing, whatever it was, or the person, whoever he was, was approaching my bed.

I threw myself back in the bed, and as I did so a mass of charred wood on the hearth fell down and sent up a flash of—I fancy sparks, that gave out a glare in the darkness, and by that—red as blood—I saw a face near me.

With a cry, over which I had as little control as the scream uttered by a sleeper in the agony of a nightmare, I called: "Who are you?"

There was an instant during which my hair bristled on my head, as in the horror of the darkness I prepared to grapple with the being at my side; when a board creaked as if someone had moved, and I heard the footsteps retreat, and again the click of the latch.

The next instant there was a rush on the stairs and Lynton burst into the room, just as he had sprung out of bed, crying: "For God's sake, what is the matter? Are you ill?"

I could not answer. Lynton struck a light and leant over the bed. Then I seized him by the arm, and said without moving: "There has been something in this room—gone in thither."

The words were hardly out of my mouth when Lynton, following the direction of my eyes, had sprung to the end of the corridor and thrown open the door there.

He went into the room beyond, looked round it, returned, and said: "You must have been dreaming."

By this time I was out of bed.

"Look for yourself," said he, and he led me into the little

room. It was bare, with cupboards and boxes, a sort of lumber-place. "There is nothing beyond this," said he, "no door, no staircase. It is a *cul-de-sac*." Then he added: "Now pull on your dressing-gown and come downstairs to my *sanctum*."

I followed him, and after he had spoken to Lady Lynton, who was standing with the door of her room ajar in a state of great agitation, he turned to me and said: "No one can have been in your room. You see my and my wife's apartments are close below, and no one could come up the spiral staircase without passing my door. You must have had a nightmare. Directly you screamed I rushed up the steps, and met no one descending; and there is no place of concealment in the lumber-room at the end of the gallery."

Then he took me into his private snuggery, blew up the fire, lighted a lamp, and said: "I shall be really grateful if you will say nothing about this. There are some in the house and neighbourhood who are silly enough as it is. You stay here, and if you do not feel inclined to go to bed, read—here are books. I must go to Lady Lynton, who is a good deal frightened, and does not like to be left alone."

He then went to his bedroom.

Sleep, as far as I was concerned, was out of the question, nor do I think that Sir Francis or his wife slept much either.

I made up the fire, and after a time took up a book, and tried to read, but it was useless.

I sat absorbed in thoughts and questionings till I heard the servants stirring in the morning. I then went to my own room, left the candle burning, and got into bed. I had just fallen asleep when my servant brought me a cup of tea at eight o'clock.

At breakfast Colonel Hampshire and his wife asked if anything had happened in the night, as they had been much disturbed by noises overhead, to which Lynton replied that I had not been very well, and had an attack of cramp, and that he had been upstairs to look after me. From his manner I could see that he wished me to be silent, and I said nothing accordingly.

In the afternoon, when everyone had gone out, Sir Francis

took me into his snuggery and said: "Halifax, I am very sorry about that matter last night. It is quite true, as my brother said, that steps have been heard about this house, but I never gave heed to such things, putting all noises down to rats. But after your experiences I feel that it is due to you to tell you something, and also to make to you an explanation. There is—there was—no one in the room at the end of the corridor, except the skeleton that was discovered in the chalk-pit when you were here many years ago. I confess I had not paid much heed to it.

"My archaeological fancies passed; I had no visits from anthropologists; the bones and skull were never shown to experts, but remained packed in a chest in that lumber-room. I confess I ought to have buried them, having no more scientific use for them, but I did not—on my word, I forgot all about them, or, at least, gave no heed to them. However, what you have gone through, and have described to me, has made me uneasy, and has also given me a suspicion that I can account for that body in a manner that had never occurred to me before."

After a pause, he added: "What I am going to tell you is known to no one else, and must not be mentioned by you—anyhow, in my lifetime, You know now that, owing to the death of my father when quite young, I and my brother and sister were brought up here with our grandfather, Sir Richard. He was an old, imperious, short-tempered man. I will tell you what I have made out of a matter that was a mystery for long, and I will tell you afterwards how I came to unravel it. My grandfather was in the habit of going out at night with a young under-keeper, of whom he was very fond, to look after the game and see if any poachers, whom he regarded as his natural enemies, were about.

"One night, as I suppose, my grandfather had been out with the young man in question, and, returning by the plantations, where the hill is steepest, and not far from that chalk-pit you remarked on yesterday, they came upon a man, who, though not actually belonging to the country, was well known in it as a sort of travelling tinker of indifferent character, and a notorious poacher. Mind this, I am not sure it was at the place I mention; I only now surmise it. On the particular night in question, my grandfather and the keeper must have caught this man setting snares; there must have been a tussle, in the course of which as subsequent circumstances have led me to imagine, the man showed fight and was knocked down by one or other of the two—my grandfather or the keeper. I believe that after having made various attempts to restore him, they found that the man was actually dead.

"They were both in great alarm and concern—my grandfather especially. He had been prominent in putting down some factory riots, and had acted as magistrate with promptitude, and had given orders to the military to fire, whereby a couple of lives had been lost. There was a vast outcry against him, and a certain political party had denounced him as an assassin. No man was more vituperated; yet, in my conscience, I believe that he acted with both discretion and pluck, and arrested a mischievous movement that might have led to much bloodshed. Be that as it may, my impression is that he lost his head over this fatal affair with the tinker, and that he and the keeper together buried the body secretly, not far from the place where he was killed. I now think it was in the chalk-pit, and that the skeleton found years after there belonged to this man."

"Good heavens!" I exclaimed, as at once my mind rushed back to the figure with the fur cap that I had seen against the window.

Sir Francis went on: "The sudden disappearance of the tramp, in view of his well-known habits and wandering mode of life, did not for some time excite surprise; but, later on, one or two circumstances having led to suspicion, an inquiry was set on foot, and among others, my grandfather's keepers were examined before the magistrates. It was remembered afterwards that the under-keeper in question was absent at the time of the inquiry, my grandfather having sent him with some dogs to a brother-in-law of his who lived upon the moors; but whether no one noticed the fact, or if they did, preferred to be silent, I know not, no observations were made. Nothing came of the investigation, and the whole subject would have dropped if it had not been that two years later, for some reasons I do not understand, but at the instigation of a magistrate recently imported into the division, whom my grandfather greatly disliked, and who was opposed to him in politics, a fresh inquiry was instituted. In the course of that inquiry it transpired that, owing to some unguarded words dropped by the under-keeper, a warrant was about to be issued for his arrest.

"My grandfather, who had had a fit of the gout, was away from home at the time, but on hearing the news he came home at once. The evening he returned he had a long interview with the young man, who left the house after he had supped in the servants' hall. It was observed that he looked much depressed. The warrant was issued the next day, but in the meantime the keeper had disappeared. My grandfather gave orders to all his own people to do everything in their power to assist the authorities in the search that was at once set on foot, but was unable himself to take any share in it.

"No trace of the keeper was found, although at a subsequent period rumours circulated that he had been heard of in America. But the man having been unmarried, he gradually dropped out of remembrance, and as my grandfather never allowed the subject to be mentioned in his presence, I should probably never have known anything about it but for the vague tradition which always attaches to such events, and for this fact: that after my grandfather's death a letter came addressed to him from somewhere in the United States from someone—the name different from that of the keeper—but alluding to the past, and implying the presence of a common secret, and, of course, with it came a request for money.

"I replied, mentioning the death of Sir Richard, and asking for an explanation. I did get an answer, and it is from that that I am able to fill in so much of the story. But I never learned *where* the man had been killed and buried, and my next letter to the fellow was returned with 'Deceased' written across it. Somehow, it never occurred to me till I heard your story that possibly the skeleton in the chalk-pit might be that of the poaching tinker. I will now most assuredly have it buried in the churchyard."

"That certainly ought to be done," said I.

"And—" said Sir Francis, after a pause, "I give you my word. After the burial of the bones, and you are gone, I will sleep for a week in the bed in the gallery, and report to you if I see or hear anything. If all be quiet, then—well, you form your own conclusions."

I left a day after. Before long I got a letter from my friend, brief but to the point: "All quiet, old boy; come again."

Little Joe Gander

(A tale from *A Book of Ghosts*)

"There's no good in him," said his stepmother, "not a mossul!" With these words she thrust little Joe forward by applying her knee to the small of his back, and thereby jerking him into the middle of the school before the master. "There's no making nothing out of him, whack him as you will."

Little Joe Lambole was a child of ten, dressed in second-hand, nay, third-hand garments that did not fit. His coat had been a soldier's scarlet uniform, that had gone when discarded to a dealer, who had dealt it to a carter, and when the carter had worn it out it was reduced and adapted to the wear of the child. The nether garments had, in like manner, served a full-grown man till worn out; then they had been cut down at the knees. Though shortened in leg, they maintained their former copiousness of seat, and served as an inexhaustible receptacle for dust. Often as little Joe was "licked" there issued from the dense mass of drapery clouds of dust. It was like beating a puff-ball.

"Only a seven-month child," said Mrs. Lambole contemptuously, "born without his nails on fingers and toes; they growed later. His wits have never come right, and a deal, a deal of larruping it will take to make 'em grow. Use the rod; we won't grumble at you for doing so."

Little Joe Lambole when he came into the world had not been expected to live. He was a poor, small, miserable baby, that could not roar, but whimpered. He had been privately baptised directly he was born, because, at the first, Mrs. Lambole said,

"The child is mine, though it be such a creetur, and I wouldn't like it, according, to be buried like a dog."

He was called Joseph. The scriptural Joseph had been sold as a bondman into Egypt; this little Joseph seemed to have been brought into the world to be a slave. In all propriety he ought to have died as a baby, and that happy consummation was almost desired, but he disappointed expectations and lived. His mother died soon after, and his father married again, and his father and stepmother loved him, doubtless; but love is manifested in many ways, and the Lamboles showed theirs in a rough way, by slaps and blows and kicks.

The father was ashamed of him because he was a weakling, and the stepmother because he was ugly, and was not her own child. He was a meagre little fellow, with a long neck and a white face and sunken cheeks, a pigeon breast, and a big stomach. He walked with his head forward and his great pale blue eyes staring before him into the far distance, as if he were always looking out of the world. His walk was a waddle, and he tumbled over every obstacle, because he never looked where he was going, always looked to something beyond the horizon.

Because of his walk and his long neck, and staring eyes and big stomach, the village children called him "Gander Joe" or "Joe Gander"; and his parents were not sorry, for they were ashamed that such a creature should be known as a Lambole.

The Lamboles were a sturdy, hearty people, with cheeks like quarrender apples, and bones set firm and knit with iron sinews. They were a hard-working, practical people who fattened pigs and kept poultry at home. Lambole was a roadmaker. In breaking stones one day a bit of one had struck his eye and blinded it. After that he wore a black patch upon it. He saw well enough out of the other; he never missed seeing his own interests. Lambole could have made a few pence with his son had his son been worth anything. He could have sent him to scrape the road, and bring the manure off it in a shovel to his garden. But Joe never took heartily to scraping the dung up. In a word, the boy was good for nothing.

He had hair like tow, and a little straw hat on his head with the top torn, so that the hair forced its way out, and as he walked the top bobbed about like the lid of a boiling saucepan.

When the whortleberries were ripe in June, Mrs. Lambole sent Joe out with other children to collect the berries in a tin can; she sold them for fourpence a quart, and any child could earn eightpence a day in whortleberry time; one that was active might earn a shilling.

But Joe would not remain with the other children. They teased him, imitated ganders and geese, and poked out their necks and uttered sounds in imitation of the voices of these birds. Moreover, they stole the berries he had picked, and put them into their own cans.

When Joe Gander left them and found himself alone in the woods, then he lay down among the brown heather and green fern, and looked up through the oak leaves at the sky, and listened to the singing of the birds. Oh, wondrous music of the woods! the hum of the summer air among the leaves, the drone of the bees about the flowers, the twittering and fluting and piping of the finches and blackbirds and thrushes, and the cool soft cooing of the wood pigeons, like the lowing of aerial oxen; then the tapping of the green woodpecker and a glimpse of its crimson head, like a carbuncle running up the tree trunk, and the powdering down of old husks of fir cones or of the tender rind of the topmost shoot of a Scottish pine; for aloft a red squirrel was barking a beautiful tree out of wantonness and frolic.

A rabbit would come forth from the bracken and sit up in the sun, and clean its face with the fore paws and stroke its long ears; then, seeing the soiled red coat, would skip up—little Joe lying very still—and screw its nose and turn its eyes from side to side, and skip nearer again, till it was quite close to Joe Gander; and then the boy laughed, and the rabbit was gone with a flash of white tail.

Happy days! days of listening to mysterious music, of looking into mysteries of sun and foliage, of spiritual intercourse with the great mother-soul of nature.

In the evenings, when Gander Joe came without his can, or with his can empty, he would say to his stepmother: "Oh, steppy! it was so nice; everything was singing."

"I'll make you sing in the chorus too!" cried Mrs. Lambole, and laid a stick across his shoulders. Experience had taught her the futility of dusting at a lower level.

Then Gander Joe cried and writhed, and promised to be more diligent in picking whortleberries in future. But when he went again into the wood it was again the same. The spell of the wood spirits was on him; he forgot about the berries at fourpence a quart, and lay on his back and listened. And the whole wood whispered and sang to him and consoled him for his beating, and the wind played lullabies among the fir spines and whistled in the grass, and the aspen clashed its myriad tiny cymbals together, producing an orchestra of sound that filled the soul of the dreaming boy with love and delight and unutterable yearning.

It fared no better in autumn, when the blackberry season set in. Joe went with his can to an old quarry where the brambles sent their runners over the masses of rubble thrown out from the pits, and warmed and ripened their fruit on the hot stones. It was a marvel to see how the blackberries grew in this deserted quarry; how large the fruit swelled, how thick they were—like mulberries. On the road side of the quarry was a belt of pines, and the sun drew out of their bark scents of unsurpassed sweetness. About the blackberries hovered spotted white and yellow and black moths, beautiful as butterflies. Butterflies did not fail either. The red admiral was there, resting on the bark of the trees, asleep in the sun with wings expanded, or drifting about the clumps of yellow ragwort, doubtful whether to perch or not.

Here, hidden behind the trees, among the leaves of overgrown rubble, was a one-story cottage of wood and clay, covered with thatch, in which lived Roger Gale, the postman.

Roger Gale had ten miles to walk every morning, delivering letters, and the same number of miles every evening, for which twenty miles he received the liberal pay of six shillings a week.

He had to be at the post office at half-past six in the morning to receive the letters, and at seven in the evening to deliver them. His work took him about six hours. The middle of the day he had to himself. Roger Gale was an old soldier, and enjoyed a pension. He occupied himself, when at home, as a shoemaker; but the walks took so much out of him, being an old man, that he had not the strength and energy to do much cobbling when at home. Therefore he idled a good deal, and he amused his idle hours with a violin.

Now, when Joe Gander came to the quarry before the return of the postman from his rounds, he picked blackberries; but no sooner had Roger Gale unlocked his door, taken down his fiddle, and drawn the bow across the strings, than Joe set down the can and listened. And when old Roger began to play an air from the *Daughter of the Regiment*, then Joe crept towards his cottage in little stages of wonderment and hunger to hear more and hear better, much in the same way as now and again in the wood the inquisitive rabbits had approached his red jacket. Presently Joe was seated on the doorstep, with his ear against the wooden door, and the blackberries and the can, and stepmother's orders and father's stick, and his hard bed and his meagre meals, even the whole world had passed away as a scroll that is rolled up and laid aside, and he lived only in the world of music.

Though his great eyes were wide he saw nothing through them; though the rain began to fall, and the north-east wind to blow, he felt nothing: he had but one faculty that was awake, and that was hearing.

One day Roger came to his door and opened it suddenly, so that the child, leaning against it, fell across his threshold.

"Whom have we here? What is this? What do you want?" asked the postman.

Then Gander Joe stood up, craning his long neck and staring out of his goggle eyes, with his rough flaxen hair standing up in a ruffle above his head and his great stomach protruded, and said nothing. So Roger burst out laughing. But he did not kick him off the step; he gave him a bit of bread and a drop of cider, and presently drew from the boy the confession that he had been listening to the fiddle. This was flattering to the postman, and it was the initiation of a friendship between them.

But when Joe came home with an empty can and said: "Oh, steppy, Master Roger Gale did fiddle so beautiful!" the woman said: "Fiddle! I'll fiddle your back pretty smartly, you idle vagabond"; and she was a truthful woman who never fell short of her word.

To break him of his bad habits—that is, of his dreaminess and uselessness—Mrs. Lambole took Joe to school.

At school he had a bad time of it. He could not learn the letters. He was mentally incapable of doing a subtraction sum. He sat on a bench staring at the teacher, and was unable to answer an ordinary question what the lesson was about. The school-children tormented him, the monitor scolded, and the master beat. Then little Joe Gander took to absenting himself from school. He was sent off every morning by his stepmother, but instead of going to the school he went to the cottage in the quarry, and listened to the fiddle of Roger Gale.

Little Joe got hold of an old box, and with a knife he cut holes in it; and he fashioned a bridge, and then a handle, and he strung horsehair over the latter, and made a bow, and drew very faint sounds from this improvised violin, that made the postman laugh, but which gave great pleasure to Joe. The sound that issued from his instrument was like the humming of flies, but he got distinct notes out of his strings, though the notes were faint.

After he had played truant for some time his father heard what he had done, and he beat the boy till he was like a battered apple that had been flung from the tree by a storm upon a road.

For a while Joe did not venture to the quarry except on Saturdays and Sundays. He was forbidden by his father to go to church, because the organ and the singing there drove him half crazed. When a beautiful, touching melody was played his eyes became clouded and the tears ran down his cheeks; and when the organ played the "Hallelujah Chorus," or some grand and stirring march, his eyes flashed, and his little body quivered, and he made such faces that the congregation were disturbed and the parson remonstrated with his mother. The child was clearly imbecile, and unfit to attend divine worship.

Mr. Lambole got an idea into his head, he would bring up Joe to be a butcher, and he informed Joe that he was going to place him with a gentleman of that profession in town. Joe cried. He turned sick at the sight of blood, and the smell of raw meat was abhorrent to him. But Joe's likings were of no account with his father, and he took him to the town and placed him with a butcher there. He was invested in a blue smock, and was informed that his duties would consist in taking meat about to the customers. Joe was left. It was the first time he had been from home, and he cried himself to sleep the first night, and he cried all the next day when sent around with meat on his shoulder.

Now on his journey through the streets he had to pass the window of a toy-shop. In the window were dolls and horses and little carts. For these Joe did not care, but there were also some little violins, some high priced, and some very low, and over these Joe lingered with loving, covetous eyes. There was one little fiddle to which his heart went out, that cost only three shillings and sixpence. Each day, as he passed the shop, he was drawn to it, and stood looking in, and longed daily more ardently than on the previous day for this three-and-sixpenny violin.

One day he was so lost in admiration and on the schemes he framed as to how he might eventually become possessed of the instrument, that he was unconscious of some boys stealing the meat out of the sort of trough on his shoulder in which he carried it about.

This was the climax of his misdeeds—he had been reprimanded for his blunders, delivering the wrong meat at the customers' doors; for his dilatory ways in going on his errands. The butcher could endure him no more, and sent him home to his father, who thrashed him, as his welcome.

But he carried home with him the haunting recollections of

that beautiful little red fiddle, with its fine black keys. The bow, he remembered, was strung with white horsehair. Joe had now a fixed ambition—something to live for. He would be perfectly happy if he could have that three-shillings-and-sixpenny fiddle. But how were three shillings and sixpence to be earned?

He confided his difficulty to postman Roger Gale, and Roger Gale said he would consider the matter.

A couple of days after the postman said to Joe—

"Gander, they want a lad to sweep the leaves in the drive at the great house. The squire's coachman told me, and I mentioned you. You'll have to do it on Saturday, and be paid sixpence."

Joe's face brightened. He went home and told his stepmother.

"For once you are going to be useful," said Mrs. Lambole. "Very well, you shall sweep the drive; then fivepence will come to us, and you shall have a penny every week to spend in sweet-stuff at the post office."

Joe tried to reckon how long it would be before he could purchase the fiddle, but the calculation was beyond his powers; so he asked the postman, who assured him it would take him forty weeks—that is, about ten months.

Little Joe was not cast down. What was time with such an end in view? Jacob served fourteen years for Rachel, and this was only forty weeks for a fiddle!

Joe was diligent every Saturday sweeping the drive. He was ordered whenever a carriage entered to dive behind the rhododendrons and laurels and disappear. He was of a too ragged and idiotic appearance to show in a gentleman's grounds.

Once or twice he encountered the squire and stood quaking, with his fingers spread out, his mouth and eyes open, and the broom at his feet. The squire spoke kindly to him, but Joe Gander was too frightened to reply.

"Poor fellow," said the squire to the gardener. "I suppose it is a charity to employ him, but I must say I should have preferred someone else with his wits about him. I will see to having him sent to an asylum for idiots in which I have some interest.

There's no knowing," said the squire, "no knowing but that with wholesome food, cleanliness, and kindness his feeble mind may be got to understand that two and two make four, which I learn he has not yet mastered."

Every Saturday evening Joe Gander brought his sixpence home to his stepmother. The woman was not so regular in allowing him his penny out.

"Your edication costs such a lot of money," she said.

"Steppy, need I go to school anymore?" He never could frame his mouth to call her mother.

"Of course you must. You haven't passed your standard."

"But I don't think that I ever shall."

"Then," said Mrs. Lambole, "what masses of good food you do eat. You're perfectly insatiable. You cost us more than it would to keep a cow."

"Oh, steppy, I won't eat so much if I may have my penny!"

"Very well. Eating such a lot does no one good. If you will be content with one slice of bread for breakfast instead of two, and the same for supper, you shall have your penny. If you are so very hungry you can always get a swede or a mangold out of Farmer Eggins's field. Swedes and mangolds are cooling to the blood and sit light on the stomick," said Mrs. Lambole.

So the compact was made; but it nearly killed Joe. His cheeks and chest fell in deeper and deeper, and his stomach protruded more than ever. His legs seemed hardly able to support him, and his great pale blue wandering eyes appeared ready to start out of his head like the horns of a snail. As for his voice, it was thin and toneless, like the notes on his improvised fiddle, on which he played incessantly.

"The child will always be a discredit to us," said Lambole. "He don't look like a human child. He don't think and feel like a Christian. The shovelfuls of dung he might have brought to cover our garden if he had only given his heart to it!"

"I've heard of changelings," said Mrs. Lambole; "and with this creetur on our hands I mainly believe the tale. They do say that the pixies steal away the babies of Christian folk, and put

73

their own bantlings in their stead. The only way to find out is to heat a poker red-hot and ram it down the throat of the child; and when you do that the door opens, and in comes the pixy mother and runs off with her own child, and leaves your proper babe behind. That's what we ought to ha' done wi' Joe."

"I doubt, wife, the law wouldn't have upheld us," said Lambole, thrusting hot coals back on to the hearth with his foot.

"I don't suppose it would," said Mrs. Lambole. "And yet we call this a land of liberty! Law ain't made for the poor, but for the rich."

"It is wickedness," argued the father. "It is just the same with colts—all wickedness. You must drive it out with the stick."

And now a great temptation fell on little Gander Joe. The squire and his family were at home, and the daughter of the house, Miss Amory, was musical. Her mother played on the piano and the young lady on the violin. The fashion for ladies to play on this instrument had come in, and Miss Amory had taken lessons from the best masters in town. She played vastly better than poor Roger Gale, and she played to an accompaniment.

Sometimes whilst Joe was sweeping he heard the music; then he stole nearer and nearer to the house, hiding behind rhododendron bushes, and listening with eyes and mouth and nostrils and ears. The music exercised on him an irresistible attraction. He forgot his obligation to work; he forgot the strict orders he had received not to approach the garden-front of the house. The music acted on him like a spell. Occasionally he was roused from his dream by the gardener, who boxed his ears, knocked him over, and bade him get back to his sweeping. Once a servant came out from Miss Amory to tell the ragged little boy not to stand in front of the drawing-room window staring in. On another occasion he was found by Miss Amory crouched behind a rose bush outside her *boudoir*, listening whilst she practised.

No one supposed that the music drew him. They thought him a fool, and that he had the inquisitiveness of the half-witted to peer in at windows and see the pretty sights within.

He was reprimanded, and threatened with dismissal. The gardener complained to the lad's father and advised a good hiding, such as Joe should not forget.

"These sort of chaps," said the gardener, "have no senses like rational beings, except only the feeling, and you must teach them as you feed the Polar bears—with the end of a stick."

One day Miss Amory, seeing how thin and hollow-eyed the child was, and hearing him cough, brought him out a cup of hot coffee and some bread.

He took it without a word, only pulling off his torn straw hat and throwing it at his feet, exposing the full shock of tow-like hair; then he stared at her out of his great eyes, speechless.

"Joe," she said, "poor little man, how old are you?"

"Dun'now," he answered.

"Can you read and write?"

"No."

"Nor do sums?"

"No."

"What can you do?"

"Fiddle."

"Have you got a fiddle?"

"Yes."

"I should like to see it, and hear you play."

Next day was Sunday. Little Joe forgot about the day, and forgot that Miss Amory would probably be in church in the morning. She had asked to see his fiddle, so in the morning he took it and went down with it to the park. The church was within the grounds, and he had to pass it. As he went by he heard the roll of the organ and the strains of the choir. He stopped to hearken, then went up the steps of the churchyard, listening. A desire came on him to catch the air on his improvised violin, and he put it to his shoulder and drew his bow across the slender cords.

The sound was very faint, so faint as to be drowned by the greater volume of the organ and the choir. Nevertheless he could hear the feeble tones close to his ear, and his heart danced at the pleasure of playing to an accompaniment, like Miss Amory.

75

The choir, the congregation, were singing the Advent hymn to Luther's tune—

Great God, what do I see and hear?
The end of things created.

Little Joe, playing his inaudible instrument, came creeping up the avenue, treading on the fallen yellow lime leaves, passing between the tombstones, drawn on by the solemn, beautiful music. Presently he stood in the porch, then he went on; he was unconscious of everything but the music and the joy of playing with it; he walked on softly into the church without even removing his ragged straw cap, though the squire and the squire's wife, and the rector and the reverend the Mrs. Rector, and the parish churchwarden and the rector's churchwarden, and the overseer and the waywarden, and all the farmers and their wives were present. He had forgotten about his broken cap in the delight that made the tears fill his eyes and trickle over his pale cheeks.

Then when with a shock the parson and the churchwardens saw the ragged urchin coming up the nave fiddling, with his hat on, regardless of the sacredness of the place, and above all of the sacredness of the presence of the squire, J.P. and D.L., the rector coughed very loud and looked hard at his churchwarden, Farmer Eggins, who turned red as the sun in a November fog, and rose. At the same instant the people's churchwarden rose, and both advanced upon Joe Gander from opposite sides of the church.

At the moment that they touched him the organ and the singing ceased; and it was to Joe a sudden wakening from a golden dream to a black and raw reality. He looked up with dazed face first at one man, then at the other: both their faces blazed with equal indignation; both were equally speechless with wrath. They conducted him, each holding an arm, out of the porch and down the avenue. Joe heard indistinctly behind him the droning of the rector's voice continuing the prayers. He looked back over his shoulder and saw the faces of the schoolchildren straining after him through the open door from their places near it.

On reaching the steps—there was a flight of five leading to the road—the people's churchwarden uttered a loud and disgusted "Ugh!" then with his heavy hand slapped the head of the child towards the parson's churchwarden, who with his still heavier hand boxed it back again; then the people's churchwarden gave him a blow which sent him staggering forward, and this was supplemented by a kick from the parson's churchwarden, which sent Joe Gander spinning down the five steps at once and cast him prostrate into the road, where he fell and crushed his extemporised violin.

Then the churchwardens turned, blew their noses, and re-entered the church, where they sat out the rest of the service, grateful in their hearts that they had been enabled that day to show that their office was no sinecure.

The churchwardens were unaware that in banging and kicking the little boy out of the churchyard and into the road they had flung him so that he fell with his head upon the kerbstone of the footpath, which stone was of slate, and sharp. They did not find this out through the prayers, nor through the sermon. But when the whole congregation left the church they were startled to find little Joe Gander insensible, with his head cut, and a pool of blood on the footway. The squire was shocked, as were his wife and daughter, and the churchwardens were in consternation. Fortunately the squire's stables were near the church, and there was a running fountain there, so that water was procured, and the child revived.

Mrs. Amory had in the meantime hastened home and returned with a roll of diachylon plaster and a pair of small scissors. Strips of the adhesive plaster were applied to the wound, and the boy was soon sufficiently recovered to stand on his feet, when the churchwardens very considerately undertook to march him home. On reaching his cottage the churchwardens described what had taken place, painting the insult offered to the worshippers in the most hideous colours, and representing the accident of the cut as due to the violent resistance offered by the culprit to their ejectment of him. Then each pressed a half-crown into the hand of Mr. Lambole and departed to his dinner.

"Now then, young shaver," exclaimed the father, "at your pranks again! How often have I told you not to go intruding into a place of worship? Church ain't for such as you. If you had'nt been punished a bit already, wouldn't I larrup you neither? Oh, no!"

Little Joe's head was bad for some days. His cheeks were flushed and his eyes bright, and he talked strangely—he who was usually so silent. What troubled him was the loss of his fiddle; he did not know what had become of it, whether it had been stolen or confiscated. He asked after it, and when at last it was produced, smashed to chips, with the strings torn and hanging loose about it like the cordage of a broken vessel, he cried bitterly.

Miss Amory came to the cottage to see him, and finding father and stepmother out, went in and pressed five shillings into his hand. Then he laughed with delight, and clapped his hands, and hid the money away in his pocket, but he said nothing, and Miss Amory went away convinced that the child was half a fool. But little Joe had sense in his head, though his head was different from those of others; he knew that now he had the money wherewith to buy the beautiful fiddle he had seen in the shop window many months before, and to get which he had worked and denied himself food.

When Miss Amory was gone, and his stepmother had not returned, he opened the door of the cottage and stole out. He was afraid of being seen, so he crept along in the hedge, and when he thought anyone was coming he got through a gate or lay down in a ditch, till he was some way on his road to the town. Then he ran till he was tired. He had a bandage round his head, and, as his head was hot, he took the rag off, dipped it in water, and tied it round his head again. Never in his life had his mind been clearer than it was now, for now he had a distinct purpose, and an object easily attainable, before him. He held the money in his hand, and looked at it, and kissed it; then pressed it to his beating heart, then ran on. He lost breath. He could run no more. He sat down in the hedge and gasped. The perspiration was streaming off his face. Then he thought he heard steps coming fast along the road he had run, and as he feared pursuit, he got up and ran on.

He went through the village four miles from home just as the children were leaving school, and when they saw him some of the elder cried out that here was "Gander Joe! quack! quack! Joe the Gander! quack! quack! quack!" and the little ones joined in the banter. The boy ran on, though hot and exhausted, and with his head swimming, to escape their merriment.

He got some way beyond the village when he came to a turnpike. There he felt dizzy, and he timidly asked if he might have a piece of bread. He would pay for it if they would change a shilling. The woman at the 'pike pitied the pale, hollow-eyed child, and questioned him; but her questions bewildered him, and he feared she would send him home, so that he either answered nothing, or in a way which made her think him distraught. She gave him some bread and water, and watched him going on towards the town till he was out of sight. The day was already declining; it would be dark by the time he reached the town. But he did not think of that.

He did not consider where he would sleep, whether he would have strength to return ten miles to his home. He thought only of the beautiful red violin with the yellow bridge hung in the shop window, and offered for three shillings and sixpence. Three-and-sixpence! Why, he had five shillings. He had money to spend on other things beside the fiddle. He had been sadly disappointed about his savings from the weekly sixpence. He had asked for them; he had earned them, not by his work only, but by his abstention from two pieces of bread *per diem*. When he asked for the money, his stepmother answered that she had put it away in the savings bank. If he had it he would waste it on sweetstuff; if it were hoarded up it would help him on in life when left to shift for himself; and if he died, why it would go towards his burying.

So the child had been disappointed in his calculations, and had worked and starved for nothing. Then came Miss Amory with her present, and he had run away with that, lest his mother should take it from him to put in the savings bank for setting him up in life or for his burying. What cared he for either? All his ambition was to have a fiddle, and a fiddle was to be had for three-and-sixpence.

Joe Gander was tired. He was fain to sit down at intervals on the heaps of stones by the roadside to rest. His shoes were very poor, with soles worn through, so that the stones hurt his feet. At this time of the year the highways were fresh metalled, and as he stumbled over the newly broken stones they cut his soles and his ankles turned. He was footsore and weary in body, but his heart never failed him. Before him shone the red violin with the yellow bridge, and the beautiful bow strung with shining white hair. When he had that all his weariness would pass as a dream; he would hunger no more, cry no more, feel no more sickness or faintness. He would draw the bow over the strings and play with his fingers on the catgut, and the waves of music would thrill and flow, and away on those melodious waves his soul would float far from trouble, far from want, far from tears, into a shining, sunny world of music.

So he picked himself up when he fell, and staggered to his feet from the stones on which he rested, and pressed on.

The sun was setting as he entered the town. He went straight to the shop he so well remembered, and to his inexpressible delight saw still in the window the coveted violin, price three shillings and sixpence.

Then he timidly entered the shop, and with trembling hand held out the money.

"What do you want?"

"It," said the boy. It. To him the shop held but one article. The dolls, the wooden horses, the tin steam-engines, the bats, the kites, were unconsidered. He had seen and remembered only one thing—the red violin. "It," said the boy, and pointed.

When little Joe had got the violin he pressed it to his shoulder, and his heart bounded as though it would have burst the pigeon breast. His dull eyes lightened, and into his white sunken cheeks shot a hectic flame. He went forth with his head erect and with firm foot, holding his fiddle to the shoulder and the bow in hand.

He turned his face homeward. Now he would return to father and stepmother, to his little bed at the head of the stairs, to his scanty meals, to the school, to the sweeping of the park drive, and to his stepmother's scoldings and his father's beatings. He had his fiddle, and he cared for nothing else.

He waited till he was out of the town before he tried it. Then, when he was on a lonely part of the road, he seated himself in the hedge, under a holly tree covered with scarlet berries, and tried his instrument. Alas! it had hung many years in the shop window, and the catgut was old and the glue had lost its tenacity. One string started; then when he tried to screw up a second, it sprang as well, and then the bridge collapsed and fell. Moreover, the hairs on the bow came out. They were unresined.

Then little Joe's spirits gave way. He laid the bow and the violin on his knees and began to cry.

As he cried he heard the sound of approaching wheels and the clatter of a horse's hoofs.

He heard, but he was immersed in sorrow and did not heed and raise his head to see who was coming. Had he done so he would have seen nothing, as his eyes were swimming with tears. Looking out of them he saw only as one sees who opens his eyes when diving.

"Halloa, young shaver! Dang you! What do you mean giving me such a cursed hunt after you as this—you as ain't worth the trouble, eh?"

The voice was that of his father, who drew up before him. Mr. Lambole had made inquiries when it was discovered that Joe was lost, first at the school, where it was most unlikely he would be found, then at the public-house, at the gardener's and the gamekeeper's; then he had looked down the well and then up the chimney. After that he went to the cottage in the quarry. Roger Gale knew nothing of him. Presently someone coming from the nearest village mentioned that he had been seen there;

whereupon Lambole borrowed Farmer Eggins's trap and went after him, peering right and left of the road with his one eye.

Sure enough he had been through the village. He had passed the turnpike. The woman there described him accurately as "a sort of a tottle" (fool).

Mr. Lambole was not a pleasant-looking man; he was as solidly built as a navvy. The backs of his hands were hairy, and his fist was so hard, and his blows so weighty, that for sport he was wont to knock down and kill at a blow the oxen sent to Butcher Robbins for slaughter, and that he did with his fist alone, hitting the animal on the head between the horns, a little forward of the horns. That was a great feat of strength, and Lambole was proud of it. He had a long back and short legs. The back was not pliable or bending; it was hard, braced with sinews tough as hawsers, and supported a pair of shoulders that could sustain the weight of an ox.

His face was of a coppery colour, caused by exposure to the air and drinking. His hair was light: that was almost the only feature his son had derived from him. It was very light, too light for his dark red face. It grew about his neck and under his chin as a Newgate collar; there was a great deal of it, and his face, encircled by the pale hair, looked like an angry moon surrounded by a fog bow.

Mr. Lambole had a queer temper. He bottled up his anger, but when it blew the cork out it spurted over and splashed all his home; it flew in the faces and soused everyone who came near him.

Mr. Lambole took his son roughly by the arm and lifted him into the tax cart. The boy offered no resistance. His spirit was broken, his hopes extinguished. For months he had yearned for the red fiddle, price three-and-six, and now that, after great pains and privations, he had acquired it, the fiddle would not sound.

"Ain't you ashamed of yourself, giving your dear dada such trouble, eh, Viper?"

Mr. Lambole turned the horse's head homeward. He had his black patch towards the little Gander, seated in the bottom of the cart, hugging his wrecked violin. When Mr. Lambole spoke he turned his face round to bring the active eye to bear on the shrinking, crouching little figure below.

The Viper made no answer, but looked up. Mr. Lambole turned his face away, and the seeing eye watched the horse's ears, and the black patch was towards a frightened, piteous, pleading little face, looking up, with the light of the evening sky irradiating it, showing how wan it was, how hollow were the cheeks, how sunken the eyes, how sharp the little pinched nose. The boy put up his arm, that held the bow, and wiped his eyes with his sleeve. In so doing he poked his father in the ribs with the end of the bow.

"Now, then!" exclaimed Mr. Lambole with an oath, "what darn'd insolence be you up to now, Gorilla?"

If he had not held the whip in one hand and the reins in the other he would have taken the bow from the child and flung it into the road. He contented himself with rapping Joe's head with the end of the whip.

"What's that you've got there, eh?" he asked.

The child replied timidly: "Please, father, a fiddle."

"Where did you get 'un—steal it, eh?"

Joe answered, trembling: "No, dada, I bought it."

"Bought it! Where did you get the money?"

"Miss Amory gave it me."

"How much?"

The Gander answered: "Her gave me five shilling."

"Five shillings! And what did that blessed" (he did not say "blessed," but something quite the reverse) "fiddle cost you?"

"Three-and-sixpence."

"So you've only one-and-six left?"

"I've none, dada."

"Why not?"

"Because I spent one shilling on a pipe for you, and sixpence on a thimble for stepmother as a present," answered the child, with a flicker of hope in his dim eyes that this would propitiate his father.

"Dash me," roared the roadmaker, "if you ain't worse nor Mr. Chamberlain, as would rob us of the cheap loaf! What in the name of Thunder and Bones do you mean squandering the precious money over fooleries like that for? I've got my pipe, black as your back shall be before tomorrow, and mother has an old thimble as full o' holes as I'll make your skin before the night is much older. Wait till we get home, and I'll make pretty music out of that there fiddle! just you see if I don't."

Joe shivered in his seat, and his head fell.

Mr. Lambole had a playful wit. He beguiled his journey home by indulging in it, and his humour flashed above the head of the child like summer lightning. "You're hardly expecting the abundance of the supper that's awaiting you," he said, with his black patch glowering down at the irresponsive heap in the corner of the cart. "No stinting of the dressing, I can tell you. You like your meat well basted, don't you? The basting shall not incur your disapproval as insufficient. Underdone? Oh, dear, no! Nothing underdone for me. Pickles? I can promise you that there is something in pickle for you, hot—very hot and stinging. Plenty of capers—mutton and capers. Mashed potatoes? Was the request for that on the tip of your tongue? Sorry I can give you only half what you want—the mash, not the potatoes. There is nothing comparable in my mind to young pig with crackling. The hide is well striped, cut in lines from the neck to the tail. I think we'll have crackling on our pig before morning."

He now threw his seeing eye into the depths of the cart, to note the effect his fun had on the child, but he was disappointed. It had evoked no hilarity. Joe had fallen asleep, exhausted by his walk, worn out with disappointments, with his head on his fiddle, that lay on his knees. The jogging of the cart, the attitude, affected his wound; the plaster had given way, and the blood was running over the little red fiddle and dripping into its hollow body through the S-hole on each side.

It was too dark for Mr. Lambole to notice this. He set his lips. His self-esteem was hurt at the child not relishing his waggery.

Mrs. Lambole observed it when, shortly after, the cart drew

up at the cottage and she lifted the sleeping child out.

"I must take the cart back to Farmer Eggins," said her husband; "duty fust, and pleasure after."

When his father was gone Mrs. Lambole said, "Now then, Joe, you've been a very wicked, bad boy, and God will never forgive you for the naughtiness you have committed and the trouble to which you have put your poor father and me." She would have spoken more sharply but that his head needed her care and the sight of the blood disarmed her. Moreover, she knew that her husband would not pass over what had occurred with a reprimand. "Get off your clothes and go to bed, Joe," she said when she had readjusted the plaster. "You may take a piece of dry bread with you, and I'll see if I can't persuade your father to put off whipping of you for a day or two."

Joe began to cry.

"There," she said, "don't cry. When wicked children do wicked things they must suffer for them. It is the law of nature. And," she went on, "you ought to be that ashamed of yourself that you'd be glad for the earth to open under you and swallow you up like Korah, Dathan, and Abiram. Running away from so good and happy a home and such tender parents! But I reckon you be lost to natural affection as you be to reason."

"May I take my fiddle with me?" asked the boy.

"Oh, take your fiddle if you like," answered his mother. "Much good may it do you. Here, it is all smeared wi' blood. Let me wipe it first, or you'll mess the bedclothes with it. There," she said as she gave him the broken instrument. "Say your prayers and go to sleep; though I reckon your prayers will never reach to heaven, coming out of such a wicked unnatural heart."

So the little Gander went to his bed. The cottage had but one bedroom and a landing above the steep and narrow flight of steps that led to it from the kitchen. On this landing was a small truckle bed, on which Joe slept. He took off his clothes and stood in his little short shirt of very coarse white linen. He knelt down and said his prayers, with both his hands spread over his fiddle. Then he got into bed, and until his stepmother fetched away the benzoline lamp he examined the instrument. He saw that the bridge might be set up again with a little glue, and that fresh catgut strings might be supplied. He would take his fiddle next day to Roger Gale and ask him to help to mend it for him. He was sure Roger would take an interest in it. Roger had been mysterious of late, hinting that the time was coming when Joey would have a first-rate instrument and learn to play like a Paganini. Yes; the case of the red fiddle was not desperate.

Just then he heard the door below open, and his father's step.

"Where is the toad?" said Mr. Lambole.

Joe held his breath, and his blood ran cold. He could hear every word, every sound in the room below.

"He's gone to bed," answered Mrs. Lambole. "Leave the poor little creetur alone tonight, Samuel; his head has been bad, and he don't look well. He's overdone."

"Susan," said the roadmaker, "I've been simmering all the way to town, and bubbling and boiling all the way back, and busting is what I be now, and bust I will."

Little Joe sat up in bed, hugging the violin, and his tow-like hair stood up on his head. His great stupid eyes stared wide with fear; in the dark the iris in each had grown big, and deep, and solemn.

"Give me my stick," said Mr. Lambole. "I've promised him a taste of it, and a taste won't suffice tonight; he must have a gorge of it."

"I've put it away," said Mrs. Lambole. "Samuel, right is right, and I'm not one to stand between the child and what he deserves, but he ain't in condition for it tonight. He wants feeding up to it."

Without wasting another word on her the roadmaker went upstairs.

The shuddering, cowering little fellow saw first the red face, surrounded by a halo of pale hair, rise above the floor, then the strong square shoulders, then the clenched hands, and then his father stood before him, revealed down to his thick boots. The child crept back in the bed against the wall, and would have disappeared through it had the wall been soft-hearted, as in fairy tales, and opened to receive him. He clasped his little violin tight to his heart, and then the blood that had fallen into it trickled out and ran down his shirt, staining it—upon the bedclothes, staining them. But the father did not see this. He was effervescing with fury. His pulses went at a gallop, and his great fists clutched spasmodically.

"You Judas Iscariot, come here!" he shouted.

But the child only pressed closer against the wall.

"What! disobedient and daring? Do you hear? Come to me!"

The trembling child pointed to a pretty little pipe on the bedclothes. He had drawn it from his pocket and taken the paper off it, and laid it there, and stuck the silver-headed thimble in the bowl for his stepmother when she came upstairs to take the lamp.

"Come here, vagabond!"

He could not; he had not the courage nor the strength.

He still pointed pleadingly to the little presents he had bought with his eighteenpence.

"You won't, you dogged, insulting being?" roared the road-maker, and rushed at him, knocking over the pipe, which fell and broke on the floor, and trampling flat the thimble. "You won't yet? Always full of sulks and defiance! Oh, you ungrateful one, you!" Then he had him by the collar of his night-shirt and dragged him from his bed, and with his violence tore the button off, and with his other hand he wrenched the violin away and beat the child over the back with it as he dragged him from the bed.

"Oh, my mammy! my mammy!" cried Joe.

He was not crying out for his stepmother. It was the agonised cry of his frightened heart for the one only being who had ever loved him, and whom God had removed from him.

Suddenly Samuel Lambole started back.

Before him, and between him and the child, stood a pale,

ghostly form, and he knew his first wife.

He stood speechless and quaking. Then, gradually recovering himself, he stumbled down the stairs, and seated himself, looking pasty and scared, by the fire below.

"What is the matter with you, Samuel?" asked his wife.

"I've seen her," he gasped. "Don't ask no more questions."

Now when he was gone, little Joe, filled with terror—not at the apparition, which he had not seen, for his eyes were too dazed to behold it, but with apprehension of the chastisement that awaited him, scrambled out of the window and dropped on the pigsty roof, and from thence jumped to the ground.

Then he ran—ran as fast as his legs could carry him, still hugging his instrument—to the churchyard; and on reaching that he threw himself on his mother's grave and sobbed: "Oh, mammy, mammy! father wants to beat me and take away my beautiful violin—but oh, mammy! my violin won't play."

And when he had spoken, from out the grave rose the form of his lost mother, and looked kindly on him.

Joe saw her, and he had no fear.

"Mammy!" said he, "mammy, my violin cost three shillings and sixpence, and I can't make it play no-ways."

Then the spirit of his mother passed a hand over the strings, and smiled. Joe looked into her eyes, and they were as stars. And he put the violin under his chin, and drew the bow across the strings—and lo! they sounded wondrously. His soul thrilled, his heart bounded, his dull eye brightened. He was as though caught up in a chariot of fire and carried to heavenly places. His bow worked rapidly, such strains poured from the little instrument as he had never heard before. It was to him as though heaven opened, and he heard the angels performing there, and he with his fiddle was taking a part in the mighty symphony. He felt not the cold, the night was not dark to him. His head no longer ached. It was as though after long seeking through life he had gained an undreamed-of prize, reached some glorious consummation.

★★★★★★

There was a musical party that same evening at the Hall. Miss Amory played beautifully, with extraordinary feeling and execution, both with and without accompaniment on the piano. Several ladies and gentlemen sang and played; there were duets and trios.

During the performances the guests talked to each other in low tones about various topics.

Said one lady to Mrs. Amory: "How strange it is that among the English lower classes there is no love of music."

"There is none at all," answered Mrs. Amory; "our rector's wife has given herself great trouble to get up parochial entertainments, but we find that nothing takes with the people but comic songs, and these, instead of elevating, vulgarise them."

"They have no music in them. The only people with music in their souls are the Germans and the Italians."

"Yes," said Mrs. Amory with a sigh; "it is sad, but true: there is neither poetry, nor picturesqueness, nor music among the English peasantry."

"You have never heard of one, self-taught, with a real love of music in this country?"

"Never: such do not exist among us."

★★★★★★

The parish churchwarden was walking along the road on his way to his farmhouse, and the road passed under the churchyard wall.

As he walked along the way—with a not too steady step, for he was returning from the public-house—he was surprised and frightened to hear music proceed from among the graves.

It was too dark for him to see any figure then, only the tombstones loomed on him in ghostly shapes. He began to quake, and finally turned and ran, nor did he slacken his pace till he reached the tavern, where he burst in shouting: "There's ghosts abroad. I've heard 'em in the churchyard making music."

The revellers rose from their cups.

"Shall we go and hear?" they asked.

"I'll go for one," said a man; "if others will go with me."

"Ay," said a third, "and if the ghosts be playing a jolly good tune, we'll chip in."

So the whole half-tipsy party reeled along the road, talking very loud, to encourage themselves and the others, till they approached the church, the spire of which stood up dark against the night sky.

"There's no lights in the windows," said one.

"No," observed the churchwarden, "I didn't notice any myself; it was from the graves the music came, as if all the dead was squeakin' like pigs."

"Hush!" All kept silence—not a sound could be heard.

"I'm sure I heard music afore," said the churchwarden. "I'll bet a gallon of ale I did."

"There ain't no music now, though," remarked one of the men.

"Nor more there ain't," said others.

"Well, I don't care—I say I heard it," asseverated the churchwarden. "Let's go up closer."

All of the party drew nearer to the wall of the graveyard. One man, incapable of maintaining his legs unaided, sustained himself on the arm of another.

"Well, I do believe, Churchwarden Eggins, as how you have been leading us a wild goose chase!" said a fellow.

Then the clouds broke, and a bright, dazzling pure ray shot down on a grave in the churchyard, and revealed a little figure lying on it.

"I do believe," said one man, "as how, if he ain't led us a goose chase, he's brought us after a Gander—surely that is little Joe."

Thus encouraged, and their fears dispelled, the whole half-tipsy party stumbled up the graveyard steps, staggered among the tombs, some tripping on the mounds and falling prostrate. All laughed, talked, joked with one another.

The only one silent there was little Joe Gander—and he was gone to join in the great symphony above.

Crowdy Marsh

I believe that one of the most desolate spots in the west is the moor about Brown Willy, and one of the most unpleasant experiences I have encountered is being lost at the fall of night on that moor late in the autumn, and when the days are short and the darkness settles down as a black pall over moor and fen, when even the tors no longer reflect the dying light, and are seen only as black profiles against a sky in which is scarce a ray or only a ghastly glare in the west.

I was out one day at the end of October with my friend Richards, shooting on the Bodmin moors, or to be more exact, we went out with the purpose of shooting blackcock, but saw not one. The fact that we had been unsuccessful tended to make us prolong our tramp, always hoping that we might see one, and always disappointed. At last I said, "Come, Richards, we must turn back; the sun has set, and I don't want to lose my way about Brown Willy and run the risk of stumbling into Crowdy Marsh."

Brown Willy, the highest of the Cornish tors is not of great height, only 1,375 feet, but with its five-homed head it proves a bold and conspicuous object, and in ancient times it was a beacon; three immense cairns are piled up on the summit on which once blazed fires to warn the country round when foreign sails appeared on the sea, and there was thought to be risk of invasion.

We were bound for Camelford, where is a comfortable hotel, and where we were aware that a good supper was awaiting us.

But then—how to get there? Now the moor about Brown Willy and his sister, Rough Tor, is peculiarly nasty with bogs, and these bogs are not to be trifled with. On the west of Rough Tor is Stannon Marsh, and below the tor it possesses a little odious morass of its own, Rough Tor Marsh, in which the De Lank River rises. Then under Buttern Hill is another much bigger, that festers in its own muck, feeding no stream at all. Due north of Rough Tor on Davidstow Moor is a tract of comparatively dry land, lying between the swamp just mentioned and the re-doubted Crowdy Marsh, but this measures only two-thirds of a mile in breadth, and Crowdy Marsh throws out a wet and oozy and into this dry moorland to grip and draw under an incautious wanderer.

Now it is no joke finding one's way by daylight from Brown Willy across this bridle path between morasses into the Camelford Road, and I did not much relish the prospect of venturing on it with night falling. So now I urged Richards to step out, as we had seven miles to walk if we went the way indicated. But there was another way over Lower Moor between Stannon Marsh and Crowdy that was much shorter, but I was not well acquainted with that portion of the moor, and did not like to venture on it in the dark. It was a mistake, as a direct line ran from the monument on Polden Down to Camelford. However, ill-luck attended us all that day, and I chose to push on over Davidstow Moor, where I knew I should strike the high road in two miles and a half, whereas by the other way I would have no main road at all, and I thought I might get lost among lanes when leaving the open moor.

We paced on for some time cheerily, and a certain failing amount of light enabled me to see that we were skirting Rough Tor; and then I said to my companion.

"Now we must look alive, and mind our steps. We have Scylla on one side and Charybdis on the other, and I do not think there is much choice in rotten apples; I would as soon be engulfed in one as in the other. Look alive, man! By Jove! I am in water."

And so I was. I floundered forward and went in to my middle.

Then I threw my gun down, cast myself across it, and drew my legs with a tremendous effort out of the slime that sucked at me, and had indeed, by suction, torn off one of my gaiters.

I called out to Richards to keep away from me, and aim for the lightest spot in the sky; as for me, I would find my way out as best I could.

The only possible way of getting out of these bogs is to aim for some point and work steadily forward towards it, for otherwise one shifts from one tussock of grass or mass of grey moss to another, and loses all knowledge of direction, and very often one travels about in a circle.

But just now it was not easy to take a direction; to the north there was nothing conspicuous at which one could aim; and yet, to the north we had to go. How I cursed my folly in taking this course instead of that from the monument. Lanes, bad though they might be and bewildering, could not swallow one up as would these bogs, if they got hold of you. Moreover, the cold of the slimy water was intense, and numbed the legs and feet. At last, creeping forward on my breast with the gun athwart me, I reached a hump of drier ground, and seated myself on it to gather breath before proceeding farther, worming my way through the mire. I called to Richards to go forward; I would follow. But I received no answer. I called again and again, but met with no response.

There was still a long tract of morass very similar in nature to that through part of which I had struggled, and I was fain to get through it in the same manner as before, writhing along like a lizard. Then my strength gave way. The strain on my muscles had been too great, and I turned dizzy. What had become of Richards I did not know. I greatly feared that he had been swallowed up. Exhausted, panting, my brow beaded with sweat, yet at the same time conscious of extreme cold from immersion, I tried to gather my senses together. I was still not out of the morass, I did not know in which direction to worm my way. The stench in my nostrils of the decomposing matter sickened me. As I thus lay prostrate, I heard the peal of a horn. A steely light still lingered in the southwest, not enough to enable me to distinguish forms at a distance. Moreover, I could not turn my head where I lay and look in the direction whence came the sound. Then I heard the deep-mouthed baying of hounds and another peal of the horn nearer than before. Next moment, to my ineffable surprise, I saw the dark form of a horseman in full gallop pass near me, over the surface of the morass, followed by a pack.

As one of the hounds swept by me, touching me, by a sudden impulse I let go my gun, and threw my arms about the body of the dog. In an instant I was whirled from the tussock of grass on which I lay, and carried forward swift as the wind, ploughing through water, course grass and moss blinding me, but I held fast desperately, and in a few moments felt that I was on firm ground; whereupon I relaxed my hold and rolled over on one side. Then I saw before me a rude stone house, thatched doubtless with rushes and heather, before which the huntsman had drawn up, and the hounds were barking about the door. There was either no window to the cottage, or that which existed had been so well closed by shutters as to allow no ray of light to appear; a streak, however, issued from below the door.

The horn rang out again. Then the door was thrown open, and in the doorway, against the red light from a peat fire within, appeared the forms of three women. Their faces I could not see, nor was there light sufficient coming from the house to enable me to distinguish the features of the horseman. But I could make out that he had saddlebags cast over the back of the steed. These, without a word of explanation or salutation, he lifted and cast at the women, who caught them and at once retired within. I could see a table, and on to this the women poured the contents of the bags that glittered, but whether from the reflection of the fire or from phosphoric light in themselves I had no means of judging.

Without a word one woman came forth, and threw the empty bags to the huntsman, who caught them dexterously, replaced them over his saddle, sounded another blast, and instantly he, followed by the pack, was off, careering over the moor, and the last I saw of him and the hounds was profiled against the dying light in the sky on the shoulder of a tor. The women had shut the door. I had been unnoticed.

I remained where I lay for a few minutes, too exhausted to rise, too perplexed to know what to do. But by degrees I recovered energy and framed resolutions; and, rising to my feet that were stiff and numbed, I went to the door, knocked, and remained awaiting a reply. None came. I knocked again; and then, impatient at the delay, unhasped the door uninvited, and entered.

The spectacle that met my eyes was sufficiently surprising to make me doubt whether I were awake or dreaming. About the table sat the three women, aged, grey and haggard, with long, lean fingers, sorting the contents of the saddlebags heaped upon it. But what that was among which their fingers moved I could not tell. There appeared to be small, flickering lights of various colour, and different degrees of brilliancy; interspersed in the heap were dark particles.

"I am sorry to intrude," said I, as the three women raised their faces and looked at me.

They were strangely alike, all much of an age, equally grey, wan and weird, with their hair hanging over their shoulders. All had their sleeves rolled up above their elbows; the nervous arms so lean that their hands at the extremities looked preternaturally large.

"I must apologise," I said. "I sank up to my shoulders in Crowdy Marsh, and I extricated myself with the utmost difficulty, and am so exhausted and so chilled that I am constrained to throw myself on your hospitality, and entreat you to allow me to rest so as to warm myself and get somewhat dry before proceeding on my way."

"You can come in and rest," said one of the sisters.

"Sit by the fire," said the second.

"Drink from the simmering cauldron," said the third.

Then without further regarding me, they proceeded with their work. I took them at their word. I drew towards the hearth, and crouched over the fire. My teeth chattered with cold. On the hob stood a mug and ladle. Without more ado I dipped the long-handled ladle into the pot, and poured the liquid it brought up into the mug and set that to my lips. The draught was fiery; it sent a glow through my arteries and inflamed my brain. It was excellent in flavour and strength, and I fell that it nerved me and enabled me to resist the chill that had invaded my members, and was stealing upon my heart. My garments began to steam. It was not judicious to dry them upon me by the fire, but what else could I do? I felt that I must drive away the numbness, so as to enable me to pursue my course; and the exertion, I trusted, would restore circulation and prevent the ill effects of my immersion in the morass.

I now looked at the sisters for sisters they certainly were. What could have induced these women to settle on the edge of the ill-savoured and unwholesome marsh? No one with common sense I should have supposed would have done that, but would have selected a habitation on higher ground, above the mists that hung over Crowdy. Possibly the moor-slope was so thickly strewn with granite masses, as to leave only a vacant spot for their hovel and little field near the brim of the morass. This alone could explain their settling in such a spot.

I puzzled my head to make out on what the sisters were engaged. At one moment I supposed that they were sorting out the crystals that go by the name of Cornish diamonds. At another I conjectured that they were collecting glow-worms; but then, I considered, these insects are not seen in October.

Two of the sisters were gathering what they collected into little heaps at their sides on the board; the third had a pan on the floor at her feet, and I noticed that she picked out and raked together only such particles as showed no light, and these she dropped into the pan.

As my chill passed off, my interest in what proceeded under my eyes increased. I could restrain my curiosity no longer, and, drawing my stool to the table, asked: "Would you mind informing me what those articles are which you arc selecting so carefully?"

"Faculties," replied the woman who sat nearest to me.

"Gifts," said the second.

"Talents," said the third.

"I am in no degree enlightened," said I. "Who was the rider who came to your door and surrendered to you his saddle-bags?"

"Dewer, the great master," answered the first.

"He gathers up the neglected, the unused, and the misused faculties," explained the second.

"In Nature nothing is lost," said the third.

"Everyone," continued the first, "is given faculties. Such as have been received and by stress of circumstances have not been brought to perfection go into my heap."

"I select all such faculties as are wilfully neglected," said the second. "They go into my heap."

"All such as are misused, turned to evil, I cast into the pan," said the third. "Look yonder where they lie, like slugs sodden in salt water."

"Mine are for redistribution," said the first.

"The same with mine," said the second.

"Mine go into Crowdy Marsh," said the third.

She stooped, lifted a trap-door, and shot the contents of her pan into the hole beneath the floor.

"That is the sewer discharging into the morass, and they run down into Crowdy, where they rot and stink."

"Dewer," said the first, "rides over the world, and collects human faculties from the souls of men and women—faculties implanted in them when they come into the world, that have been unused, neglected, or ill-used. In Nature, there is no waste."

"We sort them out for redistribution," said the second.

"Save such as have been ill-used; they go to feed Crowdy," added the third.

I was not much the wiser for their explanation.

"Excuse me," I said, "generalities are beyond my powers of comprehension; come to particulars, and then I get hold of the sense. What, for instance, is that?"

I pointed to a sparklet that the first was handling. It was luminous with a steady ray.

"That," said she, "is the faculty of the strategist. It was implanted in a man, and had circumstances been propitious he would have made a great general a Wellington, or a Napoleon. Had he been in Parliament he would have been in the Ministry before long, and have been a marvellous man for organising and holding his party together. But circumstances were unfavourable, he was to the end of his days a coalheaver. He is in no degree blameworthy. He had not the chance."

She took up a luminous drop that diffused a soft, sweet radiance.

"This," she said, "is the maternal faculty. It was disposed of to a woman who never had the offer of a man's hand, and died, sorely against her will, as an old maid. She never had the chance."

Then I turned to the other sister.

"Excuse my freedom," said I, "if I say to you what I did to your sister. Do not give me generalities, but particular instances. What is that star you hold between your finger and thumb that has in it all the prismatic colours?"

"That," said she, "is the artist's faculty. He in whom it was lodged as a child showed marked aptitude with his pencil. He could catch a likeness in a moment, and with him every stroke told. His father, like a reasonable man, saw what was the bent of his son's genius, and directed his education in conformity with his taste for art. He sent him to the Royal Academy."

"Which killed the artistic faculty in him," I interrupted.

"No; that was not so. His father died early and left him a competence; he was not rich, but in easy circumstances. He laid aside his brush and palette, and spent his time in golf, cricket, billiards, bridge and poker; in a word, became a loafer and pleasure seeker, and did nothing with the talent that was in him, and which he knew was there, but was too lazy to develop. He had the chance and threw it away. He goes to my heap."

"And that," said I, pointing to another drop.

"It is the modelling faculty," said the second sister. "It was bestowed on a woman."

"What, to make a sculptor of her?"

"No; the moulding of character. She married a very rich man, and had many children ten in all. She might have shaped their minds and characters. But she was inert. She left them to nurses and governesses, and became a great society lady, neglecting her domestic duties and the direction of her children's future. She had ten chances and threw them all away. This goes into my heap."

"See," exclaimed the third sister; "here is a pile of talents that have been, not neglected, but misused; that have been dedicated to evil only. This," taking up what looked like a dead slug, "this—"

"Stay," I interrupted, "faculties, talents, turned to bad ends are manifest enough in the world. I have come across many of them, to my cost. I need no special examples; I have seen too many of them already."

Suddenly the sisters cried out: "Throw yourselves down. He comes! He comes! As you value your eyesight do not look up."

I saw the three hags cover up their eyes and drop their faces upon the table. I obeyed, and cast myself down.

Then I heard a rushing sound, and a brilliant light filled the room; so brilliant was it, that although my face was covered, it dazzled me through my fingers and eyelids. I could not have looked up. I should have been blinded.

In a moment the light was gone; the sound had passed away. I rose and resumed my place at the table.

"He has passed through," said one sister.

"Who?" I inquired.

"The Angel of Redistribution," answered the first. "See, my pile has gone. His right hand gathered it up."

"And his left hand took up mine," said the second.

"Of mine he has taken nothing," said the third sister; "all mine goes down the drain into the slough of rottenness."

Then the sisters rose to their feet.

"The moon has risen," said the first. "It is time, stranger, for you to go."

"Keep to the right above the marsh," advised the second.

"They have come out in quest of you," said the third.

I also had risen. I was no more to remain in the cottage. That was obvious. I made my way to the door, but, standing there, I turned for the purpose of thanking the sisters; but instantly the door was slammed in my face and I was shut out.

Presently I heard my name called. I saw lights. Then I was grasped by the hand, and Richards exclaimed:

"By the living Jingo! I thought never to see you again. How did you manage to escape?"

"I escaped in a strange fashion," I replied. "But of that on a future occasion. Hark!"

I heard the blast of the horn and the baying of hounds.

"Look," I cried, as I saw the Wild Hunt sweep over the moon-lit side of a tor in mad career.

"I hear nothing and see nothing," said Richards.

"You must see—look yonder. Do you not see them?"

"See what?"

"Dewer and his pack."

"I see nothing but the broken shadows of clouds flying over the face of the moon. On my word, friend! Immersion in Crowdy Mire seems to have quickened your faculties to see and to hear what are unperceived by other eyes and ears."

"It may be so it must be so," I said meditatively. "I have had strange experiences this night, such as are not given to other men."

Glámr

(A tale from *A Book of Ghosts*)

The following story is found in the Gretla, an Icelandic Saga, composed in the thirteenth century, or that comes to us in the form then given to it; but it is a redaction of a Saga of much earlier date. Most of it is thoroughly historical, and its statements are corroborated by other Sagas. The following incident was introduced to account for the fact that the outlaw Grettir would run any risk rather than spend the long winter nights alone in the dark.

★★★★★★

At the beginning of the eleventh century there stood, a little way up the Valley of Shadows in the north of Iceland, a small farm, occupied by a worthy bonder, named Thorhall, and his wife. The farmer was not exactly a chieftain, but he was well enough connected to be considered respectable; to back up his gentility he possessed numerous flocks of sheep and a goodly drove of oxen. Thorhall would have been a happy man but for one circumstance—his sheepwalks were haunted.

Not a herdsman would remain with him; he bribed, he threatened, entreated, all to no purpose; one shepherd after another left his service, and things came to such a pass that he determined on asking advice at the next annual council. Thorhall saddled his horses, adjusted his packs, provided himself with hobbles, cracked his long Icelandic whip, and cantered along the road, and in due time reached Thingvellir.

Skapti Thorodd's son was lawgiver at that time, and as everyone considered him a man of the utmost prudence and able to give the best advice, our friend from the Vale of Shadows made straight for his booth.

"An awkward predicament, certainly—to have large droves of sheep and no one to look after them," said Skapti, nibbling the nail of his thumb, and shaking his wise head—a head as stuffed with law as a ptarmigan's crop is stuffed with blaeberries. "Now I'll tell you what—as you have asked my advice, I will help you to a shepherd; a character in his way, a man of dull intellect, to be sure but strong as a bull."

"I do not care about his wits so long as he can look after sheep," answered Thorhall.

"You may rely on his being able to do that," said Skapti. "He is a stout, plucky fellow; a Swede from Sylgsdale, if you know where that is."

Towards the break-up of the council—"Thing" they call it in Iceland—two greyish-white horses belonging to Thorhall slipped their hobbles and strayed; so the good man had to hunt after them himself, which shows how short of servants he was. He crossed Sletha-asi, thence he bent his way to Armann's-fell, and just by the Priest's Wood he met a strange-looking man driving before him a horse laden with faggots. The fellow was tall and stalwart; his face involuntarily attracted Thorhall's attention, for the eyes, of an ashen grey, were large and staring, the powerful jaw was furnished with very white protruding teeth, and around the low forehead hung bunches of coarse wolf-grey hair.

"Pray, what is your name, my man?" asked the farmer pulling up.

"Glámr, an please you," replied the wood-cutter.

Thorhall stared; then, with a preliminary cough, he asked how Glámr liked faggot-picking.

"Not much," was the answer; "I prefer shepherd life."

"Will you come with me?" asked Thorhall; "Skapti has handed you over to me, and I want a shepherd this winter uncommonly."

102

"If I serve you, it is on the understanding that I come or go as it pleases me. I tell you I am a bit truculent if things do not go just to my thinking."

"I shall not object to this," answered the bonder. "So I may count on your services?"

"Wait a moment! You have not told me whether there be any drawback."

"I must acknowledge that there is one," said Thorhall; "in fact, the sheepwalks have got a bad name for bogies."

"Pshaw! I'm not the man to be scared at shadows," laughed Glámr; "so here's my hand to it; I'll be with you at the beginning of the winter night."

Well, after this they parted, and presently the farmer found his ponies. Having thanked Skapti for his advice and assistance, he got his horses together and trotted home.

Summer, and then autumn passed, but not a word about the new shepherd reached the Valley of Shadows. The winter storms began to bluster up the glen, driving the flying snow-flakes and massing the white drifts at every winding of the vale. Ice formed in the shallows of the river; and the streams, which in summer trickled down the ribbed scarps, were now transmuted into icicles.

One gusty night a violent blow at the door startled all in the farm. In another moment Glámr, tall as a troll, stood in the hall glowering out of his wild eyes, his grey hair matted with frost, his teeth rattling and snapping with cold, his face blood-red in the glare of the fire which smouldered in the centre of the hall. Thorhall jumped up and greeted him warmly, but the housewife was too frightened to be very cordial.

Weeks passed, and the new shepherd was daily on the moors with his flock; his loud and deep-toned voice was often borne down on the blast as he shouted to the sheep driving them into fold. His presence in the house always produced gloom, and if he spoke it sent a thrill through the women, who openly proclaimed their aversion for him.

There was a church near the byre, but Glámr never crossed

the threshold; he hated psalmody; apparently he was an indifferent Christian. On the vigil of the Nativity Glámr rose early and shouted for meat.

"Meat!" exclaimed the housewife; "no man calling himself a Christian touches flesh today. Tomorrow is the holy Christmas Day, and this is a fast."

"All superstition!" roared Glámr. "As far as I can see, men are no better now than they were in the bonny heathen time. Bring me meat, and make no more ado about it."

"You may be quite certain," protested the good wife, "if Church rule be not kept, ill-luck will follow."

Glámr ground his teeth and clenched his hands. "Meat! I will have meat, or——" In fear and trembling the poor woman obeyed.

The day was raw and windy; masses of grey vapour rolled up from the Arctic Ocean, and hung in piles about the mountain-tops. Now and then a scud of frozen fog, composed of minute particles of ice, swept along the glen, covering bar and beam with feathery hoar-frost. As the day declined, snow began to fall in large flakes like the down of the eider-duck. One moment there was a lull in the wind, and then the deep-toned shout of Glámr, high up the moor slopes, was heard distinctly by the congregation assembling for the first vespers of Christmas Day. Darkness came on, deep as that in the rayless abysses of the caverns under the lava, and still the snow fell thicker. The lights from the church windows sent a yellow haze far out into the night, and every flake burned golden as it swept within the ray.

The bell in the lych-gate clanged for evensong, and the wind puffed the sound far up the glen; perhaps it reached the herds-man's ear. Hark! Someone caught a distant sound or shriek, which it was he could not tell, for the wind muttered and mumbled about the church eaves, and then with a fierce whistle scudded over the graveyard fence. Glámr had not returned when the service was over. Thorhall suggested a search, but no man would accompany him; and no wonder! it was not a night for a dog to be out in; besides, the tracks were a foot deep in snow. The family sat up all night, waiting, listening, trembling; but no Glámr came home. Dawn broke at last, wan and blear in the south. The clouds hung down like great sheets, full of snow, almost to bursting.

A party was soon formed to search for the missing man. A sharp scramble brought them to high land, and the ridge between the two rivers which join in Vatnsdalr was thoroughly examined. Here and there were found the scattered sheep, shuddering under an icicled rock, or half buried in a snowdrift. No trace yet of the keeper. A dead ewe lay at the bottom of a crag; it had staggered over in the gloom, and had been dashed to pieces.

Presently the whole party were called together about a trampled spot in the heath, where evidently a death-struggle had taken place, for earth and stone were tossed about, and the snow was blotched with large splashes of blood. A gory track led up the mountain, and the farm-servants were following it, when a cry, almost of agony, from one of the lads, made them turn. In looking behind a rock, the boy had come upon the corpse of the shepherd; it was livid and swollen to the size of a bullock. It lay on its back with the arms extended. The snow had been scrabbled up by the puffed hands in the death-agony, and the staring glassy eyes gazed out of the ashen-grey, upturned face into the vaporous canopy overhead. From the purple lips lolled the tongue, which in the last throes had been bitten through by the white fangs, and a discoloured stream which had flowed from it was now an icicle.

With trouble the dead man was raised on a litter, and carried to a gill-edge, but beyond this he could not be borne; his weight waxed more and more, the bearers toiled beneath their burden, their foreheads became beaded with sweat; though strong men they were crushed to the ground. Consequently, the corpse was left at the ravine-head, and the men returned to the farm. Next day their efforts to lift Glámr's bloated carcass, and remove it to consecrated ground, were unavailing. On the third day a priest accompanied them, but the body was nowhere to be found.

Another expedition without the priest was made, and on this occasion the corpse was discovered; so a cairn was raised over the spot.

Two nights after this one of the thralls who had gone after the cows burst into the hall with a face blank and scared; he staggered to a seat and fainted. On recovering his senses, in a broken voice he assured all who crowded about him that he had seen Glámr walking past him as he left the door of the stable. On the following evening a houseboy was found in a fit under the farmyard wall, and he remained an idiot to his dying day. Some of the women next saw a face which, though blown out and discoloured, they recognised as that of Glámr, looking in upon them through a window of the dairy. In the twilight, Thorhall himself met the dead man, who stood and glowered at him, but made no attempt to injure his master. The haunting did not end there. Nightly a heavy tread was heard around the house, and a hand feeling along the walls, sometimes thrust in at the windows, at others clutching the woodwork, and breaking it to splinters. However, when the spring came round the disturbances lessened, and as the sun obtained full power, ceased altogether.

That summer a vessel from Norway dropped anchor in the nearest bay. Thorhall visited it, and found on board a man named Thorgaut, who was in search of work.

"What do you say to being my shepherd?" asked the bonder.

"I should very much like the office," answered Thorgaut. "I am as strong as two ordinary men, and a handy fellow to boot."

"I will not engage you without forewarning you of the terrible things you may have to encounter during the winter night."

"Pray, what may they be?"

"Ghosts and hobgoblins," answered the farmer; "a fine dance they lead me, I can promise you."

"I fear them not," answered Thorgaut; "I shall be with you at cattle-slaughtering time."

At the appointed season the man came, and soon established himself as a favourite in the house; he romped with the children, chucked the maidens under the chin, helped his fellow-servants, gratified the housewife by admiring her curd, and was just as much liked as his predecessor had been detested. He was a devil-may-care fellow, too, and made no bones of his contempt for the ghost, expressing hopes of meeting him face to face, which made his master look grave, and his mistress shudderingly cross herself. As the winter came on, strange sights and sounds began to alarm the folk, but these never frightened Thorgaut; he slept too soundly at night to hear the tread of feet about the door, and was too short-sighted to catch glimpses of a grizzly monster striding up and down, in the twilight, before its cairn.

At last Christmas Eve came round, and Thorgaut went out as usual with his sheep.

"Have a care, man," urged the bonder; "go not near to the gill-head, where Glámr lies."

"Tut, tut! fear not for me. I shall be back by vespers."

"God grant it," sighed the housewife; "but 'tis not a day for risks, to be sure."

Twilight came on: a feeble light hung over the south, one white streak above the heath land to the south. Far off in southern lands it was still day, but here the darkness gathered in apace, and men came from Vatnsdalr for evensong, to herald in the night when Christ was born. Christmas Eve! How different in Saxon England! There the great ashen faggot is rolled along the hall with torch and taper; the mummers dance with their merry jingling bells; the boar's head, with gilded tusks, "bedecked with holly and rosemary," is brought in by the steward to a flourish of trumpets.

How different, too, where the Varanger cluster round the imperial throne in the mighty church of the Eternal Wisdom at this very hour. Outside, the air is soft from breathing over the Bosphorus, which flashes tremulously beneath the stars. The orange and laurel leaves in the palace gardens are still exhaling fragrance in the hush of the Christmas night.

But it is different here. The wind is piercing as a two-edged sword; blocks of ice crash and grind along the coast, and the lake waters are congealed to stone. Aloft, the Aurora flames crimson, flinging long streamers to the zenith, and then suddenly dissolving into a sea of pale green light. The natives are waiting round the church-door, but no Thorgaut has returned.

They find him next morning, lying across Glámr's cairn, with his spine, his leg, and arm-bones shattered. He is conveyed to the churchyard, and a cross is set up at his head. He sleeps peacefully. Not so Glámr; he becomes more furious than ever. No one will remain with Thorhall now, except an old cowherd who has always served the family, and who had long ago dandled his present master on his knee.

"All the cattle will be lost if I leave," said the *carle*; "it shall never be told of me that I deserted Thorhall from fear of a spectre."

Matters grew rapidly worse. Outbuildings were broken into of a night, and their woodwork was rent and shattered; the house door was violently shaken, and great pieces of it were torn away; the gables of the house were also pulled furiously to and fro.

One morning before dawn, the old man went to the stable. An hour later, his mistress arose, and taking her milking pails, followed him. As she reached the door of the stable, a terrible sound from within—the bellowing of the cattle, mingled with the deep notes of an unearthly voice—sent her back shrieking to the house. Thorhall leaped out of bed, caught up a weapon, and hastened to the cow-house. On opening the door, he found the cattle goring each other. Slung across the stone that separated the stalls was something. Thorhall stepped up to it, felt it, looked close; it was the cowherd, perfectly dead, his feet on one side of the slab, his head on the other, and his spine snapped in twain.

The bonder now moved with his family to Tunga, another farm owned by him lower down the valley; it was too venturesome living during the mid-winter night at the haunted farm; and it was not till the sun had returned as a bridegroom out of his chamber, and had dispelled night with its phantoms, that he went back to the Vale of Shadows. In the meantime, his little girl's health had given way under the repeated alarms of the winter; she became paler every day; with the autumn flowers she faded, and was laid beneath the mould of the churchyard in time for the first snows to spread a virgin pall over her small grave.

At this time Grettir —a hero of great fame, and a native of the north of the island—was in Iceland, and as the hauntings of this vale were matters of gossip throughout the district, he inquired about them, and resolved on visiting the scene. So Grettir busked himself for a cold ride, mounted his horse, and in due course of time drew rein at the door of Thorhall's farm with the request that he might be accommodated there for the night.

"Ahem!" coughed the bonder; "perhaps you are not aware——"

"I am perfectly aware of all. I want to catch sight of the troll."

"But your horse is sure to be killed."

"I will risk it. Glámr I must meet, so there's an end of it."

"I am delighted to see you," spoke the bonder; "at the same time, should mischief befall you, don't lay the blame at my door."

"Never fear, man."

So they shook hands; the horse was put into the strongest stable, Thorhall made Grettir as good cheer as he was able, and then, as the visitor was sleepy, all retired to rest.

The night passed quietly, and no sounds indicated the presence of a restless spirit. The horse, moreover, was found next morning in good condition, enjoying his hay.

"This is unexpected!" exclaimed the bonder, gleefully. "Now, where's the saddle? We'll clap it on, and then good-bye, and a merry journey to you."

"Goodbye!" echoed Grettir ; "I am going to stay here another night."

"You had best be advised," urged Thorhall; "if misfortune should overtake you, I know that all your kinsmen would visit it on my head."

"I have made up my mind to stay," said Grettir, and he looked so dogged that Thorhall opposed him no more.

All was quiet next night; not a sound roused Grettir from his slumber. Next morning he went with the farmer to the stable. The strong wooden door was shivered and driven in. They stepped across it; Grettir called to his horse, but there was no responsive whinny.

"I am afraid——" began Thorhall. Grettir leaped in, and found the poor brute dead, and with its neck broken.

"Now," said Thorhall quickly, "I've got a capital horse—a skewbald—down by Tunga, I shall not be many hours in fetching it; your saddle is here, I think, and then you will just have time to reach——"

"I stay here another night," interrupted Grettir.

"I implore you to depart," said Thorhall.

"My horse is slain!"

"But I will provide you with another."

"Friend," answered Grettir, turning so sharply round that the farmer jumped back, half frightened, "no man ever did me an injury without rueing it. Now, your demon herdsman has been the death of my horse. He must be taught a lesson."

"Would that he were!" groaned Thorhall; "but mortal must not face him. Go in peace and receive compensation from me for what has happened."

"I must revenge my horse."

"An obstinate man will have his own way! But if you run your head against a stone wall, don't be angry because you get a broken pate."

Night came on; Grettir ate a hearty supper and was right jovial; not so Thorhall, who had his misgivings. At bedtime the latter crept into his crib, which, in the manner of old Icelandic beds, opened out of the hall, as berths do out of a cabin. Grettir, however, determined on remaining up; so he flung himself on a bench with his feet against the posts of the high seat, and his back against Thorhall's crib; then he wrapped one lappet of his fur coat round his feet, the other about his head, keeping the neck-opening in front of his face, so that he could look through into the hall.

There was a fire burning on the hearth, a smouldering heap of red embers; every now and then a twig flared up and crackled, giving Grettir glimpses of the rafters, as he lay with his eyes wandering among the mysteries of the smoke-blackened roof. The wind whistled softly overhead. The clerestory windows, covered with the amnion of sheep, admitted now and then a sickly yellow glare from the full moon, which, however, shot a beam of pure silver through the smoke-hole in the roof. A dog without began to howl; the cat, which had long been sitting demurely watching the fire, stood up with raised back and bristling tail, then darted behind some chests in a corner. The hall door was in a sad plight. It had been so riven by the spectre that it was made firm by wattles only, and the moon glinted athwart the crevices. Soothingly the river, not yet frozen over, prattled over its shingly bed as it swept round the knoll on which stood the farm. Grettir heard the breathing of the sleeping women in the adjoining chamber, and the sigh of the housewife as she turned in her bed.

Click! click!—It is only the frozen turf on the roof cracking with the cold. The wind lulls completely. The night is very still without. Hark! a heavy tread, beneath which the snow yields. Every footfall goes straight to Grettir's heart. A crash on the turf overhead! By all the saints in paradise! The monster is treading on the roof. For one moment the chimney-gap is completely darkened: Glámr is looking down it; the flash of the red ash is reflected in the two lustreless eyes. Then the moon glances sweetly in once more, and the heavy tramp of Glámr is audibly moving towards the farther end of the hall. A thud—he has leaped down.

Grettir feels the board at his back quivering, for Thorhall is awake and is trembling in his bed. The steps pass round to the back of the house, and then the snapping of the wood shows that the creature is destroying some of the outhouse doors. He

111

tires of this apparently, for his footfall comes clear towards the main entrance to the hall. The moon is veiled behind a watery cloud, and by the uncertain glimmer Grettir fancies that he sees two dark hands thrust in above the door. His apprehensions are verified, for, with a loud snap, a long strip of panel breaks, and light is admitted. *Snap—snap!* another portion gives way, and the gap becomes larger. Then the wattles slip from their places, and a dark arm rips them out in bunches, and flings them away. There is a cross-beam to the door, holding a bolt which slides into a stone groove. Against the grey light, Grettir sees a huge black figure heaving itself over the bar. *Crack!* that has given way, and the rest of the door falls in shivers to the earth.

"Oh, heavens above!" exclaims the bonder.

Stealthily the dead man creeps on, feeling at the beams as he comes; then he stands in the hall, with the firelight on him. A fearful sight; the tall figure distended with the corruption of the grave, the nose fallen off, the wandering, vacant eyes, with the glaze of death on them, the sallow flesh patched with green masses of decay; the wolf-grey hair and beard have grown in the tomb, and hang matted about the shoulders and breast; the nails, too, they have grown. It is a sickening sight—a thing to shudder at, not to see.

Motionless, with no nerve quivering now, Thorhall and Grettir held their breath.

Glámr's lifeless glance strayed round the chamber; it rested on the shaggy bundle by the high seat. Cautiously he stepped towards it. Grettir felt him groping about the lower lappet and pulling at it. The cloak did not give way. Another jerk; Grettir kept his feet firmly pressed against the posts, so that the rug was not pulled off. The vampire seemed puzzled, he plucked at the upper flap and tugged. Grettir held to the bench and bed-board, so that he was not moved, but the cloak was rent in twain, and the corpse staggered back, holding half in its hands, and gazing wonderingly at it.

Before it had done examining the shred, Grettir started to his feet, bowed his body, flung his arms about the carcass, and, driving his head into the chest, strove to bend it backward and snap the spine. A vain attempt! The cold hands came down on Grettir's arms with diabolical force, riving them from their hold. Grettir clasped them about the body again; then the arms closed round him, and began dragging him along. The brave man clung by his feet to benches and posts, but the strength of the vampire was the greater; posts gave way, benches were heaved from their places, and the wrestlers at each moment neared the door. Sharply writhing loose, Grettir flung his hands round a roof-beam. He was dragged from his feet; the numbing arms clenched him round the waist, and tore at him; every tendon in his breast was strained; the strain under his shoulders became excruciating, the muscles stood out in knots.

Still he held on; his fingers were bloodless; the pulses of his temples throbbed in jerks; the breath came in a whistle through his rigid nostrils. All the while, too, the long nails of the dead man cut into his side, and Grettir could feel them piercing like knives between his ribs. Then at once his hands gave way, and the monster bore him reeling towards the porch, crashing over the broken fragments of the door. Hard as the battle had gone with him indoors, Grettir knew that it would go worse outside, so he gathered up all his remaining strength for one final desperate struggle.

The door had been shut with a swivel into a groove; this groove was in a stone, which formed the jamb on one side, and there was a similar block on the other, into which the hinges had been driven. As the wrestlers neared the opening, Grettir planted both his feet against the stone posts, holding Glámr by the middle. He had the advantage now. The dead man writhed in his arms, drove his talons into Grettir's back, and tore up great ribbons of flesh, but the stone jambs held firm.

"Now," thought Grettir, "I can break his back," and thrusting his head under the chin, so that the grizzly beard covered his eyes, he forced the face from him, and the back was bent as a hazel-rod.

"If I can but hold on," thought Grettir, and he tried to

shout for Thorhall, but his voice was muffled in the hair of the corpse.

Suddenly one or both of the door-posts gave way. Down crashed the gable trees, ripping beams and rafters from their beds; frozen clods of earth rattled from the roof and thumped into the snow. Glámr fell on his back, and Grettir staggered down on top of him. The moon was at her full; large white clouds chased each other across the sky, and as they swept before her disk she looked through them with a brown halo round her. The snow-cap of Jorundarfell, however, glowed like a planet, then the white mountain ridge was kindled, the light ran down the hillside, the bright disk stared out of the veil and flashed at this moment full on the vampire's face. Grettir's strength was failing him, his hands quivered in the snow, and he knew that he could not support himself from dropping flat on the dead man's face, eye to eye, lip to lip. The eyes of the corpse were fixed on him, lit with the cold glare of the moon. His head swam as his heart sent a hot stream to his brain. Then a voice from the grey lips said—

Thou hast acted madly in seeking to match thyself with me. Now learn that henceforth ill-luck shall constantly attend thee; that thy strength shall never exceed what it now is, and that by night these eyes of mine shall stare at thee through the darkness till thy dying day, so that for very horror thou shalt not endure to be alone.

Grettir at this moment noticed that his dirk had slipped from its sheath during the fall, and that it now lay conveniently near his hand. The giddiness which had oppressed him passed away, he clutched at the sword-haft, and with a blow severed the vampire's throat. Then, kneeling on the breast, he hacked till the head came off.

Thorhall appeared now, his face blanched with terror, but when he saw how the fray had terminated he assisted Grettir gleefully to roll the corpse on the top of a pile of faggots, which had been collected for winter fuel. Fire was applied, and soon far down the valley the flames of the pyre startled people, and made them wonder what new horror was being enacted in the upper portion of the Vale of Shadows.

Next day the charred bones were conveyed to a spot remote from the habitations of men, and were there buried.

What Glámr had predicted came to pass. Never after did Grettir dare to be alone in the dark.

Mustapha

(A tale from *A Book of Ghosts*)

1

Among the many hangers-on at the Hotel de l'Europe at Luxor—donkey-boys, porters, guides, antiquity dealers—was one, a young man named Mustapha, who proved a general favourite.

I spent three winters at Luxor, partly for my health, partly for pleasure, mainly to make artistic studies, as I am by profession a painter. So I came to know Mustapha fairly well in three stages, during those three winters.

When first I made his acquaintance he was in the transition condition from boyhood to manhood. He had an intelligent face, with bright eyes, a skin soft as brown silk, with a velvety hue on it. His features were regular, and if his face was a little too round to quite satisfy an English artistic eye, yet this was a peculiarity to which one soon became accustomed. He was unflaggingly good-natured and obliging. A mongrel, no doubt, he was; Arab and native Egyptian blood were mingled in his veins. But the result was happy; he combined the patience and gentleness of the child of Mizraim with the energy and pluck of the son of the desert.

Mustapha had been a donkey-boy, but had risen a stage higher, and looked, as the object of his supreme ambition, to become someday a dragoman, and blaze like one of these gilded beetles in lace and chains, rings and weapons. To become a dragoman—one of the most obsequious of men till engaged, one of the veriest tyrants when engaged—to what higher could an Egyptian boy aspire?

To become a dragoman means to go in broadcloth and with gold chains when his fellows are half naked; to lounge and twist the moustache when his kinsfolk are toiling under the water-buckets; to be able to extort *backsheesh* from all the tradesmen to whom he can introduce a master; to do nothing himself and make others work for him; to be able to look to purchase two, three, even four wives when his father contented himself with one; to soar out of the region of native virtues into that of foreign vices; to be superior to all instilled prejudices against spirits and wine—that is the ideal set before young Egypt through contact with the English and the American tourist.

We all liked Mustapha. No one had a bad word to say of him. Some pious individuals rejoiced to see that he had broken with the Koran, as if this were a first step towards taking up with the Bible. A free-thinking professor was glad to find that Mustapha had emancipated himself from some of those shackles which religion places on august, divine humanity, and that by getting drunk he gave pledge that he had risen into a sphere of pure emancipation, which eventuates in ideal perfection.

As I made my studies I engaged Mustapha to carry my easel and canvas, or camp-stool. I was glad to have him as a study, to make him stand by a wall or sit on a pillar that was prostrate, as artistic exigencies required. He was always ready to accompany me. There was an understanding between us that when a drove of tourists came to Luxor he might leave me for the day to pick up what he could then from the natural prey; but I found him not always keen to be off duty to me. Though he could get more from the occasional visitor than from me, he was above the ravenous appetite for *backsheesh* which consumed his fellows.

He who has much to do with the native Egyptian will have discovered that there are in him a fund of kindliness and a treasure of good qualities. He is delighted to be treated with humanity, pleased to be noticed, and ready to repay attention with touching gratitude. He is by no means as rapacious for *backsheesh* as the passing traveller supposes; he is shrewd to distinguish between man and man; likes this one, and will do anything for him unrewarded, and will do naught for another for any bribe.

The Egyptian is now in a transitional state. If it be quite true that the touch of England is restoring life to his crippled limbs, and the voice of England bidding him rise up and walk, there are occasions on which association with Englishmen is a disadvantage to him. Such an instance is that of poor, good Mustapha.

It was not my place to caution Mustapha against the pernicious influences to which he was subjected, and, to speak plainly, I did not know what line to adopt, on what ground to take my stand, if I did. He was breaking with the old life, and taking up with what was new, retaining of the old only what was bad in it, and acquiring of the new none of its good parts. Civilisation—European civilisation—is excellent, but cannot be swallowed at a gulp, nor does it wholly suit the oriental digestion.

That which impelled Mustapha still further in his course was the attitude assumed towards him by his own relatives and the natives of his own village. They were strict Moslems, and they regarded him as one on the highway to becoming a renegade. They treated him with mistrust, showed him aversion, and loaded him with reproaches. Mustapha had a high spirit, and he resented rebuke. Let his fellows grumble and objurgate, said he; they would cringe to him when he became a dragoman, with his pockets stuffed with *piastres*.

There was in our hotel, the second winter, a young fellow of the name of Jameson, a man with plenty of money, superficial good nature, little intellect, very conceited and egotistic, and this fellow was Mustapha's evil genius. It was Jameson's delight to encourage Mustapha in drinking and gambling. Time hung heavy on his hands. He cared nothing for hieroglyphics, scenery bored him, antiquities, art, had no charm for him. Natural history presented to him no attraction, and the only amusement level with his mental faculties was that of hoaxing natives, or breaking down their religious prejudices.

Matters were in this condition as regarded Mustapha, when an incident occurred during my second winter at Luxor that completely altered the tenor of Mustapha's life.

One night a fire broke out in the nearest village. It originated in a mud hovel belonging to a *fellah*; his wife had spilled some oil on the hearth, and the flames leaping up had caught the low thatch, which immediately burst into a blaze. A wind was blowing from the direction of the Arabian desert, and it carried the flames and ignited the thatch before it on other roofs; the conflagration spread, and the whole village was menaced with destruction. The greatest excitement and alarm prevailed. The inhabitants lost their heads. Men ran about rescuing from their hovels their only treasures—old sardine tins and empty marmalade pots; women wailed, children sobbed; no one made any attempt to stay the fire; and, above all, were heard the screams of the woman whose incaution had caused the mischief, and who was being beaten unmercifully by her husband.

The few English in the hotel came on the scene, and with their instinctive energy and system set to work to organise a corps and subdue the flames. The women and girls who were rescued from the menaced hovels, or plucked out of those already on fire, were in many cases unveiled, and so it came to pass that Mustapha, who, under English direction, was ablest and most vigorous in his efforts to stop the conflagration, met his fate in the shape of the daughter of Ibraim the Farrier.

By the light of the flames he saw her, and at once resolved to make that fair girl his wife.

No reasonable obstacle intervened, so thought Mustapha. He had amassed a sufficient sum to entitle him to buy a wife and set up a household of his own. A house consists of four mud walls and a low thatch, and housekeeping in an Egyptian house is as elementary and economical as the domestic architecture. The maintenance of a wife and family is not costly after the first outlay, which consists in indemnifying the father for the expense to which he has been put in rearing a daughter.

The ceremony of courting is also elementary, and the addresses of the suitor are not paid to the bride, but to her father, and not in person by the candidate, but by an intermediary.

Mustapha negotiated with a friend, a fellow hanger-on at the hotel, to open proceedings with the farrier. He was to represent to the worthy man that the suitor entertained the most ardent admiration for the virtues of Ibraim personally, that he was inspired with but one ambition, which was alliance with so distinguished a family as his. He was to assure the father of the damsel that Mustapha undertook to proclaim through Upper and Lower Egypt, in the ears of Egyptians, Arabs, and Europeans, that Ibraim was the most remarkable man that ever existed for solidity of judgment, excellence of parts, uprightness of dealing, nobility of sentiment, strictness in observance of the precepts of the Koran, and that finally Mustapha was anxious to indemnify this same paragon of genius and virtue for his condescension in having cared to breed and clothe and feed for several years a certain girl, his daughter, if Mustapha might have that daughter as his wife. Not that he cared for the daughter in herself, but as a means whereby he might have the honour of entering into alliance with one so distinguished and so esteemed of *Allah* as Ibraim the Farrier.

To the infinite surprise of the intermediary, and to the no less surprise and mortification of the suitor, Mustapha was refused. He was a bad Moslem. Ibraim would have no alliance with one who had turned his back on the Prophet and drunk bottled beer.

Till this moment Mustapha had not realised how great was the alienation between his fellows and himself—what a barrier he had set up between himself and the men of his own blood. The refusal of his suit struck the young man to the quick. He had known and played with the farrier's daughter in childhood, till she had come of age to veil her face; now that he had seen her in her ripe charms, his heart was deeply stirred and engaged. He entered into himself, and going to the mosque he there made a solemn vow that if he ever touched wine, ale, or spirits again he would cut his throat, and he sent word to Ibraim that he had done so, and begged that he would not dispose of his daughter and finally reject him till he had seen how that he who had turned in thought and manner of life from the Prophet would return with firm resolution to the right way.

<h1 style="text-align:center">2</h1>

From this time Mustapha changed his conduct. He was obliging and attentive as before, ready to exert himself to do for me what I wanted, ready also to extort money from the ordinary tourist for doing nothing, to go with me and carry my tools when I went forth painting, and to joke and laugh with Jameson; but, unless he were unavoidably detained, he said his prayers five times daily in the mosque, and no inducement whatever would make him touch anything save sherbet, milk, or water.

Mustapha had no easy time of it. The strict Mohammedans mistrusted this sudden conversion, and believed that he was playing a part. Ibraim gave him no encouragement. His relatives maintained their reserve and stiffness towards him.

His companions, moreover, who were in the transitional stage, and those who had completely shaken off all faith in *Allah* and trust in the Prophet and respect for the *Koran*, were incensed at his desertion. He was ridiculed, insulted; he was waylaid and beaten. The young fellows mimicked him, the elder scoffed at him.

Jameson took his change to heart, and laid himself out to bring him out of his pot of scruples.

"Mustapha ain't any sport at all now," said he. "I'm hanged if he has another *para* from me." He offered him bribes in gold, he united with the others in ridicule, he turned his back on him, and refused to employ him. Nothing availed. Mustapha was respectful, courteous, obliging as before, but he had returned, he said, to the faith and rule of life in which he had been brought up, and he would never again leave it.

"I have sworn," said he, "that if I do I will cut my throat."

I had been, perhaps, negligent in cautioning the young fellow the first winter that I knew him against the harm likely to be done him by taking up with European habits contrary to his law and the feelings and prejudices of his people. Now, however, I had no hesitation in expressing to him the satisfaction I felt at the courageous and determined manner in which he had broken with acquired habits that could do him no good. For one thing, we were now better acquaintances, and I felt that as one who had known him for more than a few months in the winter, I had a good right to speak. And, again, it is always easier or pleasanter to praise than to reprimand.

One day when sketching I cut my pencil with a pruning-knife I happened to have in my pocket; my proper knife of many blades had been left behind by misadventure.

Mustapha noticed the knife and admired it, and asked if it had cost a great sum.

"Not at all," I answered. "I did not even buy it. It was given me. I ordered some flower seeds from a seeds-man, and when he sent me the consignment he included this knife in the case as a present. It is not worth more than a shilling in England."

He turned it about, with looks of admiration.

"It is just the sort that would suit me," he said. "I know your other knife with many blades. It is very fine, but it is too small. I do not want it to cut pencils. It has other things in it, a hook for taking stones from a horse's hoof, a pair of tweezers for removing hairs. I do not want such, but a knife such as this, with such a curve, is just the thing."

"Then you shall have it," said I. "You are welcome. It was for rough work only that I brought the knife to Egypt with me."

I finished a painting that winter that gave me real satisfaction. It was of the great court of the temple of Luxor by evening light, with the last red glare of the sun over the distant desert hills, and the eastern sky above of a purple depth. What colours I used! the intensest on my palette, and yet fell short of the effect.

The picture was in the academy, was well hung, abominably represented in one of the illustrated guides to the galleries, as a blotch, by some sort of photographic process on gelatine; my picture sold, which concerned me most of all, and not only did it sell at a respectable figure, but it also brought me two or three orders for Egyptian pictures. So many English and Americans go up the Nile, and carry away with them pleasant reminiscences of the Land of the Pharaohs, that when in England they are fain to buy pictures which shall remind them of scenes in that land.

I returned to my hotel at Luxor in November, to spend there a third winter. The *fellaheen* about there saluted me as a friend with an affectionate delight, which I am quite certain was not assumed, as they got nothing out of me save kindly salutations. I had the Egyptian fever on me, which, when once acquired, is not to be shaken off—an enthusiasm for everything Egyptian, the antiquities, the history of the Pharaohs, the very desert, the brown Nile, the desolate hill ranges, the ever blue sky, the marvellous colorations at rise and set of sun, and last, but not least, the prosperity of the poor peasants.

I am quite certain that the very warmest welcome accorded to me was from Mustapha, and almost the first words he said to me on my meeting him again were: "I have been very good. I say my prayers. I drink no wine, and Ibraim will give me his daughter in the second Iomada—what you call January."

"Not before, Mustapha?"

"No, sir; he says I must be tried for one whole year, and he is right."

"Then soon after Christmas you will be happy!"

"I have got a house and made it ready. Yes. After Christmas there will be one very happy man—one very, very happy man in Egypt, and that will be your humble servant, Mustapha."

3

We were a pleasant party at Luxor, this third winter, not numerous, but for the most part of congenial tastes. For the most part we were keen on hieroglyphics, we admired Queen Hatasou and we hated Rameses II. We could distinguish the artistic work of one dynasty from that of another. We were learned on cartouches, and flourished our knowledge before the tourists dropping in.

One of those staying in the hotel was an Oxford don, very good company, interested in everything, and able to talk well on everything—I mean everything more or less remotely connected with Egypt. Another was a young fellow who had been an *attaché* at Berlin, but was out of health—nothing organic the matter with his lungs, but they were weak. He was keen on the political situation, and very anti-Gallican, as every man who has been in Egypt naturally is, who is not a Frenchman.

There was also staying in the hotel an American lady, fresh and delightful, whose mind and conversation twinkled like frost crystals in the sun, a woman full of good-humour, of the most generous sympathies, and so droll that she kept us ever amused.

And, alas! Jameson was back again, not entering into any of our pursuits, not understanding our little jokes, not at all content to be there. He grumbled at the food—and, indeed, that might have been better; at the monotony of the life at Luxor, at his London doctor for putting the *veto* on Cairo because of its drainage, or rather the absence of all drainage. I really think we did our utmost to draw Jameson into our circle, to amuse him, to interest him in something; but one by one we gave him up, and the last to do this was the little American lady.

From the outset he had attacked Mustapha, and endeavoured to persuade him to shake off his "squeamish nonsense," as Jameson called his resolve. "I'll tell you what it is, old fellow," he said, "life isn't worth living without good liquor, and as for that blessed Prophet of yours, he showed he was a fool when he put a bar on drinks."

But as Mustapha was not pliable he gave him up. "He's become just as great a bore as that old Rameses," said he. "I'm sick of the whole concern, and I don't think anything of fresh dates, that you fellows make such a fuss about. As for that stupid old Nile—there ain't a fish worth eating comes out of it. And those old Egyptians were arrant humbugs. I haven't seen a lotus since I came here, and they made such a fuss about them too."

The little American lady was not weary of asking questions relative to English home life, and especially to country-house living and amusements.

"Oh, my dear!" said she, "I would give my ears to spend a Christmas in the fine old fashion in a good ancient manor-house in the country."

"There is nothing remarkable in that," said an English lady.

"Not to you, maybe; but there would be to us. What we read of and make pictures of in our fancies, that is what you live. Your facts are our fairy tales. Look at your hunting."

"That, if you like, is fun," threw in Jameson. "But I don't myself think anything save Luxor can be a bigger bore than country-house life at Christmas time—when all the boys are back from school."

"With us," said the little American, "our sportsmen dress in pink like yours—the whole thing—and canter after a bag of anise seed that is trailed before them."

"Why do they not import foxes?"

"Because a fox would not keep to the road. Our farmers object pretty freely to trespass; so the hunting must of necessity be done on the highway, and the game is but a bag of anise seed. I would like to see an English meet and a run."

This subject was thrashed out after having been prolonged unduly for the sake of Jameson.

"Oh, dear me!" said the Yankee lady. "If but that chef could be persuaded to give us plum-puddings for Christmas, I would try to think I was in England."

"Plum-pudding is exploded," said Jameson. "Only children ask for it now. A good trifle or a tipsy-cake is much more to my taste; but this hanged cook here can give us nothing but his blooming custard pudding and burnt sugar."

"I do not think it would be wise to let him attempt a plum-pudding," said the English lady. "But if we can persuade him to permit me I will mix and make the pudding, and then he cannot go far wrong in the boiling and dishing up."

"That is the only thing wanting to make me perfectly happy," said the American. "I'll confront *monsieur*. I am sure I can talk him into a good humour, and we shall have our plum-pudding."

No one has yet been found, I do believe, who could resist that little woman. She carried everything before her. The cook placed himself and all his culinary apparatus at her feet. We took part in the stoning of the raisins, and the washing of the currants, even the chopping of the suet; we stirred the pudding, threw in sixpence apiece, and a ring, and then it was tied up in a cloth, and set aside to be boiled. Christmas Day came, and the English chaplain preached us a practical sermon on "Goodwill towards men." That was his text, and his sermon was but a swelling out of the words just as rice is swelled to thrice its size by boiling.

We dined. There was an attempt at roast beef—it was more like baked leather. The event of the dinner was to be the bringing in and eating of the plum-pudding.

Surely all would be perfect. We could answer for the materials and the mixing. The English lady could guarantee the boiling. She had seen the plum-pudding "on the boil," and had given strict injunctions as to the length of time during which it was to boil.

But, alas! the pudding was not right when brought on the table. It was not enveloped in lambent blue flame—it was not crackling in the burning brandy. It was sent in dry, and the brandy arrived separate in a white sauce-boat, hot indeed, and sugared, but not on fire.

There ensued outcries of disappointment. Attempts were made to redress the mistake by setting fire to the brandy in a spoon, but the spoon was cold. The flame would not catch, and finally, with a sigh, we had to take our plum-pudding as served.

"I say, chaplain!" exclaimed Jameson, "practice is better than precept, is it not?"

"To be sure it is."

"You gave us a deuced good sermon. It was short, as it ought to be; but I'll go better on it, I'll practise where you preached, and have larks, too!"

Then Jameson started from table with a plate of plum-pudding in one hand and the sauce-boat in the other. "By Jove!" he said, "I'll teach these fellows to open their eyes. I'll show them that we know how to feed. We can't turn out scarabs and cartouches in England, that are no good to anyone, but we can produce the finest roast beef in the world, and do a thing or two in puddings."

And he left the room.

We paid no heed to anything Jameson said or did. We were rather relieved that he was out of the room, and did not concern ourselves about the "larks" he promised himself, and which we were quite certain would be as insipid as were the quails of the Israelites.

In ten minutes he was back, laughing and red in the face.

"I've had splitting fun," he said. "You should have been there."

"Where, Jameson?"

"Why, outside. There were a lot of old *moolahs* and other hoky-pokies sitting and contemplating the setting sun and all that sort of thing, and I gave Mustapha the pudding. I told him I wished him to try our great national English dish, on which her Majesty the Queen dines daily. Well, he ate and enjoyed it, by George. Then I said, 'Old fellow, it's uncommonly dry, so you must take the sauce to it.' He asked if it was only sauce— flour and water. 'It's sauce, by Jove,' said I, 'a little sugar to it; no bar on the sugar, Musty.' So I put the boat to his lips and gave him a pull. By George, you should have seen his face! It was just thundering fun. 'I've done you at last, old Musty,' I said. 'It is best cognac.' He gave me such a look! He'd have eaten me, I believe—and he walked away. It was just splitting fun. I wish you had been there to see it."

I went out after dinner, to take my usual stroll along the river-bank, and to watch the evening lights die away on the columns and obelisk. On my return I saw at once that something had happened which had produced commotion among the servants of the hotel. I had reached the salon before I inquired what was the matter.

The boy who was taking the coffee round said: "Mustapha is dead. He cut his throat at the door of the mosque. He could not help himself. He had broken his vow."

I looked at Jameson without a word. Indeed, I could not speak; I was choking. The little American lady was trembling, the English lady crying. The gentlemen stood silent in the windows, not speaking a word.

Jameson's colour changed. He was honestly distressed, uneasy, and tried to cover his confusion with bravado and a jest.

"After all," he said, "it is only a nigger the less."

"Nigger!" said the American lady. "He was no nigger, but an Egyptian."

"Oh! I don't pretend to distinguish between your blacks and whity-browns any more than I do between your cartouches," returned Jameson.

"He was no black," said the American lady, standing up. "But I do mean to say that I consider you an utterly unredeemed black——"

"My dear, don't," said the Englishwoman, drawing the other down. "It's no good. The thing is done. He meant no harm."

4

I could not sleep. My blood was in a boil. I felt that I could not speak to Jameson again. He would have to leave Luxor. That was tacitly understood among us. Coventry was the place to which he would be consigned.

I tried to finish in a little sketch I had made in my notebook when I was in my room, but my hand shook, and I was constrained to lay my pencil aside. Then I took up an Egyptian grammar, but could not fix my mind on study. The hotel was very still. Everyone had gone to bed at an early hour that night, disinclined for conversation. No one was moving. There was a lamp in the passage; it was partly turned down. Jameson's room was next to mine. I heard him stir as he undressed, and talk to himself. Then he was quiet. I wound up my watch, and emptying my pocket, put my purse under the pillow. I was not in the least heavy with sleep. If I did go to bed I should not be able to close my eyes. But then—if I sat up I could do nothing.

I was about leisurely to undress, when I heard a sharp cry, or exclamation of mingled pain and alarm, from the adjoining room. In another moment there was a rap at my door. I opened, and Jameson came in. He was in his night-shirt, and looking agitated and frightened.

"Look here, old fellow," said he in a shaking voice, "there is Musty in my room. He has been hiding there, and just as I dropped asleep he ran that knife of yours into my throat."

"My knife?"

"Yes—that pruning-knife you gave him, you know. Look here—I must have the place sewn up. Do go for a doctor, there's a good chap."

"Where is the place?"

"Here on my right gill."

Jameson turned his head to the left, and I raised the lamp. There was no wound of any sort there.

I told him so.

"Oh, yes! That's fine—I tell you I felt his knife go in."

"Nonsense, you were dreaming."

"Dreaming! Not I. I saw Musty as distinctly as I now see you."

"This is a delusion, Jameson," I replied. "The poor fellow is dead."

"Oh, that's very fine," said Jameson. "It is not the first of April, and I don't believe the yarns that you've been spinning. You tried to make believe he was dead, but I know he is not. He has got into my room, and he made a dig at my throat with your pruning-knife."

"I'll go into your room with you."

"Do so. But he's gone by this time. Trust him to cut and run."

I followed Jameson, and looked about. There was no trace of anyone beside himself having been in the room. Moreover, there was no place but the nut-wood wardrobe in the bedroom in which anyone could have secreted himself. I opened this and showed that it was empty.

129

After a while I pacified Jameson, and induced him to go to bed again, and then I left his room. I did not now attempt to court sleep. I wrote letters with a hand not the steadiest, and did my accounts.

As the hour approached midnight I was again startled by a cry from the adjoining room, and in another moment Jameson was at my door.

"That blooming fellow Musty is in my room still," said he. "He has been at my throat again."

"Nonsense," I said. "You are labouring under hallucinations. You locked your door."

"Oh, by Jove, yes—of course I did; but, hang it, in this hole, neither doors nor windows fit, and the locks are no good, and the bolts nowhere. He got in again somehow, and if I had not started up the moment I felt the knife, he'd have done for me. He would, by George. I wish I had a revolver."

I went into Jameson's room. Again he insisted on my looking at his throat.

"It's very good of you to say there is no wound," said he. "But you won't gull me with words. I felt his knife in my windpipe, and if I had not jumped out of bed——"

"You locked your door. No one could enter. Look in the glass, there is not even a scratch. This is pure imagination."

"I'll tell you what, old fellow, I won't sleep in that room again. Change with me, there's a charitable buffer. If you don't believe in Musty, Musty won't hurt you, maybe—anyhow you can try if he's solid or a phantom. Blow me if the knife felt like a phantom."

"I do not quite see my way to changing rooms," I replied; "but this I will do for you. If you like to go to bed again in your own apartment, I will sit up with you till morning."

"All right," answered Jameson. "And if Musty comes in again, let out at him and do not spare him. Swear that."

I accompanied Jameson once more to his bedroom, Little as I liked the man, I could not deny him my presence and assistance at this time. It was obvious that his nerves were shaken by what had occurred, and he felt his relation to Mustapha much more than he cared to show. The thought that he had been the cause of the poor fellow's death preyed on his mind, never strong, and now it was upset with imaginary terrors.

I gave up letter writing, and brought my Baedeker's *Upper Egypt* into Jameson's room, one of the best of all guide-books, and one crammed with information. I seated myself near the light, and with my back to the bed, on which the young man had once more flung himself.

"I say," said Jameson, raising his head, "is it too late for a brandy-and-soda?"

"Everyone is in bed."

"What lazy dogs they are. One never can get anything one wants here."

"Well, try to go to sleep."

He tossed from side to side for some time, but after a while, either he was quiet, or I was engrossed in my Baedeker, and I heard nothing till a clock struck twelve. At the last stroke I heard a snort and then a gasp and a cry from the bed. I started up, and looked round. Jameson was slipping out with his feet onto the floor.

"Confound you!" said he angrily, "you are a fine watch, you are, to let Mustapha steal in on tiptoe whilst you are cartouching and all that sort of rubbish. He was at me again, and if I had not been sharp he'd have cut my throat. I won't go to bed anymore!"

"Well, sit up. But I assure you no one has been here."

"That's fine. How can you tell? You had your back to me, and these devils of fellows steal about like cats. You can't hear them till they are at you."

It was of no use arguing with Jameson, so I let him have his way.

"I can feel all the three places in my throat where he ran the knife in," said he. "And—don't you notice?—I speak with difficulty."

So we sat up together the rest of the night. He became more

reasonable as dawn came on, and inclined to admit that he had been a prey to fancies.

The day passed very much as did others—Jameson was dull and sulky. After *déjeuner* he sat on at table when the ladies had risen and retired, and the gentlemen had formed in knots at the window, discussing what was to be done in the afternoon.

Suddenly Jameson, whose head had begun to nod, started up with an oath and threw down his chair.

"You fellows!" he said, "you are all in league against me. You let that Mustapha come in without a word, and try to stick his knife into me."

"He has not been here."

"It's a plant. You are combined to bully me and drive me away. You don't like me. You have engaged Mustapha to murder me. This is the fourth time he has tried to cut my throat, and in the *salle à manger*, too, with you all standing round. You ought to be ashamed to call yourselves Englishmen. I'll go to Cairo. I'll complain."

It really seemed that the feeble brain of Jameson was affected. The Oxford don undertook to sit up in the room the following night.

The young man was fagged and sleep-weary, but no sooner did his eyes close, and clouds form about his head, than he was brought to wakefulness again by the same fancy or dream. The Oxford don had more trouble with him on the second night than I had on the first, for his lapses into sleep were more frequent, and each such lapse was succeeded by a start and a panic.

The next day he was worse, and we felt that he could no longer be left alone. The third night the *attaché* sat up to watch him.

Jameson had now sunk into a sullen mood. He would not speak, except to himself, and then only to grumble.

During the night, without being aware of it, the young *attaché*, who had taken a couple of magazines with him to read, fell asleep. When he went off he did not know. He woke just before dawn, and in a spasm of terror and self-reproach saw that

Jameson's chair was empty.

Jameson was not on his bed. He could not be found in the hotel.

At dawn he was found—dead, at the door of the mosque, with his throat cut.

A Dead Finger

(A tale from *A Book of Ghosts*)

1

Why the National Gallery should not attract so many visitors as, say, the British Museum, I cannot explain. The latter does not contain much that, one would suppose, appeals to the interest of the ordinary sightseer. What knows such of prehistoric flints and scratched bones? Of Assyrian sculpture? Of Egyptian hieroglyphics? The Greek and Roman statuary is cold and dead. The paintings in the National Gallery glow with colour, and are instinct with life. Yet, somehow, a few listless wanderers saunter yawning through the National Gallery, whereas swarms pour through the halls of the British Museum, and talk and pass remarks about the objects there exposed, of the date and meaning of which they have not the faintest conception.

I was thinking of this problem, and endeavouring to unravel it, one morning whilst sitting in the room for English masters at the great collection in Trafalgar Square. At the same time another thought forced itself upon me. I had been through the rooms devoted to foreign schools, and had then come into that given over to Reynolds, Morland, Gainsborough, Constable, and Hogarth. The morning had been for a while propitious, but towards noon a dense umber-tinted fog had come on, making it all but impossible to see the pictures, and quite impossible to do them justice. I was tired, and so seated myself on one of the chairs, and fell into the consideration first of all of—why the National Gallery is not as popular as it should be; and secondly, how it was that the British School had no beginnings, like those of Italy and the Netherlands.

We can see the art of the painter from its first initiation in the Italian peninsula, and among the Flemings. It starts on its progress like a child, and we can trace every stage of its growth. Not so with English art. It springs to life in full and splendid maturity. Who were there before Reynolds and Gainsborough and Hogarth? The great names of those portrait and subject painters who have left their canvases upon the walls of our country houses were those of foreigners—Holbein, Kneller, Van Dyck, and Lely for portraits, and Monnoyer for flower and fruit pieces. Landscapes, figure subjects were all importations, none home-grown. How came that about? Was there no limner that was native? Was it that fashion trampled on home-grown pictorial beginnings as it flouted and spurned native music?

Here was food for contemplation. Dreaming in the brown fog, looking through it without seeing its beauties, at Hogarth's painting of Lavinia Fenton as Polly Peachum, without wondering how so indifferent a beauty could have captivated the Duke of Bolton and held him for thirty years, I was recalled to myself and my surroundings by the strange conduct of a lady who had seated herself on a chair near me, also discouraged by the fog, and awaiting its dispersion.

I had not noticed her particularly. At the present moment I do not remember particularly what she was like. So far as I can recollect she was middle-aged, and was quietly yet well dressed. It was not her face nor her dress that attracted my attention and disturbed the current of my thoughts; the effect I speak of was produced by her strange movements and behaviour.

She had been sitting listless, probably thinking of nothing at all, or nothing in particular, when, in turning her eyes round, and finding that she could see nothing of the paintings, she began to study me. This did concern me greatly. A cat may look at the king; but to be contemplated by a lady is a compliment sufficient to please any gentleman. It was not gratified vanity that troubled my thoughts, but the consciousness that my appearance produced—first of all a startled surprise, then undisguised alarm, and, finally, indescribable horror.

Now a man can sit quietly leaning on the head of his umbrella, and glow internally, warmed and illumined by the consciousness that he is being surveyed with admiration by a lovely woman, even when he is middle-aged and not fashionably dressed; but no man can maintain his composure when he discovers himself to be an object of aversion and terror.

What was it? I passed my hand over my chin and upper lip, thinking it not impossible that I might have forgotten to shave that morning, and in my confusion not considering that the fog would prevent the lady from discovering neglect in this particular, had it occurred, which it had not. I am a little careless, perhaps, about shaving when in the country; but when in town, never.

The next idea that occurred to me was—a smut. Had a London black, curdled in that dense pea-soup atmosphere, descended on my nose and blackened it? I hastily drew my silk handkerchief from my pocket, moistened it, and passed it over my nose, and then each cheek. I then turned my eyes into the corners and looked at the lady, to see whether by this means I had got rid of what was objectionable in my personal appearance.

Then I saw that her eyes, dilated with horror, were riveted, not on my face, but on my leg.

My leg! What on earth could that harmless member have in it so terrifying? The morning had been dull; there had been rain in the night, and I admit that on leaving my hotel I had turned up the bottoms of my trousers. That is a proceeding not so uncommon, not so outrageous as to account for the stony stare of this woman's eyes.

If that were all I would turn my trousers down.

Then I saw her shrink from the chair on which she sat to one further removed from me, but still with her eyes fixed on my leg—about the level of my knee. She had let fall her umbrella, and was grasping the seat of her chair with both hands, as she backed from me.

I need hardly say that I was greatly disturbed in mind and feelings, and forgot all about the origin of the English schools of painters, and the question why the British Museum is more popular than the National Gallery.

Thinking that I might have been spattered by a hansom whilst crossing Oxford Street, I passed my hand down my side hastily, with a sense of annoyance, and all at once touched something cold, clammy, that sent a thrill to my heart, and made me start and take a step forward. At the same moment, the lady, with a cry of horror, sprang to her feet, and with raised hands fled from the room, leaving her umbrella where it had fallen.

There were other visitors to the Picture Gallery besides ourselves, who had been passing through the saloon, and they turned at her cry, and looked in surprise after her.

The policeman stationed in the room came to me and asked what had happened. I was in such agitation that I hardly knew what to answer. I told him that I could explain what had occurred little better than himself. I had noticed that the lady had worn an odd expression, and had behaved in most extraordinary fashion, and that he had best take charge of her umbrella, and wait for her return to claim it.

This questioning by the official was vexing, as it prevented me from at once and on the spot investigating the cause of her alarm and mine—hers at something she must have seen on my leg, and mine at something I had distinctly felt creeping up my leg.

The numbing and sickening effect on me of the touch of the object I had seen was not to be shaken off at once. Indeed, I felt as though my hand were contaminated, and that I could have no rest till I had thoroughly washed the hand, and, if possible, washed away the feeling that had been produced.

I looked on the floor, I examined my leg, but saw nothing. As I wore my overcoat, it was probable that in rising from my seat the skirt had fallen over my trousers and hidden the thing, whatever it was. I therefore hastily removed my overcoat and shook it, then I looked at my trousers. There was nothing whatever on my leg, and nothing fell from my overcoat when shaken.

Accordingly I reinvested myself, and hastily left the gallery; then took my way as speedily as I could, without actually running, to Charing Cross Station and down the narrow way leading to the Metropolitan, where I went into Faulkner's bath and hairdressing establishment, and asked for hot water to thoroughly wash my hand and well soap it. I bathed my hand in water as hot as I could endure it, employed carbolic soap, and then, after having a good brush down, especially on my left side where my hand had encountered the object that had so affected me, I left.

I had entertained the intention of going to the Princess's Theatre that evening, and of securing a ticket in the morning; but all thought of theatre-going was gone from me. I could not free my heart from the sense of nausea and cold that had been produced by the touch. I went into Gatti's to have lunch, and ordered something, I forget what, but, when served, I found that my appetite was gone. I could eat nothing; the food inspired me with disgust. I thrust it from me untasted, and, after drinking a couple of glasses of claret, left the restaurant, and returned to my hotel.

Feeling sick and faint, I threw my overcoat over the sofa-back, and cast myself on my bed.

I do not know that there was any particular reason for my doing so, but as I lay my eyes were on my great-coat.

The density of the fog had passed away, and there was light again, not of first quality, but sufficient for a Londoner to swear by, so that I could see everything in my room, though through a veil, darkly.

I do not think my mind was occupied in any way. About the only occasions on which, to my knowledge, my mind is actually passive or inert is when crossing the Channel in *The Foam* from Dover to Calais, when I am always, in every weather, abjectly seasick—and thoughtless. But as I now lay on my bed, uncomfortable, squeamish, without knowing why—I was in the same inactive mental condition. But not for long.

I saw something that startled me.

First, it appeared to me as if the lappet of my overcoat pocket were in movement, being raised. I did not pay much attention to this, as I supposed that the garment was sliding down on to the seat of the sofa, from the back, and that this displacement of gravity caused the movement I observed. But this I soon saw was not the case. That which moved the lappet was something in the pocket that was struggling to get out. I could see now that it was working its way up the inside, and that when it reached the opening it lost balance and fell down again. I could make this out by the projections and indentations in the cloth; these moved as the creature, or whatever it was, worked its way up the lining.

"A mouse," I said, and forgot my seediness; I was interested. "The little rascal! However did he contrive to seat himself in my pocket? and I have worn that overcoat all the morning!" But no—it was not a mouse. I saw something white poke its way out from under the lappet; and in another moment an object was revealed that, though revealed, I could not understand, nor could I distinguish what it was.

Now roused by curiosity, I raised myself on my elbow. In doing this I made some noise, the bed creaked. Instantly the something dropped on the floor, lay outstretched for a moment, to recover itself, and then began, with the motions of a maggot, to run along the floor.

There is a caterpillar called "The Measurer," because, when it advances, it draws its tail up to where its head is and then throws forward its full length, and again draws up its extremity, forming at each time a loop; and with each step measuring its total length. The object I now saw on the floor was advancing precisely like the measuring caterpillar. It had the colour of a cheese-maggot, and in length was about three and a half inches. It was not, however, like a caterpillar, which is flexible throughout its entire length, but this was, as it seemed to me, jointed in two places, one joint being more conspicuous than the other. For some moments I was so completely paralysed by astonishment that I remained motionless, looking at the thing as it crawled along the carpet—a dull green carpet with darker green, almost black, flowers in it.

It had, as it seemed to me, a glossy head, distinctly marked; but, as the light was not brilliant, I could not make out very clearly, and, moreover, the rapid movements prevented close scrutiny.

Presently, with a shock still more startling than that produced by its apparition at the opening of the pocket of my great-coat, I became convinced that what I saw was a finger, a human fore-finger, and that the glossy head was no other than the nail.

The finger did not seem to have been amputated. There was no sign of blood or laceration where the knuckle should be, but the extremity of the finger, or root rather, faded away to indistinctness, and I was unable to make out the root of the finger.

I could see no hand, no body behind this finger, nothing whatever except a finger that had little token of warm life in it, no coloration as though blood circulated in it; and this finger was in active motion creeping along the carpet towards a ward-robe that stood against the wall by the fireplace.

I sprang off the bed and pursued it.

Evidently the finger was alarmed, for it redoubled its pace, reached the wardrobe, and went under it. By the time I had ar-rived at the article of furniture it had disappeared. I lit a vesta match and held it beneath the wardrobe, that was raised above the carpet by about two inches, on turned feet, but I could see nothing more of the finger.

I got my umbrella and thrust it beneath, and raked forwards and backwards, right and left, and raked out flue, and nothing more solid.

2

I packed my portmanteau next day and returned to my home in the country. All desire for amusement in town was gone, and the faculty to transact business had departed as well.

A languor and qualms had come over me, and my head was in a maze. I was unable to fix my thoughts on anything. At times I was disposed to believe that my wits were deserting me, at others that I was on the verge of a severe illness. Anyhow, whether likely to go off my head or not, or take to my bed, home was the only place for me, and homeward I sped, accordingly. On reaching my country habitation, my servant, as usual, took my portmanteau to my bedroom, unstrapped it, but did not unpack it. I object to his throwing out the contents of my Gladstone bag; not that there is anything in it he may not see, but that he puts my things where I cannot find them again.

My clothes—he is welcome to place them where he likes and where they belong, and this latter he knows better than I do; but, then, I carry about with me other things than a dress suit, and changes of linen and flannel. There are letters, papers, books—and the proper destinations of these are known only to myself. A servant has a singular and evil knack of putting away literary matter and odd volumes in such places that it takes the owner half a day to find them again.

Although I was uncomfortable, and my head in a whirl, I opened and unpacked my own portmanteau. As I was thus engaged I saw something curled up in my collar-box, the lid of which had got broken in by a boot-heel impinging on it. I had pulled off the damaged cover to see if my collars had been spoiled, when something curled up inside suddenly rose on end and leapt, just like a cheese-jumper, out of the box, over the edge of the Gladstone bag, and scurried away across the floor in a manner already familiar to me.

I could not doubt for a moment what it was—here was the finger again. It had come with me from London to the country.

Whither it went in its run over the floor I do not know, I was too bewildered to observe.

Somewhat later, towards evening, I seated myself in my easy-chair, took up a book, and tried to read. I was tired with the journey, with the knocking about in town, and the discomfort and alarm produced by the apparition of the finger. I felt worn out. I was unable to give my attention to what I read, and before I was aware was asleep. Roused for an instant by the fall of the book from my hands, I speedily relapsed into unconsciousness. I am not sure that a doze in an armchair ever does good. It usually leaves me in a semi-stupid condition and with a headache. Five minutes in a horizontal position on my bed is worth thirty in a chair. That is my experience. In sleeping in a sedentary position the head is a difficulty; it drops forward or lolls on one side or the other, and has to be brought back into a position in which the line to the centre of gravity runs through the trunk, otherwise the head carries the body over in a sort of general capsize out of the chair on to the floor.

I slept, on the occasion of which I am speaking, pretty healthily, because deadly weary; but I was brought to waking, not by my head falling over the arm of the chair, and my trunk tumbling after it, but by a feeling of cold extending from my throat to my heart. When I awoke I was in a diagonal position, with my right ear resting on my right shoulder, and exposing the left side of my throat, and it was here—where the jugular vein throbs—that I felt the greatest intensity of cold. At once I shrugged my left shoulder, rubbing my neck with the collar of my coat in so doing. Immediately something fell off, upon the floor, and I again saw the finger.

My disgust—horror, were intensified when I perceived that it was dragging something after it, which might have been an old stocking, and which I took at first glance for something of the sort.

The evening sun shone in through my window, in a brilliant golden ray that lighted the object as it scrambled along. With this illumination I was able to distinguish what the object was. It is not easy to describe it, but I will make the attempt.

The finger I saw was solid and material; what it drew after it was neither, or was in a nebulous, protoplasmic condition. The finger was attached to a hand that was curdling into matter and in process of acquiring solidity; attached to the hand was an arm in a very filmy condition, and this arm belonged to a human body in a still more vaporous, immaterial condition. This was being dragged along the floor by the finger, just as a silkworm might pull after it the tangle of its web.

I could see legs and arms, and head, and coat-tail tumbling about and interlacing and disentangling again in a promiscuous manner. There were no bone, no muscle, no substance in the figure; the members were attached to the trunk, which was spineless, but they had evidently no functions, and were wholly dependent on the finger which pulled them along in a jumble of parts as it advanced.

In such confusion did the whole vaporous matter seem, that I think—I cannot say for certain it was so, but the impression left on my mind was—that one of the eyeballs was looking out at a nostril, and the tongue lolling out of one of the ears.

It was, however, only for a moment that I saw this germ-body; I cannot call by another name that which had not more substance than smoke. I saw it only so long as it was being dragged athwart the ray of sunlight. The moment it was pulled jerkily out of the beam into the shadow beyond, I could see nothing of it, only the crawling finger.

I had not sufficient moral energy or physical force in me to rise, pursue, and stamp on the finger, and grind it with my heel into the floor. Both seemed drained out of me. What became of the finger, whither it went, how it managed to secrete itself, I do not know. I had lost the power to inquire. I sat in my chair, chilled, staring before me into space.

"Please, sir," a voice said, "there's Mr. Square below, electrical engineer."

"Eh?" I looked dreamily round.

My valet was at the door.

"Please, sir, the gentleman would be glad to be allowed to go over the house and see that all the electrical apparatus is in order."

"Oh, indeed! Yes—show him up."

3

I had recently placed the lighting of my house in the hands of an electrical engineer, a very intelligent man, Mr. Square, for whom I had contracted a sincere friendship.

He had built a shed with a dynamo out of sight, and had entrusted the laying of the wires to subordinates, as he had been busy with other orders and could not personally watch every detail. But he was not the man to let anything pass unobserved, and he knew that electricity was not a force to be played with. Bad or careless workmen will often insufficiently protect the wires, or neglect the insertion of the lead which serves as a safety-valve in the event of the current being too strong. Houses may be set on fire, human beings fatally shocked, by the neglect of a bad or slovenly workman.

The apparatus for my mansion was but just completed, and Mr. Square had come to inspect it and make sure that all was right.

He was an enthusiast in the matter of electricity, and saw for it a vast perspective, the limits of which could not be predicted.

"All forces," said he, "are correlated. When you have force in one form, you may just turn it into this or that, as you like. In one form it is motive power, in another it is light, in another heat. Now we have electricity for illumination. We employ it, but not as freely as in the States, for propelling vehicles. Why should we have horses drawing our buses? We should use only electric trams. Why do we burn coal to warm our shins? There is electricity, which throws out no filthy smoke as does coal. Why should we let the tides waste their energies in the Thames? in other estuaries? There we have Nature supplying us—free *gratis*, and for nothing—with all the force we want for propelling, for heating, for lighting. I will tell you something more, my dear sir," said Mr. Square. "I have mentioned but three modes of force, and have instanced but a limited number of uses to which electricity may be turned. How is it with photography? Is not electric light becoming an artistic agent? I bet you," said he, "before long it will become a therapeutic agent as well."

"Oh, yes; I have heard of certain impostors with their life-belts."

Mr. Square did not relish this little dig I gave him. He winced, but returned to the charge. "We don't know how to direct it aright, that is all," said he. "I haven't taken the matter up, but others will, I bet; and we shall have electricity used as freely as now we use powders and pills. I don't believe in doctors' stuffs myself. I hold that disease lays hold of a man because he lacks physical force to resist it. Now, is it not obvious that you are beginning at the wrong end when you attack the disease? What you want is to supply force, make up for the lack of physical power, and force is force wherever you find it—here motive, there illuminating, and so on. I don't see why a physician should not utilise the tide rushing out under London Bridge for restoring the feeble vigour of all who are languid and a prey to disorder in the Metropolis.

"It will come to that, I bet, and that is not all. Force is force, everywhere. Political, moral force, physical force, dynamic force, heat, light, tidal waves, and so on—all are one, all is one. In time we shall know how to galvanise into aptitude and moral energy all the limp and crooked consciences and wills that need taking in hand, and such there always will be in modern civilisation. I don't know how to do it. I don't know how it will be done, but in the future the priest as well as the doctor will turn electricity on as his principal, nay, his only agent. And he can get his force anywhere, out of the running stream, out of the wind, out of the tidal wave.

"I'll give you an instance," continued Mr. Square, chuckling and rubbing his hands, "to show you the great possibilities in electricity, used in a crude fashion. In a certain great city away far west in the States, a go-ahead place, too, more so than New York, they had electric trams all up and down and along the roads to everywhere. The union men working for the company demanded that the non-unionists should be turned off. But the company didn't see it. Instead, it turned off the union men. It had up its sleeve a sufficiency of the others, and filled all places at once. Union men didn't like it, and passed word that at a given hour on a certain day every wire was to be cut. The company knew this by means of its spies, and turned on, ready for them, three times the power into all the wires. At the fixed moment, up the poles went the strikers to cut the cables, and down they came a dozen times quicker than they went up, I bet. Then there came wires to the hospitals from all quarters for stretchers to carry off the disabled men, some with broken legs, arms, ribs; two or three had their necks broken. I reckon the company was wonderfully merciful—it didn't put on sufficient force to make cinders of them then and there; possibly opinion might not have liked it. Stopped the strike, did that. Great moral effect—all done by electricity."

In this manner Mr. Square was wont to rattle on. He interested me, and I came to think that there might be something in what he said—that his suggestions were not mere nonsense. I was glad to see Mr. Square enter my room, shown in by my man. I did not rise from my chair to shake his hand, for I had not sufficient energy to do so. In a languid tone I welcomed him and signed to him to take a seat. Mr. Square looked at me with some surprise.

"Why, what's the matter?" he said. "You seem unwell. Not got the 'flue, have you?"

"I beg your pardon?"

"The influenza. Every third person is crying out that he has it, and the sale of eucalyptus is enormous, not that eucalyptus is any good. Influenza microbes indeed! What care they for eucalyptus? You've gone down some steps of the ladder of life since I saw you last, squire. How do you account for that?"

I hesitated about mentioning the extraordinary circumstances that had occurred; but Square was a man who would not allow any beating about the bush. He was downright and straight, and in ten minutes had got the entire story out of me.

"Rather boisterous for your nerves that—a crawling finger," said he. "It's a queer story taken on end."

Then he was silent, considering.

After a few minutes he rose, and said: "I'll go and look at the fittings, and then I'll turn this little matter of yours over again, and see if I can't knock the bottom out of it, I'm kinder fond of

146

these sort of things."

Mr. Square was not a Yankee, but he had lived for some time in America, and affected to speak like an American. He used expressions, terms of speech common in the States, but had none of the Transatlantic twang. He was a man absolutely without affectation in every other particular; this was his sole weakness, and it was harmless.

The man was so thorough in all he did that I did not expect his return immediately. He was certain to examine every portion of the dynamo engine, and all the connections and burners. This would necessarily engage him for some hours. As the day was nearly done, I knew he could not accomplish what he wanted that evening, and accordingly gave orders that a room should be prepared for him. Then, as my head was full of pain, and my skin was burning, I told my servant to apologise for my absence from dinner, and tell Mr. Square that I was really forced to return to my bed by sickness, and that I believed I was about to be prostrated by an attack of influenza.

The valet—a worthy fellow, who has been with me for six years—was concerned at my appearance, and urged me to allow him to send for a doctor. I had no confidence in the local practitioner, and if I sent for another from the nearest town I should offend him, and a row would perhaps ensue, so I declined. If I were really in for an influenza attack, I knew about as much as any doctor how to deal with it. Quinine, quinine—that was all. I bade my man light a small lamp, lower it, so as to give sufficient illumination to enable me to find some lime-juice at my bed head, and my pocket-handkerchief, and to be able to read my watch. When he had done this, I bade him leave me.

I lay in bed, burning, racked with pain in my head, and with my eyeballs on fire.

Whether I fell asleep or went off my head for a while I cannot tell. I may have fainted. I have no recollection of anything after having gone to bed and taken a sip of lime-juice that tasted to me like soap—till I was roused by a sense of pain in my ribs—a slow, gnawing, torturing pain, waxing momentarily more intense. In half-consciousness I was partly dreaming and partly aware of actual suffering. The pain was real; but in my fancy I thought that a great maggot was working its way into my side between my ribs. I seemed to see it. It twisted itself half round, then reverted to its former position, and again twisted itself, moving like a bradawl, not like a gimlet, which latter forms a complete revolution.

This, obviously, must have been a dream, hallucination only, as I was lying on my back and my eyes were directed towards the bottom of the bed, and the coverlet and blankets and sheet intervened between my eyes and my side. But in fever one sees without eyes, and in every direction, and through all obstructions.

Roused thoroughly by an excruciating twinge, I tried to cry out, and succeeded in throwing myself over on my right side, that which was in pain. At once I felt the thing withdrawn that was awling—if I may use the word—in between my ribs.

And now I saw, standing beside the bed, a figure that had its arm under the bedclothes, and was slowly removing it. The hand was leisurely drawn from under the coverings and rested on the eider-down coverlet, with the forefinger extended.

The figure was that of a man, in shabby clothes, with a sallow, mean face, a retreating forehead, with hair cut after the French fashion, and a moustache, dark. The jaws and chin were covered with a bristly growth, as if shaving had been neglected for a fortnight. The figure did not appear to be thoroughly solid, but to be of the consistency of curd, and the face was of the complexion of curd. As I looked at this object it withdrew, sliding backward in an odd sort of manner, and as though overweighted by the hand, which was the most substantial, indeed the only substantial portion of it. Though the figure retreated stooping, yet it was no longer huddled along by the finger, as if it had no material existence. If the same, it had acquired a consistency and a solidity which it did not possess before.

How it vanished I do not know, nor whither it went. The door opened, and Square came in.

"What!" he exclaimed with cheery voice; "influenza is it?"

"I don't know—I think it's that finger again."

4

"Now, look here," said Square, "I'm not going to have that cuss at its pranks any more. Tell me all about it."

I was now so exhausted, so feeble, that I was not able to give a connected account of what had taken place, but Square put to me just a few pointed questions and elicited the main facts. He pieced them together in his own orderly mind, so as to form a connected whole. "There is a feature in the case," said he, "that strikes me as remarkable and important. At first—a finger only, then a hand, then a nebulous figure attached to the hand, without backbone, without consistency. Lastly, a complete form, with consistency and with backbone, but the latter in a gelatinous condition, and the entire figure overweighted by the hand, just as hand and figure were previously overweighted by the finger. Simultaneously with this compacting and consolidating of the figure, came your degeneration and loss of vital force and, in a word, of health. What you lose, that object acquires, and what it acquires, it gains by contact with you. That's clear enough, is it not?"

"I dare say. I don't know. I can't think."

"I suppose not; the faculty of thought is drained out of you. Very well, I must think for you, and I will. Force is force, and see if I can't deal with your visitant in such a way as will prove just as truly a moral dissuasive as that employed on the union men on strike in—never mind where it was. That's not to the point."

"Will you kindly give me some lime-juice?" I entreated.

I sipped the acid draught, but without relief. I listened to Square, but without hope. I wanted to be left alone. I was weary of my pain, weary of everything, even of life. It was a matter of indifference to me whether I recovered or slipped out of existence.

"It will be here again shortly," said the engineer. "As the French say, *l'appetit vient en mangeant*. It has been at you thrice, it won't be content without another peck. And if it does get another, I guess it will pretty well about finish you."

Mr. Square rubbed his chin, and then put his hands into his trouser pockets. That also was a trick acquired in the States, an inelegant one. His hands, when not actively occupied, went into his pockets, inevitably they gravitated thither. Ladies did not like Square; they said he was not a gentleman. But it was not that he said or did anything "off colour," only he spoke to them, looked at them, walked with them, always with his hands in his pockets. I have seen a lady turn her back on him deliberately because of this trick.

Standing now with his hands in his pockets, he studied my bed, and said contemptuously: "Old-fashioned and bad, four-poster. Oughtn't to be allowed, I guess; unwholesome all the way round."

I was not in a condition to dispute this. I like a fourposter with curtains at head and feet; not that I ever draw them, but it gives a sense of privacy that is wanting in one of your half-tester beds.

If there is a window at one's feet, one can lie in bed without the glare in one's eyes, and yet without darkening the room by drawing the blinds. There is much to be said for a fourposter, but this is not the place in which to say it.

Mr. Square pulled his hands out of his pockets and began fiddling with the electric point near the head of my bed, attached a wire, swept it in a semicircle along the floor, and then thrust the knob at the end into my hand in the bed.

"Keep your eye open," said he, "and your hand shut and covered. If that finger comes again tickling your ribs, try it with the point. I'll manage the switch, from behind the curtain."

Then he disappeared.

I was too indifferent in my misery to turn my head and observe where he was. I remained inert, with the knob in my hand, and my eyes closed, suffering and thinking of nothing but the shooting pains through my head and the aches in my loins and back and legs.

Some time probably elapsed before I felt the finger again at work at my ribs; it groped, but no longer bored. I now felt the entire hand, not a single finger, and the hand was substantial, cold, and clammy. I was aware, how, I know not, that if the finger-point reached the region of my heart, on the left side, the hand would, so to speak, sit down on it, with the cold palm over it, and that then immediately my heart would cease to beat, and it would be, as Square might express it, "gone coon" with me.

In self-preservation I brought up the knob of the electric wire against the hand—against one of the ringers, I think—and at once was aware of a rapping, squealing noise. I turned my head languidly, and saw the form, now more substantial than before, capering in an ecstasy of pain, endeavouring fruitlessly to withdraw its arm from under the bedclothes, and the hand from the electric point.

At the same moment Square stepped from behind the curtain, with a dry laugh, and said: "I thought we should fix him. He has the coil about him, and can't escape. Now let us drop to particulars. But I shan't let you off till I know all about you."

The last sentence was addressed, not to me, but to the apparition.

Thereupon he bade me take the point away from the hand of the figure—being—whatever it was, but to be ready with it at a moment's notice. He then proceeded to catechise my visitor, who moved restlessly within the circle of wire, but could not escape from it. It replied in a thin, squealing voice that sounded as if it came from a distance, and had a querulous tone in it. I do not pretend to give all that was said. I cannot recollect everything that passed. My memory was affected by my illness, as well as my body. Yet I prefer giving the scraps that I recollect to what Square told me he had heard.

"Yes—I was unsuccessful, always was. Nothing answered with me. The world was against me. Society was. I hate society. I don't like work neither, never did. But I like agitating against what is established. I hate the Royal Family, the landed interest, the parsons, everything that is, except the people—that is, the unemployed. I always did. I couldn't get work as suited me. When I died they buried me in a cheap coffin, dirt cheap, and gave me a nasty grave, cheap, and a service rattled away cheap, and no monument. Didn't want none. Oh! there are lots of us. All discontented. Discontent! That's a passion, it is—it gets into the veins, it fills the brain, it occupies the heart; it's a sort of divine cancer that takes possession of the entire man, and makes him dissatisfied with everything, and hate everybody.

"But we must have our share of happiness at some time. We all crave for it in one way or other. Some think there's a future state of blessedness and so have hope, and look to attain to it, for hope is a cable and anchor that attaches to what is real. But when you have no hope of that sort, don't believe in any future state, you must look for happiness in life here. We didn't get it when we were alive, so we seek to procure it after we are dead. We can do it, if we can get out of our cheap and nasty coffins. But not till the greater part of us is mouldered away. If a finger or two remains, that can work its way up to the surface, those cheap deal coffins go to pieces quick enough.

"Then the only solid part of us left can pull the rest of us that has gone to nothing after it. Then we grope about after the living. The well-to-do if we can get at them—the honest working poor if we can't—we hate them too, because they are content and happy. If we reach any of these, and can touch them, then we can draw their vital force out of them into ourselves, and recuperate at their expense. That was about what I was going to do with you. Getting on famous. Nearly solidified into a new man; and given another chance in life. But I've missed it this time. Just like my luck. Miss everything. Always have, except misery and disappointment. Get plenty of that."

"What are you all?" asked Square. "Anarchists out of employ?"

"Some of us go by that name, some by other designations, but we are all one, and own allegiance to but one monarch—Sovereign discontent. We are bred to have a distaste for manual work; and we grow up loafers, grumbling at everything and quarrelling with society that is around us and the Providence that is above us."

"And what do you call yourselves now?"

"Call ourselves? Nothing; we are the same, in another condition, that is all. Folk called us once Anarchists, Nihilists, Socialists, Levellers, now they call us the Influenza. The learned talk of microbes, and bacilli, and bacteria. Microbes, bacilli, and bacteria be blowed! We are the Influenza; we the social failures, the generally discontented, coming up out of our cheap and nasty graves in the form of physical disease. We are the Influenza."

"There you are, I guess!" exclaimed Square triumphantly. "Did I not say that all forces were correlated? If so, then all negations, deficiencies of force are one in their several manifestations. Talk of Divine discontent as a force impelling to progress! Rubbish, it is a paralysis of energy. It turns all it absorbs to acid, to envy, spite, gall. It inspires nothing, but rots the whole moral system. Here you have it—moral, social, political discontent in another form, nay aspect—that is all. What Anarchism is in the body Politic, that Influenza is in the body Physical. Do you see that?"

"Ye-e-s-e-s," I believe I answered, and dropped away into the land of dreams.

I recovered. What Square did with the Thing I know not, but believe that he reduced it again to its former negative and self-decomposing condition.

The Leaden Ring
(A tale from *A Book of Ghosts*)

"It is not possible, Julia. I cannot conceive how the idea of attending the county ball can have entered your head after what has happened. Poor young Hattersley's dreadful death suffices to stop that."

"But, aunt, Mr. Hattersley is no relation of ours."

"No relation—but you know that the poor fellow would not have shot himself if it had not been for you."

"Oh, Aunt Elizabeth, how can you say so, when the verdict was that he committed suicide when in an unsound condition of mind? How could I help his blowing out his brains, when those brains were deranged?"

"Julia, do not talk like this. If he did go off his head, it was you who upset him by first drawing him on, leading him to believe that you liked him, and then throwing him over so soon as the Hon. James Lawlor appeared on the *tapis*. Consider: what will people say if you go to the assembly?"

"What will they say if I do not go? They will immediately set it down to my caring deeply for James Hattersley, and they will think that there was some sort of engagement."

"They are not likely to suppose that. But really, Julia, you were for a while all smiles and encouragement. Tell me, now, did Mr. Hattersley propose to you?"

"Well—yes, he did, and I refused him."

"And then he went and shot himself in despair. Julia, you cannot with any face go to the ball."

"Nobody knows that he proposed. And precisely because I do go everyone will conclude that he did not propose. I do not wish it to be supposed that he did."

"His family, of course, must have been aware. They will see your name among those present at the assembly."

"Aunt, they are in too great trouble to look at the paper to see who were at the dance."

"His terrible death lies at your door. How you can have the heart, Julia——"

"I don't see it. Of course, I feel it. I am awfully sorry, and awfully sorry for his father, the admiral. I cannot set him up again. I wish that when I rejected him he had gone and done as did Joe Pomeroy, marry one of his landlady's daughters."

"There, Julia, is another of your delinquencies. You lured on young Pomeroy till he proposed, then you refused him, and in a fit of vexation and mortified vanity he married a girl greatly beneath him in social position. If the *ménage* prove a failure you will have it on your conscience that you have wrecked his life and perhaps hers as well."

"I cannot throw myself away as a charity to save this man or that from doing a foolish thing."

"What I complain of, Julia, is that you encouraged young Mr. Pomeroy till Mr. Hattersley appeared, whom you thought more eligible, and then you tossed him aside; and you did precisely the same with James Hattersley as soon as you came to know Mr. Lawlor. After all, Julia, I am not so sure that Mr. Pomeroy has not chosen the better part. The girl, I dare say, is simple, fresh, and affectionate."

"Your implication is not complimentary, Aunt Elizabeth."

"My dear, I have no patience with the young lady of the present day, who is shallow, self-willed, and indifferent to the feelings and happiness of others, who craves for excitement and pleasure, and desires nothing that is useful and good. Where now will you see a girl like Viola's sister, who let concealment, like a worm i' the bud, feed on her damask cheek? Nowadays a girl lays herself at the feet of a man if she likes him, turns herself inside-out to let him and all the world read her heart."

"I have no relish to be like Viola's sister, and have my story—a blank. I never grovelled at the feet of Joe Pomeroy or James Hattersley."

"No, but you led each to consider himself the favoured one till he proposed, and then you refused him. It was like smiling at a man and then stabbing him to the heart."

"Well—I don't want people to think that James Hattersley cared for me—I certainly never cared for him—nor that he proposed; so I shall go to the ball."

Julia Demant was an orphan. She had been retained at school till she was eighteen, and then had been removed just at the age when a girl begins to take an interest in her studies, and not to regard them as drudgery. On her removal she had cast away all that she had acquired, and had been plunged into the whirl of Society. Then suddenly her father died—she had lost her mother some years before—and she went to live with her aunt, Miss Flemming. Julia had inherited a sum of about five hundred pounds a year, and would probably come in for a good estate and funds as well on the death of her aunt. She had been flattered as a girl at home, and at school as a beauty, and she certainly thought no small bones of herself.

Miss Flemming was an elderly lady with a sharp tongue, very outspoken, and very decided in her opinions; but her action was weak, and Julia soon discovered that she could bend the aunt to do anything she willed, though she could not modify or alter her opinions.

In the matter of Joe Pomeroy and James Hattersley, it was as Miss Flemming had said. Julia had encouraged Mr. Pomeroy, and had only cast him off because she thought better of the suit of Mr. Hattersley, son of an admiral of that name. She had seen a good deal of young Hattersley, had given him every encouragement, had so entangled him, that he was madly in love with her; and then, when she came to know the Hon. James Lawlor, and saw that he was fascinated, she rejected Hattersley with the consequences alluded to in the conversation above given.

Julia was particularly anxious to be present at the county ball, for she had been already booked by Mr. Lawlor for several dances, and she was quite resolved to make an attempt to bring him to a declaration.

On the evening of the ball Miss Flemming and Julia entered the carriage. The aunt had given way, as was her wont, but under protest.

For about ten minutes neither spoke, and then Miss Flemming said, "Well, you know my feelings about this dance. I do not approve. I distinctly disapprove. I do not consider your going to the ball in good taste, or, as you would put it, in good form. Poor young Hattersley——"

"Oh, dear aunt, do let us put young Hattersley aside. He was buried with the regular forms, I suppose?"

"Yes, Julia."

"Then the rector accepted the verdict of the jury at the inquest. Why should not we? A man who is unsound in his mind is not responsible for his actions."

"I suppose not."

"Much less, then, I who live ten miles away."

"I do not say that you are responsible for his death, but for the condition of mind that led him to do the dreadful deed. Really, Julia, you are one of those into whose head or heart only by a surgical operation could the thought be introduced that you could be in the wrong. A hypodermic syringe would be too weak an instrument to effect such a radical change in you. Everyone else may be in the wrong, you—never. As for me, I cannot get young Hattersley out of my head."

"And I," retorted Julia with asperity, for her aunt's words had stung her—"I, for my part, do not give him a thought."

She had hardly spoken the words before a chill wind began to pass round her. She drew the Barège shawl that was over her bare shoulders closer about her, and said—"Auntie! is the glass down on your side?"

"No, Julia; why do you ask?"

"There is such a draught."

157

"Draught!—I do not feel one; perhaps the window on your side hitches."

"Indeed, that is all right. It is blowing harder and is deadly cold. Can one of the front panes be broken?"

"No. Rogers would have told me had that been the case. Besides, I can see that they are sound."

The wind of which Julia complained swirled and whistled about her. It increased in force; it plucked at her shawl and slewed it about her throat; it tore at the lace on her dress. It snatched at her hair, it wrenched it away from the pins, the combs that held it in place; one long tress was lashed across the face of Miss Flemming. Then the hair, completely released, eddied up above the girl's head, and next moment was carried as a drift before her, blinding her. Then—a sudden explosion, as though a gun had been fired into her ear; and with a scream of terror she sank back among the cushions. Miss Flemming, in great alarm, pulled the checkstring, and the carriage stopped. The footman descended from the box and came to the side. The old lady drew down the window and said: "Oh! Phillips, bring the lamp. Something has happened to Miss Demant."

The man obeyed, and sent a flood of light into the carriage. Julia was lying back, white and senseless. Her hair was scattered over her face, neck, and shoulders; the flowers that had been stuck in it, the pins that had fastened it in place, the pads that had given shape to the convolutions lay strewn, some on her lap, some in the rug at the bottom of the carriage.

"Phillips!" ordered the old lady in great agitation, "tell Rogers to turn the horses and drive home at once; and do you run as fast as you can for Dr. Crate."

A few minutes after the carriage was again in motion, Julia revived. Her aunt was chafing her hand.

"Oh, aunt!" she said, "are all the glasses broken?"

"Broken—what glasses?"

"Those of the carriage—with the explosion."

"Explosion, my dear!"

"Yes. That gun which was discharged. It stunned me. Were

you hurt?"

"I heard no gun—no explosion."

"But I did. It was as though a bullet had been discharged into my brain. I wonder that I escaped. Who can have fired at us?"

"My dear, no one fired. I heard nothing. I know what it was. I had the same experience many years ago. I slept in a damp bed, and awoke stone deaf in my right ear. I remained so for three weeks. But one night when I was at a ball and was dancing, all at once I heard a report as of a pistol in my right ear, and immediately heard quite clearly again. It was wax."

"But, Aunt Elizabeth, I have not been deaf."

"You have not noticed that you were deaf."

"Oh! but look at my hair; it was that wind that blew it about."

"You are labouring under a delusion, Julia. There was no wind."

"But look—feel how my hair is down."

"That has been done by the motion of the carriage. There are many ruts in the road."

They reached home, and Julia, feeling sick, frightened, and bewildered, retired to bed. Dr. Crate arrived, said that she was hysterical, and ordered something to soothe her nerves. Julia was not convinced. The explanation offered by Miss Flemming did not satisfy her. That she was a victim to hysteria she did not in the least believe. Neither her aunt, nor the coachman, nor Phillips had heard the discharge of a gun. As to the rushing wind, Julia was satisfied that she had experienced it. The lace was ripped, as by a hand, from her dress, and the shawl was twisted about her throat; besides, her hair had not been so slightly arranged that the jolting of the carnage would completely disarrange it. She was vastly perplexed over what she had undergone. She thought and thought, but could get no nearer to a solution of the mystery.

Next day, as she was almost herself again, she rose and went about as usual.

In the afternoon the Hon. James Lawlor called and asked

after Miss Flemming. The butler replied that his mistress was out making calls, but that Miss Demant was at home, and he believed was on the terrace. Mr. Lawlor at once asked to see her.

He did not find Julia in the parlour or on the terrace, but in a lower garden to which she had descended to feed the goldfish in the pond.

"Oh! Miss Demant," said he, "I was so disappointed not to see you at the ball last night."

"I was very unwell; I had a fainting fit and could not go."

"It threw a damp on our spirits—that is to say, on mine. I had you booked for several dances."

"You were able to give them to others."

"But that was not the same to me. I did an act of charity and self-denial. I danced instead with the ugly Miss Burgons and with Miss Pounding, and that was like dragging about a sack of potatoes. I believe it would have been a jolly evening, but for that shocking affair of young Hattersley which kept some of the better sort away. I mean those who know the Hattersleys. Of course, for me that did not matter, we were not acquainted. I never even spoke with the fellow. You knew him, I believe? I heard some people say so, and that you had not come because of him. The supper, for a subscription ball, was not atrociously bad."

"What did they say of me?"

"Oh!—if you will know—that you did not attend the ball because you liked him very much, and were awfully cut up."

"I—I! What a shame that people should talk! I never cared a rush for him. He was nice enough in his way, not a bounder, but tolerable as young men go."

Mr. Lawlor laughed. "I should not relish to have such a qualified estimate made of me."

"Nor need you. You are interesting. He became so only when he had shot himself. It will be by this alone that he will be remembered."

"But there is no smoke without fire. Did he like you—much?"

160

"Dear Mr. Lawlor, I am not a *clairvoyante*, and never was able to see into the brains or hearts of people—least of all of young men. Perhaps it is fortunate for me that I cannot."

"One lady told me that he had proposed to you."

"Who was that? The potato-sack?"

"I will not give her name. Is there any truth in it? Did he?"

"No."

At the moment she spoke there sounded in her ear a whistle of wind, and she felt a current like a cord of ice creep round her throat, increasing in force and compression, her hat was blown off, and next instant a detonation rang through her head as though a gun had been fired into her ear. She uttered a cry and sank upon the ground.

James Lawlor was bewildered. His first impulse was to run to the house for assistance; then he considered that he could not leave her lying on the wet soil, and he stooped to raise her in his arms and to carry her within. In novels young men perform such a feat without difficulty; but in fact they are not able to do it, especially when the girl is tall and big-boned. Moreover, one in a faint is a dead weight. Lawlor staggered under his burden to the steps. It was as much as he could perform to carry her up to the terrace, and there he placed her on a seat. Panting, and with his muscles quivering after the strain, he hastened to the drawing-room, rang the bell, and when the butler appeared, he gasped: "Miss Demant has fainted; you and I and the footman must carry her within."

"She fainted last night in the carriage," said the butler.

When Julia came to her senses, she was in bed attended by the housekeeper and her maid. A few moments later Miss Flemming arrived.

"Oh, aunt! I have heard it again."

"Heard what, dear?"

"The discharge of a gun."

"It is nothing but wax," said the old lady. "I will drop a little sweet-oil into your ear, and then have it syringed with warm water."

"I want to tell you something—in private."

Miss Flemming signed to the servants to withdraw.

"Aunt," said the girl, "I must say something. This is the second time that this has happened. I am sure it is significant. James Lawlor was with me in the sunken garden, and he began to speak about James Hattersley. You know it was when we were talking about him last night that I heard that awful noise. It was precisely as if a gun had been discharged into my ear. I felt as if all the nerves and tissues of my head were being torn, and all the bones of my skull shattered—just what Mr. Hattersley must have undergone when he pulled the trigger. It was an agony for a moment perhaps, but it felt as if it lasted an hour. Mr. Lawlor had asked me point blank if James Hattersley had proposed to me, and I said, 'No.'

"I was perfectly justified in so answering, because he had no right to ask me such a question. It was an impertinence on his part, and I answered him shortly and sharply with a negative. But actually James Hattersley proposed twice to me. He would not accept a first refusal, but came next day bothering me again, and I was pretty curt with him. He made some remarks that were rude about how I had treated him, and which I will not repeat, and as he left, in a state of great agitation, he said, 'Julia, I vow that you shall not forget this, and you shall belong to no one but me, alive or dead.' I considered this great nonsense, and did not accord it another thought. But, really, these terrible annoyances, this wind and the bursts of noise, do seem to me to come from him. It is just as though he felt a malignant delight in distressing me, now that he is dead. I should like to defy him, and I will do it if I can, but I cannot bear more of these experiences—they will kill me."

Several days elapsed.

Mr. Lawlor called repeatedly to inquire, but a week passed before Julia was sufficiently recovered to receive him, and then the visit was one of courtesy and of sympathy, and the conversation turned upon her health, and on indifferent themes.

But some few days later it was otherwise. She was in the

conservatory alone, pretty much herself again, when Mr. Lawlor was announced.

Physically she had recovered, or believed that she had, but her nerves had actually received a severe shock. She had made up her mind that the phenomena of the circling wind and the explosion were in some mysterious manner connected with Hattersley.

She bitterly resented this, but she was in mortal terror of a recurrence; and she felt no compunction for her treatment of the unfortunate young man, but rather a sense of deep resentment against him. If he were dead, why did he not lie quiet and cease from vexing her?

To be a martyr was to her no gratification, for hers was not a martyrdom that provoked sympathy, and which could make her interesting.

She had hitherto supposed that when a man died there was an end of him; his condition was determined for good or for ill. But that a disembodied spirit should hover about and make itself a nuisance to the living, had never entered into her calculations.

"Julia—if I may be allowed so to call you"—began Mr. Lawlor, "I have brought you a bouquet of flowers. Will you accept them?"

"Oh!" she said, as he handed the bunch to her, "how kind of you. At this time of the year they are so rare, and aunt's gardener is so miserly that he will spare me none for my room but some miserable bits of geranium. It is too bad of you wasting your money like this upon me."

"It is no waste, if it afford you pleasure."

"It is a pleasure. I dearly love flowers."

"To give you pleasure," said Mr. Lawlor, "is the great object of my life. If I could assure you happiness—if you would allow me to hope—to seize this opportunity, now that we are alone together——"

He drew near and caught her hand. His features were agitated, his lips trembled, there was earnestness in his eyes.

At once a cold blast touched Julia and began to circle about her and to flutter her hair. She trembled and drew back. That paralysing experience was about to be renewed. She turned deadly white, and put her hand to her right ear. "Oh, James! James!" she gasped. "Do not, pray do not speak what you want to say, or I shall faint. It is coming on. I am not yet well enough to hear it. Write to me and I will answer. For pity's sake do not speak it." Then she sank upon a seat—and at that moment her aunt entered the conservatory.

On the following day a note was put into her hand, containing a formal proposal from the Hon. James Lawlor; and by return of post Julia answered with an acceptance.

There was no reason whatever why the engagement should be long; and the only alternative mooted was whether the wedding should take place before Lent or after Easter. Finally, it was settled that it should be celebrated on Shrove Tuesday. This left a short time for the necessary preparations. Miss Flemming would have to go to town with her niece concerning a trousseau, and a trousseau is not turned out rapidly any more than an armed cruiser.

There is usually a certain period allowed to young people who have become engaged, to see much of each other, to get better acquainted with one another, to build their castles in the air, and to indulge in little passages of affection, vulgarly called "spooning." But in this case the spooning had to be curtailed and postponed.

At the outset, when alone with James, Julia was nervous. She feared a recurrence of those phenomena that so affected her. But, although every now and then the wind curled and soughed about her, it was not violent, nor was it chilling; and she came to regard it as a wail of discomfiture. Moreover, there was no recurrence of the detonation, and she fondly hoped that with her marriage the vexation would completely cease.

In her heart was deep down a sense of exultation. She was defying James Hattersley and setting his prediction at naught. She was not in love with Mr. Lawlor; she liked him, in her cold manner, and was not insensible to the social advantage that would be hers when she became the Honourable Mrs. Lawlor.

The day of the wedding arrived. Happily it was fine. "Blessed is the bride the sun shines on," said the cheery Miss Flemming; "an omen, I trust, of a bright and unruffled life in your new condition."

All the neighbourhood was present at the church. Miss Flemming had many friends. Mr. Lawlor had fewer present, as he belonged to a distant county. The church path had been laid with red cloth, the church decorated with flowers, and a choir was present to twitter "The voice that breathed o'er Eden."

The rector stood by the altar, and two cushions had been laid at the chancel step. The rector was to be assisted by an uncle of the bridegroom who was in Holy Orders; the rector, being old-fashioned, had drawn on pale grey kid gloves.

First arrived the bridegroom with his best man, and stood in a nervous condition balancing himself first on one foot, then on the other, waiting, observed by all eyes.

Next entered the procession of the bride, attended by her maids, to the "Wedding March" in *Lohengrin*, on a wheezy organ. Then Julia and her intended took their places at the chancel step for the performance of the first portion of the ceremony, and the two clergy descended to them from the altar.

"Wilt thou have this woman to thy wedded wife?"

"I will."

"Wilt thou have this man to thy wedded husband?"

"I will."

"I, James, take thee, Julia, to my wedded wife, to have and to hold——"and so on.

As the words were being spoken, a cold rush of air passed over the clasped hands, numbing them, and began to creep round the bride, and to flutter her veil. She set her lips and knitted her brows. In a few minutes she would be beyond the reach of these manifestations.

When it came to her turn to speak, she began firmly: "I, Julia, take thee, James——" but as she proceeded the wind became fierce; it raged about her, it caught her veil on one side and buffeted her cheek; it switched the veil about her throat, as though strangling her with a drift of snow contracting into ice. But she persevered to the end.

Then James Lawlor produced the ring, and was about to place it on her finger with the prescribed words: "With this ring I thee wed——" when a report rang in her ear, followed by a heaving of her skull, as though the bones were being burst asunder, and she sank unconscious on the chancel step.

In the midst of profound commotion, she was raised and conveyed to the vestry, followed by James Lawlor, trembling and pale. He had slipped the ring back into his waistcoat pocket. Dr. Crate, who was present, hastened to offer his professional assistance.

In the vestry Julia rested in a Glastonbury chair, white and still, with her hands resting in her lap. And to the amazement of those present, it was seen that on the third finger of her left hand was a leaden ring, rude and solid as though fashioned out of a bullet. Restoratives were applied, but full a quarter of an hour elapsed before Julia opened her eyes, and a little colour returned to her lips and cheek. But, as she raised her hands to her brow to wipe away the damps that had formed on it, her eye caught sight of the leaden ring, and with a cry of horror she sank again into insensibility.

The congregation slowly left the church, awestruck, whispering, asking questions, receiving no satisfactory answers, forming surmises all incorrect.

"I am very much afraid, Mr. Lawlor," said the rector, "that it will be impossible to proceed with the service today; it must be postponed till Miss Demant is in a condition to conclude her part, and to sign the register. I do not see how it can be gone on with today. She is quite unequal to the effort."

The carriage which was to have conveyed the couple to Miss Flemming's house, and then, later, to have taken them to the station for their honeymoon, the horses decorated with white rosettes, the whip adorned with a white bow, had now to convey

166

Julia, hardly conscious, supported by her aunt, to her home.

No rice could be thrown. The bell-ringers, prepared to give a joyous peal, were constrained to depart.

The reception at Miss Flemming's was postponed. No one thought of attending. The cakes, the ices, were consumed in the kitchen.

The bridegroom, bewildered, almost frantic, ran hither and thither, not knowing what to do, what to say.

Julia lay as a stone for fully two hours; and when she came to herself could not speak. When conscious, she raised her left hand, looked on the leaden ring, and sank back again into senselessness.

Not till late in the evening was she sufficiently recovered to speak, and then she begged her aunt, who had remained by her bed without stirring, to dismiss the attendants. She desired to speak with her alone. When no one was in the room with her, save Miss Flemming, she said in a whisper: "Oh, Aunt Elizabeth! Oh, auntie! such an awful thing has happened. I can never marry Mr. Lawlor, never. I have married James Hattersley; I am a dead man's wife. At the time that James Lawlor was making the responses, I heard a piping voice in my ear, an unearthly voice, saying the same words. When I said: 'I, Julia, take you, James, to my wedded husband'—you know Mr. Hattersley is James as well as Mr. Lawlor—then the words applied to him as much or as well as to the other. And then, when it came to the giving of the ring, there was the explosion in my ear, as before—and the leaden ring was forced on to my finger, and not James Lawlor's golden ring. It is of no use my resisting any more. I am a dead man's wife, and I cannot marry James Lawlor."

Some years have elapsed since that disastrous day and that incomplete marriage.

Miss Demant is Miss Demant still, and she has never been able to remove the leaden ring from the third finger of her left hand. Whenever the attempt has been made, either to disengage it by drawing it off or by cutting through it, there has ensued that terrifying discharge as of a gun into her ear, causing insensibility. The prostration that has followed, the terror it has inspired, have so affected her nerves, that she has desisted from every attempt to rid herself of the ring.

She invariably wears a glove on her left hand, and it is bulged over the third finger, where lies that leaden ring.

She is not a happy woman, although her aunt is dead and has left her a handsome estate. She has not got many acquaintances. She has no friends; for her temper is unamiable, and her tongue is bitter. She supposes that the world, as far as she knows it, is in league against her.

Towards the memory of James Hattersley she entertains a deadly hate. If an incantation could lay his spirit, if prayer could give him repose, she would have recourse to none of these expedients, even though they might relieve her, so bitter is her resentment. And she harbours a silent wrath against Providence for allowing the dead to walk and to molest the living.

The Dead Trumpeter of Hurst Castle

1

In the year of our Lord God 1648, certain workmen were engaged in arranging a room in Hurst Castle, which had for a long time been unoccupied. Dark red tapestry was being suspended to the walls, whilst tables and other furniture were moved into the chambers. The quarry-glazed window was dulling, and admitted but a feeble grey light, as the day closed.

"Dykes!" quoth one of the hangers, "we shall never get the room ready in time, if the last man comes tomorrow."

"I shan't go till it is done," said Dykes; "the curtains cannot be left dragging on the hooks, we must e'en have 'em hung all round tonight, or they'll tear with their own weight, before morning."

"At what o'clock does he come?"

"Who come?—the king?"

"The—, you'd better not call him that again; faix I won't suffer it; whom I mean, is your Agag, Saul. Why it sets me against my work to think I'm preparing a room for such as he. May he have a bloody death!"

Dykes sighed, but did not answer.

"T'aint many more kings and crowns, and bishops, we shall see in Old England," continued Faggins. "We shall root them out, branch and twig; I only wish we had made shorter work, and treated the malignants, as Israel dealt with Amalek of old."

"Here, you lass, bring a light!" called Dykes to a servant who was passing.

"I'm not going to work here much longer," observed Carpenter, a third workman. "It's not such a pleasantly reported room, that I should care to wait in it after nightfall."

"Ah! I should like to know how Charles Stuart will bear the Trumpeter!" exclaimed Faggins. "Have you ever heard his horn, Carpenter?"

"Never, but I have not worked in the castle before."

"I have not heard it either," said Dykes; "but I have only been in the castle by day, and never into this room before."

"They say," quoth Faggins, "that there was a trumpeter who got together a fortune by some means or other, and that he built it into the wall of this chamber whereabouts I do not know. He was a bad enough man in his lifetime, and, I reckon, this money did not come lawfully into his hands. He never told where it was hidden, but he haunts the place, and warns folks from his treasure with a blast on his trumpet. I am a bit surprised that we haven't heard it already."

"It is I who have heard that trumpet, sure," spoke the servant, setting a candle on the table, "as I've a-been passing the door by night, it has sounded one long winding note enough to send the blood curdled to the heart."

"Did you ever see the spirit?" asked Faggins.

"No," replied the woman, "but there's th' old father Gumpthorn has; he seed 'um from the water, looking out of this window, and nodded his awful head towards him."

"I don't particularly like working here now," said Carpenter; "Here, Dykes! am I to hang the damask over this door? 1 don't know whether it leads into a room or cupboard."

"Where's the key?" asked Dykes. "You had better look afore covering it with the tapestry."

"Help me to open it," said Carpenter. "Maybe it's the closet where the Trumpeter's money is hid."

"Let us have a look, then," exclaimed Faggins, running up. "It is nailed—your pincers, Dykes!"

"I've heard a-said that the spirit got a store of gold together in its lifetime," said the servant. "Crown-dues, I've been told,

170

which he embezzled in some mysterious way; that is what he watches now so restlessly."

"Pull, Dykes, pull!" shouted Faggins, as the three tugged at the door, or worked their chisels into the openings.

"That is no good," said Carpenter, after a lug at the handle; "Just send your hammer at my punch, and I'll have this nail in two, which fastens up the door."

The hammer fell with a bang the timber cracked, and slowly the valve swung open. Within was dark—one short, furious trumpet blast snarled in the ears of the three men: back they staggered, Faggins falling over Carpenter to the ground. A face emerged from the gloom; and then, a tall figure wrapt in flowing crimson drapery, one hand lifted to hold a trumpet, stole out of the door, moved past the terrified workmen its sulphurous eyes glaring at them. Once it paused at the window and nodded, then stalked across the room, put the trumpet to its lips, the fearful ringing blast re-echoing from ceiling, door, and wall, and gradually the outlines of the figure mingled with those of the dark tapestry, and were lost.

2

The times of which I write were sad indeed. There can be no doubt that the king was greatly to be blamed, and that Iris obstinacy, and want of veracity, had done much to injure his cause. When adversity weighed heavily upon him, however, though he could not repair what was done, he sorrowed with deep contrition for it, and his character began to shine forth with true beauty and sanctity. It seems cruel to deal with him harshly for his early faults; we must remember that such as David and the Apostle Peter fell more grievously than ever did Royal Charles; and yet the one was raised from his *miserere mei,* and the other cheered after having gone out and wept bitterly.

But it is not my purpose to justify the luckless monarch; such as he was, his adherents clung to him enthusiastically; and we, in after ages, look back upon him with something of veneration and love, inclined to treat tenderly the memory of one whom

God so sharply chastened. And let those whose consciences are clear from having ever given way under strong temptation, and whose tongues are free from all deceit, let them, I say, cast at him the first stone.

Hurst Castle was a gloomy prison, its walls lapped by the tide, and rank with weeds and lichen. Now on a December night, the first of his imprisonment in the place, he sat at the table, a light burning before him; his mild yet furrowed brow resting on his hand, and his long hair, now white with sorrow, flowing over the fingers.

We can be but poor judges of the thoughts which filled the monarch's mind in the solitude of the night: the insults of foes, the coldness of false friends, were felt over again in his loneliness, with renewed pang and bitterness. The moral sickness of hope deferred, the bowing of the heart under his innumerable troubles; his griefs, as the rising tide, chill about his soul, overflowing his heart, swelling ever higher, one sorrow rousing another, one deep calling another, and all their waves and storms going heavily over him.

Perhaps it were as well not to intrude on such thoughts; sufficient for us to see that calm, pale face, that hand trembling, those goodly locks while through affliction.

All is hushed in the room. Herbert is asleep in an adjoining chamber. Charles sings to himself and to God the seventy-first Psalm:—

In Thee, O Lord, have I put my trust: let me never be put to confusion: but rid me, and deliver me in Thy righteousness: incline Thine ear unto me, and save me.

Be Thou my stronghold, whereunto I may always resort: Thou hast promised to help me, for Thou art my house of defence, and my castle.

Deliver me, O my God, out of the hand of the ungodly, out of the hand of the unrighteous and cruel man.

For Thou, O Lord God, art the thing that I long for: Thou art my hope, even from my youth—

Softly and full tenderly a horn wound the tone, as if from some distance upon the sea; rising and falling with the melody, as the king chanted. It was so faint that the monarch did not notice it, wrapped, so entirely as he was, in the utterance of his own bruised soul.

Cast me not away in the time of age: forsake me not when my strength faileth me.

For mine enemies speak against me, and they that lay wait for my soul take their counsel together, saying: God hath forsaken him; persecute him, and take him, for there is none to deliver him.

Strangely the trumpet note swelled and broke into high, sweet tenor—sometimes ringing near, sometimes very distant. The king rose in some surprise from his seat, and walked to the window—all was dark without, save that Orion was setting sideways over the downs of the Isle of Wight, and Cassiopeia in her golden chair flashed down upon the troubled sea. The rising tide shivered and plashed below, and a sea-breeze sighed against the casement.

Charles looked long out upon the waters, and his lips again took up the Psalm:—

Thou, O God, hast taught me from my youth up until now: therefore will I tell of Thy wondrous works.

Forsake me not, O God, in mine old age, when I am grey-headed—

Involuntarily his hand swept his white hair from his brow, which leaned against the window-panes, and still more sadly did he murmur:

O what great troubles and adversities hast thou showed me! and yet—

He broke off, for the trumpet sang so close to him- tenderly, very tenderly and tremulously—that he turned abruptly round.

At his side knelt a figure in a flowing grey robe, the dark head bowed towards him, and the instrument which had accompanied the Psalm drooping through the white fingers.

173

"Who art thou?" asked the king somewhat astonished.

The figure raised its colourless face a strange, livid countenance, seamed by fearful passions; but now all absorbed in awe. The eyes were closed.

King Charles shuddered; something supernatural in the kneeling figure impressed him.

Scarcely knowing why he did it, he extended his hand: the being lifted its own, bowed again, and kissed the royal hand. At the touch of the lips, a pang shot to Charles' heart, as though his fingers had been pressed by red-hot iron.

Noiselessly the apparition rose, the grey mantle falling and enveloping all but the head and right hand: then it dropped back into the deep shadows, and the only evidence of its presence was the winding of the trumpet, beginning with a faint trill, but increasing in volume, clearer, louder, more triumphant; wave and eddy of sound beating, pealing from every nook, and reverberating from every angle, till the window rattled and the walls rang.

3

Faggins was tolerably convinced that the Trumpeter's treasure was hoarded in the wall cupboard of the royal chamber, and was intent upon possessing himself of it during the daytime, when the spectre was not likely to appear.

On the plea that the tapestry required something additional to be done to it, he, Dykes and Carpenter were suffered to work in the haunted apartment during the hour the royal captive was allowed to take air.

The two men cautiously lifted the arras, and unhasped the door. In the recess all was hushed, and the light penetrated to its furthest corners.

The workmen examined the floor and walls minutely.

"Carpenter," said Faggins in a low voice; "I believe that this is the spot:—look here!" and he pointed to a stone in the wall, which had undoubtedly been notched by a tool.

"Let us chisel it away," whispered Carpenter, at the same time looking cautiously about.

A few strokes of the hammer on the implement made the block start from its place. Faggins pulled it out, and laid it on the floor. Both peered into the hollow, and compressed their lips. A metal box was just discernible, but so encased with mortar as to render it difficult to dislodge. After a few efforts, they succeeded in forcing in part of the plate which formed the exposed side, and a few pieces of gold fell out.

"Hark!" said Carpenter, suddenly desisting; "there is Dykes' signal!"

A low whistle at the room door warned them to make haste; and they had barely time to scramble the gold into their pockets, heave the stone into its place again, and emerge from the closet, when the King and his faithful companion Herbert entered the Chamber.

"On what grounds are you here?" asked Charles of the men.

"We are at work upon the tapestry," answered Carpenter; "but we have done now, and shall be off."

Faggins, bent on showing his effrontery and contempt for Royalty, began to whistle and put his hat on; but instantly, a furious trumpet blast brayed into his ears, and an invisible hand dashed the hat from his head.

The king had turned with contempt at the petty insult, like the aged lion of the fable; but at the sound he stopped abruptly and looked back.

Faggins, startled but not daunted, picked up his hat, growling forth: "So thou art in league with foul spirits too, accursed Agag;—"

A violent blow from some smooth metal instrument fell upon his mouth, and sent him reeling across the apartment. He staggered from the door, and, as he descended the stair with Carpenter and Dykes, who had been left to watch outside the room, his lips cracked and bled as though they had been touched by fire.

"I'm not going there again, for all the gold in the world," said Faggins, when he got beyond the castle walls, and had washed the blood from his mouth.

"I cannot understand," observed Carpenter, "how it is that the spectre should have suffered us to take his treasure, or part of it, without a sign of displeasure: and, faith, I reckon we should have got off pretty clear, if you had not begun to insult the king."

Faggins growled forth a curse. "We have some of the gold at any rate;—the last time I shall go *there* for any more."

"We might have gone any number of times, it is my belief," Carpenter said, "had you not angered the spirit."

"How was I to know that what I did would vex it?" asked Faggins angrily.

Carpenter shrugged his shoulders. "I reckon that the spirit has left off watching his hoard, altogether, and has taken to guarding the king," he remarked.

"I should not wonder if it were so," observed Dykes; "for Royal blood is a higher treasure than any pelf; and the spectre might well forget its gold in the presence of such a priceless jewel as a Monarch. I suppose that, next to the Sacraments of the Church, there is nothing the world contains so hallowed as the life and majesty of a king. That, at least, is my opinion."

4

Of a night Charles would be lulled to sleep by the sweet rise and fall of a horn, winding flute-like and faint; and at times, when he awoke during the watches, he could see, seated at his bedside, a tall, grey-mantled form; the night-lamp feebly irradiating its placid, though furrowed, countenance. Should the eyes meet his, there was somewhat in their tranquil light which lulled him back into a sleep no fears could trouble, nor misgivings spoil.

Once the Monarch was roused by a pang in his hand, which hung over the bedside; and on opening his eyes, he saw the same figure kneeling and pressing its lips to his fingers.

The gloom of Hurst Castle had, at first, somewhat impressed the royal prisoner with the notion that it was intended he should be there assassinated, but the presence of his spectral guard reassured him. By night and by day, he was aware of its proximity, either by some chime on the unseen instrument, or by a flash as of red light, and a bugle-snarl, should any insult be offered him.

The king was at length removed from Hurst, by order of Parliament, and conveyed by Major Harrison to Windsor, there to wait his trial.

By the shadow which stole after him, and by the sight of his mysterious guard at night, Charles knew that he was not left unprotected.

That strange face had been undergoing a slow change. It might have been likened to some bleak, torrent-rent Alpine ridge, dark and horror-inspiring; but lightly falls the snow, and some harsh outlines become smooth, dusky crags are polished as Carrara marble, and tumbled boulders lie veiled beneath drifts of whimpled silver. Yet the whiteness drops still out of heaven; and the sun, at last, comes forth on bays of tranquil light running in to the rifts, powdering the topmost icy spires with sulphur, and lying in primrose flakes on sweeps, or bending curves undinted by the foot; the rough places are made plain, and crooked paths straight tracks on frosted meadows. As yet more descends, the shoulders of the mountains are bowed in snow, sending the gleam of their purity far away to distant plains, where the poplars whiten and twinkle back grey-green in the breeze, which blows cool from that chain robed in angelic vesture. And so, somewhat thus, had an utterable calm fallen on those terrible features.

5

The 30th of January, 1649. A raw sea-fog curling over the ramparts of Hurst Castle; the heights of the Isle of Wight lost in the vapour, even the rushing tide obscured. The sentinel could see the mist driving through the battlements in streaks; the moisture stood on his pike, and trickled over his fingers, his steel cap was beaded with wet, his foot plashed as he trod the platform. The fog entered within as well; the windows were dulled with breath, fires seemed cheerlessly to smoulder without a blaze. Damp settled on woodwork, and the cement of the walls showed dark and spotty. The waves tumbled at the castle base with a roar, and retreated with a sob.

Dykes, for the nonce an inmate of the castle, sat over the embers warming a jug of beer, and looking occasionally towards the window in the hope of seeing some break in the clouds.

"I wonder," pondered he; "what they can be about in London town today? so they say that the king—God bless His Majesty!—is going to be tried for high treason. I know what that means; the Commons think to intimidate him into abdication of his Crown."

"What is that, Dykes?" asked a musketeer who was leaning against the fireplace; "try the king! I don't believe a word of it."

"There is no doubt but that Parliament is doing so now," answered Dykes; "but what Parliament intends doing with him after his trial, is another matter. God save the King! say I; and I care not who hears me."

"Did you ever hear what happened at Stretton Manor, when Master Hill (I knew him well, he was parson of that parish, and I was born there) was drinking at the king's health a few months ago?"

"I never heard."

"Well, the old man was quaffing cider in the bay-window; after filling his cup, he bared his head and rose, saying, 'God bless our Gracious Sovereign!' Just as he was going to put the mug to his lips, a swallow flew in at the window, and pitching on the brim of the little earthenware cup, sipped, and so flew out again."

"Is that really true?" asked Dykes.

Before the soldier could reply, there rang a shrill bugle shriek in the air, above the castle. Dykes started to his feet, and, followed by the musketeer, ran out of the room, and hurried up the steps to know the origin of the sound. When they reached the landing outside the room which had been the king's, they found a maid standing, pale and trembling, against the wall.

"Oh, mercy on us!" she gasped; "I've been in there, and there's the most awful sight!"

Dykes pushed the door open, and entered with the soldier.

It might have been four o'clock in the afternoon, and there was only twilight in the chamber, darkened at the best of times by its crimson hangings. A pale grey film lit the floor, which was clear of furniture.

The two men held their breath, and clutched the door. A figure in long black stole was visible in the further shadows, standing with its face towards the window, a trumpet in its left hand, dangling and touching the floor. The features were calm and majestic, but perfectly white, white as driven snow; over them hung a jet-black cowl.

The men could not stir, their eyes were riveted to the spectre.

Its lips were moving, the right hand was lifted and making signs.

"Hurt not the axe that may hurt me!" the voice said.

Dykes' heart stood still. The words seemed to sound from some vast distance, they were low, thrilling, yet perfectly distinct. The face turned towards the door, the men cowered before it, but the eyes did not rest on the intruders, they appeared absorbed, like those of a sleep-walker. The trumpet fell from the fingers, but did not ring on the floor as it dropped.

Again the voice in a deep whisper:

"I shall say but short prayers, and then thrust out my hands for a signal."

There could be no doubt but that the being was re-enacting some fearful tragedy.

Then it knelt down in the gloaming.

"Does my hair trouble you?"

The figure began to feel at the hood, draw it back, and arranged the locks, sweeping them from the neck.

A few moments, seeming hours, of stillness. The hands of the kneeling figure were folded over the face, as though it were wrapt in prayer, every stroke of the clock in the hall below sounded distinctly in that room, and the pulses of the two witnesses beat with the throb of the clock. The moan and swash of the sea, over

179

the shingle beach and about the castle base, were audible, every wave as it tumbled roared in that chamber. A draught creeping through the diamond-paned windows just stirred the folds of the drapery on the walls.

Those were awful moments, whilst the spirit was in prayer. Dykes tried to move, tried to escape, fear oppressed him insupportably; he could not stir a muscle, the sound of his own breath alarmed him.

Slowly the apparition removed its hands; the face did at that moment look strangely like the king's, as it was bowed forward: the two hands were then extended, not rapidly, but very, very slowly. A flash, a heavy fall; and all had vanished.

It was not till the news reached Hurst of what had taken place that day at Whitehall, that Dykes and the musketeer knew what had been signified by that ghastly pageant.

6

The night is cold and frosty: stand in the courtyard of Windsor, and look up into that solemn sapphire sky, set with God's jewellery; Charles's Wain is moving on its march; Jupiter is burning as a lamp, the nebulous belt of the Milky-way binds the sky with a bow of tender light, and through the haze of splendour sparkle the Pleiades; a shooting star passes over head, and goes out over Eton woods. Faith is dull and black, and all heaven so set with brilliants, that the more we look, the mightier the store appears; and yet we see, perhaps, but the outermost sprinkled verge of the treasure, the diamond dust from the imperishable crowns there laid up. How ochreous and impure seems that flare through the windows of St. George's Hall! We know whence it comes—from the flambeaux round about the coffin of the king. Look up, the corruptible crown has been exchanged for the incorruptible! Lift up your heads; see the beautiful treasure place, where neither moth corrupts nor thief breaks through and steals!

No banner flaps now from Caesar's Tower, but the low wind sings a requiem through the fretwork on the chapel roof.

A feeble murmur rises from the village. Hark! someone is singing:

Dulce domum resonemus,
Dulce, dulce, dulce domum.

The boy Mildmay has come home from Winchester for his holidays, and from very joy of heart sings about sweet home. Well, well! there is another Home besides that under the father's roof-tree, or on the mother's breast; may it be sweet to us all!

The tramp of feet. We must come back from our reverie. Look! there is a file of soldiers posted by the chapel door, and their arquebuses rattle on the flagstones, then turn your face towards the hall, and see the funeral cortege.

First went Herbert, the king's faithful friend and companion, his head bowed on his breast; immediately behind him the coffin, covered with a black velvet pall. Then walked the sad train of nobles, consisting of four only, the Duke of Richmond, the Earl of Southampton, the youthful Earl of Lindsay, and Seymour Marquis of Hertford; the rear brought up by Col. Whitchcott, the governor, and some of the officers of the castle.

With slow tread they advanced. On leaving the hall the sky had been clear, but before the court was crossed, a shower of snow began to fall.

To some, there seemed to move a strange mourner in white, now before, then alongside, *anon* behind the coffin; and yet others thought it only a whirl of snow tossed in an eddy of wind. 'There accompanied it also an unwonted wail it might have been the cry of the gale in the parapets, but the Marquis of Hertford fancied once that he caught a glimpse of a figure in snowy drapery stalking at his side, with a trumpet to its lips, he seemed then to see it glide forward, lay a wreath of thorns woven into a crown, upon the pall, and then trail its mantle over the bier, heaping on snow, tossing it on the thorn-spines till they blossomed as May, spreading it over the black velvet, shaking it into the folds, hanging it in festoons at the side, studding it on the fringes, and finally vanishing in the torch flare at the door of

St. George's Chapel.

"I am the Resurrection and the Life," began Juxon, Bishop of London, meeting the procession at the gate.

"Hold!" exclaimed Whitchcott, thrusting himself forward. "You have no licence to say anything from the Book of Common Prayer; the Directory is now alone lawful."

So without the prayers of his Church, King Charles was laid at rest.

When the bier was placed by the tomb, the pall was covered with snow; and "so," as Herbert says, "went the White King to his grave," reminding him of the time when, at his coronation, white satin, instead of the usual purple, had been his robes; also how the sermon then preached had been on the text, "Be thou faithful unto death, and I will give thee a crown of life." And all present took it as a sign from heaven, testifying as to the martyr's innocence.

As Juxon said, "Thou shalt purge me with hyssop, and I shall be clean; Thou shalt wash me, and I shall be whiter than snow," something went by him, and appeared to drop into the vault. Probably it was only the snow shelving from the pall into the tomb; yet, when the body had been lowered, the bishop stooped, and looking down, thought he saw a white figure kneeling at the head; but his eyes were aged and dim with tears, so he rose, believing himself mistaken.

Heavily the slab fell into its place again.

Through the unglazed eastern window the wind blew, and the torches guttered in the draught.

The Marquis of Hertford and the Earl of Lindsay remained whilst the tomb was being secured; all others went forth; and a single candle sent its orange gleam on the slab. The Sexton finished his work at last, and then blew out the light.

As the two noblemen lingered by the grave, the marquis said, "Lindsay, do you hear nothing?"

The earl listened: he could distinguish the playing of a trumpet, but it seemed to him very distant, and yet below.

"1 could almost fancy that it proceeded from the tomb," observed the marquis with hesitation.

Lord Lindsay listened again; "No, it cannot be," he said; "someone is playing a lullaby in a distant tower. Come, my Lord, shall we go?"

That was the last ever heard of the trumpeter.

Jean Bouchon
(A tale from *A Book of Ghosts*)

I was in Orléans a good many years ago. At the time it was my purpose to write a life of Joan of Arc, and I considered it advisable to visit the scenes of her exploits, so as to be able to give to my narrative some local colour.

But I did not find Orléans answer to my expectations. It is a dull town, very modern in appearance, but with that measly and decrepit look which is so general in French towns. There was a Place Jeanne d'Arc, with an equestrian statue of her in the midst, flourishing a banner. There was the house that the maid had occupied after the taking of the city, but, with the exception of the walls and rafters, it had undergone so much alteration and modernisation as to have lost its interest. A museum of memorials of la Pucelle had been formed, but possessed no genuine relics, only arms and tapestries of a later date.

The city walls she had besieged, the gate through which she had burst, had been levelled, and their places taken by boulevards. The very cathedral in which she had knelt to return thanks for her victory was not the same. That had been blown up by the Huguenots, and the cathedral that now stands was erected on its ruins in 1601.

There was an ormolu figure of Jeanne on the clock—never wound up—upon the mantelshelf in my room at the hotel, and there were chocolate figures of her in the confectioners' shop-windows for children to suck. When I sat down at 7 p.m. to *table d'hôte*, at my inn, I was out of heart. The result of my exploration of sites had been unsatisfactory; but I trusted on the morrow to be able to find material to serve my purpose in the municipal archives of the town library.

My dinner ended, I sauntered to a *café*.

That I selected opened on to the Place, but there was a back entrance near to my hotel, leading through a long, stone-paved passage at the back of the houses in the street, and by ascending three or four stone steps one entered the long, well-lighted *café*. I came into it from the back by this means, and not from the front.

I took my place and called for a *café-cognac*. Then I picked up a French paper and proceeded to read it—all but the *feuilleton*. In my experience I have never yet come across anyone who reads the *feuilletons* in a French paper; and my impression is that these snippets of novel are printed solely for the purpose of filling up space and disguising the lack of news at the disposal of the editors. The French papers borrow their information relative to foreign affairs largely from the English journals, so that they are a day behind ours in the foreign news that they publish.

Whilst I was engaged in reading, something caused me to look up, and I noticed standing by the white marble-topped table, on which was my coffee, a waiter, with a pale face and black whiskers, in an expectant attitude.

I was a little nettled at his precipitancy in applying for payment, but I put it down to my being a total stranger there; and without a word I set down half a *franc* and a ten *centimes* coin, the latter as his *pourboire*. Then I proceeded with my reading.

I think a quarter of an hour had elapsed, when I rose to depart, and then, to my surprise, I noticed the half-*franc* still on the table, but the *sous* piece was gone.

I beckoned to a waiter, and said: "One of you came to me a little while ago demanding payment. I think he was somewhat hasty in pressing for it; however, I set the money down, and the fellow has taken the tip, and has neglected the charge for the coffee."

"*Sapristi!*" exclaimed the *garçon*; "Jean Bouchon has been at his tricks again."

I said nothing further; asked no questions. The matter did not concern me, or indeed interest me in the smallest degree; and I left.

Next day I worked hard in the town library. I cannot say that I lighted on any unpublished documents that might serve my purpose.

I had to go through the controversial literature relative to whether Jeanne d'Arc was burnt or not, for it has been maintained that a person of the same name, and also of Arques, died a natural death some time later, and who postured as the original warrior-maid. I read a good many monographs on the Pucelle, of various values; some real contributions to history, others mere second-hand cookings-up of well-known and often-used material. The sauce in these latter was all that was new.

In the evening, after dinner, I went back to the same *café* and called for black coffee with a nip of brandy. I drank it leisurely, and then retreated to the desk where I could write some letters.

I had finished one, and was folding it, when I saw the same pale-visaged waiter standing by with his hand extended for payment. I put my hand into my pocket, pulled out a fifty *centimes* piece and a coin of two *sous*, and placed both beside me, near the man, and proceeded to put my letter in an envelope, which I then directed.

Next I wrote a second letter, and that concluded, I rose to go to one of the tables and to call for stamps, when I noticed that again the silver coin had been left untouched, but the copper piece had been taken away.

I tapped for a waiter.

"*Tiens,*" said I, "that fellow of yours has been bungling again. He has taken the tip and has left the half-*franc.*"

"Ah! Jean Bouchon once more!"

"But who is Jean Bouchon?"

The man shrugged his shoulders, and, instead of answering my query, said: "I should recommend *monsieur* to refuse to pay Jean Bouchon again—that is, supposing *monsieur* intends revisiting this *café*."

"I most assuredly will not pay such a noodle," I said; "and it passes my comprehension how you can keep such a fellow on your staff."

I revisited the library next day, and then walked by the Loire, that rolls in winter such a full and turbid stream, and in summer, with a reduced flood, exposes gravel and sand-banks. I wandered around the town, and endeavoured vainly to picture it, enclosed by walls and drums of towers, when on April 29th, 1429, Jeanne threw herself into the town and forced the English to retire, discomfited and perplexed.

In the evening I revisited the *café* and made my wants known as before. Then I looked at my notes, and began to arrange them.

Whilst thus engaged I observed the waiter, named Jean Bouchon, standing near the table in an expectant attitude as before. I now looked him full in the face and observed his countenance. He had puffy white cheeks, small black eyes, thick dark mutton-chop whiskers, and a broken nose. He was decidedly an ugly man, but not a man with a repulsive expression of face.

"No," said I, "I will give you nothing. I will not pay you. Send another *garçon* to me."

As I looked at him to see how he took this refusal, he seemed to fall back out of my range, or, to be more exact, the lines of his form and features became confused. It was much as though I had been gazing on a reflection in still water; that something had ruffled the surface, and all was broken up and obliterated. I could see him no more. I was puzzled and a bit startled, and I rapped my coffee-cup with the spoon to call the attention of a waiter. One sprang to me immediately.

"See!" said I, "Jean Bouchon has been here again; I told him that I would not pay him one *sou*, and he has vanished in a most perplexing manner. I do not see him in the room."

"No, he is not in the room."

"When he comes in again, send him to me. I want to have a word with him."

The waiter looked confused, and replied: "I do not think that Jean will return."

"How long has he been on your staff?"

"Oh! he has not been on our staff for some years."

"Then why does he come here and ask for payment for coffee and what else one may order?"

"He never takes payment for anything that has been consumed. He takes only the tips."

"But why do you permit him to do that?"

"We cannot help ourselves."

"He should not be allowed to enter the *café*."

"No one can keep him out."

"This is surpassing strange. He has no right to the tips. You should communicate with the police."

The waiter shook his head. "They can do nothing. Jean Bouchon died in 1869."

"Died in 1869!" I repeated.

"It is so. But he still comes here. He never pesters the old customers, the inhabitants of the town—only visitors, strangers."

"Tell me all about him."

"*Monsieur* must pardon me now. We have many in the place, and I have my duties."

"In that case I will drop in here tomorrow morning when you are disengaged, and I will ask you to inform me about him. What is your name?"

"At *monsieur's* pleasure—Alphonse."

Next morning, in place of pursuing the traces of the Maid of Orléans, I went to the *café* to hunt up Jean Bouchon. I found Alphonse with a duster wiping down the tables. I invited him to a table and made him sit down opposite me. I will give his story in substance, only where advisable recording his exact words.

Jean Bouchon had been a waiter at this particular *café*. Now in some of these establishments the attendants are wont to have a box, into which they drop all the tips that are received; and at the end of the week it is opened, and the sum found in it is divided *pro rata* among the waiters, the head waiter receiving a larger portion than the others. This is not customary in all such places of refreshment, but it is in some, and it was so in this *café*. The average is pretty constant, except on special occasions, as when a *fête* occurs; and the waiters know within a few *francs* what their perquisites will be.

But in the *café* where served Jean Bouchon the sum did not reach the weekly total that might have been anticipated; and after this deficit had been noted for a couple of months the waiters were convinced that there was something wrong, somewhere or somehow. Either the common box was tampered with, or one of them did not put in his tips received. A watch was set, and it was discovered that Jean Bouchon was the defaulter. When he had received a gratuity, he went to the box, and pretended to put in the coin, but no sound followed, as would have been the case had one been dropped in.

There ensued, of course, a great commotion among the waiters when this was discovered. Jean Bouchon endeavoured to brave it out, but the *patron* was appealed to, the case stated, and he was dismissed. As he left by the back entrance, one of the younger *garçons* put out his leg and tripped Bouchon up, so that he stumbled and fell headlong down the steps with a crash on the stone floor of the passage. He fell with such violence on his forehead that he was taken up insensible. His bones were fractured, there was concussion of the brain, and he died within a few hours without recovering consciousness.

"We were all very sorry and greatly shocked," said Alphonse; "we did not like the man, he had dealt dishonourably by us, but we wished him no ill, and our resentment was at an end when he was dead. The waiter who had tripped him up was arrested, and was sent to prison for some months, but the accident was due to *une mauvaise plaisanterie* and no malice was in it, so that the young fellow got off with a light sentence. He afterwards married a widow with a *café* at Vierzon, and is there, I believe, doing well.

"Jean Bouchon was buried," continued Alphonse; "and we waiters attended the funeral and held white kerchiefs to our eyes. Our head waiter even put a lemon into his, that by squeezing it he might draw tears from his eyes. We all subscribed for the interment, that it should be dignified—majestic as becomes a waiter."

"And do you mean to tell me that Jean Bouchon has haunted this *café* ever since?"

"Ever since 1869," replied Alphonse.

"And there is no way of getting rid of him?"

"None at all, *monsieur*. One of the Canons of Bourges came in here one evening. We did suppose that Jean Bouchon would not approach, molest an ecclesiastic, but he did. He took his *pourboire* and left the rest, just as he treated *monsieur*. Ah! *monsieur!* but Jean Bouchon did well in 1870 and 1871 when those pigs of Prussians were here in occupation. The officers came nightly to our *café*, and Jean Bouchon was greatly on the alert. He must have carried away half of the gratuities they offered. It was a sad loss to us."

"This is a very extraordinary story," said I.

"But it is true," replied Alphonse.

Next day I left Orléans. I gave up the notion of writing the life of Joan of Arc, as I found that there was absolutely no new material to be gleaned on her history—in fact, she had been thrashed out.

Years passed, and I had almost forgotten about Jean Bouchon, when, the other day, I was in Orléans once more, on my way south, and at once the whole story recurred to me.

I went that evening to the same *café*. It had been smartened up since I was there before. There was more plate glass, more gilding; electric light had been introduced, there were more mirrors, and there were also ornaments that had not been in the *café* before.

I called for *café-cognac* and looked at a journal, but turned my eyes on one side occasionally, on the lookout for Jean Bouchon. But he did not put in an appearance. I waited for a quarter of an hour in expectation, but saw no sign of him.

Presently I summoned a waiter, and when he came up I inquired: "But where is Jean Bouchon?"

"*Monsieur* asks after Jean Bouchon?" The man looked surprised.

"Yes, I have seen him here previously. Where is he at present?"

"*Monsieur* has seen Jean Bouchon? *Monsieur* perhaps knew him. He died in 1869."

"I know that he died in 1869, but I made his acquaintance in 1874. I saw him then thrice, and he accepted some small gratuities of me."

"*Monsieur* tipped Jean Bouchon?"

"Yes, and Jean Bouchon accepted my tips."

"*Tiens*, and Jean Bouchon died five years before."

"Yes, and what I want to know is how you have rid yourselves of Jean Bouchon, for that you have cleared the place of him is evident, or he would have been pestering me this evening." The man looked disconcerted and irresolute.

"Hold," said I; "is Alphonse here?"

"No, *monsieur*, Alphonse has left two or three years ago. And *monsieur* saw Jean Bouchon in 1874. I was not then here. I have been here only six years."

"But you can in all probability inform me of the manner of getting quit of Jean."

"*Monsieur!* I am very busy this evening, there are so many gentlemen come in."

"I will give you five *francs* if you will tell me all—all—succinctly about Jean Bouchon."

"Will *monsieur* be so good as to come here tomorrow during the morning? and then I place myself at the disposition of *monsieur*."

"I shall be here at eleven o'clock."

At the appointed time I was at the *café*. If there is an institution that looks ragged and dejected and dissipated, it is a *café* in the morning, when the chairs are turned upside-down, the waiters are in aprons and shirt-sleeves, and a smell of stale tobacco lurks about the air, mixed with various other unpleasant

191

odours.

The waiter I had spoken to on the previous evening was looking out for me. I made him seat himself at a table with me. No one else was in the saloon except another *garçon*, who was dusting with a long feather-brush.

"*Monsieur*," began the waiter, "I will tell you the whole truth. The story is curious, and perhaps everyone would not believe it, but it is well *documentée*. Jean Bouchon was at one time in service here. We had a box. When I say we, I do not mean myself included, for I was not here at the time."

"I know about the common box. I know the story down to my visit to Orléans in 1874, when I saw the man."

"*Monsieur* has perhaps been informed that he was buried in the cemetery?"

"I do know that, at the cost of his fellow-waiters."

"Well, *monsieur*, he was poor, and his fellow-waiters, though well-disposed, were not rich. So he did not have a grave *en perpétuité*. Accordingly, after many years, when the term of consignment was expired, and it might well be supposed that Jean Bouchon had mouldered away, his grave was cleared out to make room for a fresh occupant. Then a very remarkable discovery was made. It was found that his corroded coffin was crammed—literally stuffed—with five and ten *centimes* pieces, and with them were also some German coins, no doubt received from those pigs of Prussians during the occupation of Orléans.

"This discovery was much talked about. Our proprietor of the *café* and the headwaiter went to the mayor and represented to him how matters stood—that all this money had been filched during a series of years since 1869 from the waiters. And our *patron* represented to him that it should in all propriety and justice be restored to us. The mayor was a man of intelligence and heart, and he quite accepted this view of the matter, and ordered the surrender of the whole coffin-load of coins to us, the waiters of the *café*."

"So you divided it amongst you."

"Pardon, *monsieur*, we did not. It is true that the money might legitimately be regarded as belonging to us. But then those de-frauded, or most of them, had left long ago, and there were among us some who had not been in service in the *café* more than a year or eighteen months. We could not trace the old wait-ers. Some were dead, some had married and left this part of the country. We were not a corporation.

"So we held a meeting to discuss what was to be done with the money. We feared, moreover, that unless the spirit of Jean Bouchon were satisfied, he might continue revisiting the *café* and go on sweeping away the tips. It was of paramount impor-tance to please Jean Bouchon, to lay out the money in such a manner as would commend itself to his feelings. One suggested one thing, one another. One proposed that the sum should be expended on masses for the repose of Jean's soul. But the head waiter objected to that. He said that he thought he knew the mind of Jean Bouchon, and that this would not commend itself to it. He said, did our headwaiter, that he knew Jean Bouchon from head to heels. And he proposed that all the coins should be melted up, and that out of them should be cast a statue of Jean Bouchon in bronze, to be set up here in the *café*, as there were not enough coins to make one large enough to be erected in a Place. If *monsieur* will step with me he will see the statue; it is a superb work of art."

He led the way, and I followed.

In the midst of the *café* stood a pedestal, and on this basis a bronze figure about four feet high. It represented a man reeling backward, with a banner in his left hand, and the right raised towards his brow, as though he had been struck there by a bullet. A sabre, apparently fallen from his grasp, lay at his feet. I studied the face, and it most assuredly was utterly unlike Jean Bouchon with his puffy cheeks, mutton-chop whiskers, and broken nose, as I recalled him.

"But," said I, "the features do not—pardon me—at all resem-ble those of Jean Bouchon. This might be the young Augustus, or Napoleon I. The profile is quite Greek."

"It may be so," replied the waiter. "But we had no photograph to go by. We had to allow the artist to exercise his genius, and, above all, we had to gratify the spirit of Jean Bouchon."

"I see. But the attitude is inexact. Jean Bouchon fell down the steps headlong, and this represents a man staggering backwards."

"It would have been inartistic to have shown him precipitated forwards; besides, the spirit of Jean might not have liked it."

"Quite so. I understand. But the flag?"

"That was an idea of the artist. Jean could not be made holding a coffee-cup. You will see the whole makes a superb subject. Art has its exigencies. *Monsieur* will see underneath is an inscription on the pedestal."

I stooped, and with some astonishment read—

JEAN BOUCHON
MORT SUR LE CHAMP DE GLOIRE
1870
DULCE ET DECORUM EST PRO PATRIA MORI.

"Why!" objected I, "he died from falling a cropper in the back passage, not on the field of glory."

"*Monsieur!* all Orléans is a field of glory. Under S. Aignan did we not repel Attila and his Huns in 451? Under Jeanne d'Arc did we not repulse the English—*monsieur* will excuse the allusion—in 1429. Did we not recapture Orléans from the Germans in November, 1870?"

"That is all very true," I broke in. "But Jean Bouchon neither fought against Attila nor with la Pucelle, nor against the Prussians. Then '*Dulce et decorum est pro patria mori*' is rather strong, considering the facts."

"How? Does not *monsieur* see that the sentiment is patriotic and magnificent?"

"I admit that, but dispute the application."

"Then why apply it? The sentiment is all right."

"But by implication it refers to Jean Bouchon, who died, not for his country, but in a sordid coffee-house brawl. Then, again, the date is wrong. Jean Bouchon died in 1869, not in 1870."

"That is only out by a year."

"Yes, but with this mistake of a year, and with the quotation from Horace, and with the attitude given to the figure, anyone would suppose that Jean Bouchon had fallen in the retaking of Orléans from the Prussians."

"Ah! *monsieur*, who looks on a monument and expects to find thereon the literal truth relative to the deceased?"

"This is something of a sacrifice to truth," I demurred.

"Sacrifice is superb!" said the waiter. "There is nothing more noble, more heroic than sacrifice."

"But not the sacrifice of truth."

"Sacrifice is always sacrifice."

"Well," said I, unwilling further to dispute, "this is certainly a great creation out of nothing."

"Not out of nothing; out of the coppers that Jean Bouchon had filched from us, and which choked up his coffin."

"Jean Bouchon has been seen no more?"

"No, *monsieur*. And yet—yes, once, when the statue was unveiled. Our *patron* did that. The *café* was crowded. All our *habitués* were there. The *patron* made a magnificent oration; he drew a superb picture of the moral, intellectual, social, and political merits of Jean Bouchon. There was not a dry eye among the audience, and the speaker choked with emotion. Then, as we stood in a ring, not too near, we saw—I was there and I distinctly saw, so did the others—Jean Bouchon standing with his back to us, looking intently at the statue of himself. *Monsieur*, as he thus stood I could discern his black mutton-chop whiskers projecting upon each side of his head.

"Well, sir, not one word was spoken. A dead silence fell upon all. Our *patron* ceased to speak, and wiped his eyes and blew his nose. A sort of holy awe possessed us all. Then, after the lapse of some minutes, Jean Bouchon turned himself about, and we all saw his puffy pale cheeks, his thick sensual lips, his broken nose, his little pig's eyes. He was very unlike his idealised portrait in the statue; but what matters that? It gratified the deceased, and it injured no one. Well, *monsieur*, Jean Bouchon stood facing us, and he turned his head from one side to another, and gave us all what I may term a greasy smile. Then he lifted up his hands as though invoking a blessing on us all, and vanished. Since then he has not been seen."

Black Ram

(A tale from *A Book of Ghosts*)

I do not know when I had spent a more pleasant evening, or
had enjoyed a dinner more than that at Mr. Weatherwood's hos-
pitable house. For one thing, the hostess knew how to keep her
guests interested and in good-humour. The dinner was all that
could be desired, and so were the wines. But what conduced
above all to my pleasure was that at table I sat by Miss Fulton, a
bright, intelligent girl, well read and entertaining. My wife had
a cold, and had sent her excuses by me. Miss Fulton and I talked
of this, that, and everything. Towards the end of dinner she said:
"I shall be obliged to run away so soon as the ladies leave the
room to you and your cigarettes and gossip. It is rather mean,
but Mrs. Weatherwood has been forewarned, and understands.
Tomorrow is our village feast at Marksleigh, and I have a host of
things on my hand. I shall have to be up at seven, and I do object
to cut a slice off my night's rest at both ends."

"Rather an unusual time of the year for a village feast," said I.
"These things are generally got over in the summer."

"You see, our church is dedicated to St. Mark, and tomorrow
is his festival, and it has been observed in one fashion or another
in our parish from time immemorial. In your parts have they
any notions about St. Mark's eve?"

"What sort of notions?"

"That if you sit in the church porch from midnight till the
clock strikes one, you will see the apparitions pass before you of
those destined to die within the year."

"I fancy our good people see themselves, and nothing but themselves, on every day and hour throughout the twelve-month."

"Joking apart, have you any such superstition hanging on in your neighbourhood?"

"Not that I am aware of. That sort of thing belonged to the Golden Age that has passed away. Board schools have reduced us to that of lead."

"At Marksleigh the villagers believe in it, and recently their faith has received corroboration."

"How so?" I asked.

"Last year, in a fit of bravado, a young carpenter ventured to sit in the porch at the witching hour, and saw himself enter the church. He came home, looking as blank as a sheet, moped, lost flesh, and died nine months later."

"Of course he died, if he had made up his mind to do so."

"Yes—that is explicable. But how do you account for his having seen his double?"

"He had been drinking at the public-house. A good many people see double after that."

"It was not so. He was perfectly sober at the time."

"Then I give it up."

"Would you venture on a visit to a church porch on this night—St. Mark's eve?"

"Certainly I would, if well wrapped up, and I had my pipe."

"I bar the pipe," said Miss Fulton. "No apparition can stand tobacco smoke. But there is Lady Eastleigh rising. When you come to rejoin the ladies, I shall be gone."

I did not leave the house of the Weatherwoods till late. My dogcart was driven by my groom, Richard. The night was cold, or rather chilly, but I had my fur-lined overcoat, and did not mind that. The stars shone out of a frosty sky. All went smoothly enough till the road dipped into a valley, where a dense white fog hung over the river and the water-meadows. Anyone who has had much experience in driving at night is aware that in such a case the carriage lamps are worse than useless; they bewilder the horse and the driver. I cannot blame Dick if he ran his wheel over a heap of stones that upset the trap. We were both thrown out, and I fell on my head. I sang out: "Mind the cob, Dick; I am all right."

The boy at once mastered the horse. I did not rise immediately, for I had been somewhat jarred by the fall; when I did I found Dick engaged in mending a ruptured trace. One of the shafts was broken, and a carriage lamp had been shattered.

"Dick," said I, "there are a couple of steep hills to descend, and that is risky with a single shaft. I will lighten the dogcart by walking home, and do you take care at the hills."

"I think we can manage, sir."

"I should prefer to walk the rest of the way. I am rather shaken by my fall, and a good step out in the cool night will do more to put me to rights than anything else. When you get home, send up a message to your mistress that she is not to expect me at once. I shall arrive in due time, and she is not to be alarmed."

"It's a good trudge before you, sir. And I dare say we could get the shaft tied up at Fifewell."

"What—at this time of night? No, Dick, do as I say."

Accordingly the groom drove off, and I started on my walk. I was glad to get out of the clinging fog, when I reached higher ground. I looked back, and by the starlight saw the river bottom filled with the mist, lying apparently dense as snow.

After a swinging walk of a quarter of an hour I entered the outskirts of Fifewell, a village of some importance, with shops, the seat of the petty sessions, and with a small boot and shoe factory in it.

The street was deserted. Some bedroom windows were lighted, for our people have the habit of burning their paraffin lamps all night. Every door was shut, no one was stirring.

As I passed along the churchyard wall, the story of the young carpenter, told by Miss Fulton, recurred to me.

"By Jove!" thought I, "it is now close upon midnight, a rare opportunity for me to see the wonders of St. Mark's eve. I will go into the porch and rest there for a few minutes, and then I shall be able, when I meet that girl again, to tell her that I had done what she challenged me to do, without any idea that I would take her challenge up."

I turned in at the gate, and walked up the pathway. The headstones bore a somewhat ghostly look in the starlight. A cross of white stone, recently set up, I supposed, had almost the appearance of phosphorescence. The church windows were dark.

I seated myself in the roomy porch on a stone bench against the wall, and felt for my pipe. I am not sure that I contemplated smoking it then and there, partly because Miss Fulton had forbidden it, but also because I felt that it was not quite the right thing to do on consecrated ground. But it would be a satisfaction to finger it, and I might plug it, so as to be ready to light up so soon as I left the churchyard. To my vexation I found that I had lost it. The tobacco-pouch was there, and the matches. My pipe must have fallen out of my pocket when I was pitched from the trap. That pipe was a favourite of mine.

"What a howling nuisance," said I. "If I send Dick back over the road to-morrow morning, ten chances to one if he finds it, for to-morrow is market-day, and people will be passing early."

As I said this, the clock struck twelve.

I counted each stroke. I wore my fur-lined coat, and was not cold—in fact, I had been too warm walking in it. At the last stroke of twelve I noticed lines of very brilliant light appear about the door into the church. The door must have fitted well, as the light did no more than show about it, and did not gush forth at all the crevices. But from the keyhole shot a ray of intense brilliancy.

Whether the church windows were illumined I did not see—in fact, it did not occur to me to look, either then or later—but I am pretty certain that they were not, or the light streaming from them would have brought the gravestones into prominence. When you come to think of it, it was remarkable that the light of so dazzling a nature should shine through the crannies of the door, and that none should issue, as far as I could see, from the windows. At the time I did not give this a thought; my attention was otherwise taken up. For I saw distinctly Miss Venville, a very nice girl of my acquaintance, coming up the path with that swinging walk so characteristic of an English young lady.

How often it has happened to me, when I have been sitting in a public park or in the gardens of a Cursaal abroad, and some young girls have passed by, that I have said to my wife: "I bet you a bob those are English."

"Yes, of course," she has replied; "you can see that by their dress."

"I don't know anything about dress," I have said; "I judge by the walk."

Well, there was Miss Venville coming towards the porch.

"This is a joke," said I. "She is going to sit here on the look-out for ghosts, and if I stand up or speak she will be scared out of her wits. Hang it, I wish I had my pipe now; if I gave a whiff it would reveal the presence of a mortal, without alarming her. I think I shall whistle."

I had screwed up my lips to begin "Rocked in the cradle of the deep"—that is my great song I perform whenever there is a village concert, or I am asked out to dinner, and am entreated afterwards to sing—I say I had screwed up my lips to whistle, when I saw something that scared me so that I made no attempt at the melody.

The ray of light through the keyhole was shut off, and I saw standing in the porch before me the form of Mrs. Venville, the girl's mother, who had died two years before. The ray of white light arrested by her filled her as a lamp—was diffused as a mild glow from her.

"Halloo, mother, what brings you here?" asked the girl.

"Gwendoline, I have come to warn you back. You cannot enter; you have not got the key."

"The key, mother?"

"Yes, everyone who would pass within must have his or her own key."

"Well, where am I to get one?"

"It must be forged for you, Gwen. You are wholly unfit to

enter. What good have you ever done to deserve it?"

"Why, mother, everyone knows I'm an awfully good sort."

"No one in here knows it. That is no qualification."

"And I always dressed in good taste."

"Nor is that."

"And I was splendid at lawn tennis."

Her mother shook her head.

"Look here, little mummy. I won a brooch at the archery match."

"That will not do, Gwendoline. What good have you ever done to anyone else beside yourself?"

The girl considered a minute, then laughed, and said: "I put into a raffle at a bazaar—no, it was a bran-pie for an orphanage—and I drew out a pair of braces. I had rare fun over those braces, I sold them to Captain Fitzakerly for half a crown, and that I gave to the charity."

"You went for what you could get, not what you could give."

Then the mother stepped on one side, and the ray shot directly at the girl. I saw that it had something of the quality of the X-ray. It was not arrested by her garments, or her flesh or muscles. It revealed in her breast, in her brain—penetrating her whole body—a hard, dark core.

"Black Ram, I bet," said I.

Now Black Ram is the local name for a substance found in our land, especially in the low ground that ought to be the most fertile, but is not so, on account of this material found in it.

The substance lies some two or three feet below the surface, and forms a crust of the consistency of cast iron. No plough can possibly be driven through it. No water can percolate athwart it, and consequently where it is, there the superincumbent soil is resolved into a quagmire. No tree can grow in it, for the moment the taproot touches the Black Ram the tree dies.

Of what Black Ram consists is more than I can say; the popular opinion is that it is a bastard manganese. Now I happen to own several fields accursed with the presence in them of Black

Ram—fields that ought to be luxuriant meadows, but which, in consequence of its presence, are worth almost nothing at all.

"No, Gwen," said her mother, looking sorrowfully at her, "there is not a chance of your admission till you have got rid of the Black Ram that is in you."

"Sure," said I, as I slapped my knee, "I thought I knew the article, and now my opinion has been confirmed."

"How can I get rid of it?" asked the girl.

"Gwendoline, you will have to pass into little Polly Finch, and work it out of your system. She is dying of scarlet fever, and you must enter into her body, and so rid yourself in time of the Black Ram."

"Mother!—the Finches are common people."

"So much the better chance for you."

"And I am eighteen, Polly is about ten."

"You will have to become a little child if you would enter her."

"I don't like it. What is the alternative?"

"To remain without in the darkness till you come to a better mind. And now, Gwen, no time is to be lost; you must pass into Polly Finch's body before it grows cold."

"Well, then—here goes!"

Gwen Venville turned, and her mother accompanied her down the path. The girl moved reluctantly, and pouted. Passing out of the churchyard, both traversed the street and disappeared within a cottage, from the upper window of which light from behind a white blind was diffused.

I did not follow, I leaned back against the wall. I felt that my head was throbbing. I was a little afraid lest my fall had done more injury than I had at first anticipated. I put my hand to my head, and held it there for a moment.

Then it was as though a book were opened before me—the book of the life of Polly Finch—or rather of Gwendoline's soul in Polly Finch's body. It was but one page that I saw, and the figures in it were moving.

The girl was struggling under the burden of a heavy baby

brother. She coaxed him, she sang to him, she played with him, talked to him, broke off bits of her bread and butter, given to her for breakfast, and made him eat them; she wiped his nose and eyes with her pocket-handkerchief, she tried to dance him in her arms. He was a fractious urchin, and most exacting, but her patience, her good-nature, never failed. The drops stood on her brow, and her limbs tottered under the weight, but her heart was strong, and her eyes shone with love.

I drew my hand from my head. It was burning. I put my hand to the cold stone bench to cool it, and then applied it once more to my brow.

Instantly it was as though another page were revealed. I saw Polly in her widowed father's cottage. She was now a grown girl; she was on her knees scrubbing the floor. A bell tinkled. Then she put down the soap and brush, turned down her sleeves, rose and went into the outer shop to serve a customer with half a pound of tea. That done, she was back again, and the scrubbing was renewed. Again a tinkle, and again she stood up and went into the shop to a child who desired to buy a pennyworth of lemon drops.

On her return, in came her little brother crying—he had cut his finger. Polly at once applied cobweb, and then stitched a rag about the wounded member.

"There, there, Tommy! don't cry any more. I have kissed the bad place, and it will soon be well."

"Poll! it hurts! it hurts!" sobbed the boy.

"Come to me," said his sister. She drew a low chair to the fireside, took Tommy on her lap, and began to tell him the story of Jack the Giant-killer.

I removed my hand, and the vision was gone.

I put my other hand to my head, and at once saw a further scene in the life-story of Polly.

She was now a middle-aged woman, and had a cottage of her own. She was despatching her children to school. They had bright, rosy faces, their hair was neatly combed, their pinafores were white as snow. One after another, before leaving, put up the cherry lips to kiss mammy; and when they were gone, for a moment she stood in the door looking after them, then sharply turned, brought out a basket, and emptied its contents on the table. There were little girls' stockings with "potatoes" in them to be darned, torn jackets to be mended, a little boy's trousers to be reseated, pocket-handkerchiefs to be hemmed. She laboured on with her needle the greater part of the day, then put away the garments, some finished, others to be finished, and going to the flour-bin took forth flour and began to knead dough, and then to roll it out to make pasties for her husband and the children.

"Poll!" called a voice from without; she ran to the door.

"Back, Joe! I have your dinner hot in the oven."

"I must say, Poll, you are the best of good wives, and there isn't a mother like you in the shire. My word! that was a lucky day when I chose you, and didn't take Mary Matters, who was setting her cap at me. See what a slattern she has turned out. Why, I do believe, Poll, if I'd took her she'd have drove me long ago to the public-house."

I saw the mother of Gwendoline standing by me and looking out on this scene, and I heard her say: "The Black Ram is run out, and the key is forged."

All had vanished. I thought now I might as well rise and continue my journey. But before I had left the bench I observed the rector of Fifewell sauntering up the path, with uncertain step, as he fumbled in his coat-tail pockets, and said: "Where the deuce is the key?"

The Reverend William Hexworthy was a man of good private means, and was just the sort of man that a bishop delights to honour. He was one who would never cause him an hour's anxiety; he was not the man to indulge in ecclesiastical vagaries. He flattered himself that he was strictly a *via media* man. He kept dogs, he was a good judge of horses, was fond of sport. He did not hunt, but he shot and fished. He was a favourite in society, was of irreproachable conduct, and was a magistrate on the bench.

As the ray from the keyhole smote on him he seemed to be

wholly dark,—made up of nothing but Black Ram. He came on slowly, as though not very sure of his way.

"Bless me! where can be the key?" he asked.

Then from out of the graves, and from over the wall of the churchyard, came rushing up a crowd of his dead parishioners, and blocked his way to the porch.

"Please, your reverence!" said one, "you did not visit me when I was dying."

"I sent you a bottle of my best port," said the parson.

"Ay, sir, and thank you for it. But that went into my stomick, and what I wanted was medicine for my soul. You never said a prayer by me. You never urged me to repentance for my bad life, and you let me go out of the world with all my sins about me."

"And I, sir," said another, thrusting himself before Mr. Hexworthy—"I was a young man, sir, going wild, and you never said a word to restrain me; never sent for me and gave me a bit of warning and advice which would have checked me. You just shrugged your shoulders and laughed, and said that a young chap like me must sow his wild oats."

"And we," shouted the rest—"we were never taught by you anything at all."

"Now this is really too bad," said the rector. "I preached twice every Sunday."

"Oh, yes—right enough that. But precious little good it did when nothing came out of your heart, and all out of your pocket—and that you did give us was copied in your library. Why, sir, not one of your sermons ever did anybody a farthing of good."

"We were your sheep," protested others, "and you let us wander where we would! You didn't seem to know yourself that there was a fold into which to draw us."

"And we," said others, "went off to chapel, and all the good we ever got was from the dissenting minister—never a mite from you."

"And some of us," cried out others, "went to the bad altogether, through your neglect. What did you care about our souls so long as your terriers were washed and combed, and your horses well groomed? You were a fisherman, but all you fished for were trout—not souls. And if some of us turned out well, it was in spite of your neglect—no thanks to you."

Then some children's voices were raised: "Sir, you never taught us no Catechism, nor our duty to God and to man, and we grew up regular heathens."

"That was your fathers' and mothers' duty."

"But our fathers and mothers never taught us anything."

"Come, this is intolerable," shouted Mr. Hexworthy. "Get out of the way, all of you. I can't be bothered with you now. I want to go in there."

"You can't, parson! the door is shut, and you have not got your key."

Mr. Hexworthy stood bewildered and irresolute. He rubbed his chin.

"What the dickens am I to do?" he asked.

Then the crowd closed about him, and thrust him back towards the gate. "You must go whither we send you," they said.

I stood up to follow. It was curious to see a flock drive its shepherd, who, indeed, had never attempted to lead. I walked in the rear, and it seemed as though we were all swept forward as by a mighty wind. I did not gain my breath, or realise whither I was going, till I found myself in the slums of a large manufacturing town before a mean house such as those occupied by artisans, with the conventional one window on one side of the door and two windows above. Out of one of these latter shone a scarlet glow.

The crowd hustled Mr. Hexworthy in at the door, which was opened by a hospital nurse.

I stood hesitating what to do, and not understanding what had taken place. On the opposite side of the street was a mission church, and the windows were lighted. I entered, and saw that there were at least a score of people, shabbily dressed, and belonging to the lowest class, on their knees in prayer. There was a sort of door-opener or verger at the entrance, and I said to him: "What is the meaning of all this?"

"Oh, sir!" said he, "*he* is ill, he has been attacked by smallpox. It has been raging in the place, and he has been with all the sick, and now he has taken it himself, and we are terribly afraid that he is dying. So we are praying God to spare him to us."

Then one of those who was kneeling turned to me and said: "I was an hungred, and he gave me meat."

And another rose up and said: "I was a stranger, and he took me in."

Then a third said: "I was naked, and he clothed me."

And a fourth: "I was sick, and he visited me."

Then said a fifth, with bowed head, sobbing: "I was in prison, and he came to me."

Thereupon I went out and looked up at the red window, and I felt as if I must see the man for whom so many prayed. I tapped at the door, and a woman opened.

"I should so much like to see him, if I may," said I.

"Well, sir," spoke the woman, a plain, middle-aged, rough creature, but her eyes were full of tears: "Oh, sir, I think you may, if you will go up softly. There has come over him a great change. It is as though a new life had entered into him."

I mounted the narrow staircase of very steep steps and entered the sick-room. There was an all-pervading glow of red. The fire was low—no flame, and a screen was before it. The lamp had a scarlet shade over it. I stepped to the side of the bed, where stood a nurse. I looked on the patient. He was an awful object. His face had been smeared over with some dark solution, with the purpose of keeping all light from the skin, with the object of saving it from permanent disfigurement.

The sick priest lay with eyes raised, and I thought I saw in them those of Mr. Hexworthy, but with a new light, a new faith, a new fervour, a new love in them. The lips were moving in prayer, and the hands were folded over the breast. The nurse whispered to me: "We thought he was passing away, but the prayers of those he loved have prevailed. A great change has come over him. The last words he spoke were: 'God's will be done. If I live, I will live only—only for my dear sheep, and die

208

among them'; and now he is in an ecstasy, and says nothing. But he is praying still—for his people."

As I stood looking I saw what might have been tears, but seemed to be molten Black Ram, roll over the painted cheeks. The spirit of Mr. Hexworthy was in this body.

Then, without a word, I turned to the door, went through, groped my way down the steps, passed out into the street, and found myself back in the porch of Fifewell Church.

"Upon my word," said I, "I have been here long enough." I wrapped my fur coat about me, and prepared to go, when I saw a well-known figure, that of Mr. Fothergill, advancing up the path.

I knew the old gentleman well. His age must have been seventy. He was a spare man, he was rather bald, and had sunken cheeks. He was a bachelor, living in a pretty little villa of his own. He had a good fortune, and was a harmless, but self-centred, old fellow. He prided himself on his cellar and his cook. He always dressed well, and was scrupulously neat. I had often played a game of chess with him.

I would have run towards him to remonstrate with him for exposing himself to the night air, but I was forestalled. Slipping past me, his old manservant, David, went to meet him. David had died three years before. Mr. Fothergill had then been dangerously ill with typhoid fever, and the man had attended to him night and day. The old gentleman, as I heard, had been most irritable and exacting in his illness. When his malady took a turn, and he was on the way to convalescence, David had succumbed in his turn, and in three days was dead.

This man now met his master, touched his cap, and said: "Beg pardon, sir, you will not be admitted."

"Not admitted? Why not, Davie?"

"I really am very sorry, sir. If my key would have availed, you would have been welcome to it; but, sir, there's such a terrible lot of Black Ram in you, sir. That must be got out first."

"I don't understand, Davie."

"I'm sorry, sir, to have to say it; but you've never done anyone any good."

"I paid you your wages regularly."

"Yes, sir, to be sure, sir, for my services to yourself."

"And I've always subscribed when asked for money."

"Yes, that is very true, sir, but that was because you thought it was expected of you, not because you had any sympathy with those in need, and sickness, and suffering."

"I'm sure I never did anyone any harm."

"No, sir, and never anyone any good. You'll excuse me for mentioning it."

"But, Davie, what do you mean? I can't get in?"

"No, sir, not till you have the key."

"But, bless my soul! what is to become of me? Am I to stick out here?"

"Yes, sir, unless——"

"In this damp, and cold, and darkness?"

"There is no help for it, Mr. Fothergill, unless——"

"Unless what, Davie?"

"Unless you become a mother, sir!"

"What?"

"Of twins, sir."

"Fiddlesticks!"

"Indeed, it is so, sir, and you will have to nurse them."

"I can't do it. I'm physically incapable."

"It must be done, sir. Very sorry to mention it, but there is no alternative. There's Sally Bowker is approaching her confinement, and it's going terribly hard with her. The doctor thinks she'll never pull through. But if you'd consent to pass into her and become a mother——"

"And nurse the twins? Oh, Davie, I shall need a great amount of stout."

"I grieve to say it, Mr. Fothergill, but you'll be too poor to afford it."

"Is there no alternative?"

"None in the world, sir."

"I don't know my way to the place."

210

"If you'd do me the honour, sir, to take my arm, I would lead you to the house."

"It's hard—cruel hard on an old bachelor. Must it be twins? It's a rather large order."

"It really must, sir."

Then I saw David lend his arm to his former master and conduct him out of the churchyard, across the street, into the house of Seth Bowker, the shoemaker.

I was so interested in the fate of my old friend, and so curious as to the result, that I followed, and went into the cobbler's house. I found myself in the little room on the ground floor. Seth Bowker was sitting over the fire with his face in his hands, swaying himself, and moaning: "Oh dear! dear life! whatever shall I do without her? and she the best woman as breathed, and knew all my little ways."

Overhead was a trampling. The doctor and the midwife were with the woman. Seth looked up, and listened. Then he flung himself on his knees at the deal table, and prayed: "Oh, good God in heaven! have pity on me, and spare me my wife. I shall be a lost man without her—and no one to sew on my shirt-buttons!"

At the moment I heard a feeble twitter aloft, then it grew in volume, and presently became cries. Seth looked up; his face was bathed in tears. Still that strange sound like the chirping of sparrows. He rose to his feet and made for the stairs, and held on to the banister.

Forth from the chamber above came the doctor, and leisurely descended the stairs.

"Well, Bowker," said he, "I congratulate you; you have two fine boys."

"And my Sally—my wife?"

"She has pulled through. But really, upon my soul, I did fear for her at one time. But she rallied marvellously."

"Can I go up to her?"

"In a minute or two, not just now, the babes are being washed."

"And my wife will get over it?"

"I trust so, Bowker; a new life came into her as she gave birth to twins."

"God be praised!" Seth's mouth quivered, all his face worked, and he clasped his hands.

Presently the door of the chamber upstairs was opened, the nurse looked down, and said: "Mr. Bowker, you may come up. Your wife wants you. Lawk! you will see the beautifullest twins that ever was."

I followed Seth upstairs, and entered the sick-room. It was humble enough, with whitewashed walls, all scrupulously clean. The happy mother lay in the bed, her pale face on the pillow, but the eyes were lighted up with ineffable love and pride.

"Kiss them, Bowker," said she, exhibiting at her side two little pink heads, with down on them. But her husband just stooped and pressed his lips to her brow, and after that kissed the tiny morsels at her side.

"Ain't they loves!" exclaimed the midwife.

But oh! what a rapture of triumph, pity, fervour, love, was in that mother's face, and—the eyes looking on those children were the eyes of Mr. Fothergill. Never had I seen such an expression in them, not even when he had exclaimed "Checkmate" over a game of chess.

Then I knew what would follow. How night and day that mother would live only for her twins, how she would cheerfully sacrifice her night's rest to them; how she would go downstairs, even before it was judicious, to see to her husband's meals. Verily, with the mother's milk that fed those babes, the Black Ram would run out of the Fothergill soul. There was no need for me to tarry. I went forth, and as I issued into the street heard the clock strike one.

"Bless me!" I exclaimed, "I have spent an hour in the porch. What will my wife say?"

I walked home as fast as I could in my fur coat. When I arrived I found Bessie up.

"Oh, Bessie!" said I, "with your cold you ought to have been in bed."

"My dear Edward," she replied, "how could I? I had lain down, but when I heard of the accident I could not rest. Have you been hurt?"

"My head is somewhat contused," I replied.

"Let me feel. Indeed, it is burning. I will put on some cold compresses."

"But, Bessie, I have a story to tell you."

"Oh! never mind the story, we'll have that another day. I'll send for some ice from the fishmonger tomorrow for your head."

★★★★★★

I did eventually tell my wife the story of my experience in the porch of Fifewell on St. Mark's eve.

I have since regretted that I did so; for whenever I cross her will, or express my determination to do something of which she does not approve, she says: "Edward, Edward! I very much fear there is still in you too much Black Ram."

Pomps and Vanities

(A tale from *A Book of Ghosts*)

Colonel Mountjoy had an appointment in India that kept
him there permanently. Consequently he was constrained to
send his two daughters to England when they were quite children. His wife had died of cholera at Madras. The girls were
Letice and Betty. There was a year's difference in their ages, but
they were extraordinarily alike, so much so that they might have
been supposed to be twins.

Letice was given up to the charge of Miss Mountjoy, her
father's sister, and Betty to that of Lady Lacy, her maternal aunt.
Their father would have preferred that his daughters should
have been together, but there were difficulties in the way; neither of the ladies was inclined to be burdened with both, and if
both had been placed with one the other might have regarded
and resented this as a slight.

As the children grew up their likeness in feature became more
close, but they diverged exceedingly in expression. A sullenness,
an unhappy look, a towering fire of resentment characterised
that of Letice, whereas the face of Betty was open and gay.

This difference was due to the difference in their bringing
up.

Lady Lacy, who had a small house in North Devon, was a
kindly, intellectual, and broad-minded old lady, of sweet disposition but a decided will. She saw a good deal of society, and did
her best to train Betty to be an educated and liberal-minded
woman of culture and graceful manners. She did not send her to

school, but had her taught at home; and on the excuse that her eyes were weak by artificial light she made the girl read to her in the evenings, and always read books that were standard and calculated to increase her knowledge and to develop her understanding. Lady Lacy detested all shams, and under her influence Betty grew up to be thoroughly straightforward, healthy-minded, and true.

On the other hand, Miss Mountjoy was, as Letice called her, a Killjoy. She had herself been reared in the midst of the Clapham sect; had become rigid in all her ideas, narrow in all her sympathies, and a bundle of prejudices.

The present generation of young people know nothing of the system of repression that was exercised in that of their fathers and mothers. Now the tendency is wholly in the other direction, and too greatly so. It is possibly due to a revulsion of feeling against a training that is looked back upon with a shudder.

To that narrow school there existed but two categories of men and women, the Christians and the Worldlings, and those who pertained to it arrogated to themselves the former title. The Judgment had already begun with the severance of the sheep from the goats, and the saints who judged the world had their Jerusalem at Clapham.

In that school the works of the great masters of English literature, Shakespeare, Pope, Scott, Byron, were taboo; no work of imagination was tolerated save the Apocalypse, and that was degraded into a polemic by such scribblers as Elliot and Cumming.

No entertainments, not even the oratorios of Handel, were tolerated; they savoured of the world. The nearest approach to excitement was found in a missionary meeting. The Chinese contract the feet of their daughters, but those English Claphamites cramped the minds of their children. The Venetians made use of an iron prison, with gradually contracting walls, that finally crushed the life out of the captive. But these elect Christians put their sons and daughters into a school that squeezed their energies and their intelligences to death.

215

Dickens caricatured such people in Mrs. Jellyby and Mr. Chadband; but he sketched them only in their external aspect, and left untouched their private action in distorting young minds, maiming their wills, damping down all youthful buoyancy.

But the result did not answer the expectations of those who adopted this system with the young. Some daughters, indeed, of weaker wills were permanently stunted and shaped on the approved model, but nearly all the sons, and most of the daughters, on obtaining their freedom, broke away into utter frivolity and dissipation, or, if they retained any religious impressions, galloped through the Church of England, performing strange antics on the way, and plunged into the arms of Rome.

Such was the system to which the high-spirited, strong-willed Letice was subjected, and from which was no escape. The consequence was that Letice tossed and bit at her chains, and that there ensued frequent outbreaks of resentment against her aunt.

"Oh, Aunt Hannah! I want something to read."

After some demur, and disdainful rejection of more serious works, she was allowed Milton.

Then she said, "Oh! I do love *Comus*."

"*Comus!*" gasped Miss Mountjoy.

"And *L'Allegro* and *Il Penseroso*, they are not bad."

"My child. These were the compositions of the immortal bard before his eyes were opened."

"I thought, aunt, that he had dictated the *Paradise Lost and Regained* after he was blind."

"I refer to the eyes of his soul," said the old lady sternly.

"I want a story-book."

"There is the *Dairyman's Daughter*."

"I have read it, and hate it."

"I fear, Leticia, that you are in the gall of bitterness and the bond of iniquity."

Unhappily the sisters very rarely met one another. It was but occasionally that Lady Lacy and Betty came to town, and when they did, Miss Mountjoy put as many difficulties as she could in the way of their associating together.

On one such visit to London, Lady Lacy called and asked if she might take Letice with herself to the theatre. Miss Mountjoy shivered with horror, reared herself, and expressed her opinion of stage-plays and those who went to see them in strong and uncomplimentary terms. As she had the custody of Letice, she would by no persuasion be induced to allow her to imperil her soul by going to such a wicked place. Lady Lacy was fain to withdraw in some dismay and much regret.

Poor Letice, who had heard this offer made, had flashed into sudden brightness and a tremor of joy; when it was refused, she burst into a flood of tears and an ecstasy of rage. She ran up to her room, and took and tore to pieces a volume of *Clayton's Sermons*, scattered the leaves over the floor, and stamped upon them.

"Letice," said Miss Mountjoy, when she saw the devastation, "you are a child of wrath."

"Why mayn't I go where there is something pretty to see? Why may I not hear good music? Why must I be kept forever in the Doleful Dumps?"

"Because all these things are of the world, worldly."

"If God hates all that is fair and beautiful, why did He create the peacock, the humming-bird, and the bird of paradise, instead of filling the world with barn-door fowls?"

"You have a carnal mind. You will never go to heaven."

"Lucky I—if the saints there do nothing but hold missionary meetings to convert one another. Pray what else can they do?"

"They are engaged in the worship of God."

"I don't know what that means. All I am acquainted with is the worship of the congregation. At Salem Chapel the minister faces it, mouths at it, gesticulates to it, harangues, flatters, fawns at it, and, indeed, prays at it. If that be all, heaven must be a deadly dull hole."

Miss Mountjoy reared herself, she became livid with wrath. "You wicked girl."

"Aunt," said Letice, intent on further incensing her, "I do

wish you would let me go—just for once—to a Catholic church to see what the worship of God is."

"I would rather see you dead at my feet!" exclaimed the incensed lady, and stalked, rigid as a poker, out of the room.

Thus the unhappy girl grew up to woman's estate, her heart seething with rebellion.

And then a terrible thing occurred. She caught scarlet fever, which took an unfavourable turn, and her life was despaired of. Miss Mountjoy was not one to conceal from the girl that her days were few, and her future condition hopeless.

Letice fought against the idea of dying so young.

"Oh, aunt! I won't die! I can't die! I have seen nothing of the pomps and vanities. I want to just taste them, and know what they are like. Oh! save me, make the doctor give me something to revive me. I want the pomps and vanities, oh! so much. I will not, I cannot die!" But her will, her struggle, availed nothing, and she passed away into the Great Unseen.

Miss Mountjoy wrote a formal letter to her brother, who had now become a general, to inform him of the lamented decease of his eldest daughter. It was not a comforting letter. It dwelt unnecessarily on the faults of Letice, it expressed no hopes as to her happiness in the world to which she had passed. There had been no signs of resignation at the last; no turning from the world with its pomps and vanities to better things, only a vain longing after what she could not have; a bitter resentment against Providence for having denied them to her; and a steeling of her heart against good and pious influences.

A year had passed.

Lady Lacy had come to town along with her niece. A dear friend had placed her house at her disposal. She had herself gone to Dresden with her daughters to finish them off in music and German. Lady Lacy was very glad of the occasion, for Betty was now of an age to be brought out. There was to be a great ball at the house of the Countess of Belgrove, unto whom Lady Lacy was related, and at the ball Betty was to make her *début*.

The girl was in a condition of boundless excitement. A beautiful ball-dress of white satin, trimmed with rich Valenciennes lace, was laid over her chair for her to wear. Neat little white satin shoes stood on the floor, quite new, for her feet. In a flower-glass stood a red camellia that was destined to adorn her hair, and on the dressing-table, in a morocco case, was a pearl necklace that had belonged to her mother.

The maid did her hair, but the camellia, which was to be the only point of colour about her, except her rosy lips and flushed cheeks—that camellia was not to be put into her hair till the last minute.

The maid offered to help her to dress.

"No, thank you, Martha; I can do that perfectly well myself. I am accustomed to use my own hands, and I can take my own time about it."

"But really, miss, I think you should allow me."

"Indeed, indeed, no. There is plenty of time, and I shall go leisurely to work. When the carriage comes just tap at the door and tell me, and I will rejoin my aunt."

When the maid was gone, Betty locked her door. She lighted the candles beside the cheval-glass, and looked at herself in the mirror and laughed. For the first time, with glad surprise and innocent pleasure, she realised how pretty she was. And pretty she was indeed, with her pleasant face, honest eyes, finely arched brows, and twinkling smile that produced dimples in her cheeks.

"There is plenty of time," she said. "I shan't take a hundred years in dressing now that my hair is done."

She yawned. A great heaviness had come over her.

"I really think I shall have a nap first. I am dead sleepy now, and forty winks will set me up for the night."

Then she laid herself upon the bed. A numbing, over-powering lethargy weighed on her, and almost at once she sank into a dreamless sleep. So unconscious was she that she did not hear Martha's tap at the door nor the roll of the carriage as it took her aunt away.

She woke with a start. It was full day.

For some moments she did not realise this fact, nor that she was still dressed in the gown in which she had lain down the previous evening.

She rose in dismay. She had slept so soundly that she had missed the ball.

She rang her bell and unlocked the door.

"What, miss, up already?" asked the maid, coming in with a tray on which were tea and bread and butter.

"Yes, Martha. Oh! what will aunt say? I have slept so long and like a log, and never went to the ball. Why did you not call me?"

"Please, miss, you have forgotten. You went to the ball last night."

"No; I did not. I overslept myself."

The maid smiled. "If I may be so bold as to say so, I think, Miss Betty, you are dreaming still."

"No; I did not go."

The maid took up the satin dress. It was crumpled, the lace was a little torn, and the train showed unmistakable signs of having been drawn over a floor.

She then held up the shoes. They had been worn, and well worn, as if danced in all night.

"Look here, miss; here is your programme! Why, deary me! you must have had a lot of dancing. It is quite full."

Betty looked at the programme with dazed eyes; then at the camellia. It had lost some of its petals, and these had not fallen on the toilet-cover. Where were they? What was the meaning of this?

"Martha, bring me my hot water, and leave me alone."

Betty was sorely perplexed. There were evidences that her dress had been worn. The pearl necklace was in the case, but not as she had left it—outside. She bathed her head in cold water. She racked her brain. She could not recall the smallest particular of the ball. She perused the programme. A light colour came into her cheek as she recognised the initials "C. F.," those of Captain Charles Fontanel, of whom of late she had seen a good deal. Other characters expressed nothing to her mind.

"How very strange!" she said; "and I was lying on the bed in the dress I had on yesterday evening. I cannot explain it."

Twenty minutes later, Betty went downstairs and entered the breakfast-room. Lady Lacy was there. She went up to her aunt and kissed her.

"I am so sorry that I overslept myself," she said. "I was like one of the Seven Sleepers."

"My dear, I should not have minded if you had not come down till midday. After a first ball you must be tired."

"I meant—last night."

"How, last night?"

"I mean when I went to dress."

"Oh, you were punctual enough. When I was ready you were already in the hall."

The bewilderment of the girl grew apace.

"I am sure," said her aunt, "you enjoyed yourself. But you gave the lion's share of the dances to Captain Fontanel. If this had been at Exeter, it would have caused talk; but here you are known only to a few; however, Lady Belgrove observed it."

"I hope you are not very tired, auntie darling," said Betty, to change slightly the theme that perplexed her.

"Nothing to speak of. I like to go to a ball; it recalls my old dancing days. But I thought you looked white and fagged all the evening. Perhaps it was excitement."

As soon as breakfast was concluded, Betty escaped to her room. A fear was oppressing her. The only explanation of the mystery was that she had been to the dance in her sleep. She was a somnambulist. What had she said and done when unconscious? What a dreadful thing it would have been had she woke up in the middle of a dance! She must have dressed herself, gone to Lady Belgrove's, danced all night, returned, taken off her dress, put on her afternoon tea-gown, lain down and concluded her sleep—all in one long tract of unconsciousness.

"By the way," said her aunt next day, "I have taken tickets for *Carmen*, at Her Majesty's. You would like to go?"

"Oh, delighted, aunt. I know some of the music—of course, the Toreador song; but I have never heard the whole opera. It will be delightful."

"And you are not too tired to go?"

"No—ten thousand times, no—I shall love to see it."

"What dress will you go in?"

"I think my black, and put a rose in my hair."

"That will do very well. The black becomes you. I think you could not do better."

Betty was highly delighted. She had been to plays, never to a real opera.

In the evening, dinner was early, unnecessarily early, and Betty knew that it would not take her long to dress, so she went into the little conservatory and seated herself there. The scent of the heliotropes was strong. Betty called them cherry-pie. She had got the *libretto*, and she looked it over; but as she looked, her eyes closed, and without being aware that she was going to sleep, in a moment she was completely unconscious.

She woke, feeling stiff and cold.

"Goodness!" said she, "I hope I am not late. Why—what is that light?"

The glimmer of dawn shone in at the conservatory windows.

Much astonished, she left it. The hall, the staircase were dark. She groped her way to her room, and switched on the electric light.

Before her lay her black-and-white muslin dress on the bed; on the table were her white twelve-button gloves folded about her fan. She took them up, and below them, somewhat crumpled, lay the play-bill, scented.

"How very unaccountable this is," she said; and removing the dress, seated herself on the bed and thought.

"Why did they turn out the lights?" she asked herself, then sprang to her feet, switched off the electric current, and saw that actually the morning light was entering the room. She resumed her seat; put her hands to her brow.

"It cannot—it cannot be that this dreadful thing has happened again."

Presently she heard the servants stirring. She hastily undressed and retired between the sheets, but not to sleep. Her mind worked. She was seriously alarmed.

At the usual time Martha arrived with tea.

"Awake, Miss Betty!" she said. "I hope you had a nice evening. I dare say it was beautiful."

"But," began the girl, then checked herself, and said—

"Is my aunt getting up? Is she very tired?"

"Oh, miss, my lady is a wonderful person; she never seems to tire. She is always down at the same time."

Betty dressed, but her mind was in a turmoil. On one thing she was resolved. She must see a doctor. But she would not frighten her aunt, she would keep the matter close from her.

When she came into the breakfast-room, Lady Lacy said—

"I thought Maas's voice was superb, but I did not so much care for the *Carmen*. What did you think, dear?"

"Aunt," said Betty, anxious to change the topic, "would you mind my seeing a doctor? I don't think I am quite well."

"Not well! Why what is the matter with you?"

"I have such dead fits of drowsiness."

"My dearest, is that to be wondered at with this racketing about; balls and theatres—very other than the quiet life at home? But I will admit that you struck me as looking very pale last night. You shall certainly see Dr. Groves."

When the medical man arrived, Betty intimated that she wished to speak with him alone, and he was shown with her into the morning-room.

"Oh, Dr. Groves," she said nervously, "it is such a strange thing I have to say. I believe I walk in my sleep."

"You have eaten something that disagreed with you."

"But it lasted so long."

"How do you mean? Have you long been subject to it?"

"Dear, no. I never had any signs of it before I came to London this season."

"And how were you roused? How did you become aware of it?"

"I was not roused at all; the fact is I went asleep to Lady Belgrove's ball, and danced there and came back, and woke up in the morning without knowing I had been."

"What!"

"And then, last night, I went in my sleep to Her Majesty's and heard *Carmen*; but I woke up in the conservatory here at early dawn, and I remember nothing about it."

"This is a very extraordinary story. Are you sure you went to the ball and to the opera?"

"Quite sure. My dress had been used on both occasions, and my shoes and fan and gloves as well."

"Did you go with Lady Lacy?"

"Oh, yes. I was with her all the time. But I remember nothing about it."

"I must speak to her ladyship."

"Please, please do not. It would frighten her; and I do not wish her to suspect anything, except that I am a little out of sorts. She gets nervous about me."

Dr. Groves mused for some while, then he said: "I cannot see that this is at all a case of somnambulism."

"What is it, then?"

"Lapse of memory. Have you ever suffered from that previously?"

"Nothing to speak of. Of course I do not always remember everything. I do not always recollect commissions given to me, unless I write them down. And I cannot say that I remember all the novels I have read, or what was the menu at dinner yesterday."

"That is quite a different matter. What I refer to is spaces of blank in your memory. How often has this occurred?"

"Twice."

"And quite recently?"

"Yes, I never knew anything of the kind before."

"I think that the sooner you return to the country the better. It is possible that the strain of coming out and the change of entering into gay life in town has been too much for you. Take care and economise your pleasures. Do not attempt too much; and if anything of the sort happens again, send for me."

"Then you won't mention this to my aunt?"

"No, not this time. I will say that you have been a little over-wrought and must be spared too much excitement."

"Thank you so much, Dr. Groves."

Now it was that a new mystery came to confound Betty. She rang her bell.

"Martha," said she, when her maid appeared, "where is that novel I had yesterday from the circulating library? I put it on the *boudoir* table."

"I have not noticed it, miss."

"Please look for it. I have hunted everywhere for it, and it cannot be found."

"I will look in the parlour, miss, and the schoolroom."

"I have not been into the schoolroom at all, and I know that it is not in the drawing-room."

A search was instituted, but the book could not be found. On the morrow it was in the *boudoir*, where Betty had placed it on her return from Mudie's.

"One of the maids took it," was her explanation. She did not much care for the book; perhaps that was due to her preoccupation, and not to any lack of stirring incident in the story. She sent it back and took out another. Next morning that also had disappeared.

It now became customary, as surely as she drew a novel from the library, that it vanished clean away. Betty was greatly amazed. She could not read a novel she had brought home till a day or two later. She took to putting the book, so soon as it was in the house, into one of her drawers, or into a cupboard. But the result was the same. Finally, when she had locked the newly acquired volume in her desk, and it had disappeared thence also, her patience gave way. There must be one of the domestics with a ravenous appetite for fiction, which drove her to carry off a book of the sort whenever it came into the house, and even to tamper with a lock to obtain it. Betty had been most reluctant to speak of the matter to her aunt, but now she made to her a formal complaint.

The servants were all questioned, and strongly protested their innocence. Not one of them had ventured to do such a thing as that with which they were charged.

However, from this time forward the annoyance ceased, and Betty and Lady Lacy naturally concluded that this was the result of the stir that had been made.

"Betty," said Lady Lacy, "what do you say to going to the new play at the Gaiety? I hear it very highly spoken of. Mrs. Fontanel has a box and has asked if we will join her."

"I should love it," replied the girl; "we have been rather quiet of late." But her heart was oppressed with fear.

She said to her maid: "Martha, will you dress me this evening— and—pray stay with me till my aunt is ready and calls for me?"

"Yes, miss, I shall be pleased to do so." But the girl looked somewhat surprised at the latter part of the request.

Betty thought well to explain: "I don't know what it is, but I feel somewhat out of spirits and nervous, and am afraid of being left alone, lest something should happen."

"Happen, miss! If you are not feeling well, would it not be as well to stay at home?"

"Oh, not for the world! I must go. I shall be all right so soon as I am in the carriage. It will pass off then."

"Shall I get you a glass of sherry, or anything?"

"No, no, it is not that. You remain with me and I shall be myself again."

That evening Betty went to the theatre. There was no recurrence of the sleeping fit with its concomitants. Captain Fontanel was in the box, and made himself vastly agreeable. He had his seat by Betty, and talked to her not only between the acts, but also a good deal whilst the actors were on the stage. With this she could have dispensed. She was not such an *habituée* of the theatre as not to be intensely interested with what was enacted before her.

Between two of the acts he said to her: "My mother is engaging Lady Lacy. She has a scheme in her head, but wants her consent to carry it out, to make it quite too charming. And I am deputed to get you to acquiesce."

"What is it?"

"We purpose having a boat and going to the Henley Regatta. Will you come?"

"I should enjoy it above everything. I have never seen a regatta—that is to say, not one so famous, and not of this kind. There were regattas at Ilfracombe, but they were different."

"Very well, then; the party shall consist only of my mother and sister and your two selves, and young Fulwell, who is dancing attendance on Jannet, and Putsey, who is a tame cat. I am sure my mother will persuade your aunt. What a lively old lady she is, and for her years how she does enjoy life!"

"It will be a most happy conclusion to our stay in town," said Betty. "We are going back to auntie's little cottage in Devon in a few days; she wants to be at home for Good Friday and Easter Day."

So it was settled. Lady Lacy had raised no objection, and now she and her niece had to consider what Betty should wear. Thin garments were out of the question; the weather was too cold, and it would be especially chilly on the river. Betty was still in slight mourning, so she chose a silver-grey cloth costume, with a black band about her waist, and a white straw hat, with a ribbon to match her gown.

On the day of the regatta Betty said to herself; "How ignorant I am! Fancy my not knowing where Henley is! That it is on the Thames or Isis I really do not know, but I fancy on the former—yes, I am almost positive it is on the Thames. I have seen pictures in the *Graphic* and *Illustrated* of the race last year, and I know the river was represented as broad, and the Isis can only be an insignificant stream. I will run into the schoolroom and find a map of the environs of London and post myself up in the geography. One hates to look like a fool."

Without a word to anyone, Betty found her way to the apartment given up to lessons when children were in the house. It lay at the back, down a passage. Since Lady Lacy had occupied the place, neither she nor Betty had been in it more than casually and rarely; and accordingly the servants had neglected to keep it clean. A good deal of dust lay about, and Betty, laughing, wrote her name in the fine powder on the school-table, then looked at her finger, found it black, and said, "Oh, bother! I forgot that the dust of London is smut."

She went to the bookcase, and groped for a map of the Metropolis and the country round, but could not find one. Nor could she lay her hand on a gazetteer.

"This must do," said she, drawing out a large, thick *Johnston's Atlas*, "if the scale be not too small to give Henley."

She put the heavy volume on the table and opened it. England, she found, was in two parts, one map of the Northern, the second of the Southern division. She spread out the latter, placed her finger on the blue line of the Thames, and began to trace it up.

Whilst her eyes were on it, searching the small print, they closed, and without being conscious that she was sleepy, her head bowed forward on the map, and she was breathing evenly, steeped in the most profound slumber.

She woke slowly. Her consciousness returned to her little by little. She saw the atlas without understanding what it meant. She looked about her, and wondered how she could be in the schoolroom, and she then observed that darkness was closing in. Only then, suddenly, did she recall what had brought her where she was.

Next, with a rush, upon her came the remembrance that she was due at the boat-race.

She must again have overslept herself, for the evening had come on, and through the window she could see the glimmer of gaslights in the street. Was this to be accompanied by her former experiences?

With throbbing heart she went into the passage. Then she

noticed that the hall was lighted up, and she heard her aunt speaking, and the slam of the front door, and the maid say, "Shall I take off your wraps, my lady?"

She stepped forth upon the landing and proceeded to descend, when—with a shock that sent the blood coursing to her heart, and that paralysed her movements—she saw *herself* ascending the stair in her silver-grey costume and straw hat.

She clung to the banister, with convulsive grip, lest she should fall, and stared, without power to utter a sound, as she saw herself quietly mount, step by step, pass her, go beyond to her own room.

For fully ten minutes she remained rooted to the spot, unable to stir even a finger. Her tongue was stiff, her muscles set, her heart ceased to beat.

Then slowly her blood began again to circulate, her nerves to relax, power of movement returned. With a hoarse gasp she reeled from her place, and giddy, touching the banister every moment to prevent herself from falling, she crept downstairs. But when once in the hall, she had recovered flexibility. She ran towards the morning-room, whither Lady Lacy had gone to gather up the letters that had arrived by post during her absence.

Betty stood looking at her, speechless.

Her aunt raised her face from an envelope she was considering. "Why, Betty," said she, "how expeditiously you have changed your dress!"

The girl could not speak, but fell unconscious on the floor.

When she came to herself, she was aware of a strong smell of vinegar. She was lying on the sofa, and Martha was applying a moistened kerchief to her brow. Lady Lacy stood by, alarmed and anxious, with a bottle of smelling-salts in her hand.

"Oh, aunt, I saw——" then she ceased. It would not do to tell of the apparition. She would not be believed.

"My darling," said Lady Lacy, "you are overdone, and it was foolish of you tearing upstairs and scrambling into your morning-gown. I have sent for Groves. Are you able now to rise? Can

229

you manage to reach your room?"

"My room!" she shuddered. "Let me lie here a little longer. I cannot walk. Let me be here till the doctor comes."

"Certainly, dearest. I thought you looked very unlike yourself all day at the regatta. If you had felt out of sorts you ought not to have gone."

"Auntie! I was quite well in the morning."

Presently the medical man arrived, and was shown in. Betty saw that Lady Lacy purposed staying through the interview. Accordingly she said nothing to Dr. Groves about what she had seen.

"She is overdone," said he. "The sooner you move her down to Devonshire the better. Someone had better be in her room tonight."

"Yes," said Lady Lacy; "I had thought of that and have given orders. Martha can make up her bed on the sofa in the adjoining dressing-room or *boudoir*."

This was a relief to Betty, who dreaded a return to her room—her room into which her other self had gone.

"I will call again in the morning," said the medical man; "keep her in bed tomorrow, at all events till I have seen her."

When he left, Betty found herself able to ascend the stairs. She cast a frightened glance about her room. The straw hat, the grey dress were there. No one was in it.

She was helped to bed, and although laid in it with her head among the pillows, she could not sleep. Racking thoughts tortured her. What was the signification of that encounter? What of her strange sleeps? What of those mysterious appearances of herself, where she had not been? The theory that she had walked in her sleep was untenable. How was she to solve the riddle? That she was going out of her mind was no explanation.

Only towards morning did she doze off.

When Dr. Groves came, about eleven o'clock, Betty made a point of speaking to him alone, which was what she greatly desired.

She said to him: "Oh! it has been worse this last occasion, far worse than before. I do not walk in my sleep. Whilst I am buried in slumber, someone else takes my place."

"Whom do you mean? Surely not one of the maids?"

"Oh, no. I met her on the stairs last night, that is what made me faint."

"Whom did you meet?"

"Myself—my double."

"Nonsense, Miss Mountjoy."

"But it is a fact. I saw myself as clearly as I see you now. I was going down into the hall."

"You saw yourself! You saw your own pleasant, pretty face in a looking-glass."

"There is no looking-glass on the staircase. Besides, I was in my alpaca morning-gown, and my double had on my pearl-grey cloth costume, with my straw hat. She was mounting as I was descending."

"Tell me the story."

"I went yesterday—an hour or so before I had to dress—into the schoolroom. I am awfully ignorant, and I did want to see a map and find out where was Henley, because, you know, I was going to the boat-race. And I dropped off into one of those dreadful dead sleeps, with my head on the atlas. When I awoke it was evening, and the gas-lamps were lighted. I was frightened, and ran out to the landing and I heard them arrive, just come back from Henley, and as I was going down the stairs, I saw my double coming up, and we met face to face. She passed me by, and went on to my room—to this room. So you see this is proof pos. that I am not a somnambulist."

"I never said that you were. I never for a moment admitted the supposition. That, if you remember, was your own idea. What I said before is what I repeat now, that you suffer from failure of memory."

"But that cannot be so, Dr. Groves."

"Pray, why not?"

"Because I saw my double, wearing my regatta costume."

"I hold to my opinion, Miss Mountjoy. If you will listen to

me I shall be able to offer a satisfactory explanation. Satisfactory, I mean, so far as to make your experiences intelligible to you. I do not at all imply that your condition is satisfactory."

"Well, tell me. I cannot make heads or tails of this matter."

"It is this, young lady. On several recent occasions you have suffered from lapses of memory. All recollection of what you did, where you went, what you said, has been clean wiped out. But on this last—it was somewhat different. The failure took place on your return, and you forgot everything that had happened since you were engaged in the schoolroom looking at the atlas."

"Yes."

"Then, on your arrival here, as Lady Lacy told me, you ran upstairs, and in a prodigious hurry changed your clothes and put on your———"

"My alpaca."

"Your alpaca, yes. Then, in descending to the hall, your memory came back, but was still entangled with flying reminiscences of what had taken place during the intervening period. Amongst other things———"

"I remember no other things."

"You recalled confusedly one thing only, that you had mounted the stairs in your—your———"

"My pearl-grey cloth, with the straw hat and satin ribbon."

"Precisely. Whilst in your morning gown, into which you had scrambled, you recalled yourself in your regatta costume going upstairs to change. This fragmentary reminiscence presented itself before you as a vision. Actually you saw nothing. The impression on your brain of a scrap recollected appeared to you as if it had been an actual object depicted on the retina of your eye. Such things happen, and happen not infrequently. In cases of D. T.———"

"But I haven't D. T. I don't drink."

"I do not say that. If you will allow me to proceed. In cases of D. T. the patient fancies he sees rats, devils, all sorts of objects. They appear to him as obvious realities, he thinks that he sees them with his eyes. But he does not. These are mere pictures formed on the brain."

"Then you hold that I really was at the boat-race?"

"I am positive that you were."

"And that I danced at Lady Belgrove's ball?"

"Most assuredly."

"And heard *Carmen* at Her Majesty's?"

"I have not the remotest doubt that you did."

Betty drew a long breath, and remained in consideration.

Then she said very gravely: "I want you to tell me, Dr. Groves, quite truthfully, quite frankly—do not think that I shall be frightened whatever you say; I shall merely prepare for what may be—do you consider that I am going out of my mind?"

"I have not the least occasion for supposing so."

"That," said Betty, "would be the most terrible thing of all. If I thought that, I would say right out to my aunt that I wished at once to be sent to an asylum."

"You may set your mind at rest on that score."

"But loss of memory is bad, but better than the other. Will these fits of failure come on again?"

"That is more than I can prognosticate; let us hope for the best. A complete change of scene, change of air, change of association——"

"Not to leave auntie!"

"No. I do not mean that, but to get away from London society. It may restore you to what you were. You never had those fits before?"

"Never, never, till I came to town."

"And when you have left town they may not recur."

"I shall take precious good care not to revisit London if it is going to play these tricks with me."

That day Captain Fontanel called, and was vastly concerned to hear that Betty was unwell. She was not looking herself, he said, at the boat-race. He feared that the cold on the river had been too much for her. But he did trust that he might be allowed to have a word with her before she returned to Devonshire.

Although he did not see Betty, he had an hour's conversation with Lady Lacy, and he departed with a smile on his face.

On the morrow he called again. Betty had so completely recovered that she was cheerful, and the pleasant colour had returned to her cheeks. She was in the drawing-room along with her aunt when he arrived.

The captain offered his condolences, and expressed his satisfaction that her indisposition had been so quickly got over.

"Oh!" said the girl, "I am as right as a trivet. It has all passed off. I need not have soaked in bed all yesterday, but that aunt would have it so. We are going down to our home tomorrow. Yesterday auntie was scared and thought she would have to postpone our return."

Lady Lacy rose, made the excuse that she had the packing to attend to, and left the young people alone together. When the door was shut behind her, Captain Fontanel drew his chair close to that of the girl and said—

"Betty, you do not know how happy I have felt since you accepted me. It was a hurried affair in the boat-house, but really, time was running short; as you were off so soon to Devonshire, I had to snatch at the occasion when there was no one by, so I seized old Time by the forelock, and you were so good as to say 'Yes.'"

"I—I——" stammered Betty.

"But as the thing was done in such haste, I came here today to renew my offer of myself, and to make sure of my happiness. You have had time to reflect, and I trust you do not repent."

"Oh, you are so good and kind to me!"

"Dearest Betty, what a thing to say! It is I—poor, wretched, good-for-naught—who have cause to speak such words to you. Put your hand into mine; it is a short courtship of a soldier, like that of Harry V. and the fair Maid of France. 'I love you: then if you urge me farther than to say, "Do you in faith?" I wear out my suit. Give me your answer; i' faith, do: and so clap hands and a bargain.' Am I quoting aright?"

Shyly, hesitatingly, she extended her fingers, and he clasped them. Then, shrinking back and looking down, she said: "But I ought to tell you something first, something very serious, which may make you change your mind. I do not, in conscience, feel it right that you should commit yourself till you know."

"It must be something very dreadful to make me do that."

"It is dreadful. I am apt to be terribly forgetful."

"Bless me! So am I. I have passed several of my acquaintances lately and have not recognised them, but that was because I was thinking of you. And I fear I have been very oblivious about my bills; and as to answering letters—good heavens! I am a shocking defaulter."

"I do not mean that. I have lapses of memory. Why, I do not even remember——"

He sealed her lips with a kiss. "You will not forget this, at any rate, Betty."

"Oh, Charlie, no!"

"Then consider this, Betty. Our engagement cannot be for long. I am ordered to Egypt, and I positively must take my dear little wife with me and show her the Pyramids. You would like to see them, would you not?"

"I should love to."

"And the Sphynx?"

"Indeed I should."

"And Pompey's Pillar?"

"Oh, Charlie! I shall love above everything to see you every day."

"That is prettily said. I see we understand one another. Now, hearken to me, give me your close attention, and no fits of lapse of memory over what I now say, please. We must be married very shortly. I positively will not go out without you. I would rather throw up my commission."

"But what about papa's consent?"

"I shall wire to him full particulars as to my position, income, and prospects, also how much I love you, and how I will do my level best to make you happy. That is the approved formula in addressing paterfamilias, I think. Then he will telegraph back,

'Bless you, my boy'; and all is settled. I know that Lady Lacy approves."

"But dear, dear aunt. She will be so awfully lonely without me."

"She shall not be. She has no ties to hold her to the little cottage in Devon. She shall come out to us in Cairo, and we will bury the dear old girl up to her neck in the sand of the desert, and make a second Sphynx of her, and bake the rheumatism out of her bones. It will cure her of all her aches, as sure as my name is Charlie, and yours will be Fontanel."

"Don't be too sure of that."

"But I am sure—you cannot forget."

"I will try not to do so. Oh, Charlie, don't!"

★★★★★★

Mrs. Thomas, the dressmaker, and Miss Crock, the milliner, had their hands full. Betty's trousseau had to be got ready expeditiously. Patterns of materials specially adapted for a hot climate—light, beautiful, artistic, of silks and muslins and prints—had to be commanded from Liberty's. Then came the selection, then the ordering, then the discussions with the dressmaker, and the measurings. Next the fittings, for which repeated visits had to be made to Mrs. Thomas. Adjustments, alterations were made, easements under the arms, tightenings about the waist. There were fulnesses to be taken in and skimpiness to be redressed. The skirts had to be sufficiently short in front and sufficiently long behind.

As for the wedding-dress, Mrs. Thomas was not regarded as quite competent to execute such a masterpiece. For that an expedition had to be made to Exeter.

The wedding-cake must be ordered from Murch, in the cathedral city. Lady Lacy was particular that as much as possible of the outfit should be given to county tradesmen. A riding habit, tailor-made, was ordered, to fit like a glove, and a lady's saddle must be taken out to Egypt. Boxes, basket-trunks were to be procured, and a correspondence carried on as to the amount of personal luggage allowed.

Lady Lacy and Betty were constantly running up by express to Exeter about this, that, and everything.

Then ensued the sending out of the invitations, and the arrival of wedding presents, that entailed the writing of gushing letters of acknowledgment and thanks, by Betty herself. But these were not allowed to interfere with the scribbling of four pages every day to Captain Fontanel, intended for his eyes alone.

Interviews were sought by the editors or agents of local newspapers to ascertain whether reporters were desired to describe the wedding, and as to the length of the notices that were to be inserted, whether all the names of the donors of presents were to be included, and their gifts registered. Verily Lady Lacy and Betty were kept in a whirl of excitement, and their time occupied from morning till night, and their brains exercised from night to morning. Glass and china and plate had to be hired for the occasion, wine ordered. Fruit, cake, ices commanded. But all things come to an end, even the preparations for a wedding.

At last the eventful day arrived, bright and sunny, a true May morning.

The bridesmaids arrived, each wearing the pretty brooch presented by Captain Fontanel. Their costume was suitable to the season, of primrose-yellow, with hats turned up, white, with primroses. The pages were in green velvet, with knee-breeches and three-cornered hats, lace ruffles and lace fronts. The butler had made the claret-cup and the champagne-cup, and after a skirmish over the neighbourhood some borage had been obtained to float on the top. Lady Lacy was to hold a reception after the ceremony, and a marquee had been erected in the grounds, as the cottage could not contain all the guests invited. The dining-room was delivered over for the exposing of the presents. A carriage had been commanded to convey the happy couple to the station, horses and driver with white favours. With a sigh of relief in the morning, Lady Lacy declared that she believed that nothing had been forgotten.

The trunks stood ready packed, all but one, and labelled with the name of Mrs. Fontanel.

A flag flew on the church tower. The villagers had constructed a triumphal arch at the entrance to the grounds. The people from farms and cottages had all turned out, and were already congregating about the churchyard, with smiles and heartfelt wishes for the happiness of the bride, who was a mighty favourite with them, as indeed was also Lady Lacy.

The Sunday-school children had clubbed their pence, and had presented Betty, who had taught them, with a silver set of mustard-pot, pepper caster, and salt-cellar.

"Oh, dear!" said Betty, "what shall I do with all these sets of mustard- and pepper-pots? I have now received eight."

"A little later, dear," replied her aunt, "you can exchange those that you do not require."

"But never that set given me by my Sunday-school pets," said Betty.

Then came in flights of telegrams of congratulation.

And at the last moment arrived some more wedding presents.

"Good gracious me!" exclaimed the girl, "I really must manage to acknowledge these. There will be just time before I begin to dress."

So she tripped upstairs to her *boudoir*, a little room given over to herself in which to do her water-colour painting, her reading, to practise her music. A bright little room to which now, as she felt with an ache, she was to bid an eternal goodbye!

What happy hours had been spent in it! What daydreams had been spun there!

She opened her writing-case and wrote the required letters of thanks.

"There," said she, when she had signed the fifth. "This is the last time I shall subscribe myself Elizabeth Mountjoy, except when I sign my name in the church register. Oh! how my back is hurting me. I was not in bed till two o'clock and was up again at seven, and I have been on the tear for the whole week. There will be just time for me to rest it before the business of the dressing begins."

She threw herself on the sofa and put up her feet. Instantly she was asleep—in a sound, dreamless sleep.

When Betty opened her eyes she heard the church bells ringing a merry peal. Then she raised her lids, and turning her head on the sofa cushion saw—a bride, herself in full bridal dress, with the white veil and the orange-blossoms, seated at her side. The gloves had been removed and lay on the lap.

An indescribable terror held her fast. She could not cry out. She could not stir. She could only look.

Then the bride put back the veil, and Betty, studying the white face, saw that this actually was not herself; it was her dead sister, Letice.

The apparition put forth a hand and laid it on her and spoke: "Do not be frightened. I will do you no harm. I love you too dearly for that, Betty. I have been married in your name; I have exchanged vows in your name; I have received the ring for you; put it on your finger, it is not mine; it in no way belongs to me. In your name I signed the register. You are married to Charles Fontanel and not I. Listen to me. I will tell you all, and when I have told you everything you will see me no more. I will trouble you no further; I shall enter into my rest. You will see before you only the wedding garments remaining. I shall be gone. Hearken to me. When I was dying, I died in frantic despair, because I had never known what were the pleasures of life. My last cries, my last regrets, my last longings were for the pomps and vanities."

She paused, and slipped the gold hoop on to the forefinger of Betty's hand.

Then she proceeded—

"When my spirit parted from my body, it remained a while irresolute whither to go. But then, remembering that my aunt had declared that I never would go to Heaven, I resolved on forcing my way in there out of defiance; and I soared till I reached the gates of Paradise. At them stood an angel with a fiery sword drawn in his hand, and he laid it athwart the entrance. I approached, but he waved me off, and when the point of the flaming blade touched my heart, there passed a pang through it,

I know not whether of joy or of sorrow. And he said: 'Letice, you have not been a good girl; you were sullen, resentful, rebellious, and therefore are unfit to enter here. Your longings through life, and to the moment of death, were for the world and its pomps and vanities. The last throb of your heart was given to repining for them. But your faults were due largely to the mistakes of your rearing. And now hear your judgement.

"You shall not pass within these gates till you have returned to earth and partaken of and had your fill of its pomps and vanities. As for that old cat, your aunt'—but no, Betty, he did not say quite that; I put it in, and I ought not to have done so. I bear her no resentment; I wish her no ill. She did by me what she believed to be right. She acted towards me up to her lights; alas for me that the light which was in her was darkness! The angel said: 'As for your aunt, before she can enter here, she will want illumining, enlarging, and sweetening, and will have to pass through Purgatory.' And oh, Betty, that will be gall and bitterness to her, for she did not believe in Purgatory, and she wrote a controversial pamphlet against it.

"Then said the angel: 'Return, return to the pomps and vanities.' I fell on my knees, and said: 'Oh, suffer me but to have one glimpse of that which is within!' 'Be it so,' he replied. 'One glimpse only whilst I cast my sword on high.' Thereat he threw up the flaming brand, and it was as though a glorious flash of lightning filled all space. At the same moment the gates swung apart, and I saw what was beyond. It was but for one brief moment, for the sword came down, and the angel caught it by the handle, and instantly the gates were shut. Then, sorrowfully, I turned myself about and went back to earth. And, Betty, it was I who took and read your novels. It was I who went to Lady Belgrove's ball in your place.

"It was I who sat instead of you at Her Majesty's and heard *Carmen*. It was I who took your place at Henley Regatta, and I—I, instead of you, received the protestation of Charles Fontanel's affection, and there in the boat-house I received the first and last kiss of love. And it was I, Betty, as I have told you, who

240

took your place at the altar to-day. I had the pleasures that were designed for you—the ball-dress, the dances, the fair words, the music of the opera, the courtship, the excitement of the regatta, the reading of sensational novels. It was I who had what all girls most long for, their most supreme bliss of wearing the wedding-veil and the orange-blossoms. But I have reached my limit. I am full of the pomps and vanities, and I return on high. You will see me no more."

"Oh, Letice," said Betty, obtaining her speech, "you do not grudge me the joys of life?"

The fair white being at her side shook her head.

"And you desire no more of the pomps and vanities?"

"No, Betty. I have looked through the gates."

Then Betty put forth her hands to clasp the waist of her sister, as she said fervently—

"Tell me, Letice, what you saw beyond."

"Betty—everything the reverse of Salem Chapel."

The White Flag
(A tale from *A Book of Ghosts*)

A percentage of the South African Boers—how large or how small that percentage is has not been determined—is possessed of a rudimentary conscience, much as the oyster has incipient eyes, and the snake initiatory articulations for feet, which in the course of long ages may, under suitable conditions, develop into an active faculty.

If Jacob Van Heeren possessed any conscience at all it was the merest protoplasm of one.

He occupied Heerendorp, a ramshackle farmhouse under a *kopje*, and had cattle and horses, also a wife and grown-up sons and daughters.

When the war broke out Jacob hoisted the white flag at the gable, and he and his sons indulged their sporting instincts by shooting down such officers and men of the British army as went to the farm, unsuspecting treachery.

Heerendorp by this means obtained an evil notoriety, and it was ordered to be burnt, and the women of Jacob's family to be transferred to a concentration camp where they would be mollycoddled at the expense of the English taxpayer. Thus Jacob and his sons were delivered from all anxiety as to their woman-kind, and were given a free field in which to exercise their mischievous ingenuity. As to their cattle and horses that had been commandeered, they held receipts which would entitle them to claim full value for the beasts at the termination of hostilities.

Jacob and his sons might have joined one of the companies

under a Boer general, but they preferred independent action, and their peculiar tactics, which proved eminently successful.

That achievement in which Jacob exhibited most slimness, and of which he was pre-eminently proud, was as follows: feigning himself to be wounded, he rolled on the ground, waving a white kerchief, and crying out for water. A young English lieutenant at once filled a cup and ran to his assistance, when Jacob shot him through the heart.

When the war was over Van Heeren got his farm rebuilt and restocked at the expense of the British taxpayer, and received his wife and daughters from the concentration camp, plump as partridges.

So soon as the new Heerendorp was ready for occupation, Jacob took a large knife and cut seventeen notches in the door-post.

"What is that for, Jacob?" asked his wife.

"They are reminders of the Britishers I have shot."

"Well," said she, "if I hadn't killed more Rooineks than that, I'd be ashamed of myself."

"Oh, I shot more in open fight. I didn't count them; I only reckon such as I've been slim enough to befool with the white flag," said the Boer.

Now the lieutenant whom Jacob Van Heeren had killed when bringing him a cup of cold water, was Aneurin Jones, and he was the only son of his mother, and she a widow in North Wales. On Aneurin her heart had been set, in him was all her pride. Beyond him she had no ambition. About him every fibre of her heart was entwined. Life had to her no charms apart from him. When the news of his death reached her, unaccompanied by particulars, she was smitten with a sorrow that almost reached despair. The joy was gone out of her life, the light from her sky. The prospect was a blank before her. She sank into profound despondency, and would have welcomed death as an end to an aimless, a hopeless life.

But when peace was concluded, and some comrades of Aneurin returned home, the story of how he had met his death was divulged to her.

Then the passionate Welsh mother's heart became as a live coal within her breast. An impotent rage against his murderer consumed her. She did not know the name of the man who had killed him, she but ill understood where her son had fallen. Had she known, had she been able, she would have gone out to South Africa, and have gloried in being able to stab to the heart the man who had so treacherously murdered her Aneurin. But how was he to be identified?

The fact that she was powerless to avenge his death was a torture to her. She could not sleep, she could not eat, she writhed, she moaned, she bit her fingers, she chafed at her incapacity to execute justice on the murderer. A feverish flame was lit in her hollow cheeks. Her lips became parched, her tongue dry, her dark eyes glittered as if sparks of unquenchable fire had been kindled in them.

She sat with clenched hands and set teeth before her dead grate, and the purple veins swelled and throbbed in her temples.

Oh! if only she knew the name of the man who had shot her Aneurin!

Oh! if only she could find out a way to recompense him for the wrong he had done!

These were her only thoughts. And the sole passage in her Bible she could read, and which she read over and over again, was the story of the Importunate Widow who cried to the judge, "Avenge me of mine adversary!" and who was heard for her persistent asking.

Thus passed a fortnight. She was visibly wasting in flesh, but the fire within her burned only the fiercer as her bodily strength failed.

Then, all at once, an idea shot like a meteor through her brain. She remembered to have heard of the Cursing Well of St. Elian, near Colwyn. She recalled the fact that the last "Priest of the Well," an old man who had lived hard by, and who had initiated postulants into the mysteries of the well, had been brought before the magistrates for obtaining money under false pretences, and had been sent to gaol at Chester; and that the parson of Llanelian had taken a crowbar and had ripped up the wall that enclosed the spring, and had done what lay in his power to destroy it and blot out the remembrance of the powers of the well, or to ruin its efficacy.

But the spring still flowed. Had it lost its virtues? Could a parson, could magistrates bring to naught what had been for centuries?

She remembered, further, that the granddaughter of the "Priest of the Well" was then an inmate of the workhouse at Denbigh. Was it not possible that she should know the ritual of St. Elian's spring?—should be able to assist her in the desire of her heart?

Mrs. Winifred Jones resolved on trying. She went to the workhouse and sought out the woman, an old and infirm creature, and had a conference with her. She found the woman, a poor, decrepit creature, very shy of speaking about the well, very unwilling to be drawn into a confession of the extent of her knowledge, very much afraid of the magistrates and the master of the workhouse punishing her if she had anything to do with the well; but the intensity of Mrs. Jones, her vehemence in prosecuting her inquiries, and, above all, the gift of half a sovereign pressed into her palm, with the promise of another if she assisted Mrs. Winifred in the prosecution of her purpose, finally overcame her scruples, and she told all that she knew.

"You must visit St. Elian's, madam," said she, "when the moon is at the wane. You must write the name of him whose death you desire on a pebble, and drop it into the water, and recite the sixty-ninth Psalm."

"But," objected the widow, "I do not know his name, and I have no means of discovering it. I want to kill the man who murdered my son."

The old woman considered, and then said: "In this case it is different. There is a way under these circumstances. Murdered, was your son?"

"Yes, he was treacherously shot."

"Then you will have to call on your son by name, as you let fall the pebble, and say: 'Let him be wiped out of the book of the living. Avenge me of mine adversary, O my God.' And you must go on dropping in pebbles, reciting the same prayer, till you see the water of the spring boil up black as ink. Then you will know that your prayer has been heard, and that the curse has wrought."

Winifred Jones departed in some elation.

She waited till the moon changed, and then she went to the spring. It was near a hedge; there were trees by it. Apparently it had been unsought for many years. But it still flowed. About it lay scattered a few stones that had once formed the bounds.

She looked about her. No one was by. The sun was declining, and would soon set. She bent over the water—it was perfectly clear. She had collected a lapful of rounded stones.

Then she cried out: "Aneurin! come to my aid against your murderer. Let him be blotted out of the book of the living. Avenge me on my adversary, O my God!" and she dropped a pebble into the water.

Then rose a bubble. That was all.

She paused but for a moment, then again she cried: "Aneurin! come to my aid against your murderer. Let him be blotted out of the book of the living. Avenge me on my adversary, O my God!"

Once more a pebble was let fall. It splashed into the spring, but there was no change save that ripples were sent against the side.

A third—then a fourth—she went on; the sun sent a shaft of yellow glory through the trees over the spring.

Then someone passed along the road hard by, and Mrs. Winifred Jones held her breath, and desisted till the footfall had died away.

But then she continued, stone after stone was dropped, and the ritual was followed, till the seventeenth had disappeared in the well, when up rose a column of black fluid boiling as it were from below, the colour of ink; and the widow pressed her hands together, and drew a sigh of relief; her prayer had been heard, and her curse had taken effect.

She cast away the rest of the pebbles, let down her skirt, and went away rejoicing.

★★★★★★

It so fell out that on this very evening Jacob Van Heeren had gone to bed early, as he had risen before daybreak, and had been riding all day. His family were in the outer room, when they were startled by a hoarse cry from the bedroom. He was a short-tempered, imperious man, accustomed to yell at his wife and children when he needed them; but this cry was of an unusual character, it had in it the ring of alarm. His wife went to him to inquire what was the matter. She found the old Boer sitting up in bed with one leg extended, his face like dirty stained leather, his eyes starting out of his head, and his mouth opening and shutting, lifting and depressing his shaggy, grey beard, as though he were trying to speak, but could not utter words.

"Pete!" she called to her eldest son, "come here, and see what ails your father."

Pete and others entered, and stood about the bed, staring stupidly at the old man, unable to comprehend what had come over him.

"Fetch him some brandy, Pete," said the mother; "he looks as if he had a fit."

When some spirits had been poured down his throat the farmer was revived, and said huskily: "Take it away! Quick, take it off!"

"Take what away?"

"The white flag."

"There is none here."

"It is there—there, wrapped about my foot."

The wife looked at the outstretched leg, and saw nothing. Jacob became angry, he swore at her, and yelled: "Take it off; it is chilling me to the bone."

"There is nothing there."

247

"But I say it is. I saw him come in——"

"Saw whom, father?" asked one of the sons.

"I saw that Rooinek lieutenant I shot when he was bringing me drink, thinking I was wounded. He came in through the door——"

"That is not possible—he must have passed us."

"I say he did come. I saw him, and he held the white rag, and he came upon me and gave me a twist with the flag about my foot, and there it is—it numbs me. I cannot move it. Quick, quick, take it away."

"I repeat there is nothing there," said his wife.

"Pull off his stocking," said Pete Van Heeren; "he has got a chill in his foot, and fancies this nonsense. He has been dreaming."

"It was not a dream," roared Jacob; "I saw him as clearly as I see you, and he wrapped my foot up in that accursed flag."

"Accursed flag!" exclaimed Samuel, the second son. "That's a fine way to speak of it, father, when it served you so well."

"Take it off, you dogs!" yelled the old man, "and don't stand staring and barking round me."

The stocking was removed from his leg, and then it was seen that his foot—the left foot—had turned a livid white.

"Go and heat a brick," said the housewife to one of her daughters; "it is just the circulation has stopped."

But no artificial warmth served to restore the flow of blood, and the natural heat.

Jacob passed a sleepless night.

Next morning he rose, but limped; all feeling had gone out of the foot. His wife vainly urged him to keep to his bed. He was obstinate, and would get up; but he could not walk without the help of a stick. When clothed, he hobbled into the kitchen and put the numbed foot to the fire, and the stocking sole began to smoke, it was singed and went to pieces, but his foot was insensible to the heat. Then he went forth, aided by the stick, to his farmyard, hoping that movement would restore feeling and warmth; but this also was in vain. In the evening he seated himself on a bench outside the door, whilst his family ate supper. He ordered them to bring food to him. He felt easier in the open air than within doors.

Whilst his wife and children were about the table at their meal, they heard a scream without, more like that of a wounded horse than a man, and all rushed forth, to find Jacob in a paroxysm of terror only less severe than that of the preceding night.

"He came on me again," he gasped; "the same man, I do not know from whence—he seemed to spring out of the distance. I saw him first like smoke, but with a white flicker in it; and then he got nearer and became more distinct, and I knew it was he; and he had another of those white napkins in his hand. I could not call for help—I tried, I could utter no sound, till he wrapped it—that white rag—round my calf, and then, with the cold and pain, I cried out, and he vanished."

"Father," said Pete, "you fell asleep and dreamt this."

"I did not. I saw him, and I felt what he did. Give me your hand. I cannot rise. I must go within. Good Lord, when will this come to an end?"

When lifted from his seat it was seen that his left leg dragged. He had to lean heavily on his son on one side and his wife on the other, and he allowed himself, without remonstrance, to be put to bed.

It was then seen that the dead whiteness, as of a corpse, had spread from the foot up the calf.

"He is going to have a paralytic stroke, that is it," said Pete. "You, Samuel, must ride for a doctor tomorrow morning, not that he can do much good, if what I think be the case."

On the second day the old man persisted in his determination to rise. He was deaf to all remonstrance, he would get up and go about, as far as he was able. But his ability was small. In the evening, as the sun went down, he was sitting crouched over the fire. The family had finished supper, and all had left the room except his wife, who was removing the dishes, when she heard a gasping and struggling by the fire, and, turning her head, saw her husband writhing on his stool, clinging to it with his hands, with his left leg out, his mouth foaming, and he was snorting with terror or pain.

She ran to him at once.

"Jacob, what is it?"

"He is at me again! Beat him off with the broom!" he screamed. "Keep him away. He is wrapping the white flag round my knee."

Pete and the others ran in, and raised their father, who was falling out of his seat, and conveyed him to bed.

It was now seen that his knee had become hard and stiff, his calf was as if frozen; the whiteness had extended upwards to the knee.

Next day a surgeon arrived. He examined the old man, and expressed his conviction that he had a stroke. But it was a paralytic attack of an unusual character, as it had in no way affected his speech or his left arm and hand. He recommended hot fomentations.

Still the farmer would not be confined to bed; he insisted on being dressed and assisted into the kitchen.

One stick was not now sufficient for him, and Samuel contrived for him crutches. With these he could drag himself about, and on the fourth evening he laboriously worked his way to a cowstall to look at one of his beasts that was ill.

Whilst there he had a fourth attack. Pete, who was without, heard him yell and beat at the door with one of his crutches. He entered, and found his father lying on the floor, quivering with terror, and spluttering unintelligible words. He lifted him, and drew him without, then shouted to Samuel, who came up, and together they carried him to the house.

Only when there, and when he had drunk some brandy, was he able to give an account of what had taken place. He had been looking at the cow, and feeling it, when down out of the hayloft had come leaping the form of the Rooinek lieutenant, which had sprung in between him and the cow, and, stooping, had wrapped a white rag round his thigh, above the knee. And now the whole of his leg was dead and livid.

"There is nothing for it, father, but to have your leg amputated," said Pete. "The doctor told me as much. He said that mortification would set in if there was no return of circulation."

"I won't have it off! What good shall I be with only one leg?" exclaimed the old man.

"But father, it will be the sole means of saving your life."

"I won't have my leg off!" again repeated Jacob.

Pete said in a low tone to his mother: "Have you seen any dark spots on his leg? The doctor said we must look for them, and, when they come, send for him at once."

"No," she replied, "I have not noticed any, so far."

"Then we will wait till they appear."

On the fifth day the farmer was constrained to keep his bed.

He had now become a prey to abject terror. So sure as the hour of sunset came, did a new visitation occur. He listened for the clock to sound each hour of the day, and as the afternoon drew on he dreaded with unspeakable horror the advent of the moment when again the apparition would be seen, and a fresh chill be inflicted. He insisted that his wife or Pete should remain in the room with him. They took it in turns to sit by his bedside.

Through the little window the fire of the setting sun smote in and fell across the suffering man.

It was his wife's turn to be in attendance.

All at once a gurgling sound broke from his throat. His eyes started from his face, his hair bristled, and with his hands he worked himself into a sitting posture, and he heaved himself on to his pillow, and would have broken his way through the backboard of his bed, could he have done so.

"What is it, Jacob?" asked his wife, throwing down the garment which she was mending, and coming to his assistance. "Lie down again. There is nothing here."

He could not speak. His teeth were chattering, and his beard shaking, foam-bubbles formed on his lips, and great sweatdrops on his brow.

"Pete! Samuel!" she called, "come to your father."

The young men ran in, and they forcibly laid the old Boer in bed, prostrate.

And now it was found that the right foot had turned dead, like the left.

★★★★★★

On the evening of the seventeenth day after the visit to the well of Llanelian, Mrs. Winifred Jones was sitting on the side of her bed in the twilight. She had lighted no candle. She was musing, always on the same engrossing topic, the wrong that had been done to her and her son, and thirsting with a feverish thirst for vengeance on the wrongdoer.

Her confidence in the expedient to which she had resorted was beginning to fail. What was this recourse to the well but a falling in with an old superstition that had died out with the advance of knowledge, and under the influence of a wholesome feeling? Was any trust to be placed in that woman at the workhouse? Was she deceiving her for the sake of the half-sovereign? And yet—she had seen a token that her prayer would prove efficacious. There had risen through the crystal water a column of black fluid.

Could it be that a widow's prayer should meet with no response? Was wrong to prevail in the world? Were the weak and oppressed to have no means of procuring the execution of justice on the evildoers? Was not God righteous in all His ways? Would it be righteous in Him to suffer the murderer of her son to thrive? If God be merciful, He is also just. If His ear is open to the prayer for help, He must as well listen to the cry for vengeance.

Since that evening at the spring she had been unable to pray as usual, to pray for herself—her only cry had been: "Avenge me on my adversary!" If she tried to frame the words of the Lord's Prayer, she could not do so. They escaped her; her thoughts travelled to the South African veldt. Her soul could not rise to God in the ecstasy of love and devotion; it was choked with hate—an overwhelming hate.

She was in her black weeds; the hands, thin and white, were

on her lap, nervously clasping and unclasping the fingers. Had anyone been there, in the grey twilight of a summer night, he would have been saddened to see how hard and lined the face had become, how all softness had passed from the lips, how sunken were the eyes, in which was only a glitter of wrath.

Suddenly she saw standing before her, indistinct indeed, but unmistakable, the form of her lost son, her Aneurin, and he held a white napkin in his right hand, and this napkin emitted a phosphorescent glow.

She tried to cry out; to utter the beloved name; she tried to spring to her feet and throw herself into his arms! But she was unable to stir hand, or foot, or tongue. She was as one paralysed, but her heart bounded within her bosom.

"Mother," said the apparition, in a voice that seemed to come from a vast distance, yet was articulate and audible—"Mother, you called me back from the world of spirits, and sent me to discharge a task. I have done it. I have touched him on the foot and calf and knee and thigh, on hand and elbow and shoulder, on one side and on the other, on his head, and lastly on his heart, with the white flag—and now he is dead. I did it in all sixteen times, and with the sixteenth he died. I chilled him piecemeal with the white flag; the sixteenth was laid on his heart, and that stopped beating."

Then she lifted her hands slightly, and her stiffened tongue relaxed so far that she was able to murmur: "God be thanked!"

"Mother," continued the apparition, "there is a seventeenth remaining."

She tried to clasp her hands on her lap, but the fingers were no longer under her control; they had fallen to the side of the chair-bed, and hung there lifeless. Her eyes stared wildly at the spectre of her son, but without love in them; love had faded out of her heart, and given place to hate of his murderer.

"Mother," proceeded the vision, "you summoned me, and even in the world of spirits the soul of a child must respond to the cry of a mother, and I have been permitted to come back and to do your will. And now I am suffered to reveal something to you: to show you what my life would have been had it not been cut short by the shot of the Boer."

He stepped towards her, and put forth a vaporous hand and touched her eyes. She felt as though a feather had been passed over them. Then he raised the luminous sheet and shook it. Instantly all about her was changed.

Mrs. Winifred Jones was not in her little Welsh cottage; nor was it night. She was no longer alone. She stood in a court, in full daylight. She saw before her the judge on his seat, the barristers in wig and gown, the press reporters with their notebooks and pens, a dense crowd thronging every portion of the court. And she knew instinctively, before a word was spoken, without an intimation from the spirit of her son, that she was standing in the Divorce Court. And she saw there as co-respondent her son, older, changed in face, but more altered in expression. And she heard a tale unfolded—full of dishonour, and rousing disgust.

She was now able to raise her hands—she covered her ears; her face, crimson with shame, sank on her bosom. She could endure the sight, the words spoken, the revelations made, no longer, and she cried out: "Aneurin! Aneurin! for the Lord's sake, no more of this! Oh, the day, the day, that I have seen you standing here."

At once all passed; and she was again in her bedroom in Honeysuckle Cottage, North Wales, seated with folded hands on her lap, and looking before her wonderingly at the ghostly form of her son.

"Is that enough, mother?"

She lifted her hands deprecatingly.

Again he shook the glimmering white sheet, and it was as though drops of pearly fire fell out of it.

And again—all was changed.

She found herself at Monte Carlo; she knew it instinctively. She was in the great saloon, where were the gaming-tables. The electric lights glittered, and the decorations were superb. But all her attention was engrossed on her son, whom she saw at one of the tables, staking his last *napoleon.*

It was indeed her own Aneurin, but with a face on which vice and its consequent degradation were written indelibly.

He lost, and turned away, and left the hall and its lights. His mother followed him. He went forth into the gardens. The full moon was shining, and the gravel of the terraces was white as snow. The air was fragrant with the scent of oranges and myrtles. The palms cast black shadows on the soil. The sea lay still as if asleep, with a gleam over it from the moon.

Mrs. Winifred Jones tracked her son, as he stole in and out among the shrubs, amid the trees, with a sickening fear at her heart. Then she saw him pause by some oleanders, and draw a revolver from his pocket and place it at his ear. She uttered a cry of agony and horror, and tried to spring forward to dash the weapon from his hand.

Then all changed.

She was again in her little room in the dusk, and the shadowy form of Aneurin was before her.

"Mother," said the spirit, "I have been permitted to come to you and to show to you what would have been my career if I had not died whilst young, and fresh, and innocent. You have to thank Jacob Van Heeren that he saved me from such a life of infamy, and such an evil death by my own hand. You should thank, and not curse him." She was breathing heavily. Her heart beat so fast that her brain span; she fell on her knees.

"Mother," the apparition continued, "there were seventeen pebbles cast into the well."

"Yes, Aneurin," she whispered.

"And there is a seventeenth white flag. With the sixteenth Jacob Van Heeren died. The seventeenth is reserved for you."

"Aneurin! I am not fit to die."

"Mother, it must be, I must lay the white flag over your head."

"Oh! my son, my son!"

"It is so ordained," he proceeded; "but there are Love and Mercy on high, and you shall not be veiled with it till you have made your peace. You have sinned. You have thrust yourself into the council-chamber of God. You have claimed to exercise vengeance yourself, and not left it to Him to whom vengeance in right belongs."

"I know it now," breathed the widow.

"And now you must atone for the curses by prayers. You have brought Jacob Van Heeren to his death by your imprecations, and now, fold your hands and pray to God for him—for him, your son's murderer. Little have you considered that his acts were due to ignorance, resentment for what he fancied were wrongs, and to having been reared in a mutilated and debased form of Christianity. Pray for him, that God may pardon his many and great transgressions, his falsehood, his treachery, his self-righteousness. You who have been so greatly wronged are the right person to forgive and to pray for his soul. In no other way can you so fully show that your heart is turned from wrath to love. *Forgive us our trespasses as we forgive them that trespass against us.*"

She breathed a "Yes."

Then she clasped her hands. She was already on her knees, and she prayed first the great Exemplar's prayer, and then particularly for the man who had wrecked her life, with all its hopes.

And as she prayed the lines in her face softened, and the lips lost their hardness, and the fierce light passed utterly away from her eyes, in which the lamp of Charity was once more lighted, and the tears formed and rolled down her cheeks.

And still she prayed on, bathed in the pearly light from the summer sky at night. Without, in the firmament, twinkled a star; and a night-bird began to sing.

"And now, mother, pray for yourself."

Then she crossed her hands over her bosom, and bowed her head, full of self-reproach and shame; and as she prayed, the spirit of her son raised the White Flag above her and let it sail down softly, lightly over the loved head, and as it descended there fell from it as it were a dew of pale fire, and it rested on her head, and fell about her, and she sank forward with her face upon the floor. R.I.P.

The Fireman

There are certain men employed in iron-furnaces to work up the molten iron before it is run into moulds—these are called riddlers; they have huge rakes and spuds, which they strike into the smelted ore and work about, till all the earthy particles and those other things existing in hammered, but never found in cast iron, and the nature of which we hardly understand, are utterly burnt out. This life of the metal appears in keen scintillations on the surface, and, as soon as they are no longer visible, but the glowing matter preserves its uniform glare of ruddy white, the iron is considered quite dead, and fit to be run into moulds.

Now, in order that a man may be a good workman, he must become part and portion of his work, and fruit of his toil must, in like manner, become so intimately united to its artificer, that in it he should really, and not metaphorically, live.

The sculptor casts his own spirit into his carving; so that, when the framer of the statue is dead as to his body, as to his soul he lives partly in Paradise, and that part of him which he has cast into the image exists therein still; so that for centuries the artist may still do good works, when his pious handicraft excites holy aspirations in others, and thus may reap the benefit of them; he cannot be accounted dead till his handiwork is utterly destroyed.

So also with the poet, whose soul is, in part, communicated to his writings, so as to live and move, and have its being in other men's hearts, for many generations; and for every great and heroic act to which his words may impel them, he will reap his reward. Thus, alas! also, with the evil man of genius, whose soul, once imparted to his work, must remain fettered to it, till it has wrought out its full harvest of evil, when it will return loaded with those ghastly tare bundles to consume its reunited self.

The iron-workers are not quite ignorant on this score, but believe that their hopes of Salvation lie in the metal they work; and the hammered iron they find bend lithely to their will, but the molten iron to be dull and lifeless; so they have obtained a strange faith concerning the metal, which I propose illustrating.

There were many puddlers engaged upon a vast mast of ore, in a certain smelting furnace. You must know that none but the strongest and brawniest men can be employed on this work, for the fire eats into their bones and destroys them in a very few years, unless they are exceedingly powerful and healthy.

Peter Lundy was the largest made and most muscular man at the furnace, and he worked the glowing iron with gigantic force. His breast and arms were covered with dense black hair, and most of his features were similarly concealed; where they did show, they were coppered by the heat.

"Peter!" said another puddler, leaning half exhausted on his spud, "there goes a bright hope for you"; and he pointed to a vivid spark, burning in the wave of iron which Lundy was driving before his rake.

"I don't understand what you mean, Bill," said Peter, "you're ever a-calling them sparks our hopes."

"And so they be," retorted the other. "Don't you know that an iron founder's hopes of Salvation lie in hard metal, and that they leave it when he puddles molten. Every spark a man brings up in that fiery ore is some grace-hour to him; an idle work-man produces few; but some puddlers may toil all day, and not another will come after that, however much they stir the iron."

"I never heard that afore," said Peter.

"I s'pose you never learnt your Catechism," replied Bill.

"Can't say as ever I did," growled Lundy.

"I have, though," remarked a third labourer; "but never noth-ing about the hopes being in the sparks. That ain't in the Catechism nowhere."

"Then it ought to be," retorted Bill sententiously.

"I have a-heard," observed Jonas Black, an old master-man, "that there have been puddlers who've come by them sparkles in ungodly ways, and made money by them; they caught or raked them in afore they went out, and sold them for a mint of money. I can't say as how I have ever tried to get them like that, myself; for the Lord will order them if we let them alone; and I never thought of turning them into money. God forbid that a man should get rid of his hopes of Salvation that way."

"It ain't possible," said Bill; "I have tried often to draw them sparks up, and they have always gone out before they reached the edge."

That evening, Peter Lundy walked back gloomily to his hovel.

"It ain't much *I* care for my hopes of Salvation," said he to himself. "If I could only get hold of those sparkles in the iron, I'd soon swap them for a few shillings."

Peter had a son about twelve years old and a baby-daughter. The wife had died on giving birth to the little girl, so George was left ever at home to look after the child. Peter's was a miserable hut, consisting of a single dirty room lighted by a window half patched with rags and wisps of straw. At the door stood the boy to greet his father. "There's a stranger within, father," said the lad, "he's asked for a lodging here the night, when he found there was no public-house nearer than the next village; he promises to pay well." Peter pushed George aside and stepped in. An elderly man in a dark brown cloak sat on the crazy chair by the fire, and warmed his thin hands over the cinders. Peter saluted him with a slouch of the head; the stranger rose and apologised for his intrusion, repeating his request for a night's lodging.

"There's only one bed," said Lundy, "and that's at your honour's service; but we are very poor people, and haven't got good accommodation for gentlefolk."

"That does not matter," answered the elderly man; "but master, can you not give me a little more fire, I am shivering with cold?"

"George, shove on some peat and a few lumps of coke," called the puddler.

The traveller crouched over the fire, and said no more. In an hour or two he went to bed, and Peter and his children lay down on straw in a corner. The puddler did not sleep, his eyes watched the stranger by the firelight. The elderly man fidgeted about till he had disposed a packet and large purse under his pillow, and then, till he fell asleep, continually passed his hand under the bolster to assure himself of its safety. Peter soon came to the determination of robbing him and escaping with the money; as for his children, they might go to the workhouse.

Accordingly, as soon as he was convinced of the soundness of the traveller's sleep, he rose from his straw bed and stole on tiptoe across the room. The stranger breathed heavily in sleep, and Peter cautiously slipped his hand beneath the pillow to the purse. In doing so, he moved the old man's head so as partially to awaken him the eyes opened and looked into Peter's face. Instantly the puddler grasped the man's throat and pressed his fingers tightly together while he dragged the package and purse from under the bolster with the other hand. The traveller did not struggle, but by the firelight Peter saw the old cheeks creased into a horrible laugh.

"Ah, ah! Peter Lundy!" said the man without inconvenience from the gripe at his throat: "so you think to get that, do you?" The founder was startled, and dropped his arm. "The truth is, Peter," continued the stranger, "I want to have a little talk with you; pray be seated; there drag over the rickety chair." The elderly man drew his legs out of bed, and sat at his side, smiling benignantly at the terrified host. "Now give me back that parcel and purse," said the mysterious traveller. Peter mechanically obeyed. "To be candid with you," said the gentleman, "I am a bit of a naturalist, and I am in search of some curious crystals of bi-carburet of iron combined with sulphurets of alumina and cadmium. These are only to be procured when iron is at a very high temperature in fact molten. The crystals I allude to, are easily to be recognised, from their intense brightness, but they are difficult to be procured."

"Impossible," said Peter.

"I would willingly give £20 for each specimen, and for a very perfect one, we should not quarrel about the price, Peter."

"I cannot get them," growled the puddler, half frightened, half curious—"impossible."

"No! not impossible to a resolute heart, my friend," pursued the naturalist undoing his parcel; "I have here a carefully prepared ointment, which I shall be glad to present to you. You would not mind stepping into the molten iron, would you Peter?"

"Stepping in!" gasped the ironworker. "It would be instant death; I should be burned up like a wisp of straw."

"Not a bit, not a bit!" answered the elderly man with animation. "As I said before, a bold heart is all that is wanted; this little box of salve will preserve you from the fire. You must smear it over your body, and then you may with partial impunity wade through the fiery masses. Will you try?"

"I will," answered Peter after a pause.

"There is one thing to be considered by you in the first place one thing I am bound to tell you; every time you enter the melted iron your life will be shortened by a day or so, for the ointment cannot overcome the effects of the burnt air you must inhale, so that perhaps your life will be docked of a year or two; but those years which remain you will pass in affluence instead of dire poverty. Are you content?"

"Quite," replied Peter Lundy. "Two years of wealth are worth a dozen in this filthy hut."

"I have yet another remark to make: the ointment cannot preserve you from the full agony of entering the fire, each time you wade in the iron, you will feel the same anguish as if you were being consumed in it."

"Give me the stuff," said the puddler firmly.

"Here it is then, Peter," the stranger said, extending a tin box. "Take it and smear your body with it as high as your waist; it has no power to preserve the upper part of your body, so do not use it higher than your waist. You will find, Peter, that you cannot well sink in the liquid iron as deep as your middle, so you must provide yourself with stone shoes. Have an iron ladle in your hand, so as to catch the sparkles as they appear, but do not dip your hand in, or it will be charred to a cinder; the ointment remember, will only preserve the lower part of your body."

"How shall I find you, to give you the sparkles when I have got them?" asked the iron-founder.

"That can be easily managed, my dear friend," replied the stranger: "I shall call here the first Monday after every new moon, and purchase your spoils."

"Just tell me," said Lundy, "do I give up a Hope of Salvation with each spark I sell?"

The elderly naturalist drew his legs into the bed again, laughed quietly, and said, "You do not stick at such trifles as that, do you, Peter? Now suppose you leave me to take a quiet nap."

Next morning, when Peter awoke, the stranger was gone, but I here lay on the rickety chair the full purse and the tin box containing the precious unguent. A pair of stone shoes was placed by the bedside.

It was very early still, and Peter determined on trying his luck at the furnace at once. He took an old ladle with him, slipped out of the door without awaking his son or the babe, and was soon at the foundry. No one had arrived as yet, but the iron was melted, fires having been kept up during the night, so that the ore might be ready for the puddlers. The top of the colander, like the mouth of a kiln, was open, and the fused mass glared up, the brick rim being at white heat also.

Peter dressed his foot with the salve, and crept cautiously to the edge. The heat well-nigh overpowered him, but timidly he dipped in his foot. The white mass was of the consistency of honey, and closed over his instep. The agony of that tire smoked through every limb to his heart. He drew his foot hastily back. It was unconsumed, but red, as though it had been plunged into boiling water. Lundy now applied the ointment to the entire lower part of his body, drew on the stone shoes, shuddered for one instant on the verge, and then stepped in. He sunk at once to his middle; he writhed with torture; every fibre of his frame seemed at that moment torn and snapped; his hands slapped convulsively together; the blood burst out from his eyes, ears, and nose, and the drops hissed and danced in globules on the fiery surface. Little by little, as the first pangs passed off, Peter regained his sight and mental powers; then he took the ladle from the margin where he had left it, and waded further into the consuming heat. The hair on his arms and breast frizzled in the fiery breath.

Lo! one bright spark kindled before him, the ladle was plunged beneath it instantly, and the scoop rose red-hot from the fluid, but the sparkle blazed in it. Peter struggled to the verge, scrambled out, filing aside the vitrified shoes, and rolled moaning and weeping on the cool stones.

When his pains had somewhat abated, he drew his clothes over his scarlet limbs, and when the sparkle had sufficiently cooled, examined the blood-red crystal half sunk in black ore.

Shortly after, the other puddlers came to work, and Lundy set himself to his daily task, without the vigour he usually displayed, for the heat had eaten into his marrow and sinews, and the prospect of payment for his morning's work withdrew his thoughts from present business. Only, as each spark, burned white in the furnace when he stirred the iron with his spud, he cast an eager glance at it, and, but for the presence of his companions, would have plunged in again.

Next time that iron was being smelted, Peter ventured once more, and obtained two or three small crystals, which he treasured along with the first, in a cupboard at home. Lundy's skin had been copper-hued before, now it assumed a fierce red tinge, and his black beard and whiskers were singed to the roots. His eyes began to suffer and became blood-shot, brows and lashes were burnt off, and he only preserved the hair of his head by wearing a broad felt hat, which browned after the first exposure to the fire, and fell to pieces like tinder after the second. The pain never abated, so that every time Peter entered the molten iron the same crushing agony obliterated for the moment senses and reason; but his powers of endurance increased, so that, after having made several trials, he was able to support for ten minutes the all but overwhelming torture.

On the first Monday after the new moon, late at night, the stranger tapped at the window, and Peter sold him the crystals he had obtained.

"You bare up bravely, master," said the naturalist; "I do not mind paying double for that very line specimen you will soon be a rich man, that you will, Peter!"

"How many shall you want?" asked Lundy.

"These are great rarities: I can afford to purchase all you can bring me, friend," answered the stranger. "But I warn you, you will not be able to find them forever, there is not an endless store of them. Every puddler has a certain number, and they must be worked out, sooner or later. Better not waste them by useless puddling."

"What had I better do?" asked Peter.

"I should recommend you to buy a share in the foundry, and not to stir the iron yourself; the sparks rise and vanish then without being made into profitable investments. But if you husband your opportunities, and only venture into the fluid iron whenever you want to obtain one of the crystals—why, then—they may last."

At midnight the elderly man withdrew, and Peter within a few days, followed his advice, and was soon considered as a well-to-do iron-master. Whence his money had come— no one could guess.

The old hovel had been abandoned, and a small brick house was now inhabited by the iron-factor and his children. George Lundy was no model boy. Coarse and rough as his father, and endowed with much of his shrewdness, he had, moreover, some conscience and knowledge of right and wrong; his natural inquisitiveness led him soon to the conclusion that all was not right with his father, and that there was sufficient in his conduct to excite his curiosity. Peter's frequent visit to the old cupboard, which had been removed from the hovel, made George determine to examine its contents.

This he was enabled to do by means of a key fitting the lock, which he found about the house, and he was surprised to discover nothing but a heap of ore containing orange prisms, piled in a corner. George stilled his curiosity for some days, fearing to provoke an outburst of his lather's anger, by enquiring into the use of those crystals, and Peter's temper had of late grown fiery, and a dangerous matter wherewith to tamper: with a word he would blaze forth into excesses of rage, so that the workmen at the furnace shrank with terror from him.

Formerly he had been known as a deep-drinker, and his son had often seen him return reeling home; now, he never touched fermented liquor, but panted for water, the chilliest that could be procured; this he drank continually, and, of an evening, he would hurry to the shallow brook flowing through the vale, and lie for an hour or two in the stream.

His skin was hot beyond feverishness, snow dissolved instantly in his hand, and, after he had once breathed on a fuchsia George kept in the window, the plant shrivelled up and died. George was determined to get at the bottom of all the mysteries connected with his father; and one evening asked him, point blank, what was the use of those saffron crystals in the cupboard?

Peter's fiery eyes glared ominously, and his face became of a lurid scarlet, but he subdued his rising fury and asked:

"How know you anything about them sparkles, I'd like to know?"

"I saw 'em in the cupboard, father," said George. "So tell us what they be for."

"Yes, I will," answered Peter. "I've been thinking for a long while as how I had better have two to work money-making than only one."

"Are them things precious stones?" asked the boy.

"They be," replied Peter; "they's worth ten to twenty pounds a-piece, and I'll sell them at that price, come Monday next."

"Where do you get 'em?" George enquired.

"Out of the melted iron," answered the puddler; "I go in after 'em."

George whistled.

"Ay, ay! you mayn't go for to believe me," said the puddler, angrily; "but I'll do so afore your very eyes."

"How is it you don't get burned up, father?"

"Why, I've a chemical stuff with which I grease myself, and that saves me; but it is awful torment in that fire!"

George looked incredulous, but dared not utter his doubts, lest his father should break forth into a paroxysm of rage.

"There's a Hope of Salvation goes with every sparkle," continued Peter Lundy. "But, dash me, if I care, so long as it can be turned into money."

"God forbid!" exclaimed George—for he had a conscience.

"I intend you, George, to help me in getting those affairs: you are young, and will have more. I have nearly gathered in and sold all mine; they do not appear as bright, or so often as they used to; and I have been into that sweltering heat twice or thrice, and got nothing out, after all."

"I won't go, father," said George, resolutely.

"You won't! then I'll throw you in alive, you young—"

George escaped through the door, as his father slung one of his stone shoes savagely after him.

On the following day, Peter went in before his son's eyes; however much he stirred the metal, no spark appeared, and he was obliged to step out after a fruitless ten minutes of death-agony.

George had stood numbed with horror; at first he had endeavoured to make his father desist, but vainly. Then followed the wild writhing in the fire, then the settled agony on his father's countenance, as he moved about stirring the scum, his features kindled by the upward glare.

When he stepped out, and scaled from his limbs the flakes of dross which adhered, George feared to approach him; but Peter, with a wild laugh, shouted.

"Well lad! has't pluck enough to do as I have done? My grace-hours are numbered, seest thou? I could get no crystal today?"

George shook his head resolutely.

"Ah, well, well!" exclaimed the puddler, "after a little while it will not frighten you. Faix! it tried me a bit, to step in the first time!"

When George was next left alone in the cottage, he opened the chest, took away several of the specimens, and hurrying to the foundry, flung them into the iron.

As the first Monday after the new moon arrived, Peter waited impatiently for the arrival of the stranger. George, who also expected him, was on the alert as well.

At eleven, precisely, there was a tap at the window; and, on opening it, the elderly gentleman was visible in the starlight, dressed in his long brown cloak.

"You are rather short of the usual number," complained he, counting the crystals in his hand. "How comes that, Peter?"

"Well, I don't know," replied the founder; "but they are getting scarce now. I want my son George to take to the profession, but he hasn't a fancy that way."

"Well, Peter," said the naturalist, "I looked in at the foundry on my way—"

"It is locked up!" interrupted Peter.

"Nevertheless, I managed to see in as much as was requisite. It struck me that the metal was in a prime state; can you not come with me, and see if your luck, this night, will not be better? I particularly want a fine specimen, and these you have given me are so small. Come! suppose you make a trial this night."

"Well, I do not mind. George, lad! come with us; you must learn the trade."

The boy followed.

Without, the stars shone clear from a deep frosty sky to earth, and no air stirred the pensive boughs of beech; rime lay on the long bending grass: far off trilled a frog from a swamp, it was a goodly autumn night.

Lundy unlocked the silent foundry; the fires below were tended by a man all night; but the upper portion, containing the exposed metal, was kept locked.

Peter divested himself of his clothing, anointed himself as high as the waist, drew a felt cap over his head, placed his feet in the stone shoes, and took up his ladle; then he cautiously stepped into the fused iron.

George turned aside his head; but he could not stop his ears to the moans and gasps of his father. When he looked again, Peter was moving through the fire.

The stranger uttered a shout of joy. In the centre of the vat burned brightly a starry spark whiter and keener than any Peter had seen before, forward, vehemently, he waded, his ladle brandished in his right hand.

"Peter!" shouted the stranger. "Twenty pounds for that!"

"Father! dear father!" cried George, moved by a sudden impulse, "leave that one— that only one!"

"Thirty pounds for that sparkle!" yelled the elderly man, rushing frantically along the verge.

"Father, father! do y' leave it!" cried the boy once more.

"Come, Peter! I will give you fifty for it. I tell you this: that one spark is your *last* chance; you never can have one more."

Lundy redoubled his efforts to move through the treacly mass. George grasped a long-handled rake, ran forward, dashed it towards the white star, and began to drag it from his father's reach. Peter yelled forth a horrible curse.

"Get it, get it!" roared the stranger, stamping, and dashing his arms about, and running upon the white-hot bricks.

George, almost beat down by the blast of fire, dragged on still.

The puddler ploughed desperately after it. his head was reeling in that sweltering lire breath, which brought tears from the hot eyes, but dried them up on the cheeks. His ladle dropped from his fingers, was black only for a moment, and then white as the bed on which it lay.

George fell, exhausted, dragging the rake towards the edge, and the spark along with it.

Peter Lundy bent forwards.

"Catch it, man! catch it!" hallooed the stranger.

Peter dashed his hands into the metal—and fell forwards.

George caught one glimpse of a charred mass lifting itself and falling again heard the sound as it burned and he dashed through the door, and staggered to faint upon a bank of ragged-robin and bird's-eye speedwell.

The workmen, when, on the following morning they came to the foundry, saw the lower part of a man floating on the surface of the fire-vat, red, and unconsumed: but of the upper portion, there remained but some thin white dust, which, when collected, their breath blew away.

Aunt Joanna

(A tale from *A Book of Ghosts*)

In the Land's End district is the little church-town of Zennor. There is no village to speak of—a few scattered farms, and here and there a cluster of cottages. The district is bleak, the soil does not lie deep over granite that peers through the surface on exposed spots, where the furious gales from the ocean sweep the land. If trees ever existed there, they have been swept away by the blast, but the golden furze or gorse defies all winds, and clothes the moorland with a robe of splendour, and the heather flushes the slopes with crimson towards the decline of summer, and mantles them in soft, warm brown in winter, like the fur of an animal.

In Zennor is a little church, built of granite, rude and simple of construction, crouching low, to avoid the gales, but with a tower that has defied the winds and the lashing rains, because wholly devoid of sculptured detail, which would have afforded the blasts something to lay hold of and eat away. In Zennor parish is one of the finest cromlechs in Cornwall, a huge slab of unwrought stone like a table, poised on the points of standing upright blocks as rude as the mass they sustain.

Near this monument of a hoar and indeed unknown antiquity lived an old woman by herself, in a small cottage of one story in height, built of moor stones set in earth, and pointed only with lime. It was thatched with heather, and possessed but a single chimney that rose but little above the apex of the roof, and had two slates set on the top to protect the rising smoke from being blown down the chimney into the cottage when the wind was from the west or from the east. When, however, it drove from north or south, then the smoke must take care of itself. On such occasions it was wont to find its way out of the door, and little or none went up the chimney.

The only fuel burnt in this cottage was peat—not the solid black peat from deep bogs, but turf of only a spade graft, taken from the surface, and composed of undissolved roots. Such fuel gives flame, which the other does not; but, on the other hand, it does not throw out the same amount of heat, nor does it last one half the time.

The woman who lived in the cottage was called by the people of the neighbourhood Aunt Joanna. What her family name was but few remembered, nor did it concern herself much. She had no relations at all, with the exception of a grand-niece, who was married to a small tradesman, a wheelwright near the church. But Joanna and her great-niece were not on speaking terms. The girl had mortally offended the old woman by going to a dance at St. Ives, against her express orders. It was at this dance that she had met the wheelwright, and this meeting, and the treatment the girl had met with from her aunt for having gone to it, had led to the marriage. For Aunt Joanna was very strict in her Wesleyanism, and bitterly hostile to all such carnal amusements as dancing and play-acting.

Of the latter there was none in that wild west Cornish district, and no temptation ever afforded by a strolling company setting up its booth within reach of Zennor. But dancing, though denounced, still drew the more independent spirits together. Rose Penaluna had been with her great-aunt after her mother's death. She was a lively girl, and when she heard of a dance at St. Ives, and had been asked to go to it, although forbidden by Aunt Joanna, she stole from the cottage at night, and found her way to St. Ives.

Her conduct was reprehensible certainly. But that of Aunt Joanna was even more so, for when she discovered that the girl had left the house she barred her door, and refused to allow

Rose to re-enter it. The poor girl had been obliged to take refuge the same night at the nearest farm and sleep in an outhouse, and next morning to go into St. Ives and entreat an acquaintance to take her in till she could enter into service. Into service she did not go, for when Abraham Hext, the carpenter, heard how she had been treated, he at once proposed, and in three weeks married her. Since then no communication had taken place between the old woman and her grand-niece. As Rose knew, Joanna was implacable in her resentments, and considered that she had been acting aright in what she had done.

The nearest farm to Aunt Joanna's cottage was occupied by the Hockins. One day Elizabeth, the farmer's wife, saw the old woman outside the cottage as she was herself returning from market; and, noticing how bent and feeble Joanna was, she halted, and talked to her, and gave her good advice.

"See you now, auntie, you'm gettin' old and crimmed wi' rheumatics. How can you get about? An' there's no knowin' but you might be took bad in the night. You ought to have some little lass wi' you to mind you."

"I don't want nobody, thank the Lord."

"Not just now, auntie, but suppose any chance ill-luck were to come on you. And then, in the bad weather, you'm not fit to go abroad after the turves, and you can't get all you want—tay and sugar and milk for yourself now. It would be handy to have a little maid by you."

"Who should I have?" asked Joanna.

"Well, now, you couldn't do better than take little Mary, Rose Hext's eldest girl. She's a handy maid, and bright and pleasant to speak to."

"No," answered the old woman, "I'll have none o' they Hexts, not I. The Lord is agin Rose and all her family, I know it. I'll have none of them."

"But, auntie, you must be nigh on ninety."

"I be ower that. But what o' that? Didn't Sarah, the wife of Abraham, live to an hundred and seven and twenty years, and that in spite of him worritin' of her wi' that owdacious maid of hern, Hagar? If it hadn't been for their goings on, of Abraham and Hagar, it's my belief that she'd ha' held on to a hundred and fifty-seven. I thank the Lord I've never had no man to worrit me. So why I shouldn't equal Sarah's life I don't see."

Then she went indoors and shut the door.

After that a week elapsed without Mrs. Hockin seeing the old woman. She passed the cottage, but no Joanna was about. The door was not open, and usually it was. Elizabeth spoke about this to her husband. "Jabez," said she, "I don't like the looks o' this; I've kept my eye open, and there be no Auntie Joanna hoppin' about. Whativer can be up? It's my opinion us ought to go and see."

"Well, I've naught on my hands now," said the farmer, "so I reckon we will go."

The two walked together to the cottage. No smoke issued from the chimney, and the door was shut. Jabez knocked, but there came no answer; so he entered, followed by his wife.

There was in the cottage but the kitchen, with one bedroom at the side. The hearth was cold.

"There's some'ut up," said Mrs. Hockin.

"I reckon it's the old lady be down," replied her husband, and, throwing open the bedroom door, he said: "Sure enough, and no mistake—there her be, dead as a dried pilchard."

And in fact Auntie Joanna had died in the night, after having so confidently affirmed her conviction that she would live to the age of a hundred and twenty-seven.

"Whativer shall we do?" asked Mrs. Hockin.

"I reckon," said her husband, "us had better take an inventory of what is here, lest wicked rascals come in and steal anything and everything."

"Folks bain't so bad as that, and a corpse in the house," observed Mrs. Hockin.

"Don't be sure o' that—these be terrible wicked times," said the husband. "And I sez, sez I, no harm is done in seein' what the old creetur had got."

"Well, surely," acquiesced Elizabeth, "there is no harm in

that."

In the bedroom was an old oak chest, and this the farmer and his wife opened. To their surprise they found in it a silver teapot, and half a dozen silver spoons.

"Well, now," exclaimed Elizabeth Hockin, "fancy her havin' these—and me only Britannia metal."

"I reckon she came of a good family," said Jabez. "Leastwise, I've heard as how she were once well off."

"And look here!" exclaimed Elizabeth, "there's fine and beautiful linen underneath—sheets and pillow-cases."

"But look here!" cried Jabez, "blessed if the taypot bain't chock-full o' money! Whereiver did she get it from?"

"Her's been in the way of showing folk the Zennor Quoit, visitors from St. Ives and Penzance, and she's had scores o' shillings that way."

"Lord!" exclaimed Jabez. "I wish she'd left it to me, and I could buy a cow; I want another cruel bad."

"Ay, we do, terrible," said Elizabeth. "But just look to her bed, what torn and wretched linen be on that—and here these fine bedclothes all in the chest."

"Who'll get the silver taypot and spoons, and the money?" inquired Jabez.

"Her had no kin—none but Rose Hext, and her couldn't abide her. Last words her said to me was that she'd 'have never naught to do wi' the Hexts, they and all their belongings.'"

"That was her last words?"

"The very last words her spoke to me—or to anyone."

"Then," said Jabez, "I'll tell ye what, Elizabeth, it's our moral dooty to abide by the wishes of Aunt Joanna. It never does to go agin what is right. And as her expressed herself that strong, why us, as honest folks, must carry out her wishes, and see that none of all her savings go to them darned and dratted Hexts."

"But who be they to go to, then?"

"Well—we'll see. Fust us will have her removed, and provide that her be daycent buried. Them Hexts be in a poor way, and couldn't afford the expense, and it do seem to me, Elizabeth, as it would be a liberal and a kindly act in us to take all the charges on ourselves. Us is the closest neighbours."

"Ay—and her have had milk of me these ten or twelve years, and I've never charged her a penny, thinking her couldn't afford it. But her could, her were a-hoardin' of her money—and not paying me. That were not honest, and what I say is, that I have a right to some of her savin's, to pay the milk bill—and it's butter I've let her have now and then in a liberal way."

"Very well, Elizabeth. Fust of all, we'll take the silver taypot and the spoons wi' us, to get 'em out of harm's way."

"And I'll carry the linen sheets and pillow-cases. My word!— why didn't she use 'em, instead of them rags?"

All Zennor declared that the Hockins were a most neighbourly and generous couple, when it was known that they took upon themselves to defray the funeral expenses.

Mrs. Hext came to the farm, and said that she was willing to do what she could, but Mrs. Hockin replied: "My good Rose, it's no good. I seed your aunt when her was ailin', and nigh on death, and her laid it on me solemn as could be that we was to bury her, and that she'd have nothin' to do wi' the Hexts at no price."

Rose sighed, and went away.

Rose had not expected to receive anything from her aunt. She had never been allowed to look at the treasures in the oak chest. As far as she had been aware, Aunt Joanna had been extremely poor. But she remembered that the old woman had at one time befriended her, and she was ready to forgive the harsh treatment to which she had finally been subjected. In fact, she had repeatedly made overtures to her great-aunt to be reconciled, but these overtures had been always rejected. She was, accordingly, not surprised to learn from Mrs. Hockin that the old woman's last words had been as reported.

But, although disowned and disinherited, Rose, her husband, and children dressed in black, and were chief mourners at the funeral. Now it had so happened that when it came to the laying out of Aunt Joanna, Mrs. Hockin had looked at the beautiful linen sheets she had found in the oak chest, with the object of furnishing the corpse with one as a winding-sheet. But—she said to herself—it would really be a shame to spoil a pair, and where else could she get such fine and beautiful old linen as was this? So she put the sheets away, and furnished for the purpose a clean but coarse and ragged sheet such as Aunt Joanna had in common use. That was good enough to moulder in the grave. It would be positively sinful, because wasteful, to give up to corruption and the worm such fine white linen as Aunt Joanna had hoarded. The funeral was conducted, otherwise, liberally. Aunt Joanna was given an elm, and not a mean deal board coffin, such as is provided for paupers; and a handsome escutcheon of white metal was put on the lid.

Moreover, plenty of gin was drunk, and cake and cheese eaten at the house, all at the expense of the Hockins. And the conversation among those who attended, and ate and drank, and wiped their eyes, was rather anent the generosity of the Hockins than of the virtues of the departed.

Mr. and Mrs. Hockin heard this, and their hearts swelled within them. Nothing so swells the heart as the consciousness of virtue being recognised. Jabez in an undertone informed a neighbour that he weren't goin' to stick at the funeral expenses, not he; he'd have a neat stone erected above the grave with work on it, at twopence a letter. The name and the date of departure of Aunt Joanna, and her age, and two lines of a favourite hymn of his, all about earth being no dwelling-place, heaven being properly her home.

It was not often that Elizabeth Hockin cried, but she did this day; she wept tears of sympathy with the deceased, and happiness at the ovation accorded to herself and her husband. At length, as the short winter day closed in, the last of those who had attended the funeral, and had returned to the farm to recruit and regale after it, departed, and the Hockins were left to themselves.

"It were a beautiful day," said Jabez.

"Ay," responded Elizabeth, "and what a sight o' people came

276

here."

"This here buryin' of Aunt Joanna have set us up tremendous in the estimation of the neighbours."

"I'd like to know who else would ha' done it for a poor old creetur as is no relation; ay—and one as owed a purty long bill to me for milk and butter through ten or twelve years."

"Well," said Jabez, "I've allus heard say that a good deed brings its own reward wi' it—and it's a fine proverb. I feels it in my insides."

"P'raps it's the gin, Jabez."

"No—it's virtue. It's warmer nor gin a long sight. Gin gives a smouldering spark, but a good conscience is a blaze of furze."

The farm of the Hockins was small, and Hockin looked after his cattle himself. One maid was kept, but no man in the house. All were wont to retire early to bed; neither Hockin nor his wife had literary tastes, and were not disposed to consume much oil, so as to read at night.

During the night, at what time she did not know, Mrs. Hockin awoke with a start, and found that her husband was sitting up in bed listening. There was a moon that night, and no clouds in the sky. The room was full of silver light. Elizabeth Hockin heard a sound of feet in the kitchen, which was immediately under the bedroom of the couple.

"There's someone about," she whispered; "go down, Jabez."

"I wonder, now, who it be. P'raps its Sally."

"It can't be Sally—how can it, when she can't get out o' her room wi'out passin' through ours?"

"Run down, Elizabeth, and see."

"It's your place to go, Jabez."

"But if it was a woman—and me in my night-shirt?"

"And, Jabez, if it was a man, a robber—and me in my night-shirt? It 'ud be shameful."

"I reckon us had best go down together."

"We'll do so—but I hope it's not——"

"What?"

Mrs. Hockin did not answer. She and her husband crept from

bed, and, treading on tiptoe across the room, descended the stair.

There was no door at the bottom, but the staircase was boarded up at the side; it opened into the kitchen.

They descended very softly and cautiously, holding each other, and when they reached the bottom, peered timorously into the apartment that served many purposes—kitchen, sitting-room, and dining-place. The moonlight poured in through the broad, low window.

By it they saw a figure. There could be no mistaking it—it was that of Aunt Joanna, clothed in the tattered sheet that Elizabeth Hockin had allowed for her grave-clothes. The old woman had taken one of the fine linen sheets out of the cupboard in which it had been placed, and had spread it over the long table, and was smoothing it down with her bony hands.

The Hockins trembled, not with cold, though it was mid-winter, but with terror. They dared not advance, and they felt powerless to retreat.

Then they saw Aunt Joanna go to the cupboard, open it, and return with the silver spoons; she placed all six on the sheet, and with a lean finger counted them.

She turned her face towards those who were watching her proceedings, but it was in shadow, and they could not distinguish the features nor note the expression with which she regarded them.

Presently she went back to the cupboard, and returned with the silver teapot. She stood at one end of the table, and now the reflection of the moon on the linen sheet was cast upon her face, and they saw that she was moving her lips—but no sound issued from them.

She thrust her hand into the teapot and drew forth the coins, one by one, and rolled them along the table. The Hockins saw the glint of the metal, and the shadow cast by each piece of money as it rolled. The first coin lodged at the further left-hand corner and the second rested near it; and so on, the pieces were rolled, and ranged themselves in order, ten in a row. Then the next ten were run across the white cloth in the same manner, and dropped over on their sides below the first row; thus also the third ten. And all the time the dead woman was mouthing, as though counting, but still inaudibly.

The couple stood motionless observing proceedings, till suddenly a cloud passed before the face of the moon, so dense as to eclipse the light.

Then in a paroxysm of terror both turned and fled up the stairs, bolted their bedroom door, and jumped into bed.

There was no sleep for them that night. In the gloom when the moon was concealed, in the glare when it shone forth, it was the same, they could hear the light rolling of the coins along the table, and the click as they fell over. Was the supply inexhaustible? It was not so, but apparently the dead woman did not weary of counting the coins. When all had been ranged, she could be heard moving to the further end of the table, and there recommencing the same proceeding of coin-rolling.

Not till near daybreak did this sound cease, and not till the maid, Sally, had begun to stir in the inner bedchamber did Hockin and his wife venture to rise. Neither would suffer the servant girl to descend till they had been down to see in what condition the kitchen was. They found that the table had been cleared, the coins were all back in the teapot, and that and the spoons were where they had themselves placed them. The sheet, moreover, was neatly folded, and replaced where it had been before.

The Hockins did not speak to one another of their experiences during the past night, so long as they were in the house, but when Jabez was in the field, Elizabeth went to him and said: "Husband, what about Aunt Joanna?"

"I don't know—maybe it were a dream."

"Curious us should ha' dreamed alike."

"I don't know that; 'twere the gin made us dream, and us both had gin, so us dreamed the same thing."

"'Twere more like real truth than dream," observed Elizabeth.

"We'll take it as dream," said Jabez. "Mebbe it won't happen again."

But precisely the same sounds were heard on the following night. The moon was obscured by thick clouds, and neither of the two had the courage to descend to the kitchen. But they could hear the patter of feet, and then the roll and click of the coins. Again sleep was impossible.

"Whatever shall we do?" asked Elizabeth Hockin next morning of her husband. "Us can't go on like this wi' the dead woman about our house nightly. There's no tellin' she might take it into her head to come upstairs and pull the sheets off us. As we took hers, she may think it fair to carry off ours."

"I think," said Jabez sorrowfully, "we'll have to return 'em."

"But how?"

After some consultation the couple resolved on conveying all the deceased woman's goods to the churchyard, by night, and placing them on her grave.

"I reckon," said Hockin, "we'll bide in the porch and watch what happens. If they be left there till mornin', why we may carry 'em back wi' an easy conscience. We've spent some pounds over her buryin'."

"What have it come to?"

"Three pounds five and fourpence, as I make it out."

"Well," said Elizabeth, "we must risk it."

When night had fallen murk, the farmer and his wife crept from their house, carrying the linen sheets, the teapot, and the silver spoons. They did not start till late, for fear of encountering any villagers on the way, and not till after the maid, Sally, had gone to bed.

They fastened the farm door behind them. The night was dark and stormy, with scudding clouds, so dense as to make deep night, when they did not part and allow the moon to peer forth.

They walked timorously, and side by side, looking about them as they proceeded, and on reaching the churchyard gate they halted to pluck up courage before opening and venturing within. Jabez had furnished himself with a bottle of gin, to give courage to himself and his wife.

Together they heaped the articles that had belonged to Aunt Joanna upon the fresh grave, but as they did so the wind caught the linen and unfurled and flapped it, and they were forced to place stones upon it to hold it down.

Then, quaking with fear, they retreated to the church porch, and Jabez, uncorking the bottle, first took a long pull himself, and then presented it to his wife.

And now down came a tearing rain, driven by a blast from the Atlantic, howling among the gravestones, and screaming in the battlements of the tower and its bell-chamber windows. The night was so dark, and the rain fell so heavily, that they could see nothing for full half an hour. But then the clouds were rent asunder, and the moon glared white and ghastly over the churchyard.

Elizabeth caught her husband by the arm and pointed. There was, however, no need for her to indicate that on which his eyes were fixed already.

Both saw a lean hand come up out of the grave, and lay hold of one of the fine linen sheets and drag at it. They saw it drag the sheet by one corner, and then it went down underground, and the sheet followed, as though sucked down in a vortex; fold on fold it descended, till the entire sheet had disappeared.

"Her have taken it for her windin' sheet," whispered Elizabeth. "Whativer will her do wi' the rest?"

"Have a drop o' gin; this be terrible tryin'," said Jabez in an undertone; and again the couple put their lips to the bottle, which came away considerably lighter after the draughts.

"Look!" gasped Elizabeth.

Again the lean hand with long fingers appeared above the soil, and this was seen groping about the grass till it laid hold of the teapot. Then it groped again, and gathered up the spoons, that flashed in the moonbeams. Next, up came the second hand, and a long arm that stretched along the grave till it reached the other sheets. At once, on being raised, these sheets were caught by the wind, and flapped and fluttered like half-hoisted sails. The hands retained them for a while till they bellied with the wind, and then let them go, and they were swept away by the blast across the churchyard, over the wall, and lodged in the carpenter's yard that adjoined, among his timber.

"She have sent 'em to the Hexts," whispered Elizabeth.

Next the hands began to trifle with the teapot, and to shake out some of the coins.

In a minute some silver pieces were flung with so true an aim that they fell clinking down on the floor of the porch.

How many coins, how much money was cast, the couple were in no mood to estimate.

Then they saw the hands collect the pillow-cases, and proceed to roll up the teapot and silver spoons in them, and, that done, the white bundle was cast into the air, and caught by the wind and carried over the churchyard wall into the wheelwright's yard.

At once a curtain of vapour rushed across the face of the moon, and again the graveyard was buried in darkness. Half an hour elapsed before the moon shone out again. Then the Hockins saw that nothing was stirring in the cemetery.

"I reckon us may go now," said Jabez.

"Let us gather up what she chucked to us," advised Elizabeth.

So the couple felt about the floor, and collected a number of coins. What they were they could not tell till they reached their home, and had lighted a candle.

"How much be it?" asked Elizabeth.

"Three pound five and fourpence, exact," answered Jabez.

The 9.30 Up-Train
(A tale from *A Book of Ghosts*)

In a well-authenticated ghost story, names and dates should be distinctly specified. In the following story I am unfortunately able to give only the year and the month, for I have forgotten the date of the day, and I do not keep a diary. With regard to names, my own figures as a guarantee as that of the principal personage to whom the following extraordinary circumstances occurred, but the minor actors are provided with fictitious names, for I am not warranted to make their real ones public. I may add that the believer in ghosts may make use of the facts which I relate to establish his theories, if he finds that they will be of service to him—when he has read through and weighed well the startling account which I am about to give from my own experiences.

On a fine evening in June, 1860, I paid a visit to Mrs. Lyons, on my way to the Hassocks Gate Station, on the London and Brighton line. This station is the first out of Brighton.

As I rose to leave, I mentioned to the lady whom I was visiting that I expected a parcel of books from town, and that I was going to the station to inquire whether it had arrived.

"Oh!" said she, readily, "I expect Dr. Lyons out from Brighton by the 9.30 train; if you like to drive the pony chaise down and meet him, you are welcome, and you can bring your parcel back with you in it."

I gladly accepted her offer, and in a few minutes I was seated in a little low basket-carriage, drawn by a pretty iron-grey Welsh pony.

The station road commands the line of the South Downs from Chantonbury Ring, with its cap of dark firs, to Mount Harry, the scene of the memorable battle of Lewes. Woolsonbury stands out like a headland above the dark Danny woods, over which the rooks were wheeling and cawing previous to settling themselves in for the night. Ditchling beacon—its steep sides gashed with chalk-pits—was faintly flushed with light. The Clayton windmills, with their sails motionless, stood out darkly against the green evening sky. Close beneath opens the tunnel in which, not so long before, had happened one of the most fearful railway accidents on record.

The evening was exquisite. The sky was kindled with light, though the sun was set. A few gilded bars of cloud lay in the west. Two or three stars looked forth—one I noticed twinkling green, crimson, and gold, like a gem. From a field of young wheat hard by I heard the harsh, grating note of the corncrake. Mist was lying on the low meadows like a mantle of snow, pure, smooth, and white; the cattle stood in it to their knees. The effect was so singular that I drew up to look at it attentively. At the same moment I heard the scream of an engine, and on looking towards the downs I noticed the up-train shooting out of the tunnel, its red signal lamps flashing brightly out of the purple gloom which bathed the roots of the hills.

Seeing that I was late, I whipped the Welsh pony on, and proceeded at a fast trot.

At about a quarter mile from the station there is a turnpike—an odd-looking building, tenanted then by a strange old man, usually dressed in a white smock, over which his long white beard flowed to his breast. This toll-collector—he is dead now—had amused himself in bygone days by carving life-size heads out of wood, and these were stuck along the eaves. One is the face of a drunkard, round and blotched, leering out of misty eyes at the passers-by; the next has the crumpled features of a miser, worn out with toil and moil; a third has the wild scowl of a maniac; and a fourth the stare of an idiot.

I drove past, flinging the toll to the door, and shouting to the old man to pick it up, for I was in a vast hurry to reach the station before Dr. Lyons left it. I whipped the little pony on, and he began to trot down a cutting in the greensand, through which leads the station road.

Suddenly, Taffy stood still, planted his feet resolutely on the ground, threw up his head, snorted, and refused to move a peg. I "gee-uped," and "tshed," all to no purpose; not a step would the little fellow advance. I saw that he was thoroughly alarmed; his flanks were quivering, and his ears were thrown back. I was on the point of leaving the chaise, when the pony made a bound on one side and ran the carriage up into the hedge, thereby upsetting me on the road. I picked myself up, and took the beast's head. I could not conceive what had frightened him; there was positively nothing to be seen, except a puff of dust running up the road, such as might be blown along by a passing current of air. There was nothing to be heard, except the rattle of a gig or tax-cart with one wheel loose: probably a vehicle of this kind was being driven down the London road, which branches off at the turnpike at right angles. The sound became fainter, and at last died away in the distance.

The pony now no longer refused to advance. It trembled violently, and was covered with sweat.

"Well, upon my word, you have been driving hard!" exclaimed Dr. Lyons, when I met him at the station.

"I have not, indeed," was my reply; "but something has frightened Taffy, but what that something was, is more than I can tell."

"Oh, ah!" said the doctor, looking round with a certain degree of interest in his face; "so you met it, did you?"

"Met what?"

"Oh, nothing;—only I have heard of horses being frightened along this road after the arrival of the 9.30 up-train. Flys never leave the moment that the train comes in, or the horses become restive—a wonderful thing for a fly-horse to become restive, isn't it?"

"But what causes this alarm? I saw nothing!"

"You ask me more than I can answer. I am as ignorant of the cause as yourself. I take things as they stand, and make no inquiries. When the flyman tells me that he can't start for a minute or two after the train has arrived, or urges on his horses to reach the station before the arrival of this train, giving as his reason that his brutes become wild if he does not do so, then I merely say, 'Do as you think best, cabby,' and bother my head no more about the matter."

"I shall search this matter out," said I resolutely. "What has taken place so strangely corroborates the superstition, that I shall not leave it uninvestigated."

"Take my advice and banish it from your thoughts. When you have come to the end, you will be sadly disappointed, and will find that all the mystery evaporates, and leaves a dull, commonplace residuum. It is best that the few mysteries which remain to us unexplained should still remain mysteries, or we shall disbelieve in supernatural agencies altogether. We have searched out the arcana of nature, and exposed all her secrets to the garish eye of day, and we find, in despair, that the poetry and romance of life are gone. Are we the happier for knowing that there are no ghosts, no fairies, no witches, no mermaids, no wood spirits? Were not our forefathers happier in thinking every lake to be the abode of a fairy, every forest to be a bower of yellow-haired sylphs, every moorland sweep to be tripped over by elf and pixie?

"I found my little boy one day lying on his face in a fairy-ring, crying: 'You dear, dear little fairies, I *will* believe in you, though papa says you are all nonsense.' I used, in my childish days, to think, when a silence fell upon a company, that an angel was passing through the room. Alas! I now know that it results only from the subject of weather having been talked to death, and no new subject having been started. Believe me, science has done good to mankind, but it has done mischief too. If we wish to be poetical or romantic, we must shut our eyes to facts. The head and the heart wage mutual war now.

"A lover preserves a lock of his mistress's hair as a holy relic, yet he must know perfectly well that for all practical purposes a bit of rhinoceros hide would do as well—the chemical constituents are identical. If I adore a fair lady, and feel a thrill through all my veins when I touch her hand, a moment's consideration tells me that phosphate of lime No. 1 is touching phosphate of lime No. 2—nothing more. If for a moment I forget myself so far as to wave my cap and cheer for king, or queen, or prince, I laugh at my folly next moment for having paid reverence to one digesting machine above another."

I cut the doctor short as he was lapsing into his favourite subject of discussion, and asked him whether he would lend me the pony-chaise on the following evening, that I might drive to the station again and try to unravel the mystery.

"I will lend you the pony," said he, "but not the chaise, as I am afraid of its being injured should Taffy take fright and run up into the hedge again. I have got a saddle."

Next evening I was on my way to the station considerably before the time at which the train was due.

I stopped at the turnpike and chatted with the old man who kept it. I asked him whether he could throw any light on the matter which I was investigating. He shrugged his shoulders, saying that he "knowed nothink about it."

"What! Nothing at all?"

"I don't trouble my head with matters of this sort," was the reply. "People *do* say that something out of the common sort passes along the road and turns down the other road leading to Clayton and Brighton; but I pays no attention to what them people says."

"Do you ever hear anything?"

"After the arrival of the 9.30 train I does at times hear the rattle as of a mail-cart and the trot of a horse along the road; and the sound is as though one of the wheels was loose. I've a been out many a time to take the toll; but, Lor' bless 'ee! them sperits—if sperits them be—don't go for to pay toll."

"Have you never inquired into the matter?"

"Why should I? Anythink as don't go for to pay toll don't

concern me. Do ye think as I knows 'ow many people and dogs goes through this heer geatt in a day? Not I—them don't pay toll, so them's no odds to me."

"Look here, my man!" said I. "Do you object to my putting the bar across the road, immediately on the arrival of the train?"

"Not a bit! Please yersel'; but you han't got much time to lose, for theer comes thickey train out of Clayton tunnel."

I shut the gate, mounted Taffy, and drew up across the road a little way below the turnpike. I heard the train arrive—I saw it puff off. At the same moment I distinctly heard a trap coming up the road, one of the wheels rattling as though it were loose. I repeat deliberately that I *heard* it—I cannot account for it—but, though I heard it, yet I saw nothing whatever.

At the same time the pony became restless, it tossed its head, pricked up its ears, it started, pranced, and then made a bound to one side, entirely regardless of whip and rein. It tried to scramble up the sand-bank in its alarm, and I had to throw myself off and catch its head. I then cast a glance behind me at the turnpike. I saw the bar bent, as though someone were pressing against it; then, with a click, it flew open, and was dashed violently back against the white post to which it was usually hasped in the day-time. There it remained, quivering from the shock.

Immediately I heard the rattle—rattle—rattle—of the tax-cart. I confess that my first impulse was to laugh, the idea of a ghostly tax-cart was so essentially ludicrous; but the *reality* of the whole scene soon brought me to a graver mood, and, remounting Taffy, I rode down to the station.

The officials were taking their ease, as another train was not due for some while; so I stepped up to the station-master and entered into conversation with him. After a few desultory remarks, I mentioned the circumstances which had occurred to me on the road, and my inability to account for them.

"So that's what you're after!" said the master somewhat bluntly. "Well, I can tell you nothing about it; sperits don't come in my way, saving and excepting those which can be taken inwardly; and mighty comfortable warming things they be when so taken. If you ask me about other sorts of sperits, I tell you flat I don't believe in 'em, though I don't mind drinking the health of them what does."

"Perhaps you may have the chance, if you are a little more communicative," said I.

"Well, I'll tell you all I know, and that is precious little," answered the worthy man. "I know one thing for certain—that one compartment of a second-class carriage is always left vacant between Brighton and Hassocks Gate, by the 9.30 up-train."

"For what purpose?"

"Ah! that's more than I can fully explain. Before the orders came to this effect, people went into fits and that like, in one of the carriages."

"Any particular carriage?"

"The first compartment of the second-class carriage nearest to the engine. It is locked at Brighton, and I unlock it at this station."

"What do you mean by saying that people had fits?"

"I mean that I used to find men and women a-screeching and a-hollering like mad to be let out; they'd seen some'ut as had frightened them as they was passing through the Clayton tunnel. That was before they made the arrangement I told y' of."

"Very strange!" said I meditatively.

"Wery much so, but true for all that. *I* don't believe in nothing but sperits of a warming and cheering nature, and them sort ain't to be found in Clayton tunn'l to my thinking."

There was evidently nothing more to be got out of my friend. I hope that he drank my health that night; if he omitted to do so, it was his fault, not mine.

As I rode home revolving in my mind all that I had heard and seen, I became more and more settled in my determination to thoroughly investigate the matter. The best means that I could adopt for so doing would be to come out from Brighton by the 9.30 train in the very compartment of the second-class carriage from which the public were considerably excluded.

Somehow I felt no shrinking from the attempt; my curiosity

was so intense that it overcame all apprehension as to the consequences.

My next free day was Thursday, and I hoped then to execute my plan. In this, however, I was disappointed, as I found that a battalion drill was fixed for that very evening, and I was desirous of attending it, being somewhat behindhand in the regulation number of drills. I was consequently obliged to postpone my Brighton trip.

On the Thursday evening about five o'clock I started in regimentals with my rifle over my shoulder, for the drilling ground—a piece of furzy common near the railway station.

I was speedily overtaken by Mr. Ball, a corporal in the rifle corps, a capital shot and most efficient in his drill. Mr. Ball was driving his gig. He stopped on seeing me and offered me a seat beside him. I gladly accepted, as the distance to the station is a mile and three-quarters by the road, and two miles by what is commonly supposed to be the short cut across the fields.

After some conversation on volunteering matters, about which Corporal Ball was an enthusiast, we turned out of the lanes into the station road, and I took the opportunity of adverting to the subject which was uppermost in my mind.

"Ah! I have heard a good deal about that," said the corporal. "My workmen have often told me some cock-and-bull stories of that kind, but I can't say has 'ow I believed them. What you tell me is, 'owever, very remarkable. I never 'ad it on such good authority afore. Still, I can't believe that there's hanything supernatural about it."

"I do not yet know what to believe," I replied, "for the whole matter is to me perfectly inexplicable."

"You know, of course, the story which gave rise to the superstition?"

"Not I. Pray tell it me."

"Just about seven years agone—why, you must remember the circumstances as well as I do—there was a man druv over from I can't say where, for that was never exactly hascertained,—but from the Henfield direction, in a light cart. He went to the Sta-

290

tion Inn, and throwing the reins to John Thomas, the ostler, bade him take the trap and bring it round to meet the 9.30 train, by which he calculated to return from Brighton. John Thomas said as 'ow the stranger was quite unbeknown to him, and that he looked as though he 'ad some matter on his mind when he went to the train; he was a queer sort of a man, with thick grey hair and beard, and delicate white 'ands, jist like a lady's.

"The trap was round to the station door as hordered by the arrival of the 9.30 train. The ostler observed then that the man was ashen pale, and that his 'ands trembled as he took the reins, that the stranger stared at him in a wild habstracted way, and that he would have driven off without tendering payment had he not been respectfully reminded that the 'orse had been given a feed of hoats. John Thomas made a hobservation to the gent relative to the wheel which was loose, but that hobservation met with no corresponding hanswer. The driver whipped his 'orse and went off. He passed the turnpike, and was seen to take the Brighton road hinstead of that by which he had come.

"A workman hobserved the trap next on the downs above Clayton chalk-pits. He didn't pay much attention to it, but he saw that the driver was on his legs at the 'ead of the 'orse. Next, morning, when the quarrymen went to the pit, they found a shattered tax-cart at the bottom, and the 'orse and driver dead, the latter with his neck broken. What was curious, too, was that an 'andkerchief was bound round the brute's heyes, so that he must have been driven over the edge blindfold. Hodd, wasn't it? Well, folks say that the gent and his tax-cart pass along the road every hevening after the arrival of the 9.30 train; but I don't believe it; I ain't a bit superstitious—not I!"

Next week I was again disappointed in my expectation of being able to put my scheme in execution; but on the third Saturday after my conversation with Corporal Ball, I walked into Brighton in the afternoon, the distance being about nine miles. I spent an hour on the shore watching the boats, and then I sauntered round the Pavilion, ardently longing that fire might break forth and consume that architectural monstrosity. I believe that I afterwards had a cup of coffee at the refreshment-rooms of the station, and capital refreshment-rooms they are, or were—very moderate and very good. I think that I partook of a bun, but if put on my oath I could not swear to the fact; a floating reminiscence of bun lingers in the chambers of memory, but I cannot be positive, and I wish in this paper to advance nothing but reliable facts. I squandered precious time in reading the advertisements of baby-jumpers—which no mother should be without—which are indispensable in the nursery and the greatest acquisition in the parlour, the greatest discovery of modern times, etc., etc.

I perused a notice of the advantage of metallic brushes, and admired the young lady with her hair white on one side and black on the other; I studied the Chinese letter commendatory of Horniman's tea and the inferior English translation, and counted up the number of agents in Great Britain and Ireland. At length the ticket-office opened, and I booked for Hassocks Gate, second class, fare one shilling.

I ran along the platform till I came to the compartment of the second-class carriage which I wanted. The door was locked, so I shouted for a guard.

"Put me in here, please."

"Can't there, s'r; next, please, nearly empty, one woman and baby."

"I particularly wish to enter *this* carriage," said I.

"Can't be, lock'd, orders, comp'ny," replied the guard, turning on his heel.

"What reason is there for the public's being excluded, may I ask?"

"Dn'ow, 'spress ord'rs—c'n't let you in; next caridge, pl'se; now then, quick, pl'se."

I knew the guard and he knew me—by sight, for I often travelled to and fro on the line, so I thought it best to be candid with him. I briefly told him my reason for making the request, and begged him to assist me in executing my plan. He then consented, though with reluctance.

"'Ave y'r own way," said he; "only if an'thing 'appens, don't blame me!"

"Never fear," laughed I, jumping into the carriage.

The guard left the carriage unlocked, and in two minutes we were off.

I did not feel in the slightest degree nervous. There was no light in the carriage, but that did not matter, as there was twilight. I sat facing the engine on the left side, and every now and then I looked out at the downs with a soft haze of light still hanging over them. We swept into a cutting, and I watched the lines of flint in the chalk, and longed to be geologising among them with my hammer, picking out "shepherds' crowns" and sharks' teeth, the delicate rhynconella and the quaint ventriculite.

I remembered a not very distant occasion on which I had actually ventured there, and been chased off by the guard, after having brought down an avalanche of chalk *débris* in a manner dangerous to traffic whilst endeavouring to extricate a magnificent ammonite which I found, and—alas! left—protruding from the side of the cutting. I wondered whether that ammonite was still there; I looked about to identify the exact spot as we whizzed along; and at that moment we shot into the tunnel.

There are two tunnels, with a bit of chalk cutting between them. We passed through the first, which is short, and in another moment plunged into the second.

I cannot explain how it was that *now*, all of a sudden, a feeling of terror came over me; it seemed to drop over me like a wet sheet and wrap me round and round.

I felt that *someone* was seated opposite me—someone in the darkness with his eyes fixed on me.

Many persons possessed of keen nervous sensibility are well aware when they are in the presence of another, even though they can see no one, and I believe that I possess this power strongly. If I were blindfolded, I think that I should know when anyone was looking fixedly at me, and I am certain that I should instinctively know that I was not alone if I entered a dark room in which another person was seated, even though he made no noise. I remember a college friend of mine, who dabbled in anatomy, telling me that a little Italian violinist once called on him to give a lesson on his instrument. The foreigner—a singularly nervous individual—moved restlessly from the place where he had been standing, casting many a furtive glance over his shoulder at a press which was behind him. At last the little fellow tossed aside his violin, saying—

"I can note give de lesson if someone weel look at me from behind! Dare is somebodee in de cupboard, I know!"

"You are right, there is!" laughed my anatomical friend, flinging open the door of the press and discovering a skeleton.

The horror which oppressed me was numbing. For a few moments I could neither lift my hands nor stir a finger. I was tongue-tied. I seemed paralysed in every member. I fancied that I *felt* eyes staring at me through the gloom. A cold breath seemed to play over my face. I believed that fingers touched my chest and plucked at my coat. I drew back against the partition; my heart stood still, my flesh became stiff, my muscles rigid.

I do not know whether I breathed—a blue mist swam before my eyes, and my head span.

The rattle and roar of the train dashing through the tunnel drowned every other sound.

Suddenly we rushed past a light fixed against the wall in the side, and it sent a flash, instantaneous as that of lightning, through the carriage. In that moment I saw what I shall never, never forget. I saw a face opposite me, livid as that of a corpse, hideous with passion like that of a gorilla.

I cannot describe it accurately, for I saw it but for a second; yet there rises before me now, as I write, the low broad brow seamed with wrinkles, the shaggy, over-hanging grey eyebrows; the wild ashen eyes, which glared as those of a demoniac; the coarse mouth, with its fleshy lips compressed till they were white; the profusion of wolf-grey hair about the cheeks and chin; the thin, bloodless hands, raised and half-open, extended towards me as though they would clutch and tear me.

In the madness of terror, I flung myself along the seat to the further window.

Then I felt that *it* was moving slowly down, and was opposite me again. I lifted my hand to let down the window, and I touched something: I thought it was a hand—yes, yes! it *was* a hand, for it folded over mine and began to contract on it. I felt each finger separately; they were cold, dully cold. I wrenched my hand away. I slipped back to my former place in the carriage by the open window, and in frantic horror I opened the door, clinging to it with both my hands round the window-jamb, swung myself out with my feet on the floor and my head turned from the carriage. If the cold fingers had but touched my woven hands, mine would have given way; had I but turned my head and seen that hellish countenance peering out at me, I must have lost my hold.

Ah! I saw the light from the tunnel mouth; it smote on my face. The engine rushed out with a piercing whistle. The roaring echoes of the tunnel died away. The cool fresh breeze blew over my face and tossed my hair; the speed of the train was relaxed; the lights of the station became brighter. I heard the bell ringing loudly; I saw people waiting for the train; I felt the vibration as the brake was put on. We stopped; and then my fingers gave way. I dropped as a sack on the platform, and then, then—not till then—I awoke. There now! from beginning to end the whole had been a frightful dream caused by my having too many blankets over my bed. If I must append a moral—Don't sleep too hot.

A Professional Secret
(A tale from *A Book of Ghosts*)

Mr. Leveridge was in a solicitor's office at Swanton. Mr. Leveridge had been brought up well by a sensible father and an excellent mother. His principles left nothing to be desired. His father was now dead, and his mother did not reside at Swanton, but near her own relations in another part of England. Joseph Leveridge was a mild, inoffensive man, with fair hair and a full head. He was so shy that he did not move in society as he might have done had he been self-assertive. But he was fairly happy—not so happy as he might have been, for reasons to be shortly given.

Swanton was a small market-town, that woke into life every Friday, which was market-day, burst into boisterous levity at the Michaelmas fair, and then lapsed back into decorum; it was, except on Fridays, somnolent during the day and asleep at night.

Swanton was not a manufacturing town. It possessed one iron foundry and a brewery, so that it afforded little employment for the labouring classes, yet the labouring classes crowded into it, although cottage rents were high, because the farmers could not afford, owing to the hard times, to employ many hands on the land, and because their wives and daughters desired the distractions and dissipations of a town, and supposed that both were to be found in superfluity at Swanton.

There was a large town hall with a magistrates' court, where the bench sat every month once. The church, in the centre of the town, was an imposing structure of stone, very cold within.

The presentation was in the hands of the Simeonite Trustees, so that the vicar was of the theological school—if that can be called a school where nothing is taught—called Evangelical. The services ever long and dismal. The vicar slowly and impressively declaimed the prayers, preached lengthy sermons, and condemned the congregation to sing out of the Mitre hymnal.

The principal solicitor, Mr. Stork, was clerk of the petty sessions and registrar. He did a limited amount of legal work for the landed gentry round, was trustee to some widows and orphans, and was consulted by tottering yeomen as to their financial difficulties, lent them some money to relieve their immediate embarrassments, on the security of their land, which ultimately passed into his possession.

To this gentleman Mr. Leveridge had been articled. He had been induced to adopt the legal profession, not from any true vocation, but at the instigation of his mother, who had urged him to follow in the professional footsteps of his revered father. But the occupation was not one that accorded with the tastes of the young man, who, notwithstanding his apparent mildness and softness, was not deficient in brains. He was a shrewd observer, and was endowed with a redundant imagination.

From a child he had scribbled stories, and with his pencil had illustrated them; but this had brought upon him severe rebukes from his mother, who looked with disfavour on works of imagination, and his father had taken him across his knee, of course before he was adult, and had castigated him with the flat of the hairbrush for surreptitiously reading the *Arabian Nights*.

Mr. Leveridge's days passed evenly enough; there was some business coming into the office on Fridays, and none at all on Sundays, on which day he wrote a long and affectionate letter to his widowed mother.

He would have been a happy man, happy in a mild, lotus-eating way, but for three things. In the first place, he became conscious that he was not working in his proper vocation. He took no pleasure in engrossing deeds; indentures his soul abhorred. He knew himself to be capable of better things, and feared lest the higher faculties of his mind should become atrophied by lack of exercise. In the second place, he was not satisfied that his superior was a man of strict integrity. He had no reason whatever for supposing that anything dishonest went on in the office, but he had discovered that his "boss" was a daring and venturesome speculator, and he feared lest temptation should induce him to speculate with the funds of those to whom he acted as trustee. And Joseph, with his high sense of rectitude, was apprehensive lest someday something might there be done, which would cause a crash. Lastly, Joseph Leveridge had lost his heart. He was consumed by a hopeless passion for Miss Asphodel Vincent, a young lady with a small fortune of about £400 *per annum*, to whom Mr. Stork was guardian and trustee.

This young lady was tall, slender, willowy, had a sweet, Madonna-like face, and like Joseph himself was constitutionally shy; and she was unconscious of her personal and pecuniary attractions. She moved in the best society, she was taken up by the county people. No doubt she would be secured by the son of some squire, and settle down as Lady Bountiful in some parish; or else some wily curate with a moustache would step in and carry her off. But her bashfulness and her indifference to men's society had so far protected her. She loved her garden, cultivated herbaceous plants, and was specially addicted to a rockery in which she acclimatised flowers from the Alps.

As Mr. Stork was her guardian, she often visited the office, when Joseph flew, with heightened colour, to offer her a chair till Mr. Stork was disengaged. But conversation between them had never passed beyond generalities. Mr. Leveridge occasionally met her in his country walks, but never advanced in intimacy beyond raising his hat and remarking on the weather.

Probably it was the stimulus of this devouring and despairing passion which drove Mr. Leveridge to writing a novel, in which he could paint Asphodel, under another name, in all her perfections. She should move through his story diffusing an atmosphere of sweetness and saintliness, but he could not bring himself to provide her with a lover, and to conclude his romance with her union to a being of the male sex.

Impressed as he had been in early youth by the admonitions of his mother, and the applications of the hairbrush by his father, that the imagination was a dangerous and delusive gift, to be restrained, not indulged, he resolved that he would create no characters for his story, but make direct studies from life. Consequently, when the work was completed, it presented the most close portraits of a certain number of the residents in Swanton, and the town in which the scene was laid was very much like Swanton, though he called it Buzbury.

But to find a publisher was a more difficult work than to write the novel. Mr. Leveridge sent his MS. type-written to several firms, and it was declined by one after another. At last, however, it fell into the hands of an unusually discerning reader, who saw in it distinct tokens of ability. It was not one to appeal to the general public. It contained no blood-curdling episodes, no hair-breadth escapes, no risky situations; it was simply a transcript of life in a little English country town. Though not high-spiced to suit the vulgar taste, still the reader and the publisher considered that there was a discerning public, small and select, that relished good, honest work of the Jane Austen kind, and the latter resolved on risking the production. Accordingly he offered the author fifty pounds for the work, he buying all rights. Joseph Leveridge was overwhelmed at the munificence of the offer, and accepted it gratefully and with alacrity.

The next stage in the proceedings consisted in the revision of the proofs. And who that has not experienced it can judge of the sensation of exquisite delight afforded by this to the young author? After the correction of his romance—if romance such a prosaic tale can be called—in print, with characteristic modesty Leveridge insisted that his story should appear under an assumed name. What the name adopted was it does not concern the reader of this narrative to know. Some time now elapsed before the book appeared, at the usual publishing time, in October.

Eventually it came out, and Mr. Leveridge received his six copies, neatly and quietly bound in cloth. He cut and read one with avidity, and at once perceived that he had overlooked several typographical errors, and wrote to the publisher to beg that these might be corrected in the event of a second edition being called for.

On the morning following the publication and dissemination of the book, Joseph Leveridge lay in bed a little longer than usual, smiling in happy self-gratification at the thought that he had become an author. On the table by his bed stood his extinguished candle, his watch, and the book. He had looked at it the last thing before he closed his eyes in sleep. It was moreover the first thing that his eyes rested on when they opened. A fond mother could not have gazed on her new-born babe with greater pride and affection.

Whilst he thus lay and said to himself, "I really must—I positively must get up and dress!" he heard a stumping on the stairs, and a few moments later his door was burst open, and in came Major Dolgelly Jones, a retired officer, resident in Swanton, who had never before done him the honour of a call—and now he actually penetrated to Joseph's bedroom.

The major was hot in the face. He panted for breath, his cheeks quivered. The major was a man who, judging by what could be perceived of his intellectual gifts, could not have been a great acquisition to the army. He was a man who never could have been trusted to act a brilliant part. He was a creature of routine, a martinet; and since his retirement to Swanton had been a passionate golf-player and nothing else.

"What do you mean, sir? What do you mean?" spluttered he, "by putting me into your book?"

"My book!" echoed Joseph, affecting surprise. "What book do you refer to?"

"Oh! it's all very well your assuming that air of injured innocence, your trying to evade my question. Your sheepish expression does not deceive me. Why—there is the book in question by your bedside."

"I have, I admit, been reading that novel, which has recently appeared."

"You wrote it. Everyone in Swanton knows it. I don't object to your writing a book; any fool can do that—especially a novel. What I do object to is your putting me into it."

"If I remember rightly," said Joseph, quaking under the bed-clothes, and then wiping his upper lip on which a dew was forming, "If I remember aright, there is in it a major who plays golf, and does nothing else; but his name is Piper."

"What do I care about a name? It is I—I. You have put me in."

"Really, Major Jones, you have no justification in thus accusing me. The book does not bear my name on the back and title-page."

"Neither does the golfing retired military officer bear my name, but that does not matter. It is I myself. I am in your book. I would horsewhip you had I any energy left in me, but all is gone, gone with my personality into your book. Nothing is left of me—nothing but a body and a light tweed suit. I—I—have been taken out of myself and transferred to that——" he used a naughty word, "that book. How can I golf anymore? Walk the links any more with any heart? How can I putt a ball and follow it up with any feeling of interest? I am but a carcass. My soul, my character, my individuality have been burgled. You have broken into my inside, and have despoiled me of my personality." And he began to cry.

"Possibly," suggested Mr. Leveridge, "the author might——"

"The author can do nothing. I have been robbed—my fine ethereal self has been purloined. I—Dolgelly Jones—am only an outside husk. You have despoiled me of my richest jewel—myself."

"I really can do nothing, major."

"I know you can do nothing, that is the pity of it. You have sucked all my spiritual being with its concomitants out of me, and cannot put it back again. *You have used me up.*"

Then, wringing his hands, the major left the room, stumped slowly downstairs, and quitted the house.

Joseph Leveridge rose from his bed and dressed in great perturbation of mind. Here was a condition of affairs on which he had not reckoned. He was so distracted in mind that he forgot to brush his teeth.

When he reached his little sitting-room he found that the table was laid for his breakfast, and that his landlady had just brought up the usual rashers of bacon and two boiled eggs. She was sobbing.

"What is the matter, Mrs. Baker?" asked Joseph. "Has Lasinia"—that was the name of the servant—"broken any more dishes?"

"Everything has happened," replied the woman; "you have taken away my character."

"I—I never did such a thing."

"Oh, yes, sir, you have. All the time you've been writing, I've felt it going out of me like perspiration, and now it is all in your book."

"My book!"

"Yes, sir, under the name of Mrs. Brooks. But law! sir, what is there in a name? You might have taken the name of Baker and used that as you likes. There be plenty of Bakers in England and the Colonies. But it's my character, sir, you've taken away, and shoved it into your book." Then the woman wiped her eyes with her apron.

"But really, Mrs. Baker, if there be a landlady in this novel of which you complain——"

"There is, and it is me."

"But it is a mere work of fiction."

"It is not a work of fiction, it is a work of fact, and that a cruel fact. What has a poor lorn widow like me got to boast of but her character? I'm sure I've done well by you, and never boiled your eggs hard—and to use me like this."

"Good gracious, dear Mrs. Baker!"

"Don't dear me, sir. If you had loved me, if you had been decently grateful for all I have done for you, and mended your socks too, you'd not have stolen my character from me, and put it into your book. Ah, sir! you have dealt by me what I call regular shameful, and not like a gentleman. You *have used me up.*"

Joseph was silent, cowed. He turned the rashers about on the dish with his fork in an abstracted manner. All desire to eat was gone from him.

Then the landlady went on: "And it's not me only as has to complain. There are three gentlemen outside, sitting on the doorstep, awaiting of you. And they say that there they will remain, till you go out to your office. And they intend to have it out with you."

Joseph started from the chair he had taken, and went to the window, and threw up the sash.

Leaning out, he saw three hats below. It was as Mrs. Baker had intimated. Three gentlemen were seated on the doorstep. One was the vicar, another his "boss" Mr. Stork, and the third was Mr. Wotherspoon.

There could be no mistake about the vicar; he wore a chimney-pot hat of silk, that had begun to curl at the brim, anticipatory of being adapted as that of an archdeacon. Moreover, he wore extensive, well-cultivated grey whiskers on each cheek. If we were inclined to adopt the modern careless usage, we might say that he grew whiskers on *either* cheek. But in strict accuracy that would mean that the whiskers grew indifferently, or alternatively, intermittently on one cheek or the other. This, however, was not the case, consequently we say on *each* cheek. These whiskers now waved and fluttered in the light air passing up and down the street.

The second was Mr. Stork; he wore a stiff felt hat, his fiery hair showed beneath it, behind, and in front; when he lifted his head, the end of his pointed nose showed distinctly to Joseph Leveridge who looked down from above. The third, Mr. Wotherspoon, had a crushed brown cap on; he sat with his hands between his knees, dejected, and looking on the ground.

Mr. Wotherspoon lived in Swanton with his mother and three sisters. The mother was the widow of an officer, not well off. He was an agreeable man, an excellent player at lawn-tennis, croquet, golf, rackets, billiards, and cards. His age was thirty, and he had as yet no occupation. His mother gently, his sisters sharply, urged him to do something, so as to earn his livelihood. With his mother's death her pension would cease, and he could not then depend on his sisters. He always answered that something would turn up. Occasionally he ran to town to look for employment, but invariably returned without having secured any, and with his pockets empty. He was so cheerful, so good-natured, was such good company, that everyone liked him, but also everyone was provoked at his sponging on his mother and sisters.

"Really," said Mr. Leveridge, "I cannot encounter those three. It is true that I have drawn them pretty accurately in my novel, and here they are ready to take me to account for so doing. I will leave the house by the back door."

Without his breakfast, Joseph fled; and having escaped from those who had hoped to intercept him, he made his way to the river. Here were pleasant grounds, with walks laid out, and benches provided. The place was not likely to be frequented at that time of the morning, and Mr. Leveridge had half an hour to spare before he was due at the office. There, later, he was likely to meet his "boss"; but it was better to face him alone, than him accompanied by two others who had a similar grievance against him.

He seated himself on a bench and thought. He did not smoke; he had promised his "mamma" not to do so, and he was a dutiful son, and regarded his undertaking.

What should he do? He was becoming involved in serious embarrassments. Would it be possible to induce the publisher to withdraw the book from circulation and to receive back the fifty pounds? That was hardly possible. He had signed away all his rights in the novel, and the publisher had been to a considerable expense for paper, printing, binding, and advertising.

He was roused from his troubled thoughts by seeing Miss Asphodel Vincent coming along the walk towards him. Her step had lost its wonted spring, her carriage its usual buoyancy. In a minute or two she would reach him. Would she deign to speak? He felt no compunction towards her. He had made her his heroine in the tale. By not a word had he cast a shadow over her character or her abilities. Indeed, he had pictured her as the highest ideal of an English girl. She might be flattered, she could not be offended. And yet there was no flattery in his pencil—he had sketched her in as she was.

As she approached she noticed the young author. She did not hasten her step. She displayed a strange listlessness in her movements, and lack of vivacity in her eye.

When she stood over against him, Joseph Leveridge rose and removed his hat. "An early promenade, Miss Vincent," he said.

"Oh!" she said, "I am glad to meet you here where we cannot be overheard. I have something about which I must speak to you, to complain of a great injury done to me."

"You do me a high honour," exclaimed Joseph. "If I can do anything to alleviate your distress and to redress the wrong, command me."

"You can do nothing. It is impossible to undo what has already been done. You put me into your book."

"Miss Vincent," protested Leveridge with vehemence, "if I have, what then? I have not in the least overcharged the colours, by a line caricatured you." It was in vain for him further to pretend not to be the author and to have merely read the book.

"That may be, or it may not. But you have taken strange liberties with me in transferring me to your pages."

"And you really recognised yourself?"

"It is myself, my very self, who is there."

"And yet you are here, before my humble self."

"That is only my outer shell. All my individuality, all that goes to make up the Ego—I myself—has been taken from me and put into your book."

"Surely that cannot be."

"But it is so. I feel precisely as I suppose felt my doll when I was a child, when it became unstitched and all the bran ran out; it hung limp like a rag. But it is not bran you have deprived me of, it is my personality."

"In my novel is your portraiture indeed—but you yourself

are here," said Leveridge.

"It is my very self, my noblest and best part, my moral and intellectual self, which has been carried off and put into your book."

"This is quite impossible, Miss Vincent."

"A moment's thought," said she, "will convince you that it is as I say. If I pick an Alpine flower and transfer it to my blotting-book, it remains in the herbarium. It is no longer on the Alp where it bloomed."

"But——" urged Joseph.

"No," she interrupted, "you cannot undeceive me. No one can be in two places at the same time. If I am in your book, I cannot be here—except so far as goes my animal nature and frame. You have subjected me, Mr. Leveridge, to the greatest humiliation. I am by you reduced to the level of a score of girls that I know, with no pursuits, no fixed principles, no opinions of their own, no ideas. They are swayed by every fashion, they are moulded by their surroundings; they are destitute of what some would call moral fibre, and I would term character. I had all this, but you have deprived me of it, by putting it into your book. I shall henceforth be the sport of every breath, be influenced by every folly, be without self-confidence and decision, the prey to any adventurer."

"For Heaven's sake, do not say that."

"I cannot say anything other. If I had a sovereign in my purse, and a pickpocket stole it, I should no longer have the purse and sovereign, only the pocket; and I am a mere pocket now without the coin of my personality that you have filched from me. Mr. Leveridge, it was a cruel wrong you did me, *when you used me up*."

Then, sighing, Miss Asphodel went languidly on her way. Joseph was as one stunned. He buried his face in his hands. The person of all others with whom he desired to stand well, that person looked upon him as her most deadly enemy, at all events as the one who had most cruelly aggrieved her.

Presently, hearing the clock strike, he started. He was due

at the office, and Joseph Leveridge had always made a point of punctuality.

He now went to the office, and learned from his fellow-clerk that Mr. Stork had not returned; he had been there, and then had gone away to seek Leveridge at his lodgings. Joseph considered it incumbent on him to resume his hat and go in quest of his "boss."

On his way it occurred to him that there was monotony in bacon and eggs for breakfast every morning, and he would like a change. Moreover, he was hungry; he had left the house of Mrs. Baker without taking a mouthful, and if he returned now for a snack the eggs and the bacon would be cold. So he stepped into the shop of Mr. Box, the grocer, for a tin of sardines in oil.

When the grocer saw him he said: "Will you favour me with a word, sir, in the back shop?"

"I am pressed for time," replied Leveridge nervously.

"But one word; I will not detain you," said Mr. Box, and led the way. Joseph walked after him.

"Sir," said the grocer, shutting the glass door, "you have done me a prodigious wrong. You have deprived me of what I would not have lost for a thousand pounds. You have put me into your book. How my business will get on without me—I mean my intellect, my powers of organisation, my trade instincts, in a word, myself—I do not know. You have taken them from me and put them into your book. I am consigned to a novel, when I want all my powers behind the counter. Possibly my affairs for a while will go on by the weight of their own momentum, but it cannot be for long without my controlling brain. Sir, you have brought me and my family to ruin—*you have used me up.*"

Leveridge could bear this no more; he seized the handle of the door, rushed through the outer shop, precipitated himself into the street, carrying the sardine tin in his hand, and hurried to his lodgings.

But there new trouble awaited him. On the doorstep still sat the three gentlemen.

When they saw him they rose to their feet.

"I know, I know what you have to say," gasped Joseph. "In pity do not attack me all together. One at a time. With your leave, Mr. Vicar, will you step up first into my humble little sanctum, and I will receive the others later. I believe that the smell of bacon and eggs is gone from the room. I left the window open."

"I will most certainly follow you," said the Vicar of Swanton. "This is a most serious matter."

"Excuse me, will you take a chair?"

"No, thank you; I can speak best when on my legs. I lose impressiveness when seated. But I fear, alas! that gift has been taken from me. Sir! sir! you have put me into your book. My earthly tabernacle may be here, standing on your—or Mrs. Baker's drugget—but all my great oratorical powers have gone. I have been despoiled of what was in me my highest, noblest, most spiritual parts. What my preaching henceforth will be I fear to contemplate. I may be able to string together a number of texts, and tack on an application, but that is mere mechanical work. I used to dredge in much florid eloquence, to stick in the flowers of elocution between every joint. And now!—I am despoiled of all. I, the Vicar of Swanton, shall be as a mere stick; I shall no more be a power in the pulpit, a force on the platform. My prospects in the diocese are put an end to. Miserable, miserable young man, you might have pumped others, but why me? I know but too surely that *you have used me up.*" The vicar had taken off his hat, his bald forehead was beaded, his bristling grey whiskers drooped, his unctuous expression had faded away. His eyes, usually bearing the look as though turned inward in ecstatic contemplation of his personal piety, with only a watery stare on the world without, were now dull.

He turned to the door. "I will send up Stork," he said.

"Do so by all means, sir," was all that Joseph could say.

When the solicitor entered his red hair had assumed a darker dye, through the moisture that exuded from his head.

"Mr. Leveridge," said he, "this is a scurvy trick you have played me. You have put me into your book."

"I only sketched a not over-scrupulous lawyer," protested Joseph. "Why should you put the cap on your own head?"

"Because it fits. It is myself you have put into your book, and by no legal process can I get out of it. I shall not be competent to advise the magistrates on the bench, and, good heavens! what a mess they will get into. I do not know whether your fellow-clerk can carry on the business. *I have been used up.* I'll tell you what. You go away; I want you no more at the office. Whenever you revisit Swanton you will see only the ruins of the respected firm of Stork. It cannot go on when I am not in it, but in your book."

The last to arrive was Mr. Wotherspoon. He was in a most depressed condition. "There was not much in me," said he, "not at any time. You might have spared such a trifle as me, and not put me also into your book and *used me up.* Oh, dear, dear! what will my poor mother do! And how Sarah and Jane will bully me."

★★★★★★

That same day Mr. Leveridge packed up his traps and departed from Swanton for his mother's house.

That she was delighted to see him need not be said; that something was wrong, her maternal instinct told her. But it was not for some days that he confided to her so much as this: "Oh, mother, I have written a novel, and have put into it the people of Swanton—and so have had to leave."

"My dear Joe," said the old lady, "you have done wrong and made a great mistake. You never should introduce actual living personages into a work of fiction. You should pulp them first, and then run out your characters fresh from the pulp."

"I was so afraid of using my imagination," explained Joe.

Some months elapsed, and Leveridge could not resolve on an employment that would suit him and at the same time maintain him. The fifty pounds he had earned would not last long. He began to be sensible of the impulse to be again writing. He resisted it for a while, but when he got a letter from his publisher, saying that the novel had sold well, far better than had been expected, and that he would be pleased to consider another from Mr. Leveridge's pen, and could promise him for it more liberal terms, then Joseph's scruples vanished. But on one thing he was resolved. He would now create his characters. They should not be taken from observation.

Moreover, he determined to differentiate his new work from the old in other material points. His characters should be the reverse of those in the first novel. For his heroine he imagined a girl of boisterous spirits, straightforward, true, but somewhat unconventional, and given to use slang expressions. He had never met with such a girl, so that she would be a pure creation of his brain, and he made up his mind to call her Poppy. Then he would avoid drawing the portrait of an Evangelical parson, and introduce one decidedly High Church; he would have no heavy, narrow tradesman like Box, but a man full of venture and speculative push. Moreover, having used up the not over-scrupulous lawyer, he would portray one, the soul of honour, the confidant of not only the county gentry but of the county nobility. And as he had caused so much trouble by the introduction of good old Mother Baker, he would trace the line of a lively, skittish young widow, always on the hunt after admirers, and endeavouring to entangle the youths who lodged with her.

As he went on with his story, it worked out to his satisfaction, and what especially gratified him and gave repose to his mind was the consciousness that he was using no one up, with whom he was acquainted, and that all his characters were pure creations.

The work was complete, and the publisher agreed to give a hundred pounds for it. Then it passed through the press, and in due course Leveridge heard from the publisher that his six free copies had been sent off to him by train. Joseph was almost as excited over his second novel as he was over the first.

He was too impatient to wait till the parcels were sent round in the ordinary way. He hurried to the station in the evening, to meet the train from town, by which he expected his consignment; and having secured it, he hurried home, carrying the heavy parcel.

His mother's house was comparatively large; she occupied but a corner of it, and she had given over to her son a little cosy sitting-room, in which he might write and read. Into this room Joseph carried his parcel, full of impatience to cut the string and disclose the volumes.

But he had hardly passed through his door before he was startled to see that his room was full of people; all but one were seated about the table. That one who was not, lounged against the bookcase, standing on one foot. With a shock of surprise, Joseph recognised all those there gathered together. They were the characters in his book, his own creations. And that individual who stood, in an indifferent attitude, was his new heroine, Poppy. The first shock of surprise rapidly passed. Joseph Leveridge felt no fear, but rather a sense of pleasure. He was in the presence of his own creations, and knew them familiarly. There were seven in all. At his appearance they all saluted him respectfully as their creator—all except Poppy, who gave him a wink and a nod.

At the head of the table sat the High Church parson, shaven, with a long coat and a grave face, next to him, on the right, Lady Mabel Forraby, a tall, elderly, aristocratic-looking woman, the aunt of Poppy. One element of lightness in the book had consisted in the struggles of Lady Mabel to control her way-ward niece and the revolt of the latter. Mr. Leveridge had never known a person of title in his life, so that Lady Mabel was a pure creation; so also, brought up, as he had been, by a Calvinistic mother, and afterwards thrown under the ministry of the Vicar of Swanton, he had not once come across a Ritualist.

Consequently his parson, in this instance, was also a pure creation. A young gentleman, the hero of the novel, a bright intelligent fellow, full of vigour and good sense, and highly cul-tured, sat next to Lady Mabel. Joseph had never been thrown into association with men of quite this type. He had met nice respectable clerks and amusing and agreeable travellers for com-mercial houses, so that this personage also was a creation. So most certainly was the bold, pert little widow who rolled her eyes and put on winsome airs. Joseph had kept clear of all such instances, but he had heard and read of them. She could look to him as her creator.

And that naughty little Poppy! Her naughtiness was all mischief, put on to aggravate her staid old aunt, so full of daring, and yet withal so steady of heart; so full of frolic, but with principle underlying it all. Joseph had never encountered anyone like her, anyone approaching to her. The young ladies to whom his mother introduced him were all very prim and proper. At Swanton he had been little in society: the vicar's daughter was a tract distributer and a mission woman, and Mr. Stork's daughter a domestic drudge. Of all the characters in Joseph's book she was his most especial and delightful creation.

Then the white-haired family lawyer, fond of his jokes, able to tell a good story, close as a walnut relative to all matters communicated to him, strict and honourable in all his dealings, content with his small earnings, and frugally laying them by. Joseph had not met such a man, but he had idealised him as the sort of lawyer he would wish to be should he stick to his profession. He also, accordingly, was a creation. And last, but not least, was the red-faced, audacious stockbroker; a man of sharp and quick determination, who saw a chance in a moment and closed on it, who was keen of scent and smelt a risky investment the moment it came before him. Joseph knew no stockbroker—had only heard of them by rumour. He, therefore, was a creation.

"Well, my children, not of my loins, but of my brain," said the author. "What do you all want?"

"Bodies," they replied with one voice.

"Bodies!" gasped Joseph, stepping backwards. "Why, what possesses you all? You can't expect me to furnish you with them."

"But, indeed, we do, old chap," said Poppy.

"Niece!" said Lady Mabel, turning about in her chair, "address your creator with more respect."

"Stay, my lady," said the parson. "Allow me to explain matters to Mr. Leveridge. He is young and an inexperienced writer of fiction, and is therefore unaware of the exigencies of his profession. You must know, dear author of our being, that every author of a work of imagination, such as you have been, lays himself under a moral and an inexorable obligation to find bodies for all those whom he has called into existence through his fertile brain. Mr. Leveridge has not mixed in the literary world. He does not belong to the Society of Authors. He is—he will excuse the expression—raw in his profession. It is a well-known law among novelists that they must furnish bodies for such as they have called into existence out of their pure imagination. For this reason they invariably call their observation to their assistance, and they balance in their books the creations with the transcripts from life. The only exception to this rule that I am aware of," continued the parson, "is where the author is able to get his piece dramatised, in which case, of course, the difficulty ceases."

"I should love to go on the stage," threw in Poppy.

"Niece, you do not know what you say," remarked Lady Mabel, turning herself about.

"Allow me, my lady," said the parson. "What I have said is fact, is it not?"

"Most certainly," replied all. Lady Mabel said: "I suppose it is."

"Then," pursued the parson, "the situation is this: Have you secured the dramatisation of your novel?"

"I never gave it a thought," said Joseph.

"In that case, as there is no prospect of our being so accommodated, the position is this: We shall have to haunt you night and day, mainly at night, till you have accommodated us with bodies; we cannot remain as phantom creations of a highly imaginative soul such as is yours, Mr. Leveridge. If you have your rights, so have we. And we insist on ours, and will insist till we are satisfied."

At once all vanished.

Joseph Leveridge felt that he had got himself into a worse hobble than before. From his former difficulties he had escaped by flight. But there was, he feared, no flying from these seven impatient creations all clamouring for bodies, and to provide them with such was beyond his powers. All his delight in the publication of his new novel was spent. It had brought with it care and perplexity.

He went to bed.

During the night, he was troubled with his characters; they peeped in at him. Poppy got a peacock's feather and tickled his nose just as he was dropping asleep. "You bounder!" she said; "I shall give you no peace till you have settled me into a body— but oh! get me on to the stage if you can."

"Poppy, come away," called Lady Mabel. "Don't be improper. Mr. Leveridge will do his best. I want a body quite as much as do you, but I know how to ask for it properly."

"And I," said the parson, "should like to have mine before Easter, but have one I must."

Mr. Leveridge's state now was worse than the first. One or other of his creatures was ever watching him. His every movement was spied on. There was no escaping their vigilance. Sometimes they attended him in groups of two or three; sometimes they were all around him.

At meals not one was missing, and they eyed every mouthful of his food as he raised it to his lips. His mother saw nothing— the creations were invisible to all eyes save those of their creator.

If he went out for a country walk, they trotted forth with him, some before, looking round at every turn to see which way he purposed going, some following. Poppy and the skittish widow managed to attach themselves to him, one on each side. "I hate that little woman," said Poppy. "Why did you call her into being?"

"I never dreamed that things would come to this pass."

"I am convinced, creator dear, that there is a vein of wickedness in your composition, or you would never have imagined such a minx, good and amiable and butter-won't-melt-in-your-mouth though you may look. And there must be a frolicsome devil in your heart, or I should never have become."

"Indeed, Poppy, I am very glad that I gave you being. But one may have too much even of a good thing, and there are moments when I could dispense with your presence."

"I know, when you want to carry on with the widow. She is always casting sheep's eyes at you."

"But, Poppy, you forget my hero, whom I created on purpose for you."

"All my attention is now engrossed in you, and will be till you provide me with a body."

When Leveridge was in his room reading, if he raised his eyes from his book they met the stare of one of his characters. If he went up to his bedroom, he was followed. If he sat with his mother, one kept guard.

This was become so intolerable, that one evening he protested to the stockbroker, who was then in attendance. "Do, I entreat you, leave me to myself. You treat me as if I were a lunatic and about to commit *felo de se*, and you were my warders."

"We watch you, sir," said the stockbroker, "in our own interest. We cannot suffer you to give us the slip. We are all expectant and impatient for the completion of what you have begun."

Then the parson undertook to administer a lecture on duty, on responsibilities contracted to those called into partial existence by a writer of fiction. He cannot be allowed to half do his work. His creations must be realised, and can only be realised by being given a material existence.

"But what the dickens can I do? I cannot fabricate bodies for you. I never in my life even made a doll."

"Have you no thought of dramatising us?"

"I know no dramatic writers."

"Do it yourself."

"Does not this sort of work require a certain familiarity with the technique of the stage which I do not possess?"

"That might be attended to later. Pass your MS. through the hands of a dramatic expert, and pay him a percentage of your profits in recognition of his services. Only one thing I bargain for, do not present me on the stage in such a manner as to discredit my cloth."

"Have I done so in my book?"

"No, indeed, I have nothing to complain of in that. But there is no counting on what Poppy may persuade you into doing, and I fear that she is gaining influence over you. Remember, she is your creation, and you must not suffer her to mould you."

The idea took root. The suggestion was taken up, and Joseph Leveridge applied himself to his task with zest. But he had to conceal what he was about from his mother, who had no opinion of the drama, and regarded the theatre as a sink of iniquity.

But now new difficulties arose. Joseph's creations would not leave him alone for a moment. Each had a suggestion, each wanted his or her own part accentuated at the expense of the other. Each desired the heightening of the situations in which they severally appeared. The clamour, the bickering, the interference made it impossible for Joseph to collect his thoughts, keep cool, and proceed with his work.

Sunday arrived, and Joseph drew on his gloves, put on his box-hat, and offered his arm to his mother, to conduct her to chapel. All the characters were drawn up in the hall to accompany them. Joseph and his mother walking down the street to Ebenezer Chapel presented a picture of a good and dutiful son and of a pious widow not to be surpassed. Poppy and the widow entered into a struggle as to which was to walk on the unoccupied side of Joseph. If this had been introduced into the picture it would have marred it; but happily this was invisible to all eyes save those of Joseph. The rest of the imaginary party walked arm in arm behind till the chapel was reached, when the parson started back.

"I am not going in there! It is a schism-shop," he exclaimed. "Nothing in the world would induce me to cross the threshold."

"And I," said Lady Mabel, "I have no idea of attending a place of worship not of the Established Church."

"I'll go in—if only to protect Creator from the widow," said

Poppy.

Joseph and his mother entered, and occupied their pew. The characters, with the exception of the parson and the old lady, grouped themselves where they were able. The stockbroker stood in the aisle with his arms on the pew door, to ensure that Joseph was kept a prisoner there. But before the service had advanced far he had gone to sleep. This was the more to be regretted, as the minister delivered a very strong appeal to the unconverted, and if ever there was an unconverted worldling, it was that stockbroker.

The skittish widow was leering at a deacon of an amorous complexion, but as he did not, and, in fact, could not see her, all her efforts were cast away. The solicitor sat with stolid face and folded hands, and allowed the discourse to flow over him like a refreshing douche. Poppy had got very tired of the show, and had slunk away to rejoin her aunt. The hero closed his eyes and seemed resigned.

After nearly an hour had elapsed, whilst a hymn was being sung, Joseph, more to himself than to his mother, said: "Can I escape?"

"Escape what? Wretch?" inquired the widowed lady.

"I think I can do it. There's a room at the side for earnest in-quirers, or a vestry or something, with an outer door. I will risk it, and make a bolt for my liberty."

He very gently and cautiously unhasped the door of the pew, and as he slid it open, the sleeping stockbroker, still sleeping and unconscious, slipped back, and Joseph was out. He made his way into the room at the side, forth from the actual chapel, ran through it, and tried the door that opened into a side lane. It was locked, but happily the key was in its place. He turned it, plunged forth, and fell into the arms of his characters. They were all there. The solicitor had been observing him out of the corner of his eye, and had given the alarm. The stockbroker was aroused, and he, the solicitor, the hero, ran out, gave the alarm to the three without, and Joseph was intercepted, and his attempt at escape frustrated. He was reconducted home by them, himself dejected, they triumphant.

When his mother returned she was full of solicitude.

"What was the matter, Joe dear?" she inquired.

"I wasn't feeling very well," he explained. "But I shall be better presently."

"I hope it will not interfere with your appetite, Joe. I have cold lamb and mint-sauce for our early dinner."

"I shall peck a bit, I trust," said Mr. Leveridge.

But during dinner he was abstracted and silent. All at once he brought down his fist on the table. "I've hit it!" he exclaimed, and a flush of colour mantled his face to the temples.

"My dear," said his mother; "you have made all the plates and dishes jump, and have nearly upset the water-bottle."

"Excuse me, mother; I really must go to my room."

He rose, made a sign to his characters, and they all rose and trooped after him into his private apartment.

When they were within he said to his hero: "May I trouble you kindly to shut the door and turn the key? My mother will be anxious and come after me, and I want a word with you all. It will not take two minutes. I see my way to our mutual accommodation. Do not be uneasy and suspicious; I will make no further attempt at evasion. Meet me tomorrow morning at the 9.48 down train. I am going to take you all with me to Swanton."

A tap at the door.

"Open—it is my mother," said Joseph.

Mrs. Leveridge entered with a face of concern. "What is the matter with you, Joe?" she said. "If we were not both of us water-drinkers, I should say that you had been indulging in—spirits."

"Mother, I must positively be off to Swanton tomorrow morning. I see my way now, all will come right."

"How, my precious boy?"

"I cannot explain. I see my way to clearing up the unpleasantness caused by that unfortunate novel of mine. Pack my trunk, mother."

"Not on the Sabbath, lovie."

"No—tomorrow morning. I start by the 9.48 a.m. We all go together."

"We—am I to accompany you?"

"No, no. We—did I say? It is a habit I have got into as an author. Authors, like royal personages, speak of themselves as We."

Joseph Leveridge was occupied during the afternoon in writing to his victims at Swanton.

First, he penned a notice to Mrs. Baker that he would require his lodgings from the morrow, and that he had something to say to her that would afford her much gratification.

Then he wrote to the vicar, expressed his regret for having deprived him of his personality, and requested him, if he would do him the favour, to call in the evening at 7.30, at his lodgings in West Street. He had something of special importance to communicate to him. He apologised for not himself calling at the vicarage, but said that there were circumstances that made it more desirable that he should see his reverence privately in his own lodgings.

Next, he addressed an epistle to Mr. Stork. He assured him that he, Joseph Leveridge, had felt keenly the wrong he had done him, that he had forfeited his esteem, had ill repaid his kindness, had acted in a manner towards his employer that was dishonourable. But, he added, he had found a means of rectifying what was wrong. He placed himself unreservedly in the hands of Mr. Stork, and entreated him to meet him at his rooms in West Street on the ensuing Monday evening at 7.45, when he sincerely trusted that the past would be forgotten, and a brighter future would be assured.

This was followed by a formal letter couched to Mr. Box. He invited him to call at Mrs. Baker's lodgings on that same evening at 8 p.m., as he had business of an important and far-reaching nature to discuss with him. If Mr. Box considered that he, Joseph Leveridge, had done him an injury, he was ready to make what reparation lay in his power.

Taking a fresh sheet of notepaper, he now wrote a fifth letter, this to Mr. Wotherspoon, requesting the honour of a call at his "diggings" at 8.15 p.m., when matters of controversy between them could be amicably adjusted.

The ensuing letter demanded some deliberation. It was to Asphodel. He wrote it out twice before he was satisfied with the mode in which it was expressed. He endeavoured to disguise under words full of respect, yet not disguise too completely, the sentiments of his heart. But he was careful to let drop nothing at which she might take umbrage. He entreated her to be so gracious as to allow him an interview by the side of the river at the hour of 8.30 on the Monday evening. He apologised for venturing to make such a demand, but he intimated that the matter he had to communicate was so important and so urgent, that it could not well be postponed till Tuesday, and that it was also most necessary that the interview should be private. It was something he had to say that would materially—no, not materially, but morally—affect her, and would relieve his mind from a burden of remorse that had become to him wholly intolerable.

The final, the seventh letter, was to Major Dolgelly Jones, and was more brief. It merely intimated that he had something of the utmost importance to communicate to his private ear, and for this purpose he desired the favour of a call at Mrs. Baker's lodgings, at 8.45 on Monday evening.

These letters despatched, Mr. Leveridge felt easier in mind and lighter at heart. He slept well the ensuing night, better than he had for long. His creations did not so greatly disturb him. He was aware that he was still kept under surveillance, but the watch was not so strict, nor so galling as hitherto.

On the Monday morning he was at the station, and took his ticket for Swanton. One ticket sufficed, as his companions, who awaited him on the platform, were imaginary characters.

When he took his seat, they pressed into the carriage after him. Poppy secured the seat next him, but the widow placed herself opposite, and exerted all her blandishment with the hope of engrossing his whole attention. At a junction all got out, and Joseph provided himself with a luncheon-basket and mineral water. The characters watched him discussing the half-chicken and slabs of ham, with the liveliest interest, and were especially observant of his treatment of the thin paper napkin, wherewith he wiped his fingers and mouth.

At last he arrived at Swanton and engaged a cab, as he was encumbered with a portmanteau. Lady Mabel, Poppy, and the widow could be easily accommodated within, the two latter with their backs to the horses. Joseph would willingly have resigned his seat to either of these, but they would not hear of it. A gentle altercation ensued between the parson and the solicitor, as to which should ride on the box. The lawyer desired to yield the place to "the cloth," but the parson would not hear of this— the silver hairs of the other claimed precedence. The stockbroker mounted to the roof of the fly and the clerical gentleman hung on behind. The hero professed his readiness to walk.

Eventually the cab drew up at Mrs. Baker's door.

That stout, elderly lady received her old lodger without effusion, and with languid interest. The look of the house was not what it had been. It had deteriorated. The windows had not been cleaned nor the banisters dusted.

"My dear old landlady, I am so glad to see you again," said Joseph.

"Thank you, sir. You ordered no meal, but I have got two mutton chops in the larder, and can mash some potatoes. At what time would you like your supper, sir?" She had become a machine, a thing of routine.

"Not yet, thank you. I have business to transact first, and I shall not be disengaged before nine o'clock. But I have something to say to you, Mrs. Baker, and I will say it at once and get it over, if you will kindly step up into my parlour."

She did so, sighing at each step of the stairs as she ascended.

All the characters mounted as well, and entering the little sitting-room, ranged themselves against the wall facing the door.

Mrs. Baker was a portly woman, aged about forty-five, and plain featured. She had formerly been neat, now she was dowdy. Before she had lost her character she never appeared in that room without removing her apron, but on this occasion she wore it, and it was not clean.

"Widow!" said Joseph, addressing his character, "will you kindly step forward?"

"I would do anything for *you*," with a roll of the eyes.

"Dear Mrs. Baker," said Leveridge, "I feel that I have done you a grievous wrong."

"Well, sir, I ain't been myself since you put me into your book."

"My purpose is now to undo the past, and to provide you with a character."

Then, turning to the skittish widow of his creation, he said, "Now, then, slip into and occupy her."

"I don't like the tenement," said the widow, pouting.

"Whether you like it or not," protested Joseph, "you must have that or no other." He waved his hand. "Presto!" he exclaimed.

Instantly a wondrous change was effected in Mrs. Baker. She whipped off the apron, and crammed it under the sofa cushion. She wriggled in her movements, she eyed herself in the glass, and exclaimed: "Oh, my! what a fright I am. I'll be back again in a minute when I have changed my gown and done up my hair."

"We can dispense with your presence, Mrs. Baker," said Leveridge sternly. "I will ring for you when you are wanted."

At that moment a rap at the door was heard; and Mrs. Baker, having first dropped a coquettish curtsy to her lodger, tripped downstairs to admit the vicar, and to show him up to Mr. Leveridge's apartment.

"You may go, Mrs. Baker," said he; for she seemed inclined to linger.

When she had left the room, Joseph contemplated the reverend gentleman. He bore a crestfallen appearance. He looked as if he had been out in the rain all night without a paletot. His cheeks were flabby, his mouth drooped at the corners, his eyes were vacant, and his whiskers no longer stuck out horrescent and assertive.

"Dear vicar," said Leveridge, "I cannot forgive myself." In former times, Mr. Leveridge would not have dreamed of addressing the reverend gentleman in this familiar manner, but it was other now that the latter looked so limp and forlorn. "My dear vicar, I cannot forgive myself for the trouble I have brought upon you. It has weighed on me as a nightmare, for I know that it is not you only who have suffered, but also the whole parish of Swanton. Happily a remedy is at hand. I have here——" he waved to the parson of his creation, "I have here an individuality I can give to you, and henceforth, if you will not be precisely yourself again, you will be a personality in your parish and the diocese." He waved his hand. "Presto!"

In the twinkling of an eye all was changed in the Vicar of Swanton. He straightened himself. His expression altered to what it never had been before. The cheeks became firm, and lines formed about the mouth indicative of force of character and of self-restraint. The eye assumed an eager look as into far distances, as seeking something beyond the horizon.

The vicar walked to the mirror over the mantelshelf.

"Bless me!" he said, "I must go to the barber's and have these whiskers off." And he hurried downstairs.

After a little pause in the proceedings, Mrs. Baker, now very trim, with a blue ribbon round her neck hanging down in streamers behind, ushered up Mr. Stork. The lawyer had a faded appearance, as if he had been exposed to too strong sunlight; he walked in with an air of lack of interest, and sank into a chair.

"My dear old master," said Leveridge, "it is my purpose to restore to you all your former energy, and to supply you with what you may possibly have lacked previously."

He signed to the white-haired family solicitor he had called into fictitious being, and waved his hand.

At once Mr. Stork stood up and shook his legs, as though shaking out crumbs from his trousers. His breast swelled, he threw back his head, his eye shone clear and was steady.

"Mr. Leveridge," said he, "I have long had my eye on you, sir—had my eye on you. I have marked your character as one of uncompromising probity. I hate shiftiness, I abhor duplicity. I have been disappointed with my clerks. I could not always trust them to do the right thing. I want to strengthen and brace my firm. But I will not take into partnership with myself any but one of the strictest integrity. Sir! I have marked you—I have marked you, Mr. Leveridge. Call on me tomorrow morning, and we will consider the preliminaries for a partnership. Don't talk to me of buying a partnership."

"I have not done so, sir."

"I know you have not. I will take you in, sir, for your intrinsic value. An honest man is worth his weight in gold, and is as scarce as the precious metal."

Then, with dignity, Mr. Stork withdrew, and passed Mr. Box, the grocer, mounting the stairs.

"Well, Mr. Box," said Leveridge, "how wags the world with you?"

"Badly, sir, badly since you booked me. I mentioned to you, sir, that I trusted my little business would for a while go on by its own momentum. It has, sir, it has, but the momentum has been downhill. I can't control it. I have not the personality to do so, to serve as a drag, to urge it upwards. I am in daily expectation, sir, of a regular smash up."

"I am sorry to hear this," said Leveridge. "But I think I have found a means of putting all to rights. Presto!" He waved his hand and the imaginary character of the stockbroker had actualised himself in the body of Mr. Box.

"I see how to do it. By ginger, I do!" exclaimed the grocer, a spark coming into his eye. "I'll run my little concern on quite other lines. And look ye here, Mr. Leveridge. I bet you my bottom dollar that I'll run it to a tremendous success, become a second Lipton, and keep a yacht."

As Mr. Box bounced out of the room and proceeded to run downstairs, he ran against and nearly knocked over Mrs. Baker; the lady was whispering to and coquetting with Mr. Wotherspoon, who was on the landing. That gentleman, in his condition of lack of individuality, was like a teetotum spun in the hands of the designing Mrs. Baker, who put forth all the witchery she possessed, or supposed that she possessed, to entangle him in an amorous intrigue.

"Come in," shouted Joseph Leveridge, and Mr. Wotherspoon, looking hot and frightened and very shy, tottered in and sank into a chair. He was too much shaken and perturbed by the advances of Mrs. Baker to be able to speak.

"There," said Joseph, addressing his hero. "You cannot do better than animate that feeble creature. Go!"

Instantly Mr. Wotherspoon sprang to his feet. "By George!" said he. "I wonder that never struck me before. I'll at once volunteer to go out to South Africa, and have a shot at those canting, lying, treacherous Boers. If I come back with a score of their scalps at my waist, I shall have deserved well of my country. I will volunteer at once. But—I say, Leveridge—clear that hulking, fat old landlady out of the way. She blocks the stairs, and I can't kick down a woman."

When Mr. Wotherspoon was gone—"Well," said Poppy, "what have you got for me?"

"If you will come with me, Poppy dear, I will serve you as well as the rest."

"I hope better than you did that odious little widow. But she is well paid out."

"Follow me to the riverside," said Joseph; "at 8.33 p.m. I am due there, and so is another—a lady."

"And pray why did you not make her come here instead of lugging me all the way down there?"

"Because I could not make an appointment with a young lady in my bachelor's apartments."

"That's all very fine. But I am there."

"Yes, you—but you are only an imaginary character, and she is a substantial reality."

"I think I had better accompany you," said Lady Mabel.

"I think not. If your ladyship will kindly occupy my *fauteuil* till I return, that chair will ever after be sacred to me. Come along, Poppy."

"I'm game," said she.

On reaching the riverside Joseph saw that Miss Vincent was walking there in a listless manner, not straight, but swerving from side to side. She saw him, but did not quicken her pace, nor did her face light up with interest.

"Now, then," said he to Poppy, "what do you think of her?"

"She ain't bad," answered the fictitious character; "she is very pretty certainly, but inanimate."

"You will change all that."

"I'll try—you bet."

Asphodel came up. She bowed, but did not extend her hand.

"Miss Vincent," said Joseph. "How good of you to come."

"Not at all. I could not help. I have no free-will left. When you wrote Come—I came, I could do no other. I have no initiative, no power of resistance."

"I do hope, Miss Vincent, that the thing you so feared has not happened."

"What thing?"

"You have not been snapped up by a fortune-hunter?"

"No. People have not as yet found out that I have lost my individuality. I have kept very much to myself—that is to say, not to myself, as I have no proper myself left—I mean to the semblance of myself. People have thought I was anaemic."

Leveridge turned aside: "Well, Poppy!"

"Right you are."

Leveridge waved his hand. Instantly all the inertia passed away from the girl, she stood erect and firm. A merry twinkle kindled in her eye, a flush was on her cheek, and mischievous devilry played about her lips.

"I feel," said she, "as another person."

"Oh! I am so glad, Miss Vincent."

"That is a pretty speech to make to a lady! Glad I am different from what I was before."

"I did not mean that—I meant—in fact, I meant that as you were and as you are you are always charming."

"Thank you, sir!" said Asphodel, curtsying and laughing.

"Ah! Miss Vincent, at all times you have seemed to me the ideal of womanhood. I have worshipped the very ground you have trod upon."

"Fiddlesticks."

He looked at her. For the moment he was bewildered, oblivious that the old personality of Asphodel had passed into his book and that the new personality of Poppy had invaded Asphodel.

"Well," said she, "is that all you have to say to me?"

"All?—oh, no. I could say a great deal—I have ordered my supper for nine o'clock."

"Oh, how obtuse you men are! Come—is this leap year?"

"I really believe that it is."

"Then I shall take the privilege of the year, and offer you my hand and heart and fortune—there! Now it only remains with you to name the day."

"Oh! Miss Vincent, you overcome me."

"Stuff and nonsense. Call me Asphodel, do Joe."

★★★★★★

Mr. Leveridge walked back to his lodgings as if he trod on air. As he passed by the churchyard, he noticed the vicar, now shaven and shorn, labouring at a laden wheelbarrow. He halted at the rails and said: "Why, vicar, what are you about?"

"The sexton has begun a grave for old Betty Goodman, and it is unfinished. He must dig another." He turned over the wheelbarrow and shot its contents into the grave.

"But what are you doing?" again asked Joseph.

"Burying the Mitre hymnals," replied the vicar.

The clock struck a quarter to nine.

"I must hurry!" exclaimed Joseph.

On reaching his lodgings he found Major Dolgelly Jones in his sitting-room, sitting on the edge of his table tossing up a tennis-ball. In the armchair, invisible to the major, reclined Lady Mabel.

"I am so sorry to be late," apologised Joseph. "How are you, sir?"

"Below par. I have been so ever since you put me into your book. I have no appetite for golf. I can do nothing to pass the weary hours but toss up and down a tennis-ball."

"I hope——" began Joseph; and then a horror seized on him. He had no personality of his creation left but that of Lady Mabel. Would it be possible to translate that into the major?

He remained silent, musing for a while, and then said hesitatingly to the lady: "Here, my lady, is the body you are to individualise."

"But it is that of a man!"

"There is no other left."

"It is hardly delicate."

"There is no help for it." Then turning to the major, he said: "I am very sorry—it really is no fault of mine, but I have only a female personality to offer to you, and that elderly."

"It is all one to me," replied the major, "catch"—he caught the ball. "Many of our generals are old women. I am agreeable. *Place aux dames.*"

"But," protested Lady Mabel, "you made me a member of a very ancient titled house that came over with the Conqueror."

"The personality I offer you," said I to the major, "though female is noble; the family is named in the roll of Battle Abbey."

"Oh!" said Dolgelly Jones, "I descend from one of the royal families of Powys, lineally from Caswallon Llanhir and Maelgwn Gwynedd, long before the Conqueror was thought of."

"Well, then," said Leveridge, and waved his hand.

In Swanton it is known that the major now never plays golf; he keeps rabbits.

★★★★★★

It is with some scruple that I insert this record in the *Book of Ghosts*, for actually it is not a story of ghosts. But a greater scruple moved me as to whether I should be justified in revealing a professional secret, known only among such as belong to the Confraternity of Writers of Fiction. But I have observed so much perplexity arise, so much friction caused, by persons suddenly breaking out into a course of conduct, or into actions, so entirely inconsistent with their former conduct as to stagger their acquaintances and friends. Henceforth, to use a vulgarism, since I have let the cat out of the bag, they will know that such persons have been used up by novel writers that have known them, and who have replaced the stolen individualities with others freshly created. This is the explanation, and the explanation has up to the present remained a professional secret.

The Merewigs

(A tale from *A Book of Ghosts*)

During the time that I lived in Essex, I had the pleasure of knowing Major Donelly, retired on half-pay, who had spent many years in India; he was a man of great powers of observation, and possessed an inexhaustible fund of information of the most valuable quality, which he was ready to communicate to his intimates, among whom was I.

Major Donelly is now no more, and the world is thereby the poorer. Major Donelly took an interest in everything—anthropology, mechanics, archaeology, physical science, natural history, the stock market, politics. In fact, it was not possible in conversation to broach a subject with which he was wholly unacquainted, and concerning which he was not desirous of acquiring further information. A man of this description is not to be held by lightly. I grappled him to my heart.

One day when we were taking a constitutional walk together, I casually mentioned the "Red Hills." He had never heard of them, inquired, and I told him what little I knew on the matter. The Red Hills are mounds of burnt clay of a brick-red colour, found at intervals along the fringe of the marshes on the east coast. Of the date of their formation and the purpose they were destined to discharge, nothing has been certainly ascertained. Theories have been formed, and have been held to with tenacity, but these are unsupported by sound evidence. And yet, one would have supposed that these mysterious mounds would have been subjected to a careful scientific exploration to determine by the discovery of flint tools, potsherds, or coins to what epoch they belong, and that some clue should be discovered as to their purport. But at the time when I was in Essex, no such study had been attempted; whether any has been undertaken since I am unable to say.

I mentioned to Donelly some of the suppositions offered as to the origin of these Red Hills; that they represented salt-making works, that they were funereal erections, that they were artificial bases for the huts of fishers.

"That is it," said the major, "no doubt about it. To keep off the ague. Do you not know that burnt clay is a sure protection against ague, which was the curse of the Essex marsh land? In Central Africa, in the districts that lie low and there is morass, the natives are quite aware of the fact, and systematically form a bed of burnt clay as a platform on which to erect their hovels. Now look here, my dear friend, I'd most uncommonly like to take a boat along with you, and explore both sides of the Blackwater to begin with, and its inlets, and to tick down on the ordnance map every red hill we can find."

"I am quite ready," I replied. "There is one thing to remember. A vast number of these hills have been ploughed down, but you can certainly detect where they were by the colour of the soil."

Accordingly, on the next fine day we engaged a boat—not a rower—for we could manage it between us, and started on our expedition.

The country around the Blackwater is flat, and the land slides into the sea and river with so slight an incline, that a good extent of debatable ground exists, which may be reckoned as belonging to both. Vast marshes are found occasionally flooded, covered with the wild lavender, and in June flushed with the seathrift. They nourish a coarse grass, and a bastard samphire. These marshes are threaded, cobweb fashion, by myriads of lines of water and mud that intercommunicate. Woe to the man who either stumbles into, or in jumping falls into, one of these breaks in the surface of land. He sinks to his waist in mud. At certain times, when no high tides are expected, sheep are driven upon these marshes and thrive. They manage to leap the runnels, and the shepherd is aware when danger threatens, and they must be driven off.

Nearer the mainland are dykes thrown up, none know when, to reclaim certain tracts of soil, and on the land side are invariably stagnant ditches, where mosquitoes breed in myriads. Further up grow oak trees, and in summer to these the mosquitoes betake themselves in swarms, and may be seen in the evening swaying in such dense clouds above the trees that these latter seem to be on fire and smoking. Major Donelly and I leisurely paddled about, running into creeks, leaving our boat, identifying our position on the map, and marking in the position of such red hills or their traces as we lighted on.

Major Donelly and I pretty well explored the left bank up to a certain point, when he proposed that we should push across to the other.

"I should advise doing thoroughly the upper reach of the Blackwater," said he, "and we shall then have completed one section."

"All right," I responded, and we turned the boat's head to cross. Unhappily, we had not calculated that the estuary was full of mudbanks. Moreover, the tide was ebbing, and before very long we grounded.

"Confound it!" said the major, "we are on a mudbank. What a fix we are in."

We laboured with the oars to thrust off, but could touch no solid ground, to obtain purchase sufficient for our purpose.

Then said Donelly: "The only thing to be done is for one of us to step onto the bank and thrust the boat off. I will do that. I have on an old shabby pair of trousers that don't matter."

"No, indeed, you shall not. I will go," and at the word I sprang overboard. But the major had jumped simultaneously, and simultaneously we sank in the horrible slime. It had the consistency of spinach. I do not mean such as English cooks send us to table, half-mashed and often gritty, but the spinach as served at a French *table d'hôte*, that has been pulped through a fine hair sieve. And what is more, it apparently had no bottom. For aught I know it might go down a mile in depth towards the centre of the globe, and it stank abominably. We both clung to the sides of the boat to save ourselves from sinking altogether.

There we were, one on each side, clinging to the bulwarks and looking at one another. For a moment or two neither spoke. Donelly was the first to recover his presence of mind, and after wiping his mouth on the gunwale from the mud that had squirted over it, he said: "Can you get out?"

"Hardly," said I.

We tugged at the boat, it squelched about, splashing the slime over us, till it plastered our heads and faces and covered our hands.

"This will never do," said he. "We must get in together, and by instalments. Look here! when I say 'three,' throw in your left leg if you can get it out of the mud."

"I will do my best."

"And," he said further, "we must do so both at the same moment. Now, don't be a sneak and try to get in your body whilst I am putting in my leg, or you will upset the boat."

"I never was a sneak," I retorted angrily, "and I certainly will not be one in what may be the throes of death."

"All right," said the major. "One—two—three!"

Instantly both of us drew our left legs out of the mud, and projected them over the sides into the boat.

"How are you?" asked he. "Got your leg in all right?"

"All but my boot," I replied, "and that has been sucked off my foot."

"Oh, bother the boot," said the major, "so long as your leg is safe within, and has not been sucked off. That would have disturbed the equipoise. Now then—next we must have our trunks and right legs within. Take a long breath, and wait till I call 'three.'"

We paused, panting with the strain; then Donelly, in a stentorian voice, shouted: "One—two—three!"

Instantly we writhed and strained, and finally, after a convulsive effort, both were landed in the bottom of the boat. We picked ourselves up and seated ourselves, each on one bulwark, looking at one another.

We were covered with the foul slime from head to foot, our clothes were caked, so were our hands and faces. But we were secure.

"Here," said Donelly, "we shall have to remain for six hours till the tide flows, and the boat is lifted. It is of no earthly use for us to shout for help. Even if our calls were heard, no one could come out to us. Here, then, we stick and must make the best of it. Happily the sun is hot, and will cake the mud about us, and then we can pick off some of it."

The prospect was not inviting. But I saw no means of escape.

Presently Donelly said: "It is good that we brought our luncheon with us, and above all some whisky, which is the staff of life. Look here, my dear fellow. I wish it were possible to get this stinking stuff off our hands and faces; it smells like the scouring poured down the sink in Satan's own back kitchen. Is there not a bottle of claret in the basket?"

"Yes, I put one in."

"Then," said he, "the best use we can put it to is to wash our faces and hands in it. Claret is poor drink, and there is the whisky to fall back on."

"The water has all ebbed away," I remarked "We cannot clean ourselves in that."

"Then uncork the *Saint Julien*."

There was really no help for it. The smell of the mud was disgusting, and it turned one's stomach. So I pulled out the cork, and we performed our ablutions in the claret.

That done, we returned to our seats on the gunwale, one on each side, and looked sadly at one another. Six hours! That was an interminable time to spend on a mudflat in the Blackwater. Neither of us was much inclined to speak. After the lapse of a quarter of an hour, the major proposed refreshments. Accordingly we crept together into the bottom of the boat and there discussed the contents of the hamper, and we certainly did full justice to the whisky bottle. For we were wet to the skin, and beplastered from head to foot in the ill-savoured mud.

When we had done the chicken and ham, and drained the whisky jar, we returned to our several positions *vis-à-vis*. It was essential that the balance of the boat should be maintained.

Major Donelly was now in a communicative mood.

"I will say this," observed he; "that you are the best-informed and most agreeable man I have met with in Colchester and Chelmsford."

I would not record this remark but for what it led up to.

I replied—I dare say I blushed—but the claret in my face made it red, anyhow. I replied: "You flatter me."

"Not at all. I always say what I think. You have plenty of information, and you'll grow your wings, and put on rainbow colours."

"What on earth do you mean?" I inquired.

"Do you not know," said he, "that we shall all of us, some day, develop wings? Grow into angels! What do you suppose that ethereal pinions spring out of? They do not develop out of nothing. *Ex nihilo nihil fit.* You cannot think that they are the ultimate produce of ham and chicken."

"Nor of whisky."

"Nor of whisky," he repeated. "You know it is so with the grub."

"Grub is ambiguous," I observed.

"I do not mean victuals, but the caterpillar. That creature spends its short life in eating, eating, eating. Look at a cabbage-leaf, it is riddled with holes; the grub has consumed all that vegetable matter, and I will inform you for what purpose. It retires into its chrysalis, and during the winter a transformation takes place, and in spring it breaks forth as a glorious butterfly. The painted wings of the insect in its second stage of existence are the sublimated cabbage it has devoured in its condition of larva."

"Quite so. What has that to do with me?"

"We are also in our larva condition. But do not for a moment suppose that the wings we shall put on with rainbow painting are the produce of what we eat here—of ham and chicken, kidneys, beef, and the like. No, sir, certainly not. They are fashioned out of the information we have absorbed, the knowledge we have acquired during the first stage of life."

"How do you know that?"

"I will tell you," he answered. "I had a remarkable experience once. It is a rather long story, but as we have some five hours and a half to sit here looking at one another till the tide rises and floats us, I may as well tell you, and it will help to the laying on of the colours on your pinions when you acquire them. You would like to hear the tale?"

"Above all things."

"There is a sort of prologue to it," he went on. "I cannot well dispense with it as it leads up to what I particularly want to say."

"By all means let me have the prologue, if it be instructive."

"It is eminently instructive," he said. "But before I begin, just pass me the bottle, if there is any whisky left."

"It is drained," I said.

"Well, well, it can't be helped. When I was in India, I moved from one place to another, and I had pitched my tent in a certain spot. I had a native servant. I forget what his real name was, and it does not matter. I always called him Alec. He was a curious fellow, and the other servants stood in awe of him. They thought that he saw ghosts and had familiar dealings with the spiritual world. He was honest as natives go. He would not allow anyone else to rob me; but, of course, he filched things of mine himself. We are accustomed to that, and think nothing of it. But it was a satisfaction that he kept the fingers of the others off my property. Well, one night, when, as I have informed you, my tent was pitched on a spot I considered eminently convenient, I slept very uncomfortably.

"It was as though a centipede were crawling over me. Next

morning I spoke to Alec, and told him my experiences, and bade him search well my mattress and the floor of my tent. A Hindu's face is impassive, but I thought I detected in his eyes a twinkle of understanding. Nevertheless I did not give it much thought. Next night it was as bad, and in the morning I found my *panjams* slit from head to foot. I called Alec to me and held up the garment, and said how uncomfortable I had been. 'Ah! *sahib*,' said he, 'that is the doings of Abdulhamid, the blood-thirsty scoundrel!'"

"Excuse me," I interrupted. "Did he mean the present *Sultan* of Turkey?"

"No, quite another, of the same name."

"I beg your pardon," I said. "But when you mentioned him as a blood-thirsty scoundrel, I supposed it must be he."

"It was not he. It was another. Call him, if you like, the other Abdul. But to proceed with my story."

"One inquiry more," said I. "Surely Abdulhamid cannot be a Hindu name?"

"I did not say that it was," retorted the major with a touch of asperity in his tone. "He was doubtless a Mohammedan."

"But the name is rather Turkish or Arabic."

"I am not responsible for that; I was not his godfathers and godmothers at his baptism. I am merely repeating what Alec told me. If you are so captious, I shall shut up and relate no more."

"Do not take umbrage," said I. "I surely have a right to test the quality of the material I take in, out of which my wings are to be evolved. Go ahead; I will interrupt no further."

"Very well, then, let that be understood between us. Are you caking?"

"Slowly," I replied. "The sun is hot; I am drying up on one side of my body."

"I think that we had best shift sides of the boat," said the major. "It is the same with me."

Accordingly, with caution, we crossed over, and each took the seat on the gunwale lately occupied by the other.

"There," said Donelly. "How goes the enemy? My watch got

smothered in the mud, and has stopped."

"Mine," I explained, "is plastered into my waistcoat pocket, and I cannot get at it without messing my fingers, and there is no more claret left for a wash; the whisky is all inside us."

"Well," said the major, "it does not matter; there is plenty of time before us for the rest of my story. Let me see—where was I? Oh! where Alec mentioned Abdulhamid, the inferior scoundrel, not the Sultan. Alec went on to say that he was himself possessed of a remarkably keen scent for blood, even though it had been shed a century before his time, and that my tent had been pitched and my bed spread over a spot marked by a most atrocious crime. That Abdul of whom he had made mention had been a man steeped in crimes of the most atrocious character.

"Of course, he did not come up in wickedness to his illustrious namesake, but that was because he lacked the opportunities with which the other is so favoured. On the very identical spot where I then was, this same bloodstained villain had perpetrated his worst iniquity—he had murdered his father and mother, and aunt, and his children. After that he was taken and hanged. When his soul parted from his body, in the ordinary course it would have entered into the shell of a scorpion or some other noxious creature, and so have mounted through the scale of beings, by one incarnation after another, till he attained once more to the high estate of man."

"Excuse the interruption," said I, "but I think you intimated that this Abdulhamid was a Mohammedan, and the sons of the Prophet do not believe in the transmigration of souls."

"That," said Donelly, "is precisely the objection I raised to Alec. But he told me that souls after death are not accommodated with a future according to the creeds they hold, but according to Destiny: that whatever a man might suppose during life as to the condition of his future state, there was but one truth to which they would all have their eyes opened—the truth held by the Hindus, *viz.* the transmigration of souls from stage to stage, ever progressing upward to man, and then to recommence the interminable circle of reincarnation. 'So,' said I, 'it was Abdul in the form of a scorpion who was tickling my ribs all night.'

"'No, *sahib*,' replied my native servant very gravely. 'He was too wicked to be suffered to set his foot, so to speak, on the lowest rung of the ladder of existences. The doom went forth against him that he must haunt the scenes of his former crimes, till he found a man sleeping over one of them, and on that man must be a mole, and out of that mole must grow three hairs. These hairs he must pluck out and plant on the grave of his final victims, and water them with his tears. And the flowing of these first drops of penitence would enable him to pass at once into the first stage of the circle of incarnations.' 'Why,' said I, 'that un-redeemed ruffian was mole-hunting over me the last two nights! But what do you say to these slit *panjams*?'

"'*Sahib*,' replied Alec, 'he did that with his nails. I presume he turned you over, and ripped them so as to get at your back and feel for the so-much-desired mole.' 'I'll have the tent shifted,' said I. 'Nothing will induce me to sleep another night on this accursed spot.'"

Donelly paused, and proceeded to take off some flakes of mud that had formed on his sleeve. We really were beginning to get drier, but in drying we stiffened, as the mud became hard about us like pie-crust.

"So far," said I, "we have had no wings."

"I am coming to them," replied the major; "I have now con-cluded the prologue."

"Oh! that was the prologue, was it?"

"Yes. Have you anything against it? It was the prologue. Now I will go on with the main substance of my story. About a year after that incident I retired on half-pay, and returned to Eng-land. What became of Alec I did not know, nor care a hang. I had been in England for a little over two years, when one day I was walking along Great Russell Street, and passing the gates of the British Museum, I noticed a Hindu standing there, looking wretchedly cold and shabby. He had a tray containing bangles and necklaces and gewgaws, made in Germany, which he was selling as oriental works of art. As I passed, he saluted me, and, looking steadily at him, I recognised Alec. 'Why, what brings you here?' I inquired, vastly astonished.

"'*Sahib* may well ask,' he replied. 'I came over because I thought I might better my condition. I had heard speak of a Psychical Research Society established in London; and with my really extraordinary gifts, I thought that I might be of value to it, and be taken in and paid an annuity if I supplied it continuously with well-authenticated, first-hand ghost stories.' 'Well,' said I, 'and have you succeeded?' 'No, *sahib*. I cannot find it. I have inquired after it from several of the crossing-sweepers, and they could not inform me of its whereabouts; and if I applied to the police, they bade me take myself off, there was no such a thing. I should have starved, *sahib*, if it had not been that I had taken to this line'; he pointed to his tray.

"'Does that pay well?' I asked. He shook his head sadly. 'Very poorly. I can live—that is all. There goes in a Merewig.' 'How many of these rubbishy bangles can you dispose of in a day?' I inquired. 'That depends, *sahib*. It varies so greatly, and the profits are very small. So small that I can barely get along. There goes in another Merewig.' 'Where are all these things made?' I asked. 'In Germany or in Birmingham?' 'Oh, *sahib*, how can I tell? I get them from a Jew dealer. He supplies various street-hawkers. But I shall give it up—it does not pay—and shall set up a stall and dispose of Turkish Delight. There is always a run on that. You English have a sweet tooth. That's a Merewig,' and he pointed to a dowdy female, with a reticule on her arm, who, at that moment, went through the painted iron gates.

"'What do you mean by Merewigs?' said I. 'Does not *sahib* know?' Alec's face expressed genuine surprise. 'If *sahib* will go into the great reading-room, he will see scores of them there. It is their great London haunt; they pass in all day, mainly in the morning—some are in very early, so soon as the museum is open at nine o'clock. And they usually remain there all day picking up information, acquiring knowledge.' 'You mean the students.' 'Not all the students, but a large percentage of them. I know them in a moment. *Sahib* is aware that I have great gifts for the discernment of spirits.'

"By the way," broke off Donelly, "do you understand Hindustani?"

"Not a word of it," I replied.

"I am sorry for that," said he, "because I could tell you what passed between us so much easier in Hindustani. I am able to speak and understand it as readily as English, and the matter I am going to relate would come off my tongue so much easier in that language."

"You might as well speak it in Chinese. I should be none the wiser. Wait a moment. I am cracking."

It was so. The heat of the sun was sensibly affecting my crust of mud. I think I must have resembled a fine old painting, the varnish of which is stained and traversed by an infinity of minute fissures, a perfect network of cracks. I stood up and stretched myself, and split in several places. Moreover, portions of my muddy envelope began to curl at the edges.

"Don't be in too great a hurry to peel," advised Donelly.

"We have abundance of time still before us, and I want to proceed with my narrative."

"Go on, then. When are we coming to the wings?"

"Directly," replied he. "Well, then—if you cannot receive what I have to say in Hindustani, I must do my best to give you the substance of Alec's communication in the vulgar tongue. I will epitomise it. The Hindu went on to explain in this fashion. He informed me that with us, Christians and white people, it is not the same as with the dusky and the yellow races. After death we do not pass into the bodies of the lower animals, which is a great privilege and ought to afford us immense satisfaction. We at once progress into a higher condition of life. We develop wings, as does the butterfly when it emerges from its condition of grub.

"But the matter out of which the wings are produced is nothing gross. They are formed, or form themselves, out of the information with which we have filled our brains during life. We lay up, during our mortal career here, a large amount of knowl-

341

edge, of scientific, historical, philosophic, and like acquisitions, and these form the so-to-speak psychic pulp out of which, by an internal and mysterious and altogether inexplicable process, the transmutation takes place into our future wings. The more we have stored, the larger are our wings; the more varied the nature, the more radiant and coloured is their painting. When, at death, the brain is empty, there can be no wing-development. Out of nothing, nothing can arise. That is a law of nature absolutely inexorable in its application. And this is why you will never have to regret sticking in the mud today, my friend. I have supplied you with such an amount of fresh and valuable knowledge, that I believe you will have pinions painted hereafter with peacock's eyes."

"I am most obliged to you," said I, splitting into a thousand cakes with the emotion that agitated me.

Donelly proceeded. "I was so interested in what Alec told me, that I said to him, 'Come along with me into the Nineveh room, and we shall be able to thrash this matter out.' 'Ah, *sahib*,' he replied, 'they will not allow me to take in my tray.' 'Very well,' said I, 'then we will find a step before the portico, one not too much frequented by the pigeons, and will sit there.' He agreed. But the porter at the gate demurred to letting the Hindu through. He protested that no trafficking was allowed on the premises. I explained that none was purposed; that the man and I proposed a discussion on psychological topics. This seemed to content the porter, and he suffered Alec to pass through with me. We picked out as clean a portion of the steps as we could, and seated ourselves on it side by side, and then the Hindu went on with what he was saying."

Donelly and I were now drying rapidly. As we sat facing each other we must have looked very much like the chocolate men one sees in confectioners' shops—of course, I mean on a much larger scale, and not of the same warm tint, and, of course, also, we did not exhale the same aromatic odour.

"When we were seated," proceeded Donelly, "I felt the cold of the stone steps strike up into my system, and as I have had a touch or two of lumbago since I came home, I stood up again, took a copy of the *Standard* out of my pocket, folded it, and placed it between myself and the step. I did, however, pull out the inner leaf, that containing the leaders, and presented it to Alec for the same purpose. Orientals are insensible to kindness, and are deficient in the virtue of gratitude. But this delicate trait of attention did touch the benighted heathen. His lip quivered, and he became, if possible, more than ever communicative. He nudged me with his tray and said, 'There goes out a Merewig. I wonder why she leaves so soon?' I saw a middle-aged woman in a gown of grey, with greasy splotches on it, and the braid un-sewn at the skirt trailing in a loop behind.

"'What are the Merewigs?' I asked. I will give you what I learned in my own words. All men and women—I allude only to Europeans and Americans—in the first stage of their life are bound morally, and in their own interest, to acquire and store up in their brains as much information as these will hold, for it is out of this that their wings will be evolved in their second stage of existence. Of course, the more varied this information is, the better. Men inevitably accumulate knowledge. Even if they as-similate very little at school, yet, as young men, they necessar-ily take in a good deal—of course, I exempt the mashers, who never learn anything. Even in sport they obtain something; but in business, by reading, by association, by travel, they go on pil-ing up a store.

"You see that in common conversation they cannot escape doing this; politics, social questions, points of natural history, sci-entific discoveries form the staple of their talk, so that the mind of a man is necessarily kept replenished. But with women this is not the case. Young girls read nothing whatever but novels—they might as well feed on soap-bubbles. In their conversation with one another they twaddle, they do not talk."

"But," protested I, "in our civilised society young women as-sociate freely with men."

"That is true," replied he. "But to what is their dialogue limited?—to ragging, to frivolous jokes. Men do not talk to them on rational topics, for they know well enough that such topics do not interest girls, and that they are wholly incapable of applying their minds to them. It is wondered why so many Englishmen look out for American wives. That is because the American girl takes pains to cultivate her mind, becomes a rational and well-educated woman. She can enter into her husband's interests, she can converse with him on almost every topic. She becomes his companion. That the modern English girl cannot be. Her head is as hollow as a drum.

"Now, if she grows up and marries, or even remains an old maid, the case is altered; she takes to keeping poultry, she becomes passionately fond of gardening, and she acquires a fund of information on the habits and customs of the domestic servant. The consequence of this is, that the vast majority of English young women who die early, die with nothing stored up in their brains out of which the wings may be evolved. In the larva condition they have consumed nothing that can serve them to bring them into the higher state."

"So," said I, "we are all, you and I, in the larva condition as well as girls."

"Quite so, we are larvae like them, only they are more so. To proceed. When girls die, without having acquired any profitable knowledge, as you well see, they cannot rise. They become Merewigs."

"Oh, that is Merewigs," said I, greatly astonished.

"Yes, but the Merewigs I had seen pass in and out of the British Museum, whether to study the collections or to work in the reading-room, were middle-aged for the most part."

"How do you explain that?" I asked.

"I give you only what I received from Alec. There are male Merewigs, but they are few and far between, for the reasons I have given to you. I suppose there are ninety-nine female Merewigs to one male."

"You astonish me."

"I was astonished when I learned this from Alec. Now I will tell you something further. All the souls of the girls who have died empty-headed in the preceding twenty-four hours in England assemble at four o'clock every morning, or rather a few minutes before the stroke of the clock, about the statue of Queen Anne in front of St. Paul's Cathedral, with a possible sprinkling of male masher souls among them. At the stroke of the clock, off the whole swarm rushes up Holborn Hill, along Oxford Street, whither I cannot certainly say. Alec told me that it is for all the world like the rush of an army of rats in the sewers."

"But what can that Hindu know of underground London?"

"He knows because he lodges in the house of a sewer-man, with whom he has become on friendly terms."

"Then you do not know whither this galloping legion runs?"

"Not exactly, for Alec was not sure. But he tells me they tear away to the great *garde-robe* of discarded female bodies. They must get into these, so as to make up for the past, and acquire knowledge, out of which wings may be developed. Of course there is a scramble for these bodies, for there are at least half a dozen applicants. At first only the abandoned husks of old maids were given them, but the supply having proved to be altogether inadequate, they are obliged to put up with those of married women and widows. There was some demur as to this, but beggars must not be choosers. And so they become Merewigs. There are more than a sufficiency of old bachelors' outer cases hanging up in the *garde-robe*, but the girls will not get into them at any price. Now you understand what Merewigs are, and why they swarm in the reading-room of the British Museum. They are there picking up information as hard as they can pick."

"This is extremely interesting," said I, "and novel."

"I thought you would say so. How goes on the drying?"

"I have been picking off clots of clay while you have been talking."

"I hope you are interested," said Donelly.

"Interested," I replied, "is not the word for it."

"I am glad you think so," said the major; "I was intensely interested in what Alec told me, so much so that I proposed he should come with me into the reading-room, and point out to me such as he perceived by his remarkable gift of discernment of spirits were actual Merewigs. But again the difficulty of his tray was objected, and Alec further intimated that he was missing opportunities of disposing of his trinkets by spending so much time conversing with me. 'As to that,' said I, 'I will buy half a dozen of your bangles and present them to my lady friends; as coming from me, an oriental traveller, they will believe them to be genuine——'"

"As your experiences," interpolated I.

"What do you mean by that?" he inquired sharply.

"Nothing more than this," rejoined I, "that faith is grown weak among females nowadays."

"That is certainly true. It is becoming a sadly incredulous sex. I further got over Alec's difficulty about the tray by saying that it could be left in the custody of one of the officials at the entrance. Then he consented. We passed through the swing-door and deposited the tray with the functionary who presides over umbrellas and walking-sticks. Then I went forward along with my Hindu towards the reading-room. But here another hindrance arose. Alec had no ticket, and therefore might not enter beyond the glass screen interposed between the door and the readers. Some demur was made as to his being allowed to remain there for any considerable time, but I got over that by means of a little persuasion. 'Sahib,' said Alec 'I should suggest your marking the Merewigs, so as to be able to recognise them elsewhere.'

"'How can I do that?' I inquired. 'I have here with me a piece of French chalk,' he answered. 'You go within, sahib, and walk up and down by the tables, behind the chairs of the readers, or around the circular cases that contain the catalogues, and where the students are looking out for the books they desire to consult. When you pass a female, either seated or standing, glance towards the glass screen, and when you are by a Merewig I will hold up my hand above the screen, and you will know her to be one; then just scrawl a W or M, or any letter or cabalistic symbol that occurs to you, upon her back with the French chalk. Then whenever you meet her in the street, in society, at an A. B. C. place of refreshment, on a railway platform, you will recognise her infallibly.' 'Not likely,' I objected. 'Of course, so soon as she gets home, she will brush off the mark.'

"'You do not know much of the Merewigs,' he said. 'When the spirits of those frivolous girls were in their first stage of existence, they were most particular about their personal appearance, about the neatness and stylishness of their dress, and the puffing and piling up of their hair. Now all that is changed. They are so disgusted at having to get into any unsouled body that they can lay hold of in the *garde-robe*, such a body being usually plain in features, middle-aged, and with no waist to speak of, or rather too ample in the waist to be elegant, that they have abandoned all concern about dress and tidiness. Besides, they are engrossed in the acquisition of knowledge, and the burning desire that consumes them is to get out of these borrowed cases as speedily as may be.

"'Consequently, so long as they are dressed and their hair done up anyhow, that is all they care about. As to threads, or feathers, or French chalk marks on their clothes, they would not think of looking for them.' Then Alec handed to me a little piece of French chalk, such as tailors and dressmakers employ to indicate alterations when fitting on garments. So provided, I passed wholly into the spacious reading-room, leaving the Hindu behind the screen.

"I slowly strayed down the first line of desks and chairs, which were fully engaged. There were many men there, with piles of books at their sides. There were also some women. I stepped behind one, and turned my head towards the screen, but Alec made no sign. At the second, however, up went his hand above it, and I hastily scrawled M, on her back as she stooped over her studies. I had time, moreover, to see what she was engaged upon. She was working up deep-sea soundings, beginning with that recorded by Schiller in his ballad of 'The Diver,' down to the last scientific researches in the bottom of the Atlantic and the Pacific, and the dredgings in the North Sea. She was engrossed in her work, and was picking up facts at a prodigious rate. She was a woman of, I should say, forty, with a cadaverous face, a shapeless nose, and enormous hands. Her dress was grey, badly fitted, and her boots were even worse made. Her hair was drawn back and knotted in a bunch behind, with the pins sticking out.

"It might have been better brushed. I passed on behind her back; the next occupants of seats were gentlemen, so I stepped to another row of desks, and looking round saw Alec's hand go up. I was behind a young lady in a felt hat, crunched in at top, and with a feather at the side; she wore a pea-jacket, with large smoked buttons, and beneath it a dull green gown, very short in the skirt, and brown boots. Her hair was cut short like that of a man. As I halted, she looked round, and I saw that she had hard, brown eyes, like pebbles, without a gleam of tenderness or sympathy in them. I cannot say whether this was due to the body she had assumed, or to the soul which had entered into the body—whether the lack was in the organ, or in the psychic force which employed the organ. I merely state the fact.

"I looked over her shoulder to see what she was engaged upon, and found that she was working her way diligently through Herbert Spencer. I scored a W on her back and went on. The next Merewig I had to scribble on was a wizen old lady, with little grey curls on the temples, very shabby in dress, and very antiquated in costume. Her fingers were dirty with ink, and the ink did not appear to me to be all of that day's application. Besides, I saw that she had been rubbing her nose. I presume it had been tickling, and she had done this with a finger still wet with ink, so that there was a smear on her face. She was engaged on the peerage. She had Dod, Burke, and Foster before her, and was getting up the authentic pedigrees of our noble families and their ramifications. I noticed with her as with the other Merewigs, that when they had swallowed a certain amount of information they held up their heads much like fowls after drinking.

"The next that I marked was a very thin woman of an age I was quite unable to determine. She had a pointed nose, and was dressed in red. She looked like a stick of sealing-wax. The gown had probably enough been good and showy at one time, but it was ripped behind now, and the stitches showed, besides, a little bit of what was beneath. There was a frilling, or ruche, or tucker, about the throat that I think had been sewn into it three weeks before. I drew a note of interrogation on her back with my bit of French chalk. I wanted much to find out what she was studying, but could not.

"She turned round and asked sharply what I was stooping over for and breathing on the back of her neck. So I was forced to go on to the next. This was a lady fairly well dressed in the dingiest of colours, wearing spectacles. I believe that she wore divided skirts, but as she did not stand up and walk, I cannot be certain. I am particular never to make a statement of which I am not absolutely certain. She was engaged upon the subject of the land laws in various countries, on common land, and property in land; and she was at that time devoting her special attention to the constitution of the Russian *mir*, and the tenure of land under it. I scrawled on her back the zodiacal sign for Venus, the Virgin, and went further.

"But when I had marked seventeen I gave it up. I had already gone over the desks to L, beginning backward, and that sufficed, so I returned to Alec, paid him for the bangles, and we separated. I did, however, give him a letter to the Secretary of the Psychical Research Society, and addressed it, having found what I wanted in the *London Directory*, which was in the reading-room of the British Museum. Two days later I met, by appointment, my Hindu once more, and for the last time. He had not been received as he had anticipated by the Psychical Research Society, and thought of getting back to India at the first opportunity.

"It is remarkable that, a few days later, I saw in the Underground one of those I had marked. The chalk mark was still quite distinct. She was not in my compartment, but I noticed her as she stepped out on to the platform at Baker Street. I suspect she was on her way to Madame Tussaud's waxwork exhibition, to instruct her mind there. But I was more fortunate a week later when I was at St. Albans. I had an uncle living there from whom I had expectations, and I paid him a visit. Whilst there, a lecture was to be given on the spectroscope, and as my acquaintance with that remarkable invention of modern times was limited, I resolved to go. Have you, my friend, ever taken up the subject of the photosphere of the sun?"

"Never."

"Then let me press it upon you. It will really supply a large amount of wing-pulp, if properly assimilated. It is a most astonishing thought that we are able, at the remote distance at which we are from the solar orb, to detect the various incandescent metals which go to make up the luminous envelope of the sun. Not only so, but we are able to discover, by the bars in the spectroscope, of what Jupiter, Saturn, and so on are composed. What a stride astronomy has made since the days of Newton!"

"No doubt about it. But I do not want to hear about the bars, but of the chalk marks on the Merewigs."

"Well, then, I noticed two elderly ladies sitting in the row before me, and there—as distinctly as if sketched in only yesterday—were the symbols I had scribbled on their backs. I did not have an opportunity of speaking with them then; indeed, I had no introduction to them, and could hardly take on me to address them without it. I was, however, more successful a week or two later. There was a meeting of the Hertfordshire Archaelogical Society organised, to last a week, with excursions to ancient Verulam and to other objects of interest in the county. Hertfordshire is not a large county.

"It is, in fact, one of the smallest in England, but it yields to none in the points of interest that it contains, apart from the venerable abbey church that has been so fearfully mauled and maltreated by ignorant so-called restoration. One must really hope that the next generation, which will be more enlightened than our own, will undo all the villainous work that has been perpetrated to disfigure it in our own. The local secretaries and managers had arranged for *char-à-bancs* and brakes to take the party about, and men—learned, or thinking themselves to be learned, on the several antiquities—were to deliver lectures on the spot explanatory of what we saw. On three days there were to be evening gatherings, at which papers would be read. You may conceive that this was a supreme opportunity for storing the mind with information, and knowing what I did, I resolved on taking advantage of it.

"I entered my name as a subscriber to all the excursions. On the first day we went over the remains of the old Roman city of Verulam, and were shown its plan and walls, and further, the spot where the protomartyr of Britain passed over the stream, and the hill on which he was martyred. Nothing could have been more interesting and more instructive. Among those present were three middle-aged personages of the female sex, all of whom were chalk-marked on the back. One of these marks was somewhat effaced, as though the lady whose gown was scored had made a faint effort to brush it off, but had tired of the attempt and had abandoned it. The other two scorings were quite distinct.

"On this, the first day, though I sidled up to these three Merewigs, I did not succeed in ingratiating myself into their favour sufficiently to converse with them. You may well understand, my friend, that such an opportunity of getting out of them some of their Merewigian experiences was not to be allowed to slip. On the second day I was more successful. I managed to obtain a seat in a brake between two of them. We were to drive to a distant spot where was a church of considerable architectural interest.

"Well, in these excursions a sort of freemasonry exists between the archaeologists who share in them, and no ceremonious introductions are needed. For instance, you say to the lady next to you, 'Am I squeezing you?' And the ice is broken. I did not, however, attempt to draw any information from those between whom I was seated, till after luncheon, a most sumptuous repast, with champagne, liberally given to the Society by a gentleman of property, to whose house we drove up just about one o'clock. There was plenty of champagne supplied, and I did not stint myself. I felt it necessary to take in a certain amount of Dutch courage before broaching to my companions in the brake the theme that lay near my heart. When, however, we got into the conveyance, all in great spirits, after the conclusion of the lunch, I turned to my right-hand lady, and said to her: 'Well, miss, I fear it will be a long time before you become angelic.' She turned her back upon me and made no reply.

"Somewhat disconcerted, I now addressed myself to the chalk-marked lady on my left hand, and asked: 'Have you anything at all in your head except archaeology?' Instead of answering me in the kindly mood in which I spoke, she began at once to enter into a lively discussion with her neighbour on the opposite side of the carriage, and ignored me. I was not to be done in this way. I wanted information. But, of course, I could enter into the feelings of both. Merewigs do not like to converse about themselves in their former stage of existence, of which they are ashamed, nor of the efforts they are making in this transitional stage to acquire a fund of knowledge for the purpose of ultimately discarding their acquired bodies, and developing their ethereal wings as they pass into the higher and nobler condition.

"We left the carriage to go to a spot about a mile off, through lanes, muddy and rutty, for the purpose of inspecting some remarkable stones. All the party would not walk, and the conveyances could proceed no nearer. The more enthusiastic did go on, and I was of the number. What further stimulated me to do so was the fact that the third Merewig, she who had partially cleaned my scoring off her back, plucked up her skirts, and strode ahead. I hurried after and caught her up. 'I beg your pardon,' said I. 'You must excuse the interest I take in antiquities, but I suppose it is a long time since you were a girl.' Of course, my meaning was obvious; I referred to her earlier existence, before she borrowed her present body. But she stopped abruptly, gave me a withering look, and went back to rejoin another group of pedestrians. Ha! my friend, I verily believe that the boat is being lifted. The tide is flowing in."

"The tide is flowing," I said; and then added, "really, Major Donelly, your story ought not to be confined to the narrow circle of your intimates."

"That is true," he replied. "But my desire to make it known has been damped by the way in which Alec was received, or rather rejected, by the Secretary of the Society for Psychical Research."

"But I do not mean that you should tell it to the Society for Psychical Research."

"To whom, then?"

"Tell it to the Horse Marines."

The Devil's Mill

I am, what you have known me to be, a man of an inquiring mind, of broad interests, and of persistent research. It matters not whether the objects of pursuit be natural history, antiquities, ethnology I am interested in all, and when an opportunity offered to me of combining research in botany and in a special branch of archaeology, I seized it with enthusiasm. Properly the botanical study would be in a special branch also the glassworts that abound in the saltings of the mouth of the Blackwater. Here are wide tracks of soil, traversed in all directions by threads of water when the tide is in, and by rifts of mud when the tide is out; and these patches of soil, covered with sea-lavender, thrift, and various plants that live on the verge of salt water, are inundated occasionally at the very high tides. Around the coast are, moreover, the Red Hills, mysterious mounds of clay baked red, by whom, for what purpose, and at what period is wholly unknown. My purpose was, one fine day, to combine an examination of the situation of these Red Hills with a research among the glassworts.

Towards evening the weather changed, and the night came on, and found me in the labyrinth of patches of soil threaded by water channels, and I found it extremely difficult to make my way to the mainland. It is hard to say which were worse to cross the lines of water when the tide flowed, or the gulfs of horrible mud at ebb, and the rapidity with which the darkness came on caused great bewilderment in me. Were I to flounder into the mud I might sink and never come up again; some of the channels were too wide to be leaped, and when a blinding rain came on, and I could not see the low shore, I completely lost myself in the maze. I ran this way to escape, and was brought up by a wide streak of mud, impossible to pass; I turned back, and sought a point where I could tread, and in these twistings and doublings lost all knowledge of my direction. A night on the saltings in rain and mist and cold was not to be contemplated without alarm.

I became at length so fagged that I sat down in the rain, I drew out a flask of cognac, and took a long pull at it. My limbs were weary, my joints stiff. Then, feeling that if I sat much longer where I was I should become too rigid to move at all, I rose wearily and resumed my trudge. It was too dark for me to consult my watch. I tried to strike a light, but in vain the matches were extinguished the moment they developed a flame. I expected every moment to be brought up by one of the runs of water and mud, but to my inexpressible delight found that I had actually reached the mainland, but at what point I had no idea, whether on the Bradwell side, or on Mersea Island, or on that of Tollesbury. Proceed much farther I could not, so utterly exhausted was I. Happily, to my great relief, I saw before me a gleam of light. With revived courage I pushed towards it, and presently was able to distinguish the gigantic form of a windmill, with the wings revolving at a prodigious rate. I stumbled to the tail of the mill and groped my way wearily to the foot of the tall ladder.

Up this I scrambled on hands and feet and reached the door, from beneath which shot a streak of light. I shouted, and struck against the door. No answer was accorded. I was impatient, I craved for light; feeling upwards with my hand, which was cold and wet, I reached the hasp, and threw the door open. At once the light flooded me and so dazzled my eyes that I could distinguish nothing clearly at first; but I saw the figure of a man the miller, doubtless standing before me. Pulling myself together, I stated my case and solicited admission. He made no reply, and, accepting this as implying consent, I entered and shut the door behind me.

As my eyes became accustomed to the light I was better able to discern what was before me. The man was not dusted white like a miller, but was covered with sand. The eyes were black and piercing, and searched me through and through. I could see no sacks of corn, no signs of flour, nor was there in the air the pleasant odour of reduced wheat.

Presently the man asked: "What has brought you hither?"

"Science," I replied.

"Not so," said he. "Fate."

"Fate, if you will," I observed; "but an untoward one that has played the fool with me all this live-long day."

"No; it has brought you to me."

"That is true. You are the miller, I suppose?"

"Certainly; a miller."

"But I see no flour."

"I do not grind corn, I polish."

"Polish this is a marvel to me. What do you polish?"

"Glasses," he replied. "Psychoscopic lens."

"Strange—I never heard of them," I remarked.

"No; you have not heard of them because they are not yet in the market. Fate has brought you hither to make your fortune by disposing of them for me."

"I am not a rich man, far from it; and I shall be heartily glad if you will put me in the way of increasing my income. But what is the nature of your invention?"

"Come and see."

He led the way up the ladder to the storey above. Light was there also. As he ascended a shower of sand fell from him over me, and as I mounted I was constrained to close my eyes to avoid being blinded. On reaching the upper stage I saw that it was full of machinery totally unlike that of a flour mill, and all of the most delicate description, set in action by the revolutions of the sails. Some of the mechanism revolved at a rapidity so great that I could not follow it.

"For what purpose is this?" I inquired.

"Polishing glasses. Look here!" He opened a box that was fed by the machine. "Watch them as they are discharged. But the quality of the glass is the main thing; and that is my secret. There comes one complete." As he spoke an oval lens, about the size of an eye, dropped into the drawer.

"These," said he, "are psychoscopes," and he laughed a hateful, discordant laugh.

"If I am to act as your agent," said I, "I must be able to understand their special qualities. Let me try one."

He hastily put his hand between me and the box.

"No," said he. "Not now—later, as much as you will."

"Then explain their properties to me."

"They have but one property."

"And that is?"

"He who wears these glasses can see into a man's soul and read all that passes therein."

"Good heavens! I can hardly believe this possible."

"Oh, you will believe it when you come to use the spectacles. But come, you must eat and drink; follow me."

I le led the way into a narrow apartment, where was a tray on a small table, with food and wine on it. I was too hungry and thirsty not to do justice to what was provided. The wine was fiery. I would have relished my meal better had not the miller's eye been on me the whole time—a hard, cruel eye.

The generous wine had roused my spirits, and I began to take a lively interest in the invention.

"Do you mean to tell me," said I, "that by means of these glasses you can see what is passing in the mind of another?"

"You can read the thoughts as if printed in a book."

"That must be an immense advantage," said I.

"Immeasurable," acquiesced the miller. "No man will be able to deceive you—no woman either."

"A bad time for some folk," said I.

"A bad time for everyone. Everyone has got two sides, his outer side and his inner. The outer all they see, the inner he keeps to himself. My psychoscope will turn every man inside out. It is the last word of science. We are preparing a lively time for the world. There will be no more privacy; no one will relish being seen through by everyone who uses my spectacles. Children will cease to respect their parents, subjects their rulers; it will break down all discipline, all mutual regard; it will dissolve all marriages, and prevent any from being contracted. There will not be rope enough for those who would hang themselves to escape being seen through. The Thames will be choked with the corpses of those who see no other way of concealing their thoughts. A lively time, indeed! But see the dawn is creeping on, and you must be off. Turn out your bag, and let me fill it with the glasses."

I objected that the bag contained my botanical specimens.

"Bah!" said he, "glass-wort is always growing, and everywhere on the coast. You can have the glasses only from me and now."

I did as he required, and he, going to the drawer, brought out as many lens as his hands could carry, and thrust them into the receptacle; then, taking me by the shoulders, he pushed me before him to the door, opened it, made me pass through, and shut and bolted it behind me.

I descended to the ground. The day was indeed breaking, and the sails appeared white and ghost-like as they whirled.

My fatigue was gone. I pursued my way till I gained a road that eventually led me to Chelmsford, where I took the train for London. Whilst in it I had leisure for thought. My brain became calm. I opened my bag. It was stuffed with unframed glasses. I considered the matter, and saw that, as the miller had said, a great opportunity was offered me. In the train, with a stump of a pencil, I jotted down my notion of an advertisement: "The Psychoscope the latest and most wonderful of scientific discoveries. Glasses whereby the mind of any individual may be read. Fifteen guineas for a pair."

But as yet I had no office. I must secure one immediately. No sooner had I reached London than I set to work to find suitable premises, and secured an office in Mantle Street. That done, I inserted my advertisement in several papers. I had confidently expected to be besieged by applicants on the morrow; but I was disappointed. The English mind absorbs ideas slowly and with difficulty, and is cautious and suspicious. I repeated my advertisement several times, and in the meantime visited an optician and provided myself with frames, to which I fitted the lenses myself.

My first client was mistrustful. He would not buy until he had proved the quality of the glasses. I bade him mount a pair on his nose, and go into the street. He returned before very long in the utmost excitement.

"Goodness me!" he exclaimed; "it is true. I have read the thoughts of several passers-by. This is a wonderful discovery; here is the money. I must certainly secure these glasses."

After this several applicants arrived, and by evening I had sold to the amount of a hundred and twenty pounds, and I reckoned on doubling and trebling the amount on the morrow and ensuing day. I returned to my lodgings in the evening in exuberant spirits. I supposed that I would speedily dispose of all my stock, and would have to revisit the mill by the Blackwater to obtain a fresh supply. But scarcely had I settled into my office on the ensuing morning before in dashed the gentleman who had been the first purchaser, and cast the pair of spectacles on the table.

"Take these accursed things back!" said he, "and let me have my fifteen guineas again. Confound you, what do you mean by selling me such things as these?"

"Why, what is wrong with them?"

"Everything. I had them on my nose when I went home last night to dinner, and my wife came to meet me in the hall, all welcome and smiles; but curse you I saw down into her heart, and she was saying there: 'Here comes this preposterous old booby again to pester the life out of me always fuss, fuss, fuss about trifles, never content, grumbling at his food, exacting attention. I wish I had married Adolph Bloch instead of him. Adolph was at least not a fidget, and all that was against him was his German origin. Now I am mated to a dolt for the rest of my days.' That was a nice thing for me to spy out in my wife's mind. I left the spectacles after that in my study. Happening to go in there somewhat later, whom should I find there but our parlourmaid, Susan, with the spectacles on. Seeing them lying on the table, the fancy had taken her to put them across her nose and just then I entered. What she saw in me I can't say, but she became at once pert and familiar, and—" he panted for breath "I pulled the glasses off her nose, and ordered her to leave the room. Merciful power! I have not had a wink of sleep all night. I was so happy with my wife; I thought that she worshipped the very ground I trod upon and then to find out that she was still hankering after that Bloch, and despised me as a booby and a dolt. And how can I ever look Susan in the face again after what she saw, or fancied she saw, in me? Return me my money."

"That," I replied, "is too much to expect. It was a fair deal. But I will return you ten pounds, and you must forfeit the rest."

After a little demur the offer was accepted, and the gentleman departed.

The next to arrive was, by his looks, a man of business, to whom on the previous day I had sold an eyeglass. He was in a condition of excitement.

"Look here," said he, "I don't object to the glass; but it is not a pleasant thing to use. I put it to my eye yesterday when I called on my solicitor, relative to a concern I am in. He was courteous and plausible, as a lawyer always is when he thinks he can get money out of you. I read his inmost soul, and he said this, not with his lips, but in his heart: 'What a rogue this fellow is'—meaning me—'I must take care that he does not involve me in his rascalities. But I'll pick the flesh off his bones before I let him drop.' You may believe, sir, I walked out of his office and returned to mine, where I met a young fellow who was meditating the investment of a large sum of money, into which he had lately come, in a company I am floating.

"Why with an oath that fellow must have been here yesterday and bought one of your glasses, for he looked me steadily in the face; but I also had my glass to my eye, and I read his soul before the words left his lips. I saw then that he utterly mistrusted me, and that he saw through the whole bogus investment, and he had come to inform me that he would not soil his fingers by dealing with me further. So I lost the handling often thousand pounds through your confounded spectacles. Look here, old man," said he, assuming a genial and familiar tone, "I don't object to your glasses so long as you sell them only to me; but if you dispose of them to clients of mine, all I can say is that you are a howling cad, and deserve a horsewhipping. If this goes on, I may as well put up my shutters and have done with business. I'll give you a hundred pounds for your stock."

"Can't afford to do it," said I.

"Then I'm done for!" he exclaimed with an oath, and swung out of the office.

During the next hour I received three visits of inquiries concerning the glasses, but effected only one sale.

Then in bounced a lady, the only person of the weaker sex who had been a purchaser the day before. She was, obviously, a spinster, and beyond the middle age, and was clearly a person of means. She seated herself, and put up her veil. In her hand was a reticule.

"Oh, sir!" she said, "you do not know how you have upset me. These glasses have unquestionably served me well, but they have prodigiously troubled me. You may not suppose it, but I am an unmarried lady. I have been attended, as I always considered, by the most devoted servants ever attentive, forestalling my wishes, and in them I have reposed implicit confidence. My butler has been in my service fifteen years, and my lady's-maid for ten. When my maid was dressing me for dinner last night, she said to me, with sympathetic voice: 'Oh, ma'am, you should not have gone to call on Lady Dupine without your fur jacket and respirator. I am so afraid you will have one of your attacks of bronchitis again.'

"Well, I put on your spectacles, and looked into her mind, and what I saw was: 'The pestilent old cat; I only wish she would catch her death of cold, and then Thomson and I'—Thomson is my butler—'could retire, and take a public-house. It is intolerable to go on serving this selfish old woman, and we would not

361

do so but that we expect she will leave us something handsome in her will.' I read this distinctly in her mind. Inconceivable ingratitude! But this is not all. At dinner, Thomson served, and I read his mind as a book, for I wore the spectacles. I saw that he was married to my maid, Martha a thing I had never suspected—and that between them they had a deep-laid plan to rob me when I should be on my deathbed.

"I keep all my securities. I do not trust them to the bank. It was their intention, when I should be powerless, to get hold of the keys and possess themselves of such securities as they could. At dinner, when dessert was served, I had a slice of melon, with powdered ginger. Thompson's eye rested on the ginger; and I saw into his heart, and he was saying to himself: 'I wish that were arsenic. If it were not for the risk, I would spice her food for her.' Why, my life is in jeopardy. Thompson's impatience may get the better of his prudence, and he may spice my food. What can I do?"

"Really, madam, I cannot say."

"I shall put all my securities in the bank. Oh, dear! What shall I do? I shall go into rooms in the Grosvenor Hotel, and get rid of my house and servants. I shall never be happy again."

I was relieved when the lady left. As she did so she ran against a young man who was entering. After mutual apologies she went forth, but he came up to me with a firm step and with an angry frown, saying: "Do you mean to throw these glasses broadcast through society?" He flung his pair on the table. "I was a fool to buy them. You have blighted my life. I can trust nobody, respect nobody any longer. I have already seen too much with them. I have seen the seamy side of everyone through them. Is this going on?"

"Most assuredly it is," said I, "till I have disposed of my stock."

"Oh, indeed!" he exclaimed, and walked towards the door, but turned abruptly, drew a revolver from his pocket, and presented it at my head.

"Before I leave," said he, "I will settle this. I will shoot you dead as a rat unless you surrender your whole stock of psycho-scopes."

"My dear sir, my livelihood depends on the sale."

"I care not. I will rid society, the civilised world of such a terror." He pulled out his watch. "I give you five minutes. I will put a bullet through your brain unless you clear out your drawers and yield me every bit of glass that you possess."

I looked at him. He was angry. I saw deadly resolution in his eyes.

"The fool," thought I. "What if he does get possession of my stock? I can obtain a fresh supply from the miller." Happily, he had not the glasses on, and so could not read my thought.

"Come," said he; "two minutes have elapsed. Will you surrender, or must I shoot you?"

Reluctantly, with the bore of that revolver covering me, I obeyed. He swept together my whole stock-in-trade.

"A hammer," he ordered. I submitted. With his disengaged hand he set to work and smashed the glasses, nor paused till he had reduced them to small fragments. Then he returned the revolver to his pocket, cast the whole pile on the floor, and ground them to glass dust under his heel; then he departed.

I remained motionless and pondering. Then, starting up, I hurried to the station, and took a train to Chelmsford. Scruple was dead in me. I was an utterly miserable man, and in a fever to obtain a fresh supply of the glasses. Evening was coming on as I left Chelmsford and walked towards the mouth of the Blackwater. But the excitement during the previous days and the strain on my nerves were telling on me; and I was not sure of my way. I stumbled among the marshes. What cared I for glasswort now? What for the Red Hills? I caught my foot in the mud, and fell, measuring my length on the soil—and—

★★★★★★

The reciter of this story passed his hand over his face, looked vacantly at me, and said: "I can recall no more. I know *why* I am here, but how I came here I cannot say."

I had received tidings that a friend of mine was in the private lunatic asylum at Budleford, and I went to see him. He recognised me, and was glad to see me, and to me he poured forth the tale I have just recorded in his own words.

Again he passed his hand over his face, and said: "I know very well why I have been locked up in this place. It is a deep-laid plot. All the world is against me. All mankind is in alarm lest I should get a fresh supply of psychoscopic glasses; and to prevent that they have conspired against me to secure me behind bolts and bars. The world of men is afraid of being seen through. That is the secret why I am held in durance. But I cannot recall how I was got hold of and locked in here."

As I left the asylum I said to one of the keepers: "Can you tell me if there is a windmill somewhere about the mouth of the Blackwater—whereabouts I do not know?"

"The Devil's Mill. That poor gentleman was found near it— mad—quite mad."

A Happy Release

(A tale from *A Book of Ghosts*)

Mr. Benjamin Woolfield was a widower. For twelve months he put on mourning. The mourning was external, and by no means represented the condition of his feelings; for his married life had not been happy. He and Kesiah had been unequally yoked together. The Mosaic law forbade the union of the ox and the ass to draw one plough; and two more uncongenial creatures than Benjamin and Kesiah could hardly have been coupled to draw the matrimonial furrow.

She was a Plymouth Sister, and he, as she repeatedly informed him whenever he indulged in light reading, laughed, smoked, went out shooting, or drank a glass of wine, was of the earth, earthy, and a miserable worldling.

For some years Mr. Woolfield had been made to feel as though he were a moral and religious pariah. Kesiah had invited to the house and to meals, those of her own way of thinking, and on such occasions had spared no pains to have the table well served, for the elect are particular about their feeding, if indifferent as to their drinks. On such occasions, moreover, when Benjamin had sat at the bottom of his own table, he had been made to feel that he was a worm to be trodden on. The topics of conversation were such as were far beyond his horizon, and concerned matters of which he was ignorant. He attempted at intervals to enter into the circle of talk. He knew that such themes as football matches, horse races, and cricket were taboo, but he did suppose that home or foreign politics might interest the guests of Kesiah. But he soon learned that this was not the case, unless such matters tended to the fulfilment of prophecy.

When, however, in his turn, Benjamin invited home to dinner some of his old friends, he found that all provided for them was hashed mutton, cottage pie, and tapioca pudding. But even these could have been stomached, had not Mrs. Woolfield sat stern and silent at the head of the table, not uttering a word, but giving vent to occasional, very audible sighs.

When the year of mourning was well over, Mr. Woolfield put on a light suit, and contented himself, as an indication of bereavement, with a slight black band round the left arm. He also began to look about him for someone who might make up for the years during which he had felt like a crushed strawberry.

And in casting his inquiring eye about, it lighted upon Philippa Weston, a bright, vigorous young lady, well educated and intelligent. She was aged twenty-four and he was but eighteen years older, a difference on the right side.

It took Mr. Woolfield but a short courtship to reach an understanding, and he became engaged.

On the same evening upon which he had received a satisfactory answer to the question put to her, and had pressed for an early marriage, to which also consent had been accorded, he sat by his study fire, with his hands on his knees, looking into the embers and building love-castles there. Then he smiled and patted his knees.

He was startled from his honey reveries by a sniff. He looked round. There was a familiar ring in that sniff which was unpleasant to him.

What he then saw dissipated his rosy dreams, and sent his blood to his heart.

At the table sat his Kesiah, looking at him with her beady black eyes, and with stern lines in her face. He was so startled and shocked that he could not speak.

"Benjamin," said the apparition, "I know your purpose. It shall never be carried to accomplishment. I will prevent it."

"Prevent what, my love, my treasure?" he gathered up his

faculties to reply.

"It is in vain that you assume that infantile look of innocence," said his deceased wife. "You shall never—never—lead her to the hymeneal altar."

"Lead whom, my idol? You astound me."

"I know all. I can read your heart. A lost being though you be, you have still me to watch over you. When you quit this earthly tabernacle, if you have given up taking in the *Field*, and have come to realise your fallen condition, there is a chance—a distant chance—but yet one of our union becoming eternal."

"You don't mean to say so," said Mr. Woolfield, his jaw falling.

"There is—there is that to look to. That to lead you to turn over a new leaf. But it can never be if you become united to that Flibbertigibbet."

Mentally, Benjamin said: "I must hurry up with my marriage!" Vocally he said: "Dear me! Dear me!"

"My care for you is still so great," continued the apparition, "that I intend to haunt you by night and by day, till that engagement be broken off."

"I would not put you to so much trouble," said he.

"It is my duty," replied the late Mrs. Woolfield sternly.

"You are oppressively kind," sighed the widower.

At dinner that evening Mr. Woolfield had a friend to keep him company, a friend to whom he had poured out his heart. To his dismay, he saw seated opposite him the form of his deceased wife.

He tried to be lively; he cracked jokes, but the sight of the grim face and the stony eyes riveted on him damped his spirits, and all his mirth died away.

"You seem to be out of sorts tonight," said his friend.

"I am sorry that I act so bad a host," apologised Mr. Woolfield. "Two is company, three is none."

"But we are only two here tonight."

"My wife is with me in spirit."

"Which, she that was, or she that is to be?"

Mr. Woolfield looked with timid eyes towards her who sat at the end of the table. She was raising her hands in holy horror, and her face was black with frowns.

His friend said to himself when he left: "Oh, these lovers! They are never themselves so long as the fit lasts."

Mr. Woolfield retired early to bed. When a man has screwed himself up to proposing to a lady, it has taken a great deal out of him, and nature demands rest. It was so with Benjamin; he was sleepy. A nice little fire burned in his grate. He undressed and slipped between the sheets.

Before he put out the light he became aware that the late Mrs. Woolfield was standing by his bedside with a nightcap on her head.

"I am cold," said she, "bitterly cold."

"I am sorry to hear it, my dear," said Benjamin.

"The grave is cold as ice," she said. "I am going to step into bed."

"No—never!" exclaimed the widower, sitting up. "It won't do. It really won't. You will draw all the vital heat out of me, and I shall be laid up with rheumatic fever. It will be ten times worse than damp sheets."

"I am coming to bed," repeated the deceased lady, inflexible as ever in carrying out her will.

As she stepped in Mr. Woolfield crept out on the side of the fire and seated himself by the grate.

He sat there some considerable time, and then, feeling cold, he fetched his dressing-gown and enveloped himself in that.

He looked at the bed. In it lay the deceased lady with her long slit of a mouth shut like a rat-trap, and her hard eyes fixed on him.

"It is of no use your thinking of marrying, Benjamin," she said. "I shall haunt you till you give it up."

Mr. Woolfield sat by his fire all night, and only dozed off towards morning.

During the day he called at the house of Miss Weston, and was shown into the drawing-room. But there, standing behind her chair, was his deceased wife with her arms folded on the back of the seat, glowering at him.

It was impossible for the usual tender passages to ensue between the lovers with a witness present, expressing by gesture her disapproval of such matters and her inflexible determination to force on a rupture.

The dear departed did not attend Mr. Woolfield continuously during the day, but appeared at intervals. He could never say when he would be free, when she would not turn up.

In the evening he rang for the housemaid. "Jemima," he said, "put two hot bottles into my bed tonight. It is somewhat chilly."

"Yes, sir."

"And let the water be boiling—not with the chill off."

"Yes, sir."

When somewhat late Mr. Woolfield retired to his room he found, as he had feared, that his late wife was there before him. She lay in the bed with her mouth snapped, her eyes like black balls, staring at him.

"My dear," said Benjamin, "I hope you are more comfortable."

"I'm cold, deadly cold."

"But I trust you are enjoying the hot bottles."

"I lack animal heat," replied the late Mrs. Woolfield.

Benjamin fled the room and returned to his study, where he unlocked his spirit case and filled his pipe. The fire was burning. He made it up. He would sit there all night During the passing hours, however, he was not left quite alone. At intervals the door was gently opened, and the night-capped head of the late Mrs. Woolfield was thrust in.

"Don't think, Benjamin, that your engagement will lead to anything," she would say, "because it will not. I shall stop it."

So time passed. Mr. Woolfield found it impossible to escape this persecution. He lost spirits; he lost flesh.

At last, after sad thought, he saw but one way of relief, and that was to submit. And in order to break off the engagement he must have a prolonged interview with Philippa. He went to the theatre and bought two stall tickets, and sent one to her with the earnest request that she would accept it and meet him that evening at the theatre. He had something to communicate of the utmost importance.

At the theatre he knew that he would be safe; the principles of Kesiah would not suffer her to enter there.

At the proper time Mr. Woolfield drove round to Miss Weston's, picked her up, and together they went to the theatre and took their places in the stalls. Their seats were side by side.

"I am so glad you have been able to come," said Benjamin. "I have a most shocking disclosure to make to you. I am afraid that—but I hardly know how to say it—that—I really must break it off."

"Break what off?"

"Our engagement."

"Nonsense. I have been fitted for my trousseau."

"Your what?"

"My wedding-dresses."

"Oh, I beg pardon. I did not understand your French pronunciation. I thought—but it does not matter what I thought."

"Pray what is the sense of this?"

"Philippa, my affection for you is unabated. Do not suppose that I love you one whit the less. But I am oppressed by a horrible nightmare—daymare as well. I am haunted."

"Haunted, indeed!"

"Yes; by my late wife. She allows me no peace. She has made up her mind that I shall not marry you."

"Oh! Is that all? I am haunted also."

"Surely not?"

"It is a fact."

"Hush, hush!" from persons in front and at the side. Neither Ben nor Philippa had noticed that the curtain had risen and that the play had begun.

"We are disturbing the audience," whispered Mr. Woolfield. "Let us go out into the passage and promenade there, and then we can talk freely."

So both rose, left their stalls, and went into the *couloir*.

"Look here, Philippa," said he, offering the girl his arm, which she took, "the case is serious. I am badgered out of my reason, out of my health, by the late Mrs. Woolfield. She always had an iron will, and she has intimated to me that she will force me to give you up."

"Defy her."

"I cannot."

"Tut! these ghosts are exacting. Give them an inch and they take an ell. They are like old servants; if you yield to them they tyrannise over you."

"But how do you know, Philippa, dearest?"

"Because, as I said, I also am haunted."

"That only makes the matter more hopeless."

"On the contrary, it only shows how well suited we are to each other. We are in one box."

"Philippa, it is a dreadful thing. When my wife was dying she told me she was going to a better world, and that we should never meet again. *And she has not kept her word.*"

The girl laughed. "Rag her with it."

"How can I?"

"You can do it perfectly. Ask her why she is left out in the cold. Give her a piece of your mind. Make it unpleasant for her. I give Jehu no good time."

"Who is Jehu?"

"Jehu Post is the ghost who haunts me. When in the flesh he was a great admirer of mine, and in his cumbrous way tried to court me; but I never liked him, and gave him no encouragement. I snubbed him unmercifully, but he was one of those self-satisfied, self-assured creatures incapable of taking a snubbing. He was a Plymouth Brother."

"My wife was a Plymouth Sister."

"I know she was, and I always felt for you. It was so sad. Well, to go on with my story. In a frivolous mood Jehu took to a bicycle, and the very first time he scorched he was thrown, and so injured his back that he died in a week. Before he departed he entreated that I would see him; so I could not be nasty, and I went. And he told me then that he was about to be wrapped in glory. I asked him if this were so certain. 'Cocksure' was his reply; and they were his last words. And *he has not kept his word*."

"And he haunts you now?"

"Yes. He dangles about with his great ox-eyes fixed on me. But as to his envelope of glory I have not seen a fag end of it, and I have told him so."

"Do you really mean this, Philippa?"

"I do. He wrings his hands and sighs. He gets no change out of me, I promise you."

"This is a very strange condition of affairs."

"It only shows how well matched we are. I do not suppose you will find two other people in England so situated as we are, and therefore so admirably suited to one another."

"There is much in what you say. But how are we to rid ourselves of the nuisance—for it is a nuisance being thus haunted. We cannot spend all our time in a theatre."

"We must defy them. Marry in spite of them."

"I never did defy my wife when she was alive. I do not know how to pluck up courage now that she is dead. Feel my hand, Philippa, how it trembles. She has broken my nerve. When I was young I could play spellikins—my hand was so steady. Now I am quite incapable of doing anything with the little sticks."

"Well, hearken to what I propose," said Miss Weston. "I will beard the old cat——"

"Hush, not so disrespectful; she was my wife."

"Well, then, the ghostly old lady, in her den. You think she will appear if I go to pay you a visit?"

"Sure of it. She is consumed with jealousy. She had no personal attractions herself, and you have a thousand. I never knew whether she loved me, but she was always confoundedly jealous of me."

"Very well, then. You have often spoken to me about changes in the decoration of your villa. Suppose I call on you tomorrow afternoon, and you shall show me what your schemes are."

"And your ghost, will he attend you?"

"Most probably. He also is as jealous as a ghost can well be."

"Well, so be it. I shall await your coming with impatience. Now, then, we may as well go to our respective homes."

A cab was accordingly summoned, and after Mr. Woolfield had handed Philippa in, and she had taken her seat in the back, he entered and planted himself with his back to the driver.

"Why do you not sit by me?" asked the girl.

"I can't," replied Benjamin. "Perhaps you may not see, but I do, my deceased wife is in the cab, and occupies the place on your left."

"Sit on her," urged Philippa.

"I haven't the effrontery to do it," gasped Ben.

"Will you believe me," whispered the young lady, leaning over to speak to Mr. Woolfield, "I have seen Jehu Post hovering about the theatre door, wringing his white hands and turning up his eyes. I suspect he is running after the cab."

As soon as Mr. Woolfield had deposited his bride-elect at her residence he ordered the cabman to drive him home. Then he was alone in the conveyance with the ghost. As each gaslight was passed the flash came over the cadaverous face opposite him, and sparks of fire kindled momentarily in the stony eyes.

"Benjamin!" she said, "Benjamin! Oh, Benjamin! Do not suppose that I shall permit it. You may writhe and twist, you may plot and contrive how you will, I will stand between you and her as a wall of ice."

Next day, in the afternoon, Philippa Weston arrived at the house. The late Mrs. Woolfield had, however, apparently obtained an inkling of what was intended, for she was already there, in the drawing-room, seated in an armchair with her hands raised and clasped, looking stonily before her. She had a white face, no lips that showed, and her dark hair was dressed in two black slabs, one on each side of the temples. It was done in a knot behind. She wore no ornaments of any kind.

In came Miss Weston, a pretty girl, coquettishly dressed in

colours, with sparkling eyes and laughing lips. As she had predicted, she was followed by her attendant spectre, a tall, gaunt young man in a black frock-coat, with a melancholy face and large ox-eyes. He shambled in shyly, looking from side to side. He had white hands and long, lean fingers. Every now and then he put his hands behind him, up his back, under the tails of his coat, and rubbed his spine where he had received his mortal injury in cycling. Almost as soon as he entered he noticed the ghost of Mrs. Woolfield that was, and made an awkward bow. Her eyebrows rose, and a faint wintry smile of recognition lighted up her cheeks.

"I believe I have the honour of saluting Sister Kesiah," said the ghost of Jehu Post, and he assumed a posture of ecstasy.

"It is even so, Brother Jehu."

"And how do you find yourself, sister—out of the flesh?"

The late Mrs. Woolfield looked disconcerted, hesitated a moment, as if she found some difficulty in answering, and then, after a while, said: "I suppose, much as do you, brother."

"It is a melancholy duty that detains me here below," said Jehu Post's ghost.

"The same may be said of me," observed the spirit of the deceased Mrs. Woolfield. "Pray take a chair."

"I am greatly obliged, sister. My back——"

Philippa nudged Benjamin, and unobserved by the ghosts, both slipped into the adjoining room by a doorway over which hung velvet curtains.

In this room, on the table, Mr. Woolfield had collected patterns of chintzes and books of wall-papers.

There the engaged pair remained, discussing what curtains would go with the chintz coverings of the sofa and chairs, and what papers would harmonise with both.

"I see," said Philippa, "that you have plates hung on the walls. I don't like them: it is no longer in good form. If they be worth anything you must have a cabinet with glass doors for the china. How about the carpets?"

"There is the drawing-room," said Benjamin.

"No, we won't go in there and disturb the ghosts," said Philippa. "We'll take the drawing-room for granted."

"Well—come with me to the dining-room. We can reach it by another door."

In the room they now entered the carpet was in fairly good condition, except at the head and bottom of the table, where it was worn. This was especially the case at the bottom, where Mr. Woolfield had usually sat. There, when his wife had lectured, moralised, and harangued, he had rubbed his feet up and down and had fretted the nap off the Brussels carpet.

"I think," remarked Philippa, "that we can turn it about, and by taking out one width and putting that under the bookcase and inserting the strip that was there in its room, we can save the expense of a newcarpet. But—the engravings—those Landseers. What do you think of them, Ben, dear?"

She pointed to the two familiar engravings of the "Deer in Winter," and "Dignity and Impudence."

"Don't you think, Ben, that one has got a little tired of those pictures?"

"My late wife did not object to them, they were so perfectly harmless."

"But your coming wife does. We will have something more up-to-date in their room. By the way, I wonder how the ghosts are getting on. They have let us alone so far. I will run back and have a peep at them through the curtains."

The lively girl left the dining apartment, and her husband-elect, studying the pictures to which Philippa had objected. Presently she returned.

"Oh, Ben! such fun!" she said, laughing. "My ghost has drawn up his chair close to that of the late Mrs. Woolfield, and is fondling her hand. But I believe that they are only talking goody-goody."

"And now about the china," said Mr. Woolfield. "It is in a closet near the pantry—that is to say, the best china. I will get a benzoline lamp, and we will examine it. We had it out only when Mrs. Woolfield had a party of her elect brothers and sisters.

I fear a good deal is broken. I know that the soup tureen has lost a lid, and I believe we are short of vegetable dishes. How many plates remain I do not know. We had a parlourmaid, Dorcas, who was a sad smasher, but as she was one who had made her election sure, my late wife would not part with her."

"And how are you off for glass?"

"The wine-glasses are fairly complete. I fancy the cut-glass decanters are in a bad way. My late wife chipped them, I really believe out of spite."

It took the couple some time to go through the china and the glass.

"And the plate?" asked Philippa.

"Oh, that is right. All the real old silver is at the bank, as Kesiah preferred plated goods."

"How about the kitchen utensils?"

"Upon my word I cannot say. We had a rather nice-looking cook, and so my late wife never allowed me to step inside the kitchen."

"Is she here still?" inquired Philippa sharply.

"No; my wife, when she was dying, gave her the sack."

"Bless me, Ben!" exclaimed Philippa. "It is growing dark. I have been here an age. I really must go home. I wonder the ghosts have not worried us. I'll have another look at them."

She tripped off.

In five minutes she was back. She stood for a minute looking at Mr. Woolfield, laughing so heartily that she had to hold her sides.

"What is it, Philippa?" he inquired.

"Oh, Ben! A happy release. They will never dare to show their faces again. They have eloped together."

H. P.

(A tale from *A Book of Ghosts*)

The river Vézère leaps to life among the granite of the Limousin, forms a fine cascade, the Saut de la Virolle, then after a rapid descent over mica-schist, it passes into the region of red sandstone at Brive, and swelled with affluents it suddenly penetrates a chalk district, where it has scooped out for itself a valley between precipices some two to three hundred feet high.

These precipices are not perpendicular, but overhang, because the upper crust is harder than the stone it caps; and atmospheric influences, rain and frost, have gnawed into the chalk below, so that the cliffs hang forward as penthouse roofs, forming shelters beneath them. And these shelters have been utilised by man from the period when the first occupants of the district arrived at a vastly remote period, almost uninterruptedly to the present day. When peasants live beneath these roofs of nature's providing, they simply wall up the face and ends to form houses of the cheapest description of construction, with the earth as the floor, and one wall and the roof of living rock, into which they burrow to form cupboards, bedplaces, and cellars.

The refuse of all ages is superposed, like the leaves of a book, one stratum above another in orderly succession. If we shear down through these beds, we can read the history of the land, so far as its manufacture goes, beginning at the present day and going down, down to the times of primeval man. Now, after every meal, the peasant casts down the bones he has picked, he does not stoop to collect and cast forth the sherds of a broken

377

pot, and if a *sou* falls and rolls away, in the dust of these gloomy habitations it gets trampled into the soil, to form another token of the period of occupation.

When the first man settled here the climatic conditions were different. The mammoth or woolly elephant, the hyena, the cave bear, and the reindeer ranged the land. Then naked savages, using only flint tools, crouched under these rocks. They knew nothing of metals and of pottery. They hunted and ate the horse; they had no dogs, no oxen, no sheep. Glaciers covered the centre of France, and reached down the Vézère valley as far as to Brive.

These people passed away, whither we know not. The reindeer retreated to the north, the hyena to Africa, which was then united to Europe. The mammoth became extinct altogether.

After long ages another people, in a higher condition of culture, but who also used flint tools and weapons, appeared on the scene, and took possession of the abandoned rock shelters. They fashioned their implements in a different manner by flaking the flint in place of chipping it. They understood the art of the potter. They grew flax and wove linen. They had domestic animals, and the dog had become the friend of man. And their flint weapons they succeeded in bringing to a high polish by incredible labour and perseverance.

Then came in the Age of Bronze, introduced from abroad, probably from the East, as its great *depôt* was in the basin of the Po. Next arrived the Gauls, armed with weapons of iron. They were subjugated by the Romans, and Roman Gaul in turn became a prey to the Goth and the Frank. History has begun and is in full swing.

The medieval period succeeded, and finally the modern age, and man now lives on top of the accumulation of all preceding epochs of men and stages of civilisation. In no other part of France, indeed of Europe, is the story of man told so plainly, that he who runs may read; and ever since the middle of last century, when this fact was recognised, the district has been studied, and explorations have been made there, some slovenly, others scientifically.

A few years ago I was induced to visit this remarkable region and to examine it attentively. I had been furnished with letters of recommendation from the authorities of the great Museum of National Antiquities at St. Germain, to enable me to prosecute my researches unmolested by over-suspicious gendarmes and ignorant mayors.

Under one over-hanging rock was a cabaret or tavern, announcing that wine was sold there, by a withered bush above the door.

The place seemed to me to be a probable spot for my exploration. I entered into an arrangement with the proprietor to enable me to dig, he stipulating that I should not undermine and throw down his walls. I engaged six labourers, and began proceedings by driving a tunnel some little way below the tavern into the vast bed of *débris*.

The upper series of deposits did not concern me much. The point I desired to investigate, and if possible to determine, was the approximate length of time that had elapsed between the disappearance of the reindeer hunters and the coming on the scene of the next race, that which used polished stone implements and had domestic animals.

Although it may seem at first sight as if both races had been savage, as both lived in the Stone Age, yet an enormous stride forward had been taken when men had learned the arts of weaving, of pottery, and had tamed the dog, the horse, and the cow. These new folk had passed out of the mere wild condition of the hunter, and had become pastoral and to some extent agricultural.

Of course, the data for determining the length of a period might be few, but I could judge whether a very long or a very brief period had elapsed between the two occupations by the depth of *débris*—chalk fallen from the roof, brought down by frost, in which were no traces of human workmanship.

It was with this distinct object in view that I drove my adit into the slope of rubbish some way below the cabaret, and I chanced to have hit on the level of the deposits of the men of bronze. Not that we found much bronze—all we secured was a broken pin—but we came on fragments of pottery marked with the chevron and nail and twisted thong ornament peculiar to that people and age.

My men were engaged for about a week before we reached the face of the chalk cliff. We found the work not so easy as I had anticipated. Masses of rock had become detached from above and had fallen, so that we had either to quarry through them or to circumvent them. The soil was of that curious coffee colour so inseparable from the chalk formation. We found many things brought down from above, a coin commemorative of the storming of the Bastille, and some small pieces of the later Roman emperors. But all of these were, of course, not in the solid ground below, but near the surface.

When we had reached the face of the cliff, instead of sinking a shaft I determined on carrying a gallery down an incline, keeping the rock as a wall on my right, till I reached the bottom of all.

The advantage of making an incline was that there was no hauling up of the earth by a bucket let down over a pulley, and it was easier for myself to descend.

I had not made my tunnel wide enough, and it was tortuous. When I began to sink, I set two of the men to smash up the masses of fallen chalk rock, so as to widen the tunnel, so that I might use barrows. I gave strict orders that all the material brought up was to be picked over by two of the most intelligent of the men, outside in the blaze of the sun. I was not desirous of sinking too expeditiously; I wished to proceed slowly, cautiously, observing every stage as we went deeper.

We got below the layer in which were the relics of the Bronze Age and of the men of polished stone, and then we passed through many feet of earth that rendered nothing, and finally came on the traces of the reindeer period.

To understand how that there should be a considerable depth of the *débris* of the men of the rude stone implements, it must be explained that these men made their hearths on the bare ground, and feasted around their fires, throwing about them the bones they had picked, and the ashes, and broken and disused implements, till the ground was inconveniently encumbered. Then they swept all the refuse together over their old hearth, and established another on top. So the process went on from generation to generation.

For the scientific results of my exploration I must refer the reader to the journals and memoirs of learned societies. I will not trouble him with them here.

On the ninth day after we had come to the face of the cliff, and when we had reached a considerable depth, we uncovered some human bones. I immediately adopted special precautions, so that these should not be disturbed. With the utmost care the soil was removed from over them, and it took us half a day to completely clear a perfect skeleton. It was that of a full-grown man, lying on his back, with the skull supported against the wall of chalk rock. He did not seem to have been buried. Had he been so, he would doubtless have been laid on his side in a contracted posture, with the chin resting on the knees.

One of the men pointed out to me that a mass of fallen rock lay beyond his feet, and had apparently shut him in, so that he had died through suffocation, buried under the earth that the rock had brought down with it.

I at once despatched a man to my hotel to fetch my camera, that I might by flashlight take a photograph of the skeleton as it lay; and another I sent to get from the chemist and grocer as much gum arabic and isinglass as could be procured. My object was to give to the bones a bath of gum to render them less brittle when removed, restoring to them the gelatine that had been absorbed by the earth and lime in which they lay.

Thus I was left alone at the bottom of my passage, the four men above being engaged in straightening the adit and sifting the earth.

I was quite content to be alone, so that I might at my ease search for traces of personal ornament worn by the man who had thus met his death. The place was somewhat cramped, and there really was not room in it for more than one person to work freely.

Whilst I was thus engaged, I suddenly heard a shout, followed by a crash, and, to my dismay, an avalanche of rubble shot down the inclined passage of descent. I at once left the skeleton, and hastened to effect my exit, but found that this was impossible. Much of the superincumbent earth and stone had fallen, dislodged by the vibrations caused by the picks of the men smashing up the chalk blocks, and the passage was completely choked. I was sealed up in the hollow where I was, and thankful that the earth above me had not fallen as well, and buried me, a man of the present enlightened age, along with the primeval savage of eight thousand years ago.

A large amount of matter must have fallen, for I could not hear the voices of the men.

I was not seriously alarmed. The workmen would procure assistance and labour indefatigably to release me; of that I could be certain. But how much earth had fallen? How much of the passage was choked, and how long would they take before I was released? All that was uncertain. I had a candle, or, rather, a bit of one, and it was not probable that it would last till the passage was cleared. What made me most anxious was the question whether the supply of air in the hollow in which I was enclosed would suffice.

My enthusiasm for prehistoric research failed me just then. All my interests were concentrated on the present, and I gave up groping about the skeleton for relics. I seated myself on a stone, set the candle in a socket of chalk I had scooped out with my pocket-knife, and awaited events with my eyes on the skeleton.

Time passed somewhat wearily. I could hear an occasional thud, thud, when the men were using the pick; but they mostly employed the shovel, as I supposed. I set my elbows on my knees and rested my chin in my hands. The air was not cold, nor was the soil damp; it was dry as snuff. The flicker of my light played over the man of bones, and especially illumined the skull. It may have been fancy on my part, it probably was fancy, but it seemed to me as though something sparkled in the eye-sockets. Drops of water possibly lodged there, or crystals formed within the skull; but the effect was much as of eyes leering and winking at me. I lighted my pipe, and to my disgust found that my supply of matches was running short. In France the manufacture belongs to the state, and one gets but sixty *allumettes* for a penny.

I had not brought my watch with me below ground, fearing lest it might meet with an accident; consequently I was unable to reckon how time passed. I began counting and ticking off the minutes on my fingers, but soon tired of doing this.

My candle was getting short; it would not last much longer, and then I should be in the dark. I consoled myself with the thought that with the extinction of the light the consumption of the oxygen in the air would be less rapid. My eyes now rested on the flame of the candle, and I watched the gradual diminution of the composite. It was one of those abominable *bougies* with holes in them to economise the wax, and which consequently had less than the proper amount of material for feeding and maintaining a flame. At length the light went out, and I was left in total darkness. I might have used up the rest of my matches, one after another, but to what good?—they would prolong the period of illumination for but a very little while.

A sense of numbness stole over me, but I was not as yet sensible of deficiency of air to breathe. I found that the stone on which I was seated was pointed and hard, but I did not like to shift my position for fear of getting among and disturbing the bones, and I was still desirous of having them photographed *in situ* before they were moved.

I was not alarmed at my situation; I knew that I must be released eventually. But the tedium of sitting there in the dark and on a pointed stone was becoming intolerable.

Some time must have elapsed before I became, dimly at first, and then distinctly, aware of a bluish phosphorescent emanation from the skeleton. This seemed to rise above it like a faint smoke, which gradually gained consistency, took form, and became distinct; and I saw before me the misty, luminous form of a naked man, with wolfish countenance, prognathous jaws, glaring at me out of eyes deeply sunk under projecting brows. Although I thus describe what I saw, yet it gave me no idea of substance; it was vaporous, and yet it was articulate. Indeed, I cannot say at this moment whether I actually saw this apparition with my eyes, or whether it was a dream-like vision of the brain. Though luminous, it cast no light on the walls of the cave; if I raised my hand it did not obscure any portion of the form presented to me. Then I heard: "I will tear you with the nails of my fingers and toes, and rip you with my teeth."

"What have I done to injure and incense you?" I asked.

And here I must explain. No word was uttered by either of us; no word could have been uttered by this vaporous form. It had no material lungs, nor throat, nor mouth to form vocal sounds. It had but the semblance of a man. It was a spook, not a human being. But from it proceeded thought-waves, odylic force which smote on the tympanum of my mind or soul, and thereon registered the ideas formed by it. So in like manner I thought my replies, and they were communicated back in the same manner. If vocal words had passed between us neither would have been intelligible to the other.

No dictionary was ever compiled, or would be compiled, of the tongue of prehistoric man; moreover, the grammar of the speech of that race would be absolutely incomprehensible to man now. But thoughts can be interchanged without words. When we think we do not think in any language. It is only when we desire to communicate our thoughts to other men that we shape them into words and express them vocally in structural, grammatical sentences. The beasts have never attained to this, yet they can communicate with one another, not by language, but by thought vibrations.

I must further remark that when I give what ensued as a conversation, I have to render the thought intercommunication that passed between the *Homo Præhistoricus*—the prehistoric man—and me, in English as best I can render it. I knew as we conversed that I was not speaking to him in English, nor in

French, nor Latin, nor in any tongue whatever. Moreover, when I use the words "said" or "spoke," I mean no more than that the impression was formed on my brain-pan or the receptive drum of my soul, was produced by the rhythmic, orderly sequence of thought-waves. When, however, I express the words "screamed" or "shrieked," I signify that those vibrations came sharp and swift; and when I say "laughed," that they came in a choppy, irregular fashion, conveying the idea, not the sound of laughter.

"I will tear you! I will rend you to bits and throw you in pieces about this cave!" shrieked the *Homo Præhistoricus*, or primeval man.

Again I remonstrated, and inquired how I had incensed him. But yelling with rage, he threw himself upon me. In a moment I was enveloped in a luminous haze, strips of phosphorescent vapour laid themselves about me, but I received no injury whatever, only my spiritual nature was subjected to something like a magnetic storm. After a few moments the spook disengaged itself from me, and drew back to where it was before, screaming broken exclamations of meaningless rage, and jabbering savagely. It rapidly cooled down.

"Why do you wish me ill?" I asked again.

"I cannot hurt you. I am spirit, you are matter, and spirit cannot injure matter; my nails are psychic phenomena. Your soul you can lacerate yourself, but I can effect nothing, nothing."

"Then why have you attacked me? What is the cause of your impotent resentment?"

"Because you are a son of the twentieth century, and I lived eight thousand years ago. Why are you nursed in the lap of luxury? Why do you enjoy comforts, a civilisation that we knew nothing of? It is not just. It is cruel on us. We had nothing, nothing, literally nothing, not even lucifer matches!"

Again he fell to screaming, as might a caged monkey rendered furious by failure to obtain an apple which he could not reach.

"I am very sorry, but it is no fault of mine."

"Whether it be your fault or not does not matter to me. You

have these things—we had not. Why, I saw you just now strike a light on the sole of your boot. It was done in a moment. We had only flint and iron-stone, and it took half a day with us to kindle a fire, and then it flayed our knuckles with continuous knocking. No! we had nothing, nothing—no lucifer matches, no commercial travellers, no Benedictine, no pottery, no metal, no education, no elections, no *chocolat menier.*"

"How do you know about these products of the present age, here, buried under fifty feet of soil for eight thousand years?"

"It is my spirit which speaks with your spirit. My spook does not always remain with my bones. I can go up; rocks and stones and earth heaped over me do not hold me down. I am often above. I am in the tavern overhead. I have seen men drink there. I have seen a bottle of Benedictine. I have applied my psychical lips to it, but I could taste, absorb nothing. I have seen commercial travellers there, cajoling the patron into buying things he did not want. They are mysterious, marvellous beings, their powers of persuasion are little short of miraculous. What do you think of doing with me?"

"Well, I propose first of all photographing you, then soaking you in gum arabic, and finally transferring you to a museum."

He screamed as though with pain, and gasped: "Don't! don't do it. It will be torture insufferable."

"But why so? You will be under glass, in a polished oak or mahogany box."

"Don't! You cannot understand what it will be to me—a spirit more or less attached to my body, to spend ages upon ages in a museum with *fibulæ, triskelli, palstaves, celts, torques, scarabs.* We cannot travel very far from our bones—our range is limited. And conceive of my feelings for centuries condemned to wander among glass cases containing prehistoric antiquities, and to hear the talk of scientific men alone. Now here, it is otherwise. Here I can pass up when I like into the tavern, and can see men get drunk, and hear commercial travellers hoodwink the patron, and then when the taverner finds he has been induced to buy what he did not want, I can see him beat his wife and smack his children. There is something human, humorous, in that, but *fibulæ, palstaves, torques*—bah!"

"You seem to have a lively knowledge of antiquities," I observed.

"Of course I have. There come archæologists here and eat their sandwiches above me, and talk prehistoric antiquities till I am sick. Give me life! Give me something interesting!"

"But what do you mean when you say that you cannot travel far from your bones?"

"I mean that there is a sort of filmy attachment that connects our psychic nature with our mortal remains. It is like a spider and its web. Suppose the soul to be the spider and the skeleton to be the web. If you break the thread the spider will never find its way back to its home. So it is with us; there is an attachment, a faint thread of luminous spiritual matter that unites us to our earthly husk. It is liable to accidents. It sometimes gets broken, sometimes dissolved by water. If a blackbeetle crawls across it it suffers a sort of paralysis. I have never been to the other side of the river, I have feared to do so, though very anxious to look at that creature like a large black caterpillar called the Train."

"This is news to me. Do you know of any cases of rupture of connection?"

"Yes," he replied. "My old father, after he was dead some years, got his link of attachment broken, and he wandered about disconsolate. He could not find his own body, but he lighted on that of a young female of seventeen, and he got into that. It happened most singularly that her spook, being frolicsome and inconsiderate, had got its bond also broken, and she, that is her spirit, straying about in quest of her body, lighted on that of my venerable parent, and for want of a better took possession of it. It so chanced that after a while they met and became chummy. In the world of spirits there is no marriage, but there grow up spiritual attachments, and these two got rather fond of each other, but never could puzzle it out which was which and what each was; for a female soul had entered into an old male body, and a male soul had taken up its residence in a female body. Neither could riddle out of which sex each was. You see they had no education. But I know that my father's soul became quite sportive in that young woman's skeleton."

"Did they continue chummy?"

"No; they quarrelled as to which was which, and they are not now on speaking terms. I have two great-uncles. Theirs is a sad tale. Their souls were out wandering one day, and inadvertently they crossed and recrossed each other's tracks so that their spiritual threads of attachment got twisted. They found this out, and that they were getting tangled up. What one of them should have done would have been to have stood still and let the other jump over and dive under his brother's thread till he had cleared himself. But my maternal great-uncles—I think I forgot to say they were related to me through my mother—they were men of peppery tempers and they could not understand this. They had no education. So they jumped one this way and one another, each abusing the other, and made the tangle more complete. That was about six thousand years ago, and they are now so knotted up that I do not suppose they will be clear of one another till time is no more."

He paused and laughed.

Then I said: "It must have been very hard for you to be without pottery of any sort."

"It was," replied H. P. (this stands for *Homo Præhistoricus*, not for House-Parlourmaid or Hardy Perennial), "very hard. We had skins for water and milk——"

"Oh! you had milk. I supposed you had no cows."

"Nor had we, but the reindeer were beginning to get docile and be tamed. If we caught young deer we brought them up to be pets for our children. And so it came about that as they grew up we found out that we could milk them into skins. But that gave it a smack, and whenever we desired a fresh draught there was nothing for it but to lie flat on the ground under a doe reindeer and suck for all we were worth. It was hard. Horses were hunted. It did not occur to us that they could be tamed and saddled and mounted. Oh! it was not right. It was not fair that you

388

should have everything and we nothing—nothing—nothing! Why should you have all and we have had naught?"

"Because I belong to the twentieth century. Thirty-three generations go to a thousand years. There are some two hundred and sixty-four or two hundred and seventy generations intervening between you and me. Each generation makes some discovery that advances civilisation a stage, the next enters on the discoveries of the preceding generations, and so culture advances stage by stage. Man is infinitely progressive, the brute beast is not."

"That is true," he replied. "I invented butter, which was unknown to my ancestors, the unbuttered man."

"Indeed!"

"It was so," he said, and I saw a flush of light ripple over the emanation. I suppose it was a glow of self-satisfaction. "It came about thus. One of my wives had nearly let the fire out. I was very angry, and catching up one of the skins of milk, I banged her about the head with it till she fell insensible to the earth. The other wives were very pleased and applauded. When I came to take a drink, for my exertions had heated me, I found that the milk was curdled into butter. At first I did not know what it was, so I made one of my other wives taste it, and as she pronounced it to be good, I ate the rest myself. That was how butter was invented. For four hundred years that was the way it was made, by banging a milk-skin about the head of a woman till she was knocked down insensible. But at last a woman found out that by churning the milk with her hand butter could be made equally well, and then the former process was discontinued except by some men who clung to ancestral customs."

"But," said I, "nowadays you would not be suffered to knock your wife about, even with a milk-skin."

"Why not?"

"Because it is barbarous. You would be sent to gaol."

"But she was my wife."

"Nevertheless it would not be tolerated. The law steps in and protects women from ill-usage."

"How shameful! Not allowed to do what you like with your own wife!"

"Most assuredly not. Then you remarked that this was how you dealt with one of your wives. How many did you possess?"

"Off and on, seventeen."

"*Now*, no man is suffered to have more than one."

"What—one at a time?"

"Yes," I replied.

"Ah, well. Then if you had an old and ugly wife, or one who was a scold, you could kill her and get another, young and pretty."

"That would not be allowed."

"Not even if she were a scold?"

"No, you would have to put up with her to the bitter end."

"Humph!" H. P. remained silent for a while wrapped in thought. Presently he said: "There is one thing I do not understand. In the wine-shop overhead the men get very quarrelsome, others drunk, but they never kill one another."

"No. If one man killed another he would have his head cut off—here in France—unless extenuating circumstances were found. With us in England he would be hanged by the neck till he was dead."

"Then—what is your sport?"

"We hunt the fox."

"The fox is bad eating. I never could stomach it. If I did kill a fox I made my wives eat it, and had some mammoth meat for myself. But hunting is business with us—or was so—not sport."

"Nevertheless with us it is our great sport."

"Business is business and sport is sport," he said. "Now, we hunted as business, and had little fights and killed one another as our sport."

"We are not suffered to kill one another."

"But take the case," said he, "that a man has a nose-ring, or a pretty wife, and you want one or the other. Surely you might kill him and possess yourself of what you so ardently covet?"

"By no means. Now, to change the topic," I went on, "you

390

are totally destitute of clothing. You do not even wear the traditional garment of fig leaves."

"What avail fig leaves? There is no warmth in them."

"Perhaps not—but out of delicacy."

"What is that? I don't understand." There was clearly no corresponding sensation in the vibrating *tympanum* of his psychic nature.

"Did you never wear clothes?" I inquired.

"Certainly, when it was cold we wore skins, skins of the beasts we killed. But in summer what is the use of clothing? Besides, we only wore them out of doors. When we entered our homes, made of skins hitched up to the rock overhead, we threw them off. It was hot within, and we perspired freely."

"What, were naked in your homes! you and your wives?"

"Of course we were. Why not? It was very warm within with the fire always kept up."

"Why—good gracious me!" I exclaimed, "that would never be tolerated nowadays. If you attempted to go about the country unclothed, even get out of your clothes freely at home, you would be sent to a lunatic asylum and kept there."

"Humph!" He again lapsed into silence.

Presently he exclaimed: "After all, I think that we were better off as we were eight thousand years ago, even without your matches, Benedictine, education, *chocolat menier*, and commercials, for then we were able to enjoy real sport—we could kill one another, we could knock old wives on the head, we could have a dozen or more squaws according to our circumstances, young and pretty, and we could career about the country or sit and enjoy a social chat at home, stark naked. We were best off as we were. There are compensations in life at every period of man. *Vive la liberté!*"

At that moment I heard a shout—saw a flash of light. The workmen had pierced the barrier. A rush of fresh air entered. I staggered to my feet.

"*Oh! mon Dieu! Monsieur vit encore!*"

I felt dizzy. Kind hands grasped me. I was dragged forth.

Brandy was poured down my throat. When I came to myself I gasped: "Fill in the hole! Fill it all up. Let H. P. lie where he is. He shall not go to the British Museum. I have had enough of prehistoric antiquities. *Adieu, pour toujours la Vézère.*"

McAlister

(A tale from *A Book of Ghosts*)

The city of Bayonne, lying on the left bank of the Adour, and serving as its port, is one that ought to present much interest to the British tourist, on account of its associations. For three hundred years, along with Bordeaux, it belonged to the English crown. The cathedral, a noble structure of the fourteenth century, was reared by the English, and on the bosses of its vaulting are carved the arms of England, of the Talbots, and of other great English noble families. It was probably designed by English architects, for it possesses, in its vaulting, the long central rib so characteristic of English architecture, and wholly unlike what was the prevailing French fashion of vaulting in compartments, and always without that connecting rib, like the inverted keel of a ship, with which we are acquainted in our English minsters. Under some of the modern houses in the town are cellars of far earlier construction, also vaulted, and in them as well may be seen the arms of the English noble families which had their dwellings above.

But Bayonne has later associations with us. At the close of the Peninsular War, when Wellington had driven Marshal Soult and the French out of Spain, and had crossed the Pyrenees, his forces, under Sir John Hope, invested the citadel. In February, 1814, Sir John threw a bridge of boats across the Adour, boats being provided by the fleet of Admiral Penrose, in the teeth of a garrison of 15,000 men, and French gunboats which guarded the river and raked the English whilst conducting this hazardous and masterly achievement. This brilliant exploit was effected whilst Wellington engaged the attention of Soult about the Gaves, affluents of the Adour, near Orthez. It is further interesting, with a tragic interest, on account of an incident in that campaign which shall be referred to presently.

The cathedral of Bayonne, some years ago, possessed no towers—the English were driven out of Aquitaine before these had been completed. The west front was mean to the last degree, masked by a shabby penthouse, plastered white, or rather dirty white, on which in large characters was inscribed, "*Liberté égalité et fraternité.*"

This has now disappeared, and a modern west front and twin towers and spires have been added, in passable architecture. When I was at Bayonne, more years ago than I care to say, I paid a visit to the little cemetery on the north bank of the river, in which were laid the English officers who fell during the investment of Bayonne.

The north bank is in the department of the Landes, whereas that on the south is in the department of the Basses Pyrénées.

About the time when the English were expelled from France, and lost Aquitaine, the Adour changed its course. Formerly it had turned sharply round at the city, and had flowed north and found an outlet some miles away at Cap Breton, but the entrance was choked by the moving sand-dunes, and the impatient river burst its way into the Bay of Biscay by the mouth through which it still flows. But the old course is marked by lagoons of still blue water in the midst of a vast forest of pines and cork trees. I had spent a day wandering among these tree-covered *landes*, seeking out the lonely lakes, and in the evening I returned in the direction of Bayonne, diverging somewhat from my course to visit the cemetery of the English. This was a square walled enclosure with an iron gate, rank with weeds, utterly neglected, and with the tombstones, some leaning, some prostrate, all covered with lichen and moss. I could not get within to decipher the inscriptions, for the gate was locked and I had not the key, and was quite ignorant who was the custodian of the place.

Being tired with my trudge in the sand, I sat down outside, with my back to the wall, and saw the setting sun paint with saffron the boles of the pines. I took out my Murray that I had in my knapsack, and read the following passage:—

"To the N., rises the citadel, the most formidable of the works laid out by Vauban, and greatly strengthened, especially since 1814, when it formed the key to an entrenched camp of Marshal Soult, and was invested by a detachment of the army of the Duke of Wellington, but not taken, the peace having put a stop to the siege after some bloody encounters. The last of these, a dreadful and useless expenditure of human life, took place after peace was declared, and the British forces put off their guard in consequence. They were thus entirely taken by surprise by a sally of the garrison, made early on the morning of April 14th; which, though repulsed, was attended with the loss of 830 men of the British, and by the capture of their commander, Sir John Hope, whose horse was shot under him, and himself wounded. The French attack was supported by the fire of their gunboats on the river, which opened indiscriminately on friend and foe. Nine hundred and ten of the French were killed."

When I had concluded, the sun had set, and already a grey mist began to form over the course of the Adour. I thought that now it was high time for me to return to Bayonne, and to *table d'hôte*, which is at 7.30 p.m., but for which I knew I should be late. However, before rising, I pulled out my flask of Scotch whisky, and drained it to the last drop.

I had scarcely finished, and was about to heave myself to my feet, when I heard a voice from behind and above me say—"It is grateful, varra grateful to a Scotchman."

I turned myself about, and drew back from the wall, for I saw a very remarkable object perched upon it. It was the upper portion of a man in military accoutrements. He was not sitting on the wall, for, if so, his legs would have been dangling over on the outside. And yet he could not have heaved himself up to the level of the parapet, with the legs depending inside, for he appeared to be on the wall itself down to the middle.

"Are you a Scotchman or an Englishman?" he inquired.

"An Englishman," I replied, hardly knowing what to make of the apparition.

"It's mabbe a bit airly in the nicht for me to be stirring," he said; "but the smell of the whisky drew me from my grave."

"From your grave!" I exclaimed.

"And pray, what is the blend?" he asked.

I answered.

"Weel," said he, "ye might do better, but it's guid enough. I am Captain Alister McAlister of Auchimachie, at your service, that is to say, his superior half. I fell in one of the attacks on the citadel. Those"—he employed a strong qualification which need not be reproduced—"those Johnny Crapauds used chain-shot; and they cut me in half at the waistbelt, and my legs are in Scotland."

Having somewhat recovered from my astonishment, I was able to take a further look at him, and could not restrain a laugh. He so much resembled Humpty Dumpty, who, as I had learned in childhood, did sit on a wall.

"Is there anything so rideeculous about me?" asked Captain McAlister in a tone of irritation. "You seem to be in a jocular mood, sir."

"I assure you," I responded, "I was only laughing from joy of heart at the happy chance of meeting you, Alister McAlister."

"Of Auchimachie, and my title is Captain," he said. "There is only half of me here—the *etceteras* are in the family vault in Scotland."

I expressed my genuine surprise at this announcement. "You must understand, sir," continued he, "that I am but the speeritual presentment of my buried trunk. The speeritual presentment of my nether half is not here, and I should scorn to use those of Captain O'Hooligan."

I pressed my hand to my brow. Was I in my right senses? Had the hot sun during the day affected my brain, or had the last drain of whisky upset my reason?

"You may be pleased to know," said the half-captain, "that

my father, the Laird of Auchimachie, and Colonel Graham of Ours, were on terms of the greatest intimacy. Before I started for the war under Wellington—he was at the time but Sir Arthur Wellesley—my father took Colonel Graham apart and confided to him: 'If anything should happen to my son in the campaign, you'll obleege me greatly if you will forward his remains to Auchimachie. I am a staunch Presbyterian, and I shouldn't feel happy that his poor body should lie in the land of idolaters, who worship the Virgin Mary. And as to the expense, I will manage to meet that; but be careful not to do the job in an extravagant manner.'"

"And the untoward Fates cut you short?"

"Yes, the chain-shot did, but not in the Peninsula. I passed safely through that, but it was here. When we were makin' the bridge, the enemy's ships were up the river, and they fired on us with chain-shot, which ye ken are mainly used for cutting the rigging of vessels. But they employed them on us as we were engaged over the pontoons, and I was just cut in half by a pair of these shot at the junction of the tunic and the trews."

"I cannot understand how that your legs should be in Scotland and your trunk here."

"That's just what I'm aboot to tell you. There was a Captain O'Hooligan and I used to meet; we were in the same detachment. I need not inform you, if you're a man of understanding, that O'Hooligan is an Irish name, and Captain Timothy O'Hooligan was a born Irishman and an ignorant papist to boot. Now, I am by education and conveection a staunch Presbyterian. I believe in John Calvin, John Knox, and Jeannie Geddes. That's my creed; and if ye are disposed for an argument——"

"Not in the least."

"Weel, then, it was other with Captain O'Hooligan, and we often had words; but he hadn't any arguments at all, only assertions, and he lost his temper accordingly, and I was angry at the unreasonableness of the man. I had had an ancestor in Derry at the siege and at the Battle of the Boyne, and he spitted three Irish kerns on his sabre. I glory in it, and I told O'Hooligan as much, and I drank a glass of toddy to the memory of William III., and I shouted out Lillibulero! I believe in the end we would have fought a duel, after the siege was over, unless one of us had thought better of it. But it was not to be. At the same time that I was cut in half, so was he also by chain-shot."

"And is he buried here?"

"The half of him—his confounded legs, and the knees that have bowed to the image of Baal."

"Then, what became of his body?"

"If you'll pay me reasonable attention, and not interrupt, I'll tell you the whole story. But—sure enough! Here come those legs!"

Instantly the half-man rolled off the wall, on the outside, and heaving himself along on his hands, scuttled behind a tree-trunk.

Next moment I saw a pair of nimble lower limbs, in white ducks and straps under the boots, leap the wall, and run about, up and down, much like a setter after a partridge.

I did not know what to make of this.

Then the head of McAlister peered from behind the tree, and screamed "Lillibulero! God save King William!" Instantly the legs went after him, and catching him up kicked him like a football about the enclosure. I cannot recall precisely how many times the circuit was made, twice or thrice, but all the while the head of McAlister kept screaming "Lillibulero!" and "D—— the Pope!"

Recovering myself from my astonishment, and desirous of putting a term to this not very edifying scene, I picked up a leaf of shamrock, that grew at my feet, and ran between the legs and the trunk, and presented the symbol of St. Patrick to the former. The legs at once desisted from pursuit, and made a not ungrace-ful bow to the leaf, and as I advanced they retired, still bowing reverentially, till they reached the wall, which they stepped over with the utmost ease.

The half-Scotchman now hobbled up to me on his hands, and said: "I'm varra much obleeged to you for your intervention, sir."Then he scrambled, by means of the rails of the gate, to his former perch on the wall.

"You must understand, sir," said McAlister, settling himself comfortably, "that this produces no pheesical inconvenience to me at all. For O'Hooligan's boots are speeritual, and so is my trunk speeritual. And at best it only touches my speeritual feelings. Still, I thank you."

"You certainly administered to him some spiritual aggravation," I observed.

"Ay, ay, sir, I did. And I glory in it."

"And now, Captain McAlister, if it is not troubling you too greatly, after this interruption would you kindly explain to me how it comes about that the nobler part of you is here and the less noble in Scotland?"

"I will do so with pleasure. Captain O'Hooligan's upper story is at Auchimachie."

"How came that about?"

"If you had a particle of patience, you would not interrupt me in my narrative. I told you, did I not, that my dear father had enjoined on Colonel Graham, should anything untoward occur, that he should send my body home to be interred in the vault of my ancestors? Well, this is how it came about that the awkward mistake was made. When it was reported that I had been killed, Colonel Graham issued orders that my remains should be carefully attended to and put aside to be sent home to Scotland."

"By boat, I presume?"

"Certainly, by boat. But, unfortunately, he commissioned some Irishmen of his company to attend to it. And whether it was that they wished to do honour to their own countryman, or whether it was that, like most Irishmen, they could not fail to blunder in the discharge of their duty, I cannot say. They might have recognised me, even if they hadn't known my face, by my goold repeater watch; but some wretched camp-followers had been before them. On the watch were engraved the McAlister arms. But the watch had been stolen. So they picked up—either out of purpose, or by mistake—O'Hooligan's trunk, and my nether portion, and put them together into one case. You see, a man's legs are not so easily identified. So his body and my lower limbs were made ready together to be forwarded to Scotland."

"But how—did not Colonel Graham see personally to the matter?"

"He could not. He was so much engaged over regimental duties. Still, he might have stretched a point, I think."

"It must have been difficult to send the portions so far. Was the body embalmed?"

"Embalmed! no. There was no one in Bayonne who knew how to do it. There was a bird-stuffer in the Rue Pannceau, but he had done nothing larger than a seagull. So there could be no question of embalming. We, that is, the bit of O'Hooligan and the bit of me, were put into a cask of *eau-de-vie*, and so forwarded by a sailing-vessel. And either on the way to Southampton, or on another boat from that port to Edinburgh, the sailors ran a gimlet into the barrel, and inserted a straw, and drank up all the spirits. It was all gone by the time the hogshead reached Auchimachie. Whether O'Hooligan gave a smack to the liquor I cannot say, but I can answer for my legs, they would impart a grateful flavour of whisky.

"I was always a drinker of whisky, and when I had taken a considerable amount it always went to my legs; they swerved, and gave way under me. That is proof certain that the liquor went to my extremities and not to my head. Trust to a Scotchman's head for standing any amount of whisky. When the remains arrived at Auchimachie for interment, it was supposed that some mistake had been made. My hair is sandy, that of O'Hooligan is black, or nearly so; but there was no knowing what chemical action the alcohol might have on the hair in altering its colour. But my mother identified the legs past mistake, by a mole on the left calf and a varicose vein on the right. Anyhow, half a loaf is better than no bread, so all the mortal relics were consigned to the McAlister vault. It was aggravating to my feelings that the minister should pronounce a varra eloquent and moving discourse on the occasion over the trunk of a confounded Irishman and a papist."

"You must really excuse me," interrupted I, "but how the dickens do you know all this?"

"There is always an etherial current of communication between the parts of a man's body," replied McAlister, "and there is speeritual intercommunication between a man's head and his toes, however pairted they may be. I tell you, sir, in the speeritual world we know a thing or two."

"And now," said I, "what may be your wishes in this most unfortunate matter?"

"I am coming to that, if you'll exercise a little rational patience. This that I tell you of occurred in 1814, a considerable time ago. I shall be varra pleased if, on your return to England, you will make it your business to run up to Scotland, and interview my great-nephew. I am quite sure he will do the right thing by me, for the honour of the family, and to ease my soul. He never would have come into the estate at all if it had not been for my lamented decease. There's another little unpleasantness to which I desire you to call his attention. A tombstone has been erected over my trunk and O'Hooligan's legs, here in this cemetery, and on it is: 'Sacred to the Memory of Captain Timothy O'Hooligan, who fell on the field of Glory. R. I. P.' Now this is liable to a misunderstanding for it is me—I mean I, to be grammatical—who lies underneath. I make no account of the Irishman's nether extremities.

"And being a convinced and zealous Presbyterian, I altogether conscientiously object to having 'Requiescat in pace' inscribed over my bodily remains. And my great-nephew, the present laird, if he be true to the principles of the Covenant, will object just as strongly as myself. I know very weel those letters are attached to the name of O'Hooligan, but they mark the place of deposition of my body rather than his. So I wish you just to put it clearly and logically to the laird, and he will take steps, at any cost, to have me transferred to Auchimachie. What he may do with the relics of that Irish rogue I don't care for, not one stick of barley sugar."

I promised solemnly to fulfil the commission entrusted to me, and then Captain McAlister wished me a good night, and retired behind the cemetery wall.

I did not quit the South of France that same year, for I spent the winter at Pau. In the following May I returned to England, and there found that a good many matters connected with my family called for my immediate attention. It was accordingly just a year and five months after my interview with Captain McAlister that I was able to discharge my promise. I had never forgotten my undertaking—I had merely postponed it. Charity begins at home, and my own concerns engrossed my time too fully to allow me the leisure for a trip to the North.

However, in the end I did go. I took the express to Edinburgh. That city, I think candidly, is the finest for situation in the world, as far as I have seen of it. I did not then visit it. I never had previously been in the Athens of the North, and I should have liked to spend a couple of days at least in it, to look over the castle and to walk through Holyrood. But duty stands before pleasure, and I went on directly to my destination, postponing acquaintance with Edinburgh till I had accomplished my undertaking.

I had written to Mr. Fergus McAlister to inform him of my desire to see him. I had not entered into the matter of my communication. I thought it best to leave this till I could tell him the whole story by word of mouth. I merely informed him by letter that I had something to speak to him about that greatly concerned his family.

On reaching the station his carriage awaited me, and I was driven to his house.

He received me with the greatest cordiality, and offered me the kindest hospitality.

The house was large and rambling, not in the best repair, and the grounds, as I was driven through them, did not appear to be trimly kept. I was introduced to his wife and to his five daughters, fair-haired, freckled girls, certainly not beautiful, but pleasing enough in manner. His eldest son was away in the army, and his second was in a lawyer's office in Edinburgh; so I saw nothing of them.

After dinner, when the ladies had retired, I told him the entire story as freely and as fully as possible, and he listened to me with courtesy, patience, and the deepest attention.

"Yes," he said, when I had concluded, "I was aware that doubts had been cast on the genuineness of the trunk. But under the circumstances it was considered advisable to allow the matter to stand as it was. There were insuperable difficulties in the way of an investigation and a certain identification. But the legs were all right. And I hope to show you tomorrow, in the kirk, a very handsome tablet against the wall, recording the name and the date of decease of my great-uncle, and some very laudatory words on his character, beside an appropriate text from the Screeptures."

"Now, however, that the facts are known, you will, of course, take steps for the translation of the half of Captain Alister to your family vault."

"I foresee considerable difficulties in the way," he replied. "The authorities at Bayonne might raise objections to the exhuming of the remains in the grave marked by the tombstone of Captain O'Hooligan. They might very reasonably say: 'What the hang has Mr. Fergus McAlister to do with the body of Captain O'Hooligan?' We must consult the family of that officer in Ireland."

"But," said I, "a representation of the case—of the mistake made—would render all clear to them. I do not see that there is any necessity for complicating the story by saying that you have only half of your relative here, and that the other half is in O'Hooligan's grave. State that orders had been given for the transmission of the body of your great-uncle to Auchimachie, and that, through error, the corpse of Captain O'Hooligan had been sent, and Captain McAlister buried by mistake as that of the Irishman. That makes a simple, intelligible, and straightforward tale. Then you could dispose of the superfluous legs when they arrived in the manner you think best."

The laird remained silent for a while, rubbing his chin, and looking at the tablecloth.

Presently he stood up, and going to the sideboard, said: "I'll just take a wash of whisky to clear my thoughts. Will you have some?"

"Thank you; I am enjoying your old and excellent port."

Mr. Fergus McAlister returned leisurely to the table after his "wash," remained silent a few minutes longer, then lifted his head and said: "I don't see that I am called upon to transport those legs."

"No," I answered; "but you had best take the remains in a lump and sort them on their arrival."

"I am afraid it will be seriously expensive. My good sir, the property is not now worth what it was in Captain Alister's time. Land has gone down in value, and rents have been seriously reduced. Besides, farmers are now more exacting than formerly; they will not put up with the byres that served their fathers. Then my son in the army is a great expense to me, and my second son is not yet earning his livelihood, and my daughters have not yet found suitors, so that I shall have to leave them something on which to live; besides"—he drew a long breath—"I want to build on to the house a billiard-room."

"I do not think," protested I, "that the cost would be very serious."

"What do you mean by serious?" he asked.

"I think that these relics of humanity might be transported to Auchimachie in a hogshead of cognac, much as the others were."

"What is the price of cognac down there?" asked he.

"Well," I replied, "that is more than I can say as to the cask. Best cognac, three stars, is five *francs* fifty *centimes* a bottle."

"That's a long price. But one star?"

"I cannot say; I never bought that. Possibly three *francs* and a half."

"And how many bottles to a cask?"

"I am not sure, something over two hundred litres."

"Two hundred three shillings," mused Mr. Fergus; and then

looking up, "there is the duty in England, very heavy on spirits, and charges for the digging-up, and fees to the officials, and the transport by water——" He shook his head.

"You must remember," said I, "that your relative is subjected to great indignities from those legs, getting toed three or four times round the enclosure." I said three or four, but I believe it was only twice or thrice. "It hardly comports with the family honour to suffer it."

"I think," replied Mr. Fergus, "that you said it was but the speeritual presentment of a boot, and that there was no pheesical inconvenience felt, only a speeritual impression?"

"Just so."

"For my part, judging from my personal experience," said the laird, "speeritual impressions are most evanescent."

"Then," said I, "Captain Alister's trunk lies in a foreign land."

"But not," replied he, "in Roman Catholic consecrated soil. That is a great satisfaction."

"You, however, have the trunk of a Roman Catholic in your family vault."

"It is so, according to what you say. But there are a score of McAlisters there, all staunch Presbyterians, and if it came to an argument among them—I won't say he would not have a leg to stand on, as he hasn't those anyhow, but he would find himself just nowhere."

Then Mr. Fergus McAlister stood up and said: "Shall we join the ladies? As to what you have said, sir, and have recommended, I assure you that I will give it my most serious consideration."

The Red-Haired Girl
A Wife's Story
(A tale from *A Book of Ghosts*)

In 1876 we took a house in one of the best streets and parts of B———. I do not give the name of the street or the number of the house, because the circumstances that occurred in that place were such as to make people nervous, and shy—unreasonably so—of taking those lodgings, after reading our experiences therein.

We were a small family—my husband, a grown-up daughter, and myself; and we had two maids—a cook, and the other was house- and parlour-maid in one. We had not been a fortnight in the house before my daughter said to me one morning: "Mamma, I do not like Jane"—that was our house-parlour-maid.

"Why so?" I asked. "She seems respectable, and she does her work systematically. I have no fault to find with her, none whatever."

"She may do her work," said Bessie, my daughter, "but I dislike inquisitiveness."

"Inquisitiveness!" I exclaimed. "What do you mean? Has she been looking into your drawers?"

"No, mamma, but she watches me. It is hot weather now, and when I am in my room, occasionally, I leave my door open whilst writing a letter, or doing any little bit of needlework, and then I am almost certain to hear her outside. If I turn sharply round, I see her slipping out of sight. It is most annoying. I really was unaware that I was such an interesting personage as to make it worth anyone's while to spy out my proceedings."

"Nonsense, my dear. You are sure it is Jane?"

"Well—I suppose so." There was a slight hesitation in her voice. "If not Jane, who can it be?"

"Are you sure it is not cook?"

"Oh, no, it is not cook; she is busy in the kitchen. I have heard her there, when I have gone outside my room upon the landing, after having caught that girl watching me."

"If you have caught her," said I, "I suppose you spoke to her about the impropriety of her conduct."

"Well, caught is the wrong word. I have not actually *caught* her at it. Only today I distinctly heard her at my door, and I saw her back as she turned to run away, when I went towards her."

"But you followed her, of course?"

"Yes, but I did not find her on the landing when I got outside."

"Where was she, then?"

"I don't know."

"But did you not go and see?"

"She slipped away with astonishing celerity," said Bessie.

"I can take no steps in the matter. If she does it again, speak to her and remonstrate."

"But I never have a chance. She is gone in a moment."

"She cannot get away so quickly as all that."

"Somehow she does."

"And you are sure it is Jane?" again I asked; and again she replied: "If not Jane, who else can it be? There is no one else in the house."

So this unpleasant matter ended, for the time. The next intimation of something of the sort proceeded from another quarter—in fact, from Jane herself. She came to me some days later and said, with some embarrassment in her tone—

"If you please, ma'am, if I do not give satisfaction, I would rather leave the situation."

"Leave!" I exclaimed. "Why, I have not given you the slightest cause. I have not found fault with you for anything as yet, have I, Jane? On the contrary, I have been much pleased with the thoroughness of your work. And you are always tidy and obliging."

"It isn't that, ma'am; but I don't like being watched whatever I do."

"Watched!" I repeated. "What do you mean? You surely do not suppose that I am running after you when you are engaged on your occupations. I assure you I have other and more important things to do."

"No, ma'am, I don't suppose you do."

"Then who watches you?"

"I think it must be Miss Bessie."

"Miss Bessie!" I could say no more, I was so astounded.

"Yes, ma'am. When I am sweeping out a room, and my back is turned, I hear her at the door; and when I turn myself about, I just catch a glimpse of her running away. I see her skirts——"

"Miss Bessie is above doing anything of the sort."

"If it is not Miss Bessie, who is it, ma'am?"

There was a tone of indecision in her voice.

"My good Jane," said I, "set your mind at rest. Miss Bessie could not act as you suppose. Have you seen her on these occasions and assured yourself that it is she?"

"No, ma'am, I've not, so to speak, seen her face; but I know it ain't cook, and I'm sure it ain't you, ma'am; so who else can it be?"

I considered for some moments, and the maid stood before me in dubious mood.

"You say you saw her skirts. Did you recognise the gown? What did she wear?"

"It was a light cotton print—more like a maid's morning dress."

"Well, set your mind at ease; Miss Bessie has not got such a frock as you describe."

"I don't think she has," said Jane; "but there was someone at the door, watching me, who ran away when I turned myself about."

"Did she run upstairs or down?"

"I don't know. I did go out on the landing, but there was no one there. I'm sure it wasn't cook, for I heard her clattering the dishes down in the kitchen at the time."

"Well, Jane, there is some mystery in this. I will not accept your notice; we will let matters stand over till we can look into this complaint of yours and discover the rights of it."

"Thank you, ma'am. I'm very comfortable here, but it is unpleasant to suppose that one is not trusted, and is spied on wherever one goes and whatever one is about."

A week later, after dinner one evening, when Bessie and I had quitted the table and left my husband to his smoke, Bessie said to me, when we were in the drawing-room together: "Mamma, it is not Jane."

"What is not Jane?" I asked.

"It is not Jane who watches me."

"Who can it be, then?"

"I don't know."

"And how is it that you are confident that you are not being observed by Jane?"

"Because I have seen her—that is to say, her head."

"When? where?"

"Whilst dressing for dinner, I was before the glass doing my hair, when I saw in the mirror someone behind me. I had only the two candles lighted on the table, and the room was otherwise dark. I thought I heard someone stirring—just the sort of stealthy step I have come to recognise as having troubled me so often. I did not turn, but looked steadily before me into the glass, and I could see reflected therein someone—a woman with red hair. Then I moved from my place quickly. I heard steps of some person hurrying away, but I saw no one then."

"The door was open?"

"No, it was shut."

"But where did she go?"

"I do not know, mamma. I looked everywhere in the room and could find no one. I have been quite upset. I cannot tell what to think of this. I feel utterly unhinged."

"I noticed at table that you did not appear well, but I said nothing about it. Your father gets so alarmed, and fidgets and fusses, if he thinks that there is anything the matter with you. But this is a most extraordinary story."

"It is an extraordinary fact," said Bessie.

"You have searched your room thoroughly?"

"I have looked into every corner."

"And there is no one there?"

"No one. Would you mind, mamma, sleeping with me to-night? I am so frightened. Do you think it can be a ghost?"

"Ghost? Fiddlesticks!"

I made some excuse to my husband and spent the night in Bessie's room. There was no disturbance that night of any sort, and although my daughter was excited and unable to sleep till long after midnight, she did fall into refreshing slumber at last, and in the morning said to me: "Mamma, I think I must have fancied that I saw something in the glass. I dare say my nerves were over-wrought."

I was greatly relieved to hear this, and I arrived at much the same conclusion as did Bessie, but was again bewildered, and my mind unsettled by Jane, who came to me just before lunch, when I was alone, and said—

"Please, ma'am, it's only fair to say, but it's not Miss Bessie."

"What is not Miss Bessie? I mean, who is not Miss Bessie?"

"Her as is spying on me."

"I told you it could not be she. Who is it?"

"Please, ma'am, I don't know. It's a red-haired girl."

"But, Jane, be serious. There is no red-haired girl in the house."

"I know there ain't, ma'am. But for all that, she spies on me."

"Be reasonable, Jane," I said, disguising the shock her words produced on me. "If there be no red-haired girl in the house, how can you have one watching you?"

"I don't know; but one does."

"How do you know that she is red-haired?"

"Because I have seen her."

"When?"

"This morning."

"Indeed?"

"Yes, ma'am. I was going upstairs, when I heard steps coming softly after me—the backstairs, ma'am; they're rather dark and steep, and there's no carpet on them, as on the front stairs, and I was sure I heard someone following me; so I twisted about, thinking it might be cook, but it wasn't. I saw a young woman in a print dress, and the light as came from the window at the side fell on her head, and it was carrots—reg'lar carrots."

"Did you see her face?"

"No, ma'am; she put her arm up and turned and ran downstairs, and I went after her, but I never found her."

"You followed her—how far?"

"To the kitchen. Cook was there. And I said to cook, says I: 'Did you see a girl come this way?' And she said, short-like: 'No.'"

"And cook saw nothing at all?"

"Nothing. She didn't seem best pleased at my axing. I suppose I frightened her, as I'd been telling her about how I was followed and spied on."

I mused a moment only, and then said solemnly—

"Jane, what you want is a *pill*. You are suffering from hallucinations. I know a case very much like yours; and take my word for it that, in your condition of liver or digestion, a pill is a sovereign remedy. Set your mind at rest; this is a mere delusion, caused by pressure on the optic nerve. I will give you a pill tonight when you go to bed, another to-morrow, a third on the day after, and that will settle the red-haired girl. You will see no more of her."

"You think so, ma'am?"

"I am sure of it."

On consideration, I thought it as well to mention the matter to the cook, a strange, reserved woman, not given to talking, who did her work admirably, but whom, for some inexplicable reason, I did not like. If I had considered a little further as to how to broach the subject, I should perhaps have proved more successful; but by not doing so I rushed the question and obtained no satisfaction.

I had gone down to the kitchen to order dinner, and the difficult question had arisen how to dispose of the scraps from yesterday's joint.

"Rissoles, ma'am?"

"No," said I, "not rissoles. Your master objects to them."

"Then perhaps croquettes?"

"They are only rissoles in disguise."

"Perhaps cottage pie?"

"No; that is inorganic rissole, a sort of protoplasm out of which rissoles are developed."

"Then, ma'am, I might make a hash."

"Not an ordinary, barefaced, rudimentary hash?"

"No, ma'am, with French mushrooms, or truffles, or tomatoes."

"Well—yes—perhaps. By the way, talking of tomatoes, who is that red-haired girl who has been about the house?"

"Can't say, ma'am."

I noticed at once that the eyes of the cook contracted, her lips tightened, and her face assumed a half-defiant, half-terrified look.

"You have not many friends in this place, have you, cook?"

"No, ma'am, none."

"Then who can she be?"

"Can't say, ma'am."

"You can throw no light on the matter? It is very unsatisfactory having a person about the house—and she has been seen upstairs—of whom one knows nothing."

"No doubt, ma'am."

"And you cannot enlighten me?"

"She is no friend of mine."

"Nor is she of Jane's. Jane spoke to me about her. Has she remarked concerning this girl to you?"

"Can't say, ma'am, as I notice all Jane says. She talks a good deal."

"You see, there must be someone who is a stranger and who has access to this house. It is most awkward."

"Very so, ma'am."

I could get nothing more from the cook. I might as well have talked to a log; and, indeed, her face assumed a wooden look as I continued to speak to her on the matter. So I sighed, and said—

"Very well, hash with tomato," and went upstairs.

A few days later the house-parlour-maid said to me, "Please, ma'am, may I have another pill?"

"Pill!" I exclaimed. "Why?"

"Because I have seen her again. She was behind the curtains, and I caught her putting out her red head to look at me."

"Did you see her face?"

"No; she up with her arm over it and scuttled away."

"This is strange. I do not think I have more than two podophyllin pills left in the box, but to those you are welcome. Only I should recommend a different treatment. Instead of taking them yourself, the moment you see, or fancy that you see, the red-haired girl, go at her with the box and threaten to administer the pills to her. That will rout her, if anything will."

"But she will not stop for the pills."

"The threat of having them forced on her every time she shows herself will disconcert her. Conceive, I am supposing, that on each occasion Miss Bessie, or I, were to meet you on the stairs, in a room, on the landing, in the hall, we were to rush on you and force, let us say, castor-oil globules between your lips. You would give notice at once."

"Yes; so I should, ma'am."

"Well, try this upon the red-haired girl. It will prove infallible."

"Thank you, ma'am; what you say seems reasonable."

Whether Bessie saw more of the puzzling apparition, I cannot say. She spoke no further on the matter to me; but that may have been so as to cause me no further uneasiness. I was unable to resolve the question to my own satisfaction—whether what had been seen was a real person, who obtained access to the house in some unaccountable manner, or whether it was, what I have called it, an apparition.

As far as I could ascertain, nothing had been taken away. The movements of the red-haired girl were not those of one who sought to pilfer. They seemed to me rather those of one not in her right mind; and on this supposition I made inquiries in the neighbourhood as to the existence in our street, in any of the adjoining houses, of a person wanting in her wits, who was suffered to run about at will. But I could obtain no information that at all threw light on a point to me so perplexing.

Hitherto I had not mentioned the topic to my husband. I knew so well that I should obtain no help from him, that I made no effort to seek it. He would "Pish!" and "Pshaw!" and make some slighting reference to women's intellects, and not further trouble himself about the matter.

But one day, to my great astonishment, he referred to it himself.

"Julia," said he, "do you observe how I have cut myself in shaving?"

"Yes, dear," I replied. "You have cotton-wool sticking to your jaw, as if you were growing a white whisker on one side."

"It bled a great deal," said he.

"I am sorry to hear it."

"And I mopped up the blood with the new toilet-cover."

"Never!" I exclaimed. "You haven't been so foolish as to do that?"

"Yes. And that is just like you. You are much more concerned about your toilet-cover being stained than about my poor cheek which is gashed."

"You were very clumsy to do it," was all I could say. Married people are not always careful to preserve the amenities in private life. It is a pity, but it is so.

"It was due to no clumsiness on my part," said he; "though I do allow my nerves have been so shaken, broken, by married life, that I cannot always command my hand, as was the case when I was a bachelor. But this time it was due to that new, stupid, red-haired servant you have introduced into the house without consulting me or my pocket."

"Red-haired servant!" I echoed.

"Yes, that red-haired girl I have seen about. She thrusts herself into my study in a most offensive and objectionable way. But the climax of all was this morning, when I was shaving. I stood in my shirt before the glass, and had lathered my face, and was engaged on my right jaw, when that red-haired girl rushed between me and the mirror with both her elbows up, screening her face with her arms, and her head bowed. I started back, and in so doing cut myself."

"Where did she come from?"

"How can I tell? I did not expect to see anyone."

"Then where did she go?"

"I do not know; I was too concerned about my bleeding jaw to look about me. That girl must be dismissed."

"I wish she could be dismissed," I said.

"What do you mean?"

I did not answer my husband, for I really did not know what answer to make.

I was now the only person in the house who had not seen the red-haired girl, except possibly the cook, from whom I could gather nothing, but whom I suspected of knowing more concerning this mysterious apparition than she chose to admit. That what had been seen by Bessie and Jane was a supernatural visitant, I now felt convinced, seeing that it had appeared to that least imaginative and most commonplace of all individuals, my husband. By no mental process could he have been got to imagine anything. He certainly did see this red-haired girl, and that no living, corporeal maid had been in his dressing-room at the time I was perfectly certain.

I was soon, however, myself to be included in the number of those before whose eyes she appeared. It was in this wise.

Cook had gone out to do some marketing. I was in the breakfast-room, when, wanting a funnel to fill a little phial of brandy I always keep on the washstand in case of emergencies, I went to the head of the kitchen stairs, to descend and fetch what I required. Then I was aware of a great clattering of the fire-irons below, and a banging about of the boiler and grate. I went down the steps very hastily and entered the kitchen.

There I saw a figure of a short, set girl in a shabby cotton gown, not over clean, and slipshod, stooping before the stove, and striking the fender with the iron poker. She had fiery red hair, very untidy.

I uttered an exclamation.

Instantly she dropped the poker, and covering her face with her arms, uttering a strange, low cry, she dashed round the kitchen table, making nearly the complete circuit, and then swept past me, and I heard her clattering up the kitchen stairs.

I was too much taken aback to follow. I stood as one petrified. I felt dazed and unable to trust either my eyes or my ears.

Something like a minute must have elapsed before I had sufficiently recovered to turn and leave the kitchen. Then I ascended slowly and, I confess, nervously. I was fearful lest I should find the red-haired girl cowering against the wall, and that I should have to pass her.

But nothing was to be seen. I reached the hall, and saw that no door was open from it except that of the breakfast-room. I entered and thoroughly examined every recess, corner, and conceivable hiding-place, but could find no one there. Then I ascended the staircase, with my hand on the balustrade, and searched all the rooms on the first floor, without the least success. Above were the servants' apartments, and I now resolved on mounting to them. Here the staircase was uncarpeted. As I was ascending, I heard Jane at work in her room. I then heard her come out hastily upon the landing. At the same moment, with a rush past me, uttering the same moan, went the red-haired girl. I am sure I felt her skirts sweep my dress. I did not notice her till she was close upon me, but I did distinctly see her as she passed.

I turned, and saw no more.

I at once mounted to the landing where was Jane.

"What is it?" I asked.

"Please, ma'am, I've seen the red-haired girl again, and I did as you recommended. I went at her rattling the pill-box, and she turned and ran downstairs. Did you see her, ma'am, as you came up?"

"How inexplicable!" I said. I would not admit to Jane that I had seen the apparition.

The situation remained unaltered for a week. The mystery was unsolved. No fresh light had been thrown on it. I did not again see or hear anything out of the way; nor did my husband, I presume, for he made no further remarks relative to the extra servant who had caused him so much annoyance. I presume he supposed that I had summarily dismissed her. This I conjectured from a smugness assumed by his face, such as it always acquired when he had carried a point against me—which was not often.

However, one evening, abruptly, we had a new sensation. My husband, Bessie, and I were at dinner, and we were partaking of the soup, Jane standing by, waiting to change our plates and to remove the tureen, when we dropped our spoons, alarmed by fearful screams issuing from the kitchen. By the way, characteristically, my husband finished his soup before he laid down the spoon and said—

"Good gracious! What is that?"

Bessie, Jane, and I were by this time at the door, and we rushed together to the kitchen stairs, and one after the other ran down them. I was the first to enter, and I saw cook wrapped in flames, and a paraffin lamp on the floor broken, and the blazing oil flowing over it.

I had sufficient presence of mind to catch up the cocoanut matting which was not impregnated with the oil, and to throw it round cook, wrap her tightly in it, and force her down on the floor where not overflowed by the oil. I held her thus, and Bessie succoured me. Jane was too frightened to do other than scream. The cries of the burnt woman were terrible. Presently my husband appeared.

"Dear me! Bless me! Good gracious!" he said.

"You go away and fetch a doctor," I called to him; "you can be of no possible service here—you only get in our way."

"But the dinner?"

"Bother the dinner! Run for a surgeon."

In a little while we had removed the poor woman to her room, she shrieking the whole way upstairs; and, when there, we laid her on the bed, and kept her folded in the cocoanut matting till a medical man arrived, in spite of her struggles to be free. My husband, on this occasion, acted with commendable promptness; but whether because he was impatient for the completion of his meal, or whether his sluggish nature was for once touched with human sympathy, it is not for me to say.

All I know is that, so soon as the surgeon was there, I dismissed Jane with "There, go and get your master the rest of his dinner, and leave us with cook."

The poor creature was frightfully burnt. She was attended to devotedly by Bessie and myself, till a nurse was obtained from the hospital. For hours she was as one mad with terror as much as with pain.

Next day she was quieter and sent for me. I hastened to her, and she begged the nurse to leave the room. I took a chair and seated myself by her bedside, and expressed my profound commiseration, and told her that I should like to know how the accident had taken place.

"Ma'am, it was the red-haired girl did it."

"The red-haired girl!"

"Yes, ma'am. I took a lamp to look how the fish was getting on, and all at once I saw her rush straight at me, and I—I backed, thinking she would knock me down, and the lamp fell over and smashed, and my clothes caught, and——"

"Oh, cook! you should not have taken the lamp."

"It's done. And she would never leave me alone till she had burnt or scalded me. You needn't be afraid—she don't haunt the house. It is *me* she has haunted, because of what I did to her."

"Then you know her?"

"She was in service with me, as kitchenmaid, at my last place, near Cambridge. I took a sort of hate against her, she was such a slattern and so inquisitive. She peeped into my letters, and turned out my box and drawers, she was ever prying; and when I spoke to her, she was that saucy! I reg'lar hated her. And one day she was kneeling by the stove, and I was there, too, and I suppose the devil possessed me, for I upset the boiler as was on the hot-plate right upon her, just as she looked up, and it poured over her face and bosom, and arms, and scalded her that dreadful, she died. And since then she has haunted me. But she'll do so no more. She won't trouble you further. She has done for me, as she has always minded to do, since I scalded her to death."

The unhappy woman did not recover.

"Dear me! no hope?" said my husband, when informed that the surgeon despaired of her. "And good cooks are so scarce. By the way, that red-haired girl?"

"Gone—gone forever," I said.

Master Sacristan Eberhart

The much respected Master Eberhart, Sacristan of the ancient church of S. Sebaldus, lived, as others of his profession have done before, and do still on the continent, in the tower, above the big bells. His office was to keep his keen eye upon the villages around; and, should he detect the rising smoke and flame from a house on fire, to sound the alarum on a separate bell in the turret above his chamber.

This chamber, by the way, requires description. It formed one stage in the square tower; four windows commanded the points of the compass, glazed with the coarse old-fashioned glass, called in some places, "bull's eye," with the exception of one light in each, that was filled with quarries, and that was just the one to peep through In the corner of this room rose a crazy wooden stair, leading to the leads; below it, descended another to the belfry. There was a table of common deal, a large slope-backed armchair, and another chair for visitors, if they should come, but they didn't. Against the wall, as is the custom with some pious people abroad, there hung a crucifix.

Now, the Sacristan was a pious man, though he was odd too at least, "the people down below" called him so; *I* think he was very sensible, but as we may differ on the point, I leave you to judge for yourself. The good old man lived very much to himself up there in the windy old steeple, and very seldom descended into the wicked world, except to hear Mass of a morning, and to fetch his bread and milk; and these were brought for him as far as to the lower door. No one ever thought of going up the three hundred and sixty-five steps leading to the Sacristan's room, except the bell-ringers just occasionally; and they tried the old man's temper dreadfully—they were so earthy; and the priest called now and then, but Master Eberhart, although he respected and honoured him (I said before he was very pious) yet from being only associated with the birds and the old gargoyles (those are the old carved spouts) he talked to him, not as if he were flesh and blood, but as if he were a stone man; not a gargoyle exactly, but a church monument. I don't think the priest quite liked that.

Maser Eberhart had a way of making friends too; but then they were not the ordinary friends "people down below" make. You shall hear who they were. On the top of the tower below the broach of the spire, were four carved figures, life-size; one was a horse, another a dragon, a third an eagle, the fourth a monk, and the frost had taken his nose off. These statues had their mouths wide open, and were intended to spout the water off from the spire; but they never did, the rain always ran off another way down an ugly lead pipe. Yellow lichens marbled these grotesques all over, even over their faces.

The monk turned west, and at sunset a red light covered him. He looked very terrible then, as if dipped in blood. It was not to be expected that Master Eberhart should care much for the three animals, at least not more than the people below would for their horses—they haven't got dragons or eagles—or for their guinea-pigs and fancy pigeons. But it was quite another matter with regard to the monk: the Sacristan loved him dearly, and had long conversations with him only the talking was all on one side, but that was the pleasanter.

On a sunny day, it was so agreeable to sit on the leads, leaning against the battlements, right over against the monk, and discuss the world below: a genial light irradiated the stone face, and it looked quite smiling; if it had not lost the nose, it would have been even handsome. On a moon-bright night also, when the lights were going out, one after another, in the windows far below, like sparks on a bit of tinder, the Sacristan loved to kneel in the shadow of the stone man, whose cowl and mutilated face would be cutting the moon's disc, and chant clearly some beautiful psalm, finishing with his hymn *"Te lucis ante terminim."* The old man thought sometimes that the shooting lips of the figure moved; but, or course, we who live on the earth, know well enough that it was only his fancy. For a long time Master Eberhart did not know his friend's name, as he had never told him, but he found it out at last; for one day the priest of S. Sebaldus came up lo visit him, bringing under his arm a big book bound in hogskin, and having a quantity of leaves in it.

The Sacristan had never seen more; he thought there must be about a thousand five hundred and something over. The priest talked to the old man a great deal, chiefly about some Egyptian saint whose life he was going to read to him. The Sacristan loved stories, so he listened with all his cars; the life was that of S. Simon Stylites, who lived—I don't know how long—on the top of a pillar, ate nothing but leeks, and was never once blown off, however high the wind was. As he heard the account, a clear gleam of light shot into the old man's brain, and looking up through the little door at the top of the stairs, at the monk who was just visible, nodded friendly to him, with a "Good morrow, Father Simon!" After that day, the Sacristan always called the gargoyle man "Father Simon".

Master Eberhart had his notions concerning things in general; they were bright and expansive, as the view from his belfry; but as in that he looked over the rising gables of the church below, each topped with a cross, so in every view he took of earthly matters, the cross was in them. It was quite wonderful how clear and panoramic his ideas were; quaint fancies surrounded them, and they were like the gargoyles, from among which he saw the earth. We do not get these broad theories below, for somehow, a neighbour's garden wall, or a granary fable, or sometimes merely a twig, debars us from taking a general sweep of the horizon.

The old man was one day sitting on the leads, looking up to his stone monk. "I think," he said, "that the people down below are very self-sufficient, they fancy that all Creation is made to do them service; for that purpose called into being, and may be trimmed and pruned just as suits their wayward fancies; as if the handiwork of God were not made first to do Him praise and glory, and only secondly to rejoice the heart of man. I wish the folk down on earth would know their *Benedicite* a little better, and remember that all God's works praise him! Do you not agree with me, father Simon? I know you do; why—a scud of rain cannot break over this fair spire, and the water trickle down these runnels, but the men down there think it is sent just to clear their gutters and sewers; as if there were not first the yellow lichen stain to rejoice and the pretty moss to make glad before it ever reaches them."

A ripple of golden sunlight ran over the weathered face of the gargoyle: "Heaven knows," sighed the old man, "I do not, the exact way in which all the works of God praise Him; perhaps it may be in being always cheerful; perhaps in fulfilling what their mission is; perhaps in having no thought of themselves; but being beautiful; they work so steadily till they have done all they can, and till they are perfectly beautiful—and how cheerful they always are! There are those men down below! They seek their own interests, their self-advancement, and, if they be the least religious, their own feelings, forgetting all about the duty of praise; and that lifeless—I mean what *they* would call lifeless—things which cannot praise any other way, praise by lining their duty."

A bird perched on the monk's cowl, and sent forth a stream of song; "There! There!" exclaimed the Sacristan—and he was undoubtedly going on to moralise, when, for the first time, he noticed a long crack at the back of the old carved spout. "Bless me," gasped the good man in alarm, "Father Simon is breaking from the spire: what shall I do? The next high wind or frost, and he will be off—horrible! into the naughty world below. I will save him from that: what shall I do?"

Master Eberhart rushed down the stairs; and catching the rope, sent forth peal after peal on the alarm bell. The folk on earth said, "There surely must be a whole village on fire somewhere"—but it was only the gargoyle that was cracked. Up the stairs ran the sexton to know what was the matter; and the terrified Sacristan implored him to send a mason and his men at once, that his friend the monk might be saved. The sexton growled and went down the tower, he was quite disappointed that *that* was all; he had made up his mind that Altdorf was in flames. What men we are!

Well! next day there came the mason and one man; and they pulled down the stone man, and laid him on the leads. "You had better bring him into my room," said Master Eberhart.

"What shall we do next?" asked the mason, when he had done so.

"Put him in my visitor's chair, wait one moment—let me move my cash box." The Sacristan pulled a tin coffer containing all his savings from the seat, and laid it on the table; then the gargoyle was lifted into the place.

"When shall he be put up again?" asked the old man.

"Put up!" exclaimed the mason. "He ain't worth the expense. What's the good of an ugly bit of stone like that, up aloft? Why, he might have tumbled and welcome, but that people feared for their heads."

"Not put back again!" groaned the Sacristan; "Never mind my box, leave it alone," said he sharply, to the mason's man, who was lifting it. "I don't care what it costs, I'll pay for him; and if I haven't enough, why the monk will wait till my death, and all my savings shall go to put him back again; he shall be my monument." The mason laughed, and would have brought his hammer down on the head of the monk, but the Sacristan withheld his hand.

"You haven't got enough to pay for replacing that thing," said the mason's man.

"I do not know that," answered the old man. "What would it cost?"

"Why there's a new block to be let into the spire, and the figure to be rivetted with iron clamps."

"Iron clamps!" moaned the Sacristan.

"Don't know what it would come to exactly," replied the

mason. "Good evening, master."

Eberhart sat down to supper, in his slope-backed chair, on one side of the table; on the other, in the visitor's chair, the stone friar squatted on his haunches, hands on knees, head thrust forward, the mouth protruding and wide open, the cowl half drawn over the dull eyes; the nose, I said before, was gone. The wind moaned at the window, but that it always did; the little fire burned brightly; and Master Eberhart looked lovingly and with a serene brow on his guest. "I never have a meal quite to myself," said he. "There's a mouse or two generally comes out at supper time, and a robin is at the window of a morning; it is very strange that my mice do not come tonight! I cannot eat all by myself, I should feel as if doing wrong, not to share with some creature. Father Simon, will you have some?" he laid a piece of bread before him, but the courtesy passed without any acknowledgement.

"I always say my prayers after supper," said the Sacristan, "and then to bed; would that you could join!" Then he cleared the victuals from his table, moved to it his book of devotions, swept away the crumbs, and knelt down. Long and earnestly did the old man pray, his silver hair trailing over his thin fingers. He said his prayers aloud and sang a psalm or two on his knees, then remained silent for a moment or two. A shadow fell along his book; something cold touched his head; he felt two heavy hands on his hair—like a priest's, blessing him; then they were withdrawn and Master Eberhart rose joyously from his knees. "That is just as it ought to have been," murmured he in his happy heart.

Afterwards he undressed and went to bed. It might have been three hours after this that the old man awoke; hearing a heavy tread about the floor, he opened his eyes. The moon lighted up the interior of the room, shining in at one of the four windows: in the corner stood Father Simon, going down the staircase into the belfry. Shortly after. Master Eberhart heard him groping among the bells, every touch of his fingers sounding on them, for those fingers were stone; then up he came again. The old man chuckled, and said to himself "Father Simon is curious to know how the bells are hung and worked; he has heard them so very long without having seen them." The figure was again in the room; crossed it and coming up to the bedside laid itself down on it.

The old Sacristan did feel a little startled, the weight seemed so great, bending down the outside of the bed; and, as he put his hand to the figure, it was so cold, so bitterly cold; but he drove away these foolish fears, and said, "Father, if you are chilly take the coverlid"; the statue remained immovable, so the old man sitting up, folded the counterpane over his bedfellow, then turning his face to the wall, tried to sleep. Now and then, however, he cast a furtive back-glance at the monk. The moon was on his face; that was cold, white and rigid with deep shadows in the eye sockets, the monstrous mouth gaping wide.

Master Eberhart dozed off, and when morning dawned, the figure was crouching in the visitor's chair, looking before it out of the opposite window. The day passed, as days usually passed in the lower top; at half-past seven the old man went down to hear Mass, after which he received his bread, milk, and leeks at the door. Breakfast followed; but the bird was not at the window ledge, as was its wont; nor did the mice appear all day. In the evening, the fire was lighted, and Master Eberhart warmed himself at the blaze; he would have moved the monk to the fire, only he was not strong enough.

At nine a bell rung in a distant church tower; they had no clock in S. Sebaldus' steeple, but that of S. Lorenz had one. The Sacristan wiped his table, brought out his book and said his evening prayers. Again the shadow fell across the page, and two cold hands were laid in benediction on his head. Strengthened heart and soul, the old man rose from his knees, undressed by the fire; for some time he remained sitting before it, meditating, till at last he grew sleepy (people generally do get sleepy sitting over the grate), and crept to bed. Ten o'clock struck faintly and sweetly in the distant tower, and then the chimes began to play *'Willkommen du seliger Abend,'* plaintively, "I am thankful we have no chimes in S. Sebaldus," muttered the Sacristan, half dozing.

"They are like emperors playing spellikens. Bells were made to be pealed, not to be hammered about with little knockers."

Somehow, now that he was in bed, he could not sleep, first he turned his face to the wall, then the other way; then with great misgivings tried his back. In that position he may have slept for half an hour or an hour; I do not know, nor did he; but he was again awake, and his eyes opening fell on the fireplace. Then he brisked up thoroughly, for he saw, seated before the hearth, the monk, his hands on his knees, the crimson glare of the embers seeming to saturate his maimed face, cowl, and robe with blood, red, red blood. He had the blue grey of the room for a background, and through the window, the indigo sky, in which sparkled one bright frosty star.

The foregoing night, Eberhart had felt but little fear; but now, a cold shudder quivered his old flesh; it was so awful, the face of his friend was changed, the brow seemed to be contracted over eyes no longer dull, but burning as iron from a forge; the vast mouth was closed and the lips firmly set. The features were no longer grotesque, but resolute, inflexible, determined; that was what paralysed the Sacristan. The monk had some errand to perform; he saw it in that unwavering face, on which the reflection of the embers was steady, however it might flicker on cowl and robe.

The clock of S. Lorenz struck twelve, and then the chimes played a simple hymn, now sounding clearly as the wind bore the notes, then feebler as it died away. A falling star glided past the opposite window without haste. The bright star was beyond the window frame, another appeared. A slight clatter from below reached the Sacristan's ears; an owl must have got in among the bells; but for that stone figure he would have risen to drive the bird out. Slowly the monk rose from his seat and walked deliberately to the head of the stair ladder, stationing himself a little on one side, slightly back. On the other side there was but a narrow strip of flooring to the wall, sufficiently wide for a chest to stand, on which was placed the Sacristan's cash box.

Again a noise below. "Well," said the old man, half audibly,

427

"Father Simon will not hurt me, I know; and I must see what is going on among the bells; those owls and jackdaws"—he put one leg out of the bed, "No—! I hear a step on the stair." The monk turned his head cautiously round and beckoned with his stone finger. Master Eberhart understood his meaning and settled himself in bed again. There *was* a stealthy tread on the stair. Surprised and terrified the old man sat up in bed. Thirteen-fourteen-fifteen; whoever it might be, he must be near the top: there!—a head rose through the opening in the floor, and Eberhart recognised the mason's man by the firelight. The shadow of the slope-backed armchair crossed the corner where the old man sat so as to conceal him.

The fellow crept nearly to the top; a large knife was in one of his hands; his eyes roved about the room, seeking something in the obscurity: in an instant they kindled up; he saw, and put out his hand to grasp the money coffer. A heavy tread behind him made him turn sharply round, and a fearful shriek broke from him, as his eyes encountered the stone monk leaning towards him, the cold eyes fixed on his, the granite hands extended, the knees bent as if for a leap. The mason stood benumbed with horror the knife fell from his fingers and clattered down the steps, till it struck a bell. The gargoyle stooped further forward, sloping towards him; the cold hand touched his throat: in a moment those fingers collapsed; the figure became rigid; there was a gurgle, a fall, a furious bounding and crashing down the ladder; one wild jangle on a tenor bell, droning off fainter, fainter, faint, lost.

Not a sound to be heard, but the breath of the wind on the window panes, and its hum through traceried battlements over head, an Æliolian wail. Then, scarcely audible, came the horn of the watch from the great square; a bat dashed against the glass; all was still again. One o'clock struck far off in S. Lorenz tower: something moved on the bed, it was only a mouse, it scrambled down the coverlid and trotted across the floor. The last embers grew cold. A moth fluttered against the window top, and would not be still; the death watch ticked in an old beam; the cinders fell together in the grate! Morning came at last: "Thank God" sighed the Sacristan. The chair was in front of the extinguished fire; the cash box safe; no gargoyle-monk to be seen. "It cannot have been a dream," faltered Master Eberhart. Then he rose from his pallet, slowly dressed, said his prayers, and hesitated at the top of the stairs, for he feared to descend. First he peeped down, but there was only sufficient light to distinguish huge rounded shapes of bells and massive rafters. "will wait until it is a little lighter," muttered he.

The sun rose, bars of yellow shone through the luffer-boards on the bells. "I must go and ring for Mass," said the old man; "that is a duty, I *must* go now;" so down he went. In the belfry, under one of the largest bells. lay a heap:—the stone monk on top, crouching, one hand on his knee, the other clenched at the mason's throat, the large mouth gaping as of old; and the man— he lay, his feet doubled under his back, his hands clutching the stone arm, the head slung unnaturally on one side, for his neck was broken. The gargoyle too, was snapped in half.

The old man said gravely to himself, "I dare say that all creatures *in* nature, or in art, whatever they may be, cheerful flowers, happy birds, or only bits of stone, may become to us angels of good, if we only love them with true heart and reverence; but then we must love them because they are true, and good, and not because we may see in them reflections of our own selves, our feelings, and passions."

The "Bold Venture"
(A tale from *A Book of Ghosts*)

The little fisher-town of Portstephen comprised two strings of houses facing each other at the bottom of a narrow valley, down which the merest trickle of a stream decanted into the harbour. The street was so narrow that it was at intervals alone that sufficient space was accorded for two wheeled vehicles to pass one another, and the roadway was for the most part so narrow that each house door was set back in the depth of the wall, to permit the foot-passenger to step into the recess to avoid being overrun by the wheels of a cart that ascended or descended the street.

The inhabitants lived upon the sea and its produce. Such as were not fishers were mariners, and but a small percentage remained that were neither—the butcher, the baker, the smith, and the doctor; and these also lived by the sea, for they lived upon the sailors and fishermen.

For the most part, the seafaring men were furnished with large families. The net in which they drew children was almost as well filled as the seine in which they trapped pilchards.

Jonas Rea, however, was an exception; he had been married for ten years, and had but one child, and that a son.

"You've a very poor haul, Jonas," said to him his neighbour, Samuel Carnsew; "I've been married so long as you and I've twelve. My wife has had twins twice."

"It's not a poor haul for me, Samuel," replied Jonas, "I may have but one child, but he's a buster."

Jonas had a mother alive, known as Old Betty Rea. When he married, he had proposed that his mother, who was a widow, should live with him. But man proposes and woman disposes. The arrangement did not commend itself to the views of Mrs. Rea, junior—that is to say, of Jane, Jonas's wife.

Betty had always been a managing woman. She had managed her house, her children, and her husband; but she speedily was made aware that her daughter-in-law refused to be managed by her.

Jane was, in her way, also a managing woman: she kept her house clean, her husband's clothes in order, her child neat, and herself the very pink of tidiness. She was a somewhat hard woman, much given to grumbling and finding fault.

Jane and her mother-in-law did not come to an open and flagrant quarrel, but the fret between them waxed intolerable; and the curtain-lectures, of which the text and topic was Old Betty, were so frequent and so protracted that Jonas convinced himself that there was smoother water in the worst sea than in his own house.

He was constrained to break to his mother the unpleasant information that she must go elsewhere; but he softened the blow by informing her that he had secured for her residence a tiny cottage up an alley, that consisted of two rooms only, one a kitchen, above that a bedchamber.

The old woman received the communication without annoyance. She rose to the offer, for she had also herself considered that the situation had become unendurable. Accordingly, with goodwill, she removed to her new quarters, and soon made the house look keen and cosy.

But, so soon as Jane gave indications of becoming a mother, it was agreed that Betty should attend on her daughter-in-law. To this Jane consented. After all, Betty could not be worse than another woman, a stranger.

And when Jane was in bed, and unable to quit it, then Betty once more reigned supreme in the house and managed everything—even her daughter-in-law.

But the time of Jane's lying upstairs was brief, and at the earliest possible moment she reappeared in the kitchen, pale indeed and weak, but resolute, and with firm hand withdrew the reins from the grasp of Betty.

In leaving her son's house, the only thing that Betty regretted was the baby. To that she had taken a mighty affection, and she did not quit till she had poured forth into the deaf ear of Jane a thousand instructions as to how the babe was to be fed, clothed, and reared.

As a devoted son, Jonas never returned from sea without visiting his mother, and when on shore saw her every day. He sat with her by the hour, told her of all that concerned him—except about his wife—and communicated to her all his hopes and wishes. The babe, whose name was Peter, was a topic on which neither weaned of talking or of listening; and often did Jonas bring the child over to be kissed and admired by his grandmother.

Jane raised objections—the weather was cold and the child would take a chill; grandmother was inconsiderate, and upset its stomach with sweetstuff; it had not a tidy dress in which to be seen: but Jonas overruled all her objections. He was a mild and yielding man, but on this one point he was inflexible—his child should grow up to know, love, and reverence his mother as sincerely as did he himself. And these were delightful hours to the old woman, when she could have the infant on her lap, croon to it, and talk to it all the delightful nonsense that flows from the lips of a woman when caressing a child.

Moreover, when the boy was not there, Betty was knitting socks or contriving pin-cases, or making little garments for him; and all the small savings she could gather from the allowance made by her son, and from the sale of some of her needlework, were devoted to the same grandchild.

As the little fellow found his feet and was allowed to toddle, he often wanted to "go to granny," not much to the approval of Mrs. Jane. And, later, when he went to school, he found his way to her cottage before he returned home so soon as his work hours in class were over. He very early developed a love for the sea and ships.

This did not accord with Mrs. Jane's ideas; she came of a family that had ever been on the land, and she disapproved of the sea. "But," remonstrated her husband, "he is my son, and I and my father and grandfather were all of us sea-dogs, so that, naturally, my part in the boy takes to the water."

And now an idea entered the head of Old Betty. She resolved on making a ship for Peter. She provided herself with a stout piece of deal of suitable size and shape, and proceeded to fashion it into the form of a cutter, and to scoop out the interior. At this Peter assisted. After school hours he was with his grandmother watching the process, giving his opinion as to shape, and how the boat was to be rigged and furnished. The aged woman had but an old knife, no proper carpentering tools, consequently the progress made was slow.

Moreover, she worked at the ship only when Peter was by. The interest excited in the child by the process was an attraction to her house, and it served to keep him there. Further, when he was at home, he was being incessantly scolded by his mother, and the preference he developed for granny's cottage caused many a pang of jealousy in Jane's heart.

Peter was now nine years old, and remained the only child, when a sad thing happened. One evening, when the little ship was rigged and almost complete, after leaving his grandmother, Peter went down to the port. There happened to be no one about, and in craning over the quay to look into his father's boat, he overbalanced, fell in, and was drowned.

The grandmother supposed that the boy had returned home, the mother that he was with his grandmother, and a couple of hours passed before search for him was instituted, and the body was brought home an hour after that. Mrs. Jane's grief at losing her child was united with resentment against Old Betty for having drawn the child away from home, and against her husband for having encouraged it. She poured forth the vials of her wrath upon Jonas. He it was who had done his utmost to have the boy killed, because he had allowed him to wander at large, and had provided him with an excuse by allowing him to tarry with Old Betty after leaving school, so that no one knew where he was. Had Jonas been a reasonable man, and a docile husband, he would have insisted on Peter returning promptly home every day, in which case this disaster would not have occurred. "But," said Jane bitterly, "you never have considered my feelings, and I believe you did not love Peter, and wanted to be rid of him."

The blow to Betty was terrible; her heart-strings were wrapped about the little fellow; and his loss was to her the eclipse of all light, the death of all her happiness.

When Peter was in his coffin, then the old woman went to the house, carrying the little ship. It was now complete with sails and rigging.

"Jane," said she, "I want thickey ship to be put in with Peter. 'Twere made for he, and I can't let another have it, and I can't keep it myself."

"Nonsense," retorted Mrs. Rea, junior. "The boat can be no use to he, now."

"I wouldn't say that. There's naught revealed on them matters. But I'm cruel certain that up aloft there'll be a rumpus if Peter wakes up and don't find his ship."

"You may take it away; I'll have none of it," said Jane.

So the old woman departed, but was not disposed to accept discomfiture. She went to the undertaker.

"Mr. Matthews, I want you to put this here boat in wi' my gran'child Peter. It will go in fitty at his feet."

"Very sorry, ma'am, but not unless I break off the bowsprit. You see the coffin is too narrow."

"Then put'n in sideways and longways."

"Very sorry, ma'am, but the mast is in the way. I'd be forced to break that so as to get the lid down."

Disconcerted, the old woman retired; she would not suffer Peter's boat to be maltreated.

On the occasion of the funeral, the grandmother appeared as one of the principal mourners. For certain reasons, Mrs. Jane did not attend at the church and grave.

As the procession left the house, Old Betty took her place beside her son, and carried the boat in her hand. At the close of the service at the grave, she said to the sexton: "I'll trouble you, John Hext, to put this here little ship right o' top o' his coffin. I made'n for Peter, and Peter'll expect to have'n." This was done, and not a step from the grave would the grandmother take till the first shovelfuls had fallen on the coffin and had partially buried the white ship.

When Granny Rea returned to her cottage, the fire was out. She seated herself beside the dead hearth, with hands folded and the tears coursing down her withered cheeks. Her heart was as dead and dreary as that hearth. She had now no object in life, and she murmured a prayer that the Lord might please to take her, that she might see her Peter sailing his boat in paradise.

Her prayer was interrupted by the entry of Jonas, who shouted: "Mother, we want your help again. There's Jane took bad; wi' the worrit and the sorrow it's come on a bit earlier than she reckoned, and you're to come along as quick as you can. 'Tisn't the Lord gave and the Lord hath taken away, but topsy-turvy, the Lord hath taken away and is givin' again."

Betty rose at once, and went to the house with her son, and again—as nine years previously—for a while she assumed the management of the house; and when a baby arrived, another boy, she managed that as well.

The reign of Betty in the house of Jonas and Jane was not for long. The mother was soon downstairs, and with her reappearance came the departure of the grandmother.

And now began once more the same old life as had been initiated nine years previously. The child carried to its grandmother, who dandled it, crooned and talked to it. Then, as it grew, it was supplied with socks and garments knitted and cut out and put together by Betty; there ensued the visits of the toddling child, and the remonstrances of the mother. School time arrived, and with it a break in the journey to or from school at granny's house, to partake of bread and jam, hear stories, and, finally, to assist at the making of a new ship.

If, with increase of years, Betty's powers had begun to fail, there had been no corresponding decrease in energy of will. Her eyes were not so clear as of old, nor her hearing so acute, but her hand was not unsteady. She would this time make and rig a schooner and not a cutter.

Experience had made her more able, and she aspired to accomplish a greater task than she had previously undertaken. It was really remarkable how the old course was resumed almost in every particular. But the new grandson was called Jonas, like his father, and Old Betty loved him, if possible, with a more intense love than had been given to the first child. He closely resembled his father, and to her it was a renewal of her life long ago, when she nursed and cared for the first Jonas. And, if possible, Jane became more jealous of the aged woman, who was drawing to her so large a portion of her child's affection. The schooner was nearly complete. It was somewhat rude, having been worked with no better tool than a penknife, and its masts being made of knitting-pins.

On the day before little Jonas's ninth birthday, Betty carried the ship to the painter.

"Mr. Elway," said she, "there be one thing I do want your help in. I cannot put the name on the vessel. I can't fashion the letters, and I want you to do it for me."

"All right, ma'am. What name?"

"Well, now," said she, "my husband, the father of Jonas, and the grandfather of the little Jonas, he always sailed in a schooner, and the ship was the *Bold Venture*."

"The *Bonaventura*, I think. I remember her."

"I'm sure she was the *Bold Venture*."

"I think not, Mrs. Rea."

"It must have been the *Bold Venture* or *Bold Adventurer*. What sense is there in such a name as *Boneventure*? I never heard of no such venture, unless it were that of Jack Smithson, who jumped out of a garret window, and sure enough he broke a bone of his leg. No, Mr. Elway, I'll have her entitled the *Bold Venture*."

"I'll not gainsay you. *Bold Venture* she shall be."

Then the painter very dexterously and daintily put the name in black paint on the white strip at the stern.

"Will it be dry by tomorrow?" asked the old woman. "That's the little lad's birthday, and I promised to have his schooner ready for him to sail her then."

"I've put dryers in the paint," answered Mr. Elway, "and you may reckon it will be right for tomorrow."

That night Betty was unable to sleep, so eager was she for the day when the little boy would attain his ninth year and become the possessor of the beautiful ship she had fashioned for him with her own hands, and on which, in fact, she had been engaged for more than a twelvemonth.

Nor was she able to eat her simple breakfast and noonday meal, so thrilled was her old heart with love for the child and expectation of his delight when the *Bold Venture* was made over to him as his own.

She heard his little feet on the cobblestones of the alley: he came on, dancing, jumping, fidgeted at the lock, threw the door open and burst in with a shout—

"See! see, granny! my new ship! Mother has give it me. A real frigate—with three masts, all red and green, and cost her seven shillings at Camelot Fair yesterday." He bore aloft a very magnificent toy ship. It had pennants at the mast-top and a flag at stern. "Granny! look! look! ain't she a beauty? Now I shan't want your drashy old schooner when I have my grand new frigate."

"Won't you have your ship—the *Bold Venture*?"

"No, granny; chuck it away. It's a shabby bit o' rubbish, mother says; and see! there's a brass cannon, a real cannon that will go off with a bang, on my frigate. Ain't it a beauty?"

"Oh, Jonas! look at the *Bold Venture*!"

"No, granny, I can't stay. I want to be off and swim my beautiful seven-shilling ship."

Then he dashed away as boisterous as he had dashed in, and forgot to shut the door. It was evening when the elder Jonas returned home, and he was welcomed by his son with exclamations of delight, and was shown the new ship.

"But, daddy, her won't sail; over her will flop in the water."

"There is no lead on the keel," remarked the father. "The vessel is built for show only."

Then he walked away to his mother's cottage. He was vexed. He knew that his wife had bought the toy with the deliberate intent of disappointing and wounding her mother-in-law; and he was afraid that he would find the old lady deeply mortified and incensed. As he entered the dingy lane, he noticed that her door was partly open.

The aged woman was on the seat by the table at the window, lying forward clasping the ship, and the two masts were run through her white hair; her head rested, partly on the new ship and partly on the table.

"Mother!" said he. "Mother!"

There was no answer.

The feeble old heart had given way under the blow, and had ceased to beat.

★★★★★★

I was accustomed, a few summers past, to spend a couple of months at Portstephen. Jonas Rea took me often in his boat, either mackerel fishing, or on excursions to the islets off the coast, in quest of wild birds. We became familiar, and I would now and then spend an evening with him in his cottage, and talk about the sea, and the chances of a harbour of refuge being made at Portstephen, and sometimes we spoke of our own family affairs. Thus it was that, little by little, the story of the ship *Bold Venture* was told me.

Mrs. Jane was no more in the house.

"It's a curious thing," said Jonas Rea, "but the first ship my mother made was no sooner done than my boy Peter died, and when she made another, with two masts, as soon as ever it was finished she died herself, and shortly after my wife, Jane, who took a chill at mother's funeral. It settled on her chest, and she died in a fortnight."

"Is that the boat?" I inquired, pointing to a glass case on a cupboard, in which was a rudely executed schooner.

"That's her," replied Jonas; "and I'd like you to have a look close at her."

I walked to the cupboard and looked.

"Do you see anything particular?" asked the fisherman.

"I can't say that I do."

"Look at her masthead. What is there?"

After a pause I said: "There is a grey hair, that is all, like a pennant."

"I mean that," said Jonas. "I can't say whether my old mother put a hair from her white head there for the purpose, or whether it caught and fixed itself when she fell forward clasping the boat, and the masts and spars and shrouds were all tangled in her hair. Anyhow, there it be, and that's one reason why I've had the *Bold Venture* put in a glass case—that the white hair may never by no chance get brushed away from it. Now, look again. Do you see nothing more?"

"Can't say I do."

"Look at the bows."

I did so. Presently I remarked: "I see nothing except, perhaps, some bruises, and a little bit of red paint."

"Ah! that's it, and where did the red paint come from?"

I was, of course, quite unable to suggest an explanation.

Presently, after Mr. Rea had waited—as if to draw from me the answer he expected—he said: "Well, no, I reckon you can't tell. It was thus. When mother died, I brought the *Bold Venture* here and set her where she is now, on the cupboard, and Jonas, he had set the new ship, all red and green, the *Saucy Jane* it was called, on the bureau. Will you believe me, next morning when I came downstairs the frigate was on the floor, and some of her spars broken and all the rigging in a muddle."

"There was no lead on the bottom. It fell down."

"It was not once that happened. It came to the same thing every night; and what is more, the *Bold Venture* began to show signs of having fouled her."

"How so?"

"Run against her. She had bruises, and had brought away some of the paint of the *Saucy Jane*. Every morning the frigate, if she were'nt on the floor, were rammed into a corner, and battered as if she'd been in a bad sea."

"But it is impossible."

"Of course, lots o' things is impossible, but they happen all the same."

"Well, what next?"

"Jane, she was ill, and took wus and wus, and just as she got wus so it took wus as well with the *Saucy Jane*. And on the night she died, I reckon that there was a reg'lar pitched sea-fight."

"But not at sea."

"Well, no; but the frigate seemed to have been rammed, and she was on the floor and split from stem to stern."

"And, pray, has the *Bold Venture* made no attempt since? The glass case is not broken."

"There's been no occasion. I chucked what remained of the *Saucy Jane* into the fire."

The Mother of Pansies

(A tale from *A Book of Ghosts*)

Anna Voss, of Siebenstein, was the prettiest girl in her village. Never was she absent from a fair or a dance. No one ever saw her abroad anything but merry. If she had her fits of bad temper, she kept them for her mother, in the secrecy of the house. Her voice was like that of the lark, and her smile like the May morning. She had plenty of suitors, for she was possessed of what a young peasant desires more in a wife than beauty, and that is money.

But of all the young men who hovered about her, and sought her favour, none was destined to win it save Joseph Arler, the ranger, a man in a government position, whose duty was to watch the frontier against smugglers, and to keep an eye on the game against poachers.

The eve of the marriage had come.

One thing weighed on the pleasure-loving mind of Anna. She dreaded becoming a mother of a family which would keep her at home, and occupy her from morn to eve in attendance on her children, and break the sweetness of her sleep at night.

So she visited an old hag named Schändelwein, who was a reputed witch, and to whom she confided her trouble.

The old woman said that she had looked into the mirror of destiny, before Anna arrived, and she had seen that Providence had ordained that Anna should have seven children, three girls and four boys, and that one of the latter was destined to be a priest.

But Mother Schändelwein had great powers; she could set at naught the determinations of Providence; and she gave to Anna seven pips, very much like apple-pips, which she placed in a cornet of paper; and she bade her cast these one by one into the mill-race, and as each went over the mill-wheel, it ceased to have a future, and in each pip was a child's soul.

So Anna put money into Mother Schändelwein's hand and departed, and when it was growing dusk she stole to the wooden bridge over the mill-stream, and dropped in one pip after another. As each fell into the water she heard a little sigh.

But when it came to casting in the last of the seven she felt a sudden qualm, and a battle in her soul.

However, she threw it in, and then, overcome by an impulse of remorse, threw herself into the stream to recover it, and as she did so she uttered a cry.

But the water was dark, the floating pip was small, she could not see it, and the current was rapidly carrying her to the mill-wheel, when the miller ran out and rescued her.

On the following morning she had completely recovered her spirits, and laughingly told her bridesmaids how that in the dusk, in crossing the wooden bridge, her foot had slipped, she had fallen into the stream, and had been nearly drowned. "And then," added she, "if I really had been drowned, what would Joseph have done?"

The married life of Anna was not unhappy. It could hardly be that in association with so genial, kind, and simple a man as Joseph. But it was not altogether the ideal happiness anticipated by both. Joseph had to be much away from home, sometimes for days and nights together, and Anna found it very tedious to be alone. And Joseph might have calculated on a more considerate wife. After a hard day of climbing and chasing in the mountains, he might have expected that she would have a good hot supper ready for him. But Anna set before him whatever came to hand and cost least trouble. A healthy appetite is the best of sauces, she remarked.

Moreover, the nature of his avocation, scrambling up rocks

and breaking through an undergrowth of brambles and thorns, produced rents and fraying of stockings and cloth garments. Instead of cheerfully undertaking the repairs, Anna grumbled over each rent, and put out his garments to be mended by others. It was only when repair was urgent that she consented to undertake it herself, and then it was done with sulky looks, muttered reproaches, and was executed so badly that it had to be done over again, and by a hired workwoman.

But Joseph's nature was so amiable, and he was so fond of his pretty wife, that he bore with those defects, and turned off her murmurs with a joke, or sealed her pouting lips with a kiss.

There was one thing about Joseph that Anna could not relish. Whenever he came into the village, he was surrounded, besieged by the children. Hardly had he turned the corner into the square, before it was known that he was there, and the little ones burst out of their parents' houses, broke from their sister nurse's arms, to scamper up to Joseph and to jump about him. For Joseph somehow always had nuts or almonds or sweets in his pockets, and for these he made the children leap, or catch, or scramble, or sometimes beg, by putting a sweet on a boy's nose and bidding him hold it there, till he said "Catch!"

Joseph had one particular favourite among all this crew, and that was a little lame boy with a white, pinched face, who hobbled about on crutches.

Him Joseph would single out, take him on his knee, seat himself on the steps of the village cross or of the churchyard, and tell him stories of his adventures, of the habits of the beasts of the forest.

Anna, looking out of her window, could see all this; and see how before Joseph set the poor cripple down, the child would throw its arms round his neck and kiss him.

Then Joseph would come home with his swinging step and joyous face.

Anna resented that his first attention should be given to the children, regarding it as her due, and she often showed her displeasure by the chill of her reception of her husband. She did not reproach him in set words, but she did not run to meet him, jump into his arms, and respond to his warm kisses.

Once he did venture on a mild expostulation. "Anna! why do you not knit my socks or stocking-legs? Home-made is heart-made. It is a pity to spend money on buying what is poor stuff, when those made by you would not only last on my calves and feet, but warm the cockles of my heart."

To which she replied testily: "It is you who set the example of throwing money away on sweet things for those pestilent little village brats."

One evening Anna heard an unusual hubbub in the square, shouts and laughter, not of children alone, but of women and men as well, and next moment into the house burst Joseph very red, carrying a cradle on his head.

"What is this fooling for?" asked Anna, turning crimson.

"An experiment, Anna dearest," answered Joseph, setting down the cradle. "I have heard it said that a wife who rocks an empty cradle soon rocks a baby into it. So I have bought this and brought it to you. Rock, rock, rock, and when I see a little rosebud in it among the snowy linen, I shall cry for joy."

Never before had Anna known how dull and dead life could be in an empty house. When she had lived with her mother, that mother had made her do much of the necessary work of the house; now there was not much to be done, and there was no one to exercise compulsion.

If Anna ran out and visited her neighbours, they proved to be disinclined for a gossip. During the day they had to scrub and bake and cook, and in the evening they had their husbands and children with them, and did not relish the intrusion of a neighbour.

The days were weary days, and Anna had not the energy or the love of work to prompt her to occupy herself more than was absolutely necessary. Consequently, the house was not kept scrupulously clean. The glass and the pewter and the saucepans did not shine. The window-panes were dull. The house linen was unhemmed.

One evening Joseph sat in a meditative mood over the fire, looking into the red embers, and what was unusual with him, he did not speak.

Anna was inclined to take umbrage at this, when all at once he looked round at her with his bright pleasant smile and said, "Anna! I have been thinking. One thing is wanted to make us supremely happy—a baby in the house. It has not pleased God to send us one, so I propose that we both go on pilgrimage to Mariahilf to ask for one."

"Go yourself—I want no baby here," retorted Anna.

A few days after this, like a thunderbolt out of a clear sky, came the great affliction on Anna of her husband's death.

Joseph had been found shot in the mountains. He was quite dead. The bullet had pierced his heart. He was brought home borne on green fir-boughs interlaced, by four fellow-*jägers*, and they carried him into his house. He had, in all probability, met his death at the hand of smugglers.

With a cry of horror and grief Anna threw herself on Joseph's body and kissed his pale lips. Now only did she realise how deeply all along she had loved him—now that she had lost him.

Joseph was laid in his coffin preparatory to the interment on the morrow. A crucifix and two candles stood at his head on a little table covered with a white cloth. On a stool at his feet was a bowl containing holy water and a sprig of rue.

A neighbour had volunteered to keep company with Anna during the night, but she had impatiently, without speaking, repelled the offer. She would spend the last night that he was above ground alone with her dead—alone with her thoughts.

And what were those thoughts?

Now she remembered how indifferent she had been to his wishes, how careless of his comforts; how little she had valued his love, had appreciated his cheerfulness, his kindness, his forbearance, his equable temper.

Now she recalled studied coldness on her part, sharp words, mortifying gestures, outbursts of unreasoning and unreasonable petulance.

Now she recalled Joseph scattering nuts among the children, addressing kind words to old crones, giving wholesome advice to giddy youths.

She remembered now little endearments shown to her, the presents brought her from the fair, the efforts made to cheer her with his pleasant stories and quaint jokes. She heard again his cheerful voice as he strove to interest her in his adventures of the chase.

As she thus sat silent, numbed by her sorrow, in the faint light cast by the two candles, with the shadow of the coffin lying black on the floor at her feet, she heard a stumping without; then a hand was laid on the latch, the door was timidly opened, and in upon his crutches came the crippled boy. He looked wistfully at her, but she made no sign, and then he hobbled to the coffin and burst into tears, and stooped and kissed the brow of his dead friend.

Leaning on his crutches, he took his rosary and said the prayers for the rest of her and his Joseph's soul; then shuffled awkwardly to the foot, dipped the spray of rue, and sprinkled the dead with the blessed water.

Next moment the ungainly creature was stumping forth, but after he had passed through the door, he turned, looked once more towards the dead, put his hand to his lips, and wafted to it his final farewell.

Anna now took her beads and tried to pray, but her prayers would not leave her lips; they were choked and driven back by the thoughts which crowded up and bewildered her. The chain fell from her fingers upon her lap, lay there neglected, and then slipped to the floor. How the time passed she knew not, neither did she care. The clock ticked, and she heard it not; the hours sounded, and she regarded them not till in at her ear and through her brain came clear the call of the wooden cuckoo announcing midnight.

Her eyes had been closed. Now suddenly she was roused, and they opened and saw that all was changed.

The coffin was gone, but by her instead was the cradle that

446

years ago Joseph had brought home, and which she had chopped up for firewood. And now in that cradle lay a babe asleep, and with her foot she rocked it, and found a strange comfort in so doing.

She was conscious of no sense of surprise, only a great welling up of joy in her heart. Presently she heard a feeble whimper and saw a stirring in the cradle; little hands were put forth gropingly. Then she stooped and lifted the child to her lap, and clasped it to her heart. Oh, how lovely was that tiny creature! Oh, how sweet in her ears its appealing cry! As she held it to her bosom the warm hands touched her throat, and the little lips were pressed to her bosom. She pressed it to her. She had entered into a new world, a world of love and light and beauty and happiness unspeakable. Oh! the babe—the babe—the babe! She laughed and cried, and cried and laughed and sobbed for very exuberance of joy. It brought warmth to her heart, it made every vein tingle, it ingrained her brain with pride. It was hers!—her own!—her very own! She could have been content to spend an eternity thus, with that little one close, close to her heart.

Then as suddenly all faded away—the child in her arms was gone as a shadow; her tears congealed, her heart was cramped, and a voice spoke within her: "It is not, because you would not. You cast the soul away, and it went over the mill-wheel."

Wild with terror, uttering a despairing cry, she started up, straining her arms after the lost child, and grasping nothing. She looked about her. The light of the candles flickered over the face of her dead Joseph. And tick, tick, tick went the clock.

She could endure this no more. She opened the door to leave the room, and stepped into the outer chamber and cast herself into a chair. And lo! it was no more night. The sun, the red evening sun, shone in at the window, and on the sill were pots of pinks and mignonette that filled the air with fragrance.

And there at her side stood a little girl with shining fair hair, and the evening sun was on it like the glory about a saint. The child raised its large blue eyes to her, pure innocent eyes, and said: "Mother, may I say my Catechism and prayers before I go to bed?"

Then Anna answered and said: "Oh, my darling! My dearest Bärbchen! All the Catechism is comprehended in this: Love God, fear God, always do what is your duty. Do His will, and do not seek only your own pleasure and ease. And this will give you peace—peace—peace."

The little girl knelt and laid her golden head on her folded hands upon Anna's knee and began: "God bless dear father, and mother, and all my dear brothers and sisters."

Instantly a sharp pang as a knife went through the heart of Anna, and she cried: "Thou hast no father and no mother and no brothers and no sisters, for thou art not, because I would not have thee. I cast away thy soul, and it went over the mill-wheel."

The cuckoo called one. The child had vanished. But the door was thrown open, and in the doorway stood a young couple—one a youth with fair hair and the down of a moustache on his lip, and oh, in face so like to the dead Joseph. He held by the hand a girl, in black bodice and with white sleeves, looking modestly on the ground. At once Anna knew what this signified. It was her son Florian come to announce that he was engaged, and to ask his mother's sanction.

Then said the young man, as he came forward leading the girl: "Mother, sweetest mother, this is Susie, the baker's daughter, and child of your old and dear friend Vronie. We love one another; we have loved since we were little children together at school, and did our lessons out of one book, sitting on one bench. And, mother, the bakehouse is to be passed on to me and to Susie, and I shall bake for all the parish. The good Jesus fed the multitude, distributing the loaves through the hands of His apostles. And I shall be His minister feeding His people here. Mother, give us your blessing."

Then Florian and the girl knelt to Anna, and with tears of happiness in her eyes she raised her hands over them. But ere she could touch them all had vanished. The room was dark, and a voice spake within her: "There is no Florian; there would have

448

been, but you would not. You cast his soul into the water, and it passed away forever over the mill-wheel."

In an agony of terror Anna sprang from her seat. She could not endure the room, the air stifled her; her brain was on fire. She rushed to the back door that opened on a kitchen garden, where grew the pot-herbs and cabbages for use, tended by Joseph when he returned from his work in the mountains.

But she came forth on a strange scene. She was on a battlefield. The air was charged with smoke and the smell of gunpowder. The roar of cannon and the rattle of musketry, the cries of the wounded, and shouts of encouragement rang in her ears in a confused din.

As she stood, panting, her hands to her breast, staring with wondering eyes, before her charged past a battalion of soldiers, and she knew by their uniforms that they were Bavarians. One of them, as he passed, turned his face towards her; it was the face of an Arler, fired with enthusiasm, she knew it; it was that of her son Fritz.

Then came a withering volley, and many of the gallant fellows fell, among them he who carried the standard. Instantly, Fritz snatched it from his hand, waved it over his head, shouted, "Charge, brothers, fill up the ranks! Charge, and the day is ours!"

Then the remnant closed up and went forward with bayonets fixed, tramp, tramp. Again an explosion of firearms and a dense cloud of smoke rolled before her and she could not see the result.

She waited, quivering in every limb, holding her breath— hoping, fearing, waiting. And as the smoke cleared she saw men carrying to the rear one who had been wounded, and in his hand he grasped the flag. They laid him at Anna's feet, and she recognised that it was her Fritz. She fell on her knees, and snatching the kerchief from her throat and breast, strove to stanch the blood that welled from his heart. He looked up into her eyes, with such love in them as made her choke with emotion, and he said faintly: "*Mütterchen*, do not grieve for me; we have stormed the redoubt, the day is ours. Be of good cheer. They fly, they fly, those French rascals! Mother, remember me—I die for the dear Fatherland."

And a comrade standing by said: "Do not give way to your grief, Anna Arler; your son has died the death of a hero."

Then she stooped over him, and saw the glaze of death in his eyes, and his lips moved. She bent her ear to them and caught the words: "I am not, because you would not. There is no Fritz; you cast my soul into the brook and I was carried over the mill-wheel."

All passed away, the smell of the powder, the roar of the cannon, the volumes of smoke, the cry of the battle, all—to a dead hush. Anna staggered to her feet, and turned to go back to her cottage, and as she opened the door, heard the cuckoo call two.

But, as she entered, she found herself to be, not in her own room and house—she had strayed into another, and she found herself not in a lone chamber, not in her desolate home, but in the midst of a strange family scene.

A woman, a mother, was dying. Her head reposed on her husband's breast as he sat on the bed and held her in his arms.

The man had grey hair, his face was overflowed with tears, and his eyes rested with an expression of devouring love on her whom he supported, and whose brow he now and again bent over to kiss.

About the bed were gathered her children, ay, and also her grandchildren, quite young, looking on with solemn, wondering eyes on the last throes of her whom they had learned to cling to and love with all the fervour of their simple hearts. One mite held her doll, dangling by the arm, and the forefinger of her other hand was in her mouth. Her eyes were brimming, and sobs came from her infant breast. She did not understand what was being taken from her, but she wept in sympathy with the rest.

Kneeling by the bed was the eldest daughter of the expiring woman, reciting the Litany of the Dying, and the sons and another daughter and a daughter-in-law repeated the responses in voices broken with tears.

When the recitation of the prayers ceased, there ensued for a while a great stillness, and all eyes rested on the dying woman. Her lips moved, and she poured forth her last petitions, that left her as rising flakes of fire, kindled by her pure and ardent soul. "O God, comfort and bless my dear husband, and ever keep Thy watchful guard over my children and my children's children, that they may walk in the way that leads to Thee, and that in Thine own good time we may all—all be gathered in Thy Paradise together, united for evermore. Amen."

A spasm contracted Anna's heart. This woman with ecstatic, upturned gaze, this woman breathing forth her peaceful soul on her husband's breast, was her own daughter Elizabeth, and in the fine outline of her features was Joseph's profile.

All again was hushed. The father slowly rose and quitted his position on the bed, gently laid the head on the pillow, put one hand over the eyes that still looked up to heaven, and with the fingers of the other tenderly arranged the straggling hair on each side of the brow. Then standing and turning to the rest, with a subdued voice he said: "My children, it has pleased the Lord to take to Himself your dear mother and my faithful companion. The Lord's will be done."

Then ensued a great burst of weeping, and Anna's eyes brimmed till she could see no more. The church bell began to toll for a departing spirit. And following each stroke there came to her, as the after-clang of the boom: "There is not, there has not been, an Elizabeth. There would have been all this—but thou wouldest it not. For the soul of thy Elizabeth thou didst send down the mill-stream and over the wheel."

Frantic with shame, with sorrow, not knowing what she did, or whither she went, Anna made for the front door of the house, ran forth and stood in the village square.

To her unutterable amazement it was vastly changed. Moreover, the sun was shining brightly, and it gleamed over a new parish church, of cut white stone, very stately, with a gilded spire, with windows of wondrous lacework. Flags were flying, festoons of flowers hung everywhere. A triumphal arch of leaves and young birch trees was at the graveyard gate. The square was crowded with the peasants, all in their holiday attire.

Silent, Anna stood and looked around. And as she stood she heard the talk of the people about her.

One said: "It is a great thing that Johann von Arler has done for his native village. But see, he is a good man, and he is a great architect."

"But why," asked another, "do you call him Von Arler? He was the son of that Joseph the *jäger* who was killed by the smugglers in the mountains."

"That is true. But do you not know that the king has ennobled him? He has done such great things in the Residenz. He built the new Town Hall, which is thought to be the finest thing in Bavaria. He added a new wing to the Palace, and he has rebuilt very many churches, and designed mansions for the rich citizens and the nobles. But although he is such a famous man his heart is in the right place. He never forgets that he was born in Siebenstein. Look what a beautiful house he has built for himself and his family on the mountain-side. He is there in summer, and it is furnished magnificently. But he will not suffer the old, humble Arler cottage here to be meddled with. They say that he values it above gold. And this is the new church he has erected in his native village—that is good."

"Oh! he is a good man is Johann; he was always a good and serious boy, and never happy without a pencil in his hand. You mark what I say. Some day hence, when he is dead, there will be a statue erected in his honour here in this market-place, to commemorate the one famous man that has been produced by Siebenstein. But see—see! Here he comes to the dedication of the new church."

Then, through the throng advanced a blonde, middle-aged man, with broad forehead, clear, bright blue eyes, and a flowing light beard. All the men present plucked off their hats to him, and made way for him as he advanced. But, full of smiles, he had a hand and a warm pressure, and a kindly word and a question as to family concerns, for each who was near.

All at once his eye encountered that of Anna. A flash of recognition and joy kindled it up, and, extending his arms, he thrust his way towards her, crying: "My mother! my own mother!"

Then—just as she was about to be folded to his heart, all faded away, and a voice said in her soul: "He is no son of thine, Anna Arler. He is not, because thou wouldest not. He might have been, God had so purposed; but thou madest His purpose of none effect. Thou didst send his soul over the mill-wheel."

And then faintly, as from a far distance, sounded in her ear the call of the cuckoo—three.

The magnificent new church had shrivelled up to the original mean little edifice Anna had known all her life. The square was deserted, the cold faint glimmer of coming dawn was visible over the eastern mountain-tops, but stars still shone in the sky.

With a cry of pain, like a wounded beast, Anna ran hither and thither seeking a refuge, and then fled to the one home and resting-place of the troubled soul—the church. She thrust open the swing-door, pushed in, sped over the uneven floor, and flung herself on her knees before the altar.

But see! before that altar stood a priest in a vestment of black-and-silver; and a serving-boy knelt on his right hand on a lower stage. The candles were lighted, for the priest was about to say Mass. There was a rustling of feet, a sound as of people entering, and many were kneeling, shortly after, on each side of Anna, and still they came on; she turned about and looked and saw a great crowd pressing in, and strange did it seem to her eyes that all— men, women, and children, young and old—seemed to bear in their faces something, a trace only in many, of the Arler or the Voss features. And the little serving-boy, as he shifted his position, showed her his profile—it was like her little brother who had died when he was sixteen.

Then the priest turned himself about, and said, "*Oremus.*" And she knew him—he was her own son—her Joseph, named after his dear father.

The Mass began, and proceeded to the "*Sursum corda*"—"Lift

up your hearts!"—when the celebrant stood facing the congregation with extended arms, and all responded: "We lift them up unto the Lord."

But then, instead of proceeding with the accustomed invocation, he raised his hands high above his head, with the palms towards the congregation, and in a loud, stern voice exclaimed—

"Cursed is the unfruitful field!"

"Amen."

"Cursed is the barren tree!"

"Amen."

"Cursed is the empty house!"

"Amen."

"Cursed is the fishless lake!"

"Amen."

"Forasmuch as Anna Arler, born Voss, might have been the mother of countless generations, as the sand of the seashore for number, as the stars of heaven for brightness, of generations unto the end of time, even of all of us now gathered together here, but she would not—therefore shall she be alone, with none to comfort her; sick, with none to minister to her; broken in heart, with none to bind up her wounds; feeble, and none to stay her up; dead, and none to pray for her, for she would not—she shall have an unforgotten and unforgettable past, and have no future; remorse, but no hope; she shall have tears, but no laughter—for she would not. Woe! woe! woe!"

He lowered his hands, and the tapers were extinguished, the celebrant faded as a vision of the night, the server vanished as an incense-cloud, the congregation disappeared, melting into shadows, and then from shadows to nothingness, without stirring from their places, and without a sound.

And Anna, with a scream of despair, flung herself forward with her face on the pavement, and her hands extended.

★★★★★★

Two years ago, during the first week in June, an English traveller arrived at Siebenstein and put up at the "*Krone*," where, as he was tired and hungry, he ordered an early supper. When that was discussed, he strolled forth into the village square, and leaned against the wall of the churchyard. The sun had set in the valley, but the mountain-peaks were still in the glory of its rays, surrounding the place as a golden crown. He lighted a cigar, and, looking into the cemetery, observed there an old woman, bowed over a grave, above which stood a cross, inscribed "Joseph Arler," and she was tending the flowers on it, and laying over the arms of the cross a little wreath of heart's-ease or pansy. She had in her hand a small basket. Presently she rose and walked towards the gate, by which stood the traveller.

As she passed, he said kindly to her: "*Grüss Gott, Mütterchen*."

She looked steadily at him and replied: "Honoured sir! that which is past may be repented of, but can never be undone!" and went on her way.

He was struck with her face. He had never before seen one so full of boundless sorrow—almost of despair.

His eyes followed her as she walked towards the mill-stream, and there she took her place on the wooden bridge that crossed it, leaning over the handrail, and looking down into the water. An impulse of curiosity and of interest led him to follow her at a distance, and he saw her pick a flower, a pansy, out of her basket, and drop it into the current, which caught and carried it forward. Then she took a second, and allowed it to fall into the water. Then, after an interval, a third—a fourth; and he counted seven in all. After that she bowed her head on her hands; her grey hair fell over them, and she broke into a paroxysm of weeping.

The traveller, standing by the stream, saw the seven pansies swept down, and one by one pass over the revolving wheel and vanish.

He turned himself about to return to his inn, when, seeing a grave peasant near, he asked: "Who is that poor old woman who seems so broken down with sorrow?"

"That," replied the man, "is the Mother of Pansies."

"The Mother of Pansies!" he repeated.

"Well—it is the name she has acquired in the place. Actually, she is called Anna Arler, and is a widow. She was the wife of one Joseph Arler, a *jäger*, who was shot by smugglers. But that is many, many years ago. She is not right in her head, but she is harmless. When her husband was brought home dead, she insisted on being left alone in the night by him, before he was buried alone,—with his coffin. And what happened in that night no one knows. Some affirm that she saw ghosts. I do not know— she may have had thoughts. The French word for these flowers is *pensées*—thoughts—and she will have none others. When they are in her garden she collects them, and does as she has done now. When she has none, she goes about to her neighbours and begs them. She comes here every evening and throws in seven— just seven, no more and no less—and then weeps as one whose heart would split. My wife on one occasion offered her forget-me-nots. 'No,' she said; 'I cannot send forget-me-nots after those who never were, I can send only Pansies.'"

On the Leads

(A tale from *A Book of Ghosts*)

Having realised a competence in Australia, and having a hankering after country life for the remainder of my days in the old home, on my return to England I went to an agent with the object of renting a house with shooting attached, over at least three thousand acres, with the option of a purchase should the place suit me. I was no more intending to buy a country seat without having tried what it was like, than is a king disposed to go to war without knowing something of the force that can be brought against him. I was rather taken with photographs of a manor called Fernwood, and I was still further engaged when I saw the place itself on a beautiful October day, when St. Luke's summer was turning the country into a world of rainbow tints under a warm sun, and a soft vaporous blue haze tinted all shadows cobalt, and gave to the hills a stateliness that made them look like mountains.

Fernwood was an old house, built in the shape of the letter H, and therefore, presumably, dating from the time of the early Tudor monarchs. The porch opened into the hall which was on the left of the cross-stroke, and the drawing-room was on the right. There was one inconvenience about the house; it had a staircase at each extremity of the cross-stroke, and there was no upstair communication between the two wings of the mansion. But, as a practical man, I saw how this might be remedied. The front door faced the south, and the hall was windowless on the north. Nothing easier than to run a corridor along at the back, giving communication both upstairs and downstairs, without passing through the hall. The whole thing could be done for, at the outside, two hundred pounds, and would be no disfigurement to the place. I agreed to become tenant of Fernwood for a twelvemonth, in which time I should be able to judge whether the place would suit me, the neighbours be pleasant, and the climate agree with my wife. We went down to Fernwood at once, and settled ourselves comfortably in by the first week in November.

The house was furnished; it was the property of an elderly gentleman, a bachelor named Framett, who lived in rooms in town, and spent most of his time at the club. He was supposed to have been jilted by his intended, after which he eschewed female society, and remained unmarried.

I called on him before taking up our residence at Fernwood, and found him a somewhat *blasé*, languid, cold-blooded creature, not at all proud of having a noble manor-house that had belonged to his family for four centuries; very willing to sell it, so as to spite a cousin who calculated on coming in for the estate, and whom Mr. Framett, with the malignity that is sometimes found in old people, was particularly desirous of disappointing.

"The house has been let before, I suppose?" said I.

"Oh, yes," he replied indifferently, "I believe so, several times."

"For long?"

"No—o. I believe, not for long."

"Have the tenants had any particular reasons for not remaining on there—if I may be so bold as to inquire?"

"All people have reasons to offer, but what they offer you are not supposed to receive as genuine."

I could get no more from him than this. "I think, sir, if I were you I would not go down to Fernwood till after November was out."

"But," said I, "I want the shooting."

"Ah, to be sure—the shooting, ah! I should have preferred if you could have waited till December began."

458

"That would not suit me," I said, and so the matter ended.

When we were settled in, we occupied the right wing of the house. The left or west wing was but scantily furnished and looked cheerless, as though rarely tenanted. We were not a large family, my wife and myself alone; there was consequently ample accommodation in the east wing for us. The servants were placed above the kitchen, in a portion of the house I have not yet described. It was a half-wing, if I may so describe it, built on the north side parallel with the upper arm of the western limb of the hall and the [Symbol: H]. This block had a gable to the north like the wings, and a broad lead valley was between them, that, as I learned from the agent, had to be attended to after the fall of the leaf, and in times of snow, to clear it.

Access to this valley could be had from within by means of a little window in the roof, formed as a dormer. A short ladder allowed anyone to ascend from the passage to this window and open or shut it. The western staircase gave access to this passage, from which the servants' rooms in the new block were reached, as also the untenanted apartments in the old wing. And as there were no windows in the extremities of this passage that ran due north and south, it derived all its light from the aforementioned dormer window.

One night, after we had been in the house about a week, I was sitting up smoking, with a little whisky-and-water at my elbow, reading a review of an absurd, ignorantly written book on New South Wales, when I heard a tap at the door, and the parlourmaid came in, and said in a nervous tone of voice: "Beg your pardon, sir, but cook nor I, nor none of us dare go to bed."

"Why not?" I asked, looking up in surprise.

"Please, sir, we dursn't go into the passage to get to our rooms."

"Whatever is the matter with the passage?"

"Oh, nothing, sir, with the passage. Would you mind, sir, just coming to see? We don't know what to make of it."

I put down my review with a grunt of dissatisfaction, laid my pipe aside, and followed the maid.

She led me through the hall, and up the staircase at the western extremity.

On reaching the upper landing I saw all the maids there in a cluster, and all evidently much scared.

"Whatever is all this nonsense about?" I asked.

"Please, sir, will you look? We can't say."

The parlourmaid pointed to an oblong patch of moonlight on the wall of the passage. The night was cloudless, and the full moon shone slanting in through the dormer and painted a brilliant silver strip on the wall opposite. The window being on the side of the roof to the east, we could not see that, but did see the light thrown through it against the wall. This patch of reflected light was about seven feet above the floor.

The window itself was some ten feet up, and the passage was but four feet wide. I enter into these particulars for reasons that will presently appear.

The window was divided into three parts by wooden mullions, and was composed of four panes of glass in each compartment.

Now I could distinctly see the reflection of the moon through the window with the black bars up and down, and the division of the panes. But I saw more than that: I saw the shadow of a lean arm with a hand and thin, lengthy fingers across a portion of the window, apparently groping at where was the latch by which the casement could be opened.

My impression at the moment was that there was a burglar on the leads trying to enter the house by means of this dormer.

Without a minute's hesitation I ran into the passage and looked up at the window, but could see only a portion of it, as in shape it was low, though broad, and, as already stated, was set at a great height. But at that moment something fluttered past it, like a rush of flapping draperies obscuring the light.

I had placed the ladder, which I found hooked up to the wall, in position, and planted my foot on the lowest rung, when my wife arrived. She had been alarmed by the housemaid, and now she clung to me, and protested that I was not to ascend without my pistol.

To satisfy her I got my Colt's revolver that I always kept loaded, and then, but only hesitatingly, did she allow me to mount. I ascended to the casement, unhasped it, and looked out. I could see nothing. The ladder was over-short, and it required an effort to heave oneself from it through the casement on to the leads. I am stout, and not so nimble as I was when younger. After one or two efforts, and after presenting from below an appearance that would have provoked laughter at any other time, I succeeded in getting through and upon the leads.

I looked up and down the valley—there was absolutely nothing to be seen except an accumulation of leaves carried there from the trees that were shedding their foliage.

The situation was vastly puzzling. As far as I could judge there was no way off the roof, no other window opening into the valley; I did not go along upon the leads, as it was night, and moonlight is treacherous. Moreover, I was wholly unacquainted with the arrangement of the roof, and had no wish to risk a fall.

I descended from the window with my feet groping for the upper rung of the ladder in a manner even more grotesque than my ascent through the casement, but neither my wife—usually extremely alive to anything ridiculous in my appearance—nor the domestics were in a mood to make merry. I fastened the window after me, and had hardly reached the bottom of the ladder before again a shadow flickered across the patch of moonlight.

I was fairly perplexed, and stood musing. Then I recalled that immediately behind the house the ground rose; that, in fact, the house lay under a considerable hill. It was just possible by ascending the slope to reach the level of the gutter and rake the leads from one extremity to the other with my eye.

I mentioned this to my wife, and at once the whole set of maids trailed down the stairs after us. They were afraid to remain in the passage, and they were curious to see if there was really some person on the leads.

We went out at the back of the house, and ascended the bank till we were on a level with the broad gutter between the gables. I now saw that this gutter did not run through, but stopped against the hall roof; consequently, unless there were some opening of which I knew nothing, the person on the leads could not leave the place, save by the dormer window, when open, or by swarming down the fall pipe.

It at once occurred to me that if what I had seen were the shadow of a burglar, he might have mounted by means of the rain-water pipe. But if so—how had he vanished the moment my head was protruded through the window? and how was it that I had seen the shadow flicker past the light immediately after I had descended the ladder? It was conceivable that the man had concealed himself in the shadow of the hall roof, and had taken advantage of my withdrawal to run past the window so as to reach the fall pipe, and let himself down by that.

I could, however, see no one running away, as I must have done, going outside so soon after his supposed descent.

But the whole affair became more perplexing when, looking towards the leads, I saw in the moonlight something with fluttering garments running up and down them.

There could be no mistake—the object was a woman, and her garments were mere tatters. We could not hear a sound.

I looked round at my wife and the servants,—they saw this weird object as distinctly as myself. It was more like a gigantic bat than a human being, and yet, that it was a woman we could not doubt, for the arms were now and then thrown above the head in wild gesticulation, and at moments a profile was presented, and then we saw, or thought we saw, long flapping hair, unbound.

"I must go back to the ladder," said I; "you remain where you are, watching."

"Oh, Edward! not alone," pleaded my wife.

"My dear, who is to go with me?"

I went. I had left the back door unlocked, and I ascended the staircase and entered the passage. Again I saw the shadow flicker past the moonlit patch on the wall opposite the window.

I ascended the ladder and opened the casement.

Then I heard the clock in the hall strike one.

I heaved myself up to the sill with great labour, and I endeavoured to thrust my short body through the window, when I heard feet on the stairs, and next moment my wife's voice from below, at the foot of the ladder. "Oh, Edward, Edward! please do not go out there again. It has vanished. All at once. There is nothing there now to be seen."

I returned, touched the ladder tentatively with my feet, refastened the window, and descended—perhaps inelegantly. I then went down with my wife, and with her returned up the bank, to the spot where stood clustered our servants.

They had seen nothing further; and although I remained on the spot watching for half an hour, I also saw nothing more.

The maids were too frightened to go to bed, and so agreed to sit up in the kitchen for the rest of the night by a good fire, and I gave them a bottle of sherry to mull, and make themselves comfortable upon, and to help them to recover their courage.

Although I went to bed, I could not sleep. I was completely baffled by what I had seen. I could in no way explain what the object was and how it had left the leads.

Next day I sent for the village mason and asked him to set a long ladder against the well-head of the fall pipe, and examine the valley between the gables. At the same time I would mount to the little window and contemplate proceedings through that.

The man had to send for a ladder sufficiently long, and that occupied some time. However, at length he had it planted, and then mounted. When he approached the dormer window—

"Give me a hand," said I, "and haul me up; I would like to satisfy myself with my own eyes that there is no other means of getting upon or leaving the leads."

He took me under both shoulders and heaved me out, and I stood with him in the broad lead gutter.

"There's no other opening whatever," said he, "and, Lord love you, sir, I believe that what you saw was no more than this," and he pointed to a branch of a noble cedar that grew hard by the west side of the house.

"I warrant, sir," said he, "that what you saw was this here bough as has been carried by a storm and thrown here, and the wind last night swept it up and down the leads."

"But was there any wind?" I asked. "I do not remember that there was."

"I can't say," said he; "before twelve o'clock I was fast asleep, and it might have blown a gale and I hear nothing of it."

"I suppose there must have been some wind," said I, "and that I was too surprised and the women too frightened to observe it," I laughed. "So this marvellous spectral phenomenon receives a very prosaic and natural explanation. Mason, throw down the bough and we will burn it tonight."

The branch was cast over the edge, and fell at the back of the house. I left the leads, descended, and going out picked up the cedar branch, brought it into the hall, summoned the servants, and said derisively: "Here is an illustration of the way in which weak-minded women get scared. Now we will burn the burglar or ghost that we saw. It turns out to be nothing but this branch, blown up and down the leads by the wind."

"But, Edward," said my wife, "there was not a breath stirring."

"There must have been. Only where we were we were sheltered and did not observe it. Aloft, it blew across the roofs, and formed an eddy that caught the broken bough, lifted it, carried it first one way, then spun it round and carried it the reverse way. In fact, the wind between the two roofs assumed a spiral movement. I hope now you are all satisfied. I am."

So the bough was burned, and our fears—I mean those of the females—were allayed.

In the evening, after dinner, as I sat with my wife, she said to me: "Half a bottle would have been enough, Edward. Indeed, I think half a bottle would be too much; you should not give the girls a liking for sherry, it may lead to bad results. If it had been

464

elderberry wine, that would have been different."

"But there is no elderberry wine in the house," I objected.

"Well, I hope no harm will come of it, but I greatly mistrust——"

"Please, sir, it is there again."

The parlourmaid, with a blanched face, was at the door.

"Nonsense," said I, "we burnt it."

"This comes of the sherry," observed my wife. "They will be seeing ghosts every night."

"But, my dear, you saw it as well as myself!"

I rose, my wife followed, and we went to the landing as before, and, sure enough, against the patch of moonlight cast through the window in the roof, was the arm again, and then a flutter of shadows, as if cast by garments.

"It was not the bough," said my wife. "If this had been seen immediately after the sherry I should not have been surprised, but—as it is now it is most extraordinary."

"I'll have this part of the house shut up," said I. Then I bade the maids once more spend the night in the kitchen, "and make yourselves lively on tea," I said—for I knew my wife would not allow another bottle of sherry to be given them. "Tomorrow your beds shall be moved to the east wing."

"Beg pardon," said the cook, "I speaks in the name of all. We don't think we can remain in the house, but must leave the situation."

"That comes of the tea," said I to my wife. "Now," to the cook, "as you have had another fright, I will let you have a bottle of mulled port to-night."

"Sir," said the cook, "if you can get rid of the ghost, we don't want to leave so good a master. We withdraw the notice."

Next day I had all the servants' goods transferred to the east wing, and rooms were fitted up for them to sleep in. As their portion of the house was completely cut off from the west wing, the alarm of the domestics died away.

A heavy, stormy rain came on next week, the first token of winter misery.

I then found that, whether caused by the cedar bough, or by the nailed boots of the mason, I cannot say, but the lead of the valley between the roofs was torn, and water came in, streaming down the walls, and threatening to severely damage the ceilings. I had to send for a plumber as soon as the weather mended. At the same time I started for town to see Mr. Framett. I had made up my mind that Fernwood was not suitable, and by the terms of my agreement I might be off my bargain if I gave notice the first month, and then my tenancy would be for the six months only. I found the squire at his club.

"Ah!" said he, "I told you not to go there in November. No one likes Fernwood in November; it is all right at other times."

"What do you mean?"

"There is no bother except in November."

"Why should there be bother, as you term it, then?"

Mr. Framett shrugged his shoulders. "How the deuce can I tell you? I've never been a spirit, and all that sort of thing. Mme. Blavatsky might possibly tell you. I can't. But it is a fact."

"What is a fact?"

"Why, that there is no apparition at any other time It is only in November, when she met with a little misfortune. That is when she is seen."

"Who is seen?"

"My aunt Eliza—I mean my great-aunt."

"You speak mysteries."

"I don't know much about it, and care less," said Mr. Framett, and called for a lemon squash. "It was this: I had a great-aunt who was deranged. The family kept it quiet, and did not send her to an asylum, but fastened her in a room in the west wing. You see, that part of the house is partially separated from the rest. I believe she was rather shabbily treated, but she was difficult to manage, and tore her clothes to pieces. Somehow, she succeeded in getting out on the roof, and would race up and down there. They allowed her to do so, as by that means she obtained fresh air. But one night in November she scrambled up and, I believe, tumbled over. It was hushed up. Sorry you went there in November. I should have liked you to buy the place. I am sick of it."

I did buy Fernwood.What decided me was this: the plumbers, in mending the leads, with that ingenuity to do mischief which they sometimes display, succeeded in setting fire to the roof, and the result was that the west wing was burnt down. Happily, a wall so completely separated the wing from the rest of the house, that the fire was arrested.The wing was not rebuilt, and I, thinking that with the disappearance of the leads I should be freed from the apparition that haunted them, purchased Fern-wood. I am happy to say we have been undisturbed since.

Only a Ghost!
By Irenaeus the Deacon
(Attributed to Sabine Baring-Gould)

Chapter 1
Why I Came To London

I am a ghost. Reader, don't be alarmed, but nevertheless I repeat, I am a, ghost. A ghost of 1520 years' standing; for in the year 347 I was still a deacon of the Church of the Holy Cross, at Jerusalem, under the Blessed Cyril, bishop of the same. And why I am I now in London? Why have I left the holy shades and the company of blessed spirits to glide about this black and by no means saintly city? Before I disappear into my peaceful abode I will place on record why I left it, and who induced me to commit such an act of folly. On his release from the flesh and his appearance in the world of spirits, the Rev. Edward Starch, Hector of Grubbington-in-the Clay, told me that if I wished to see primitive Christianity, set forth as in the times when I lived I on earth, I had only to go to Great Britain and listen to the performance of the "incomparable liturgy" there used.

Of course, as a faithful though unworthy deacon of St. Cyril's Church, I took a grave and sympathising interest in all the holy Churches over the world at all times and in all countries; and though I should have preferred visiting Jerusalem once more, or Antioch, or Constantinople, I heard the spirit of the Ancient Church was in England, and to England accordingly I went. to London I was told I should find the true spirit of primitive Christianity, for many ware the epithets of grace lavished upon it. I heard England called the most religious country in the world, and London the city of enlightenment. I heard that all its inhabitants were interested in the spread of the Gospel, and that they considered themselves the most godly people on the earth. So to London methought I would go, to find churches like the Holy Cross, and bishops like St. Cyril reigning over each.

Now, as a ghost, of course I am invisible, but when I wish for information I have the power of investing myself with the outward appearance of an intelligent stranger, and of assuming the language of the country in which I am sojourning. People who would naturally be shy of a Greek-speaking ghost, might have no objection to impart information to a quiet looking stranger dressed in black, and indulging in broken English. When necessary, I can immediately resume my invisibility. I need scarcely say that this when done suddenly, and on the impulse of the moment, has been productive of much embarrassment to my earthly companions, but has relieved me sometimes from positions which might have become slightly disagreeable.

One fine day then, I found myself in the streets of London, amongst a hurrying crowd all seemingly too busy to give a poor ghost the slightest particle of information. I ran up against an elderly gentleman of mild and prepossessing appearance, whose hat I knocked off quite by accident; "I beg your pardon, sir," said I, returning it to him, "I am a stranger here, could you give me any information on the state of religion in London?"

Religion! you *should* have seen his face, he started at the word as if he had been shot. (They didn't shoot in my day, but I heard of such things afterwards.) I was surprised at the effect the mere pronouncing of the word had in "the most religious city in the world." He turned and walked with me up the street. If he had only had the remotest idea that I was the deacon Irenaeus of Jerusalem in the 4th century he would, I feel persuaded, have fled as fast as his legs would carry him. But he thought I was only an intelligent stranger, and so he put his arm through mine and walked on. He seemed to be a confiding sort of person, and somehow or other I have always remarked that I possessed a supernatural power of fascination, which drew out the hearts and brains of those I met with.

"I am a stranger here," I again said; "could you give me any information on the state of religion in England?"

"Religion," said my stout friend; "humph! what's your line?"

"Line?" what could he mean? "I don't exactly understand your method of expressing yourself," I replied.

"Eh? I mean what sort do you affect?"

"Affect?" said I, "I did not know religion was a matter of affectation. In *my* day it was a very real thing, and often cost a man his life."

"Ah, poor things, overwork I suppose; should learn to take it easy, no use killing oneself for an idea."

"Idea?" more incomprehensible still. "But you have not answered my question about religion?"

"Religion?" replied my friend; "Ah, yes to be sure. Which do you prefer?"

"*Which?*" said I in amazement; "why the Christian religion to be sure."

"Yes, but there are such a lot of them," replied my friend. "High and Low, and Puseyite and Ritualist, and Papist and Baptist, and Wesleyan and Methodist, and Calvinist and Independent, and Bible Christians and . . . ."

Stop, stop," replied I, "you puzzle me more than ever; who may you be? are you a deacon?" hoping I might find a kindred spirit in my new acquaintance.

"My name's Boodle; and as to being a Deacon, I'd as soon be a chimney sweep."

I *was* astonished. To speak thus of an office I had always looked upon as one of the chiefest honours the Christian Church had to bestow. As for myself I had never considered myself worthy to fill it, but had been persuaded into accepting it by the blessed Cyril himself. He vainly tried to ordain me priest, but I considered myself too highly honoured already, and nothing would induce me to accept that awful dignity.

For a moment I forgot I was a ghost

"I was a deacon once," I said, "the deacon Irenae...." I stopped in time, "One of seven belonging to the Church of Holy Cross, and—"

"What, seven to one church?" said Boodle, "that must have been a precious long way off, we should have cut you down."

"Cut me down? There were a hundred to S. Sophia, in Constantinople."

"What, all in residence ?" asked Boodle.

"Of course;" what could he mean?

"What frightful extravagance! Reduction is the order of the day; *we* should make very short work of that. But you spoke of Holy Cross Church. Where may that be, pray?"

"In Jerusalem," I replied.

"Ha! Palestine Exploration Fund and all that; yes, I know; perhaps you were dug out with the rest?"

"Dug out with the rest ?"

"Yes, with the lamp and the dishes, and all the things they found, you know;" and off Boodle went into a Ha, ha, ha! which took him some minutes to recover.

I did not know what he meant, and thought I had met with an unfortunate man afflicted by the loss of his reasoning powers. However, as I am a ghost it did not matter to me, for should he become violent I had nothing to do but to disappear.

"But you want to know something about the last new thing in religion?"

I did not at all like his way of putting it, but thought I had better humour him, so said "Yes."

"Well, the swell thing now is to go and hear a gospel address in the Drill Hall."

"Is that a church?"

"Dear me, no; but you don't know the meaning of the word church. A church is an assembly of faithful people. Well, Delia Perkins gives the next gospel address."

"And who is Delia Perkins?"

"Delia Perkins *was*—a very wicked woman; Delia Perkins *is*—a saint."

"Poor soul! poor soul! Was her time of penance and probation long?"

"Penance? what for?"

"Why you said she sinned and then repented; she lapsed, I imagine, in the persecution. For how long was she put out of the Church?"

"Don't talk nonsense," replied Boodle, "the Church considers itself extremely honoured by having her bright eyes in it."

"But of course the priest absolved her first?"

"How provoking you are. We have none of that ritualistic nonsense here. She says she can do her own soul without any of your priests and rubbish."

"*Anon! Anon!* then will I lend her the *Treatise of S. John Chrysostom the Golden Mouthed upon the Priesthood*; it came after my time, but I doubt not I procure it, and she will see how great is the office she despises."

"Read? my dear fellow, I should like to see her do it! No one has any time to read now. By the time we have done our *Times*, and our *Pall Mall*, and our *Temple Bar*, we have read enough to float our minds for the day, and a big book sends the best of us into a fit of sulks."

"But stay; has not S. Paul a passage forbidding women to speak in the Church? Perhaps though you never heard of S. Paul?" for my mind misgave me, my informant appealing so very ignorant on some points.

"Oh, yes I have, and I know the passage you refer to. But there S, Paul speaks of the Church; now the Drill Hall isn't a church,"

"But if I understood you rightly, you said just now it is. You said a church was an assembly of faithful people. Pardon me, is not this arguing in a circle?"

"Oh bother!" replied my illogical friend, "how you worry one, I never was brought up to theology."

"Then why talk about it, if you have, no time to read about it?" Here I remembered the saying, that every Englishman considers himself born a farmer and a theologian, however ignorant he may be on every other subject.

"My dear sir, if we only talked about what we understood, our conversation would be extremely limited. But to tell you the truth, I am glad you have no fancy for the renowned Delia, for I am in reality an old fashioned Anglican, and don't approve of all these new lights. Moderation say I, moderation, and leave these frights and fervours to Happy Tommy and the rest of them."

"And who is Happy Tommy?"

"A converted collier. He tells exciting tales of how he dragged his grandmother round the room by her white hair when he was drunk and multitudes crowd to hear him, for the greater the sinner the greater the saint."

"And was this man baptized before he perpetrated these atrocities?"

"I suppose so."

I was aghast. "The Blessed Cyril would have insisted on years of lowly penitence before he readmitted him to Christian fellowship. You would have seen such a man when truly repentant fall at the feet of the faithful and implore their prayers. You would have seen him in the porch weeping scalding tears, and counting himself unworthy even to hear the prayers, much less to join in them: you would have seen"—

"Well, I don't know anything about your friend the Blessed Cyril, but I *do* know that people here I don't make such a fuss about repentance. The more atrocious the crimes, the more they like to talk about them, and the more people crowd to hear them."

"Do you not remember how we read that holy Paul, when converted, went into the wilderness for three years to fit himself to preach the gospel?"

"My dear fellow, we've got no desert here, except one of brick and mortar, and there is no glory to be gained by hiding oneself."

"Of course not. But what has a Christian to do with glory? Read Tertullian's *De Corona* and you will see, though afterwards he lapsed into heresy, how nobly and beautifully he speaks in that treatise of the glory which is our Master's alone."

"What's the gentleman's name? Tertullian? Oh, ah, something ritualistic I suppose. Tomorrow's Sunday: you had better come to *my* church, St. Silas."

"With pleasure. What hour does the great Liturgy begin?"

"Eleven o'clock."

"Surely that is rather late?"

"Not at all. Quite early enough. Some very extreme people assemble at seven or eight o'clock, but it's not considered at all the thing. In fact it's very extreme."

I thought something about the extreme of laziness, but said nothing, especially as Boodle held out his card in the kindest manner. I promised to be faithful to the appointment, and having waited till my friend had turned the corner of the street, for fear of startling him by my sudden disappearance, I dropped the intelligent stranger and subsided into the ghost.

CHAPTER 2
HOW I WENT TO CHURCH WITH BOODLE

Punctual to my appointment, I was at the door of St. Silas's a little before eleven. Crowds were streaming in at the three doors which led into the church. "This looks well," thought I, "devotion to the Christian Faith seems to have a home within this city. I wonder if they have had a persecution here lately." Boodle was late, and a roll of distant thunder from within told me that something had begun. I soon saw my fat friend puffing up the steps.

"Come along," he said, "I'm late. They don't keep seats beyond the first lesson."

"Keep seats!" I did not understand him. He spoke as if he were talking of the amphitheatre. The Gentiles always had their seats kept for them there, but I scarcely thought Christians would in this matter imitate the unbelievers: and "the lesson," lesson of what? There was no time to ask questions though, and we hurried into church. They had not yet begun, though a mighty instrument of music, perched on high, was giving forth a roll of harmony.

"Confound it," said Boodle, "they've stuffed an old woman into my seat, and I've only one, too; they might have waited a few minutes."

"*My* seat again." I was so aghast at his profane language in the holy precincts that I *could* not ask him for an explanation. But what I saw explained itself. The whole building was mapped out into little divisions with high but thin walls between. These little divisions were lined with seats, some had crimson cushions, and some had not. I imagined the thin walls were to prevent any pushing and quarrelling that might take place (for I had always heard that the English were the most pugnacious people in the world), and I also judged that the cushions were for the comforts of invalids. I could not help thinking what an advance civilization had made since my time.

My stout friend beckoned to a busy-looking gentleman in a short black gown and a stick, and told him to "put us into a seat." Now I could speedily have dispensed with the attentions of the busy gentleman by dropping the intelligent stranger and resuming the ghost, but I was again afraid of the effect such a proceeding might have upon Boodle, whose nerves I perceived were not of the strongest order. However, I saw a row of seats without backs or cushions, and I said to him, "Why cannot we sit here?"

"My dear fellow," he replied, "they are the free seats," and his tone of contempt showed me that somehow or other they "were not the thing."

"Oh, I understand," a ray of light shooting across my mind, "those are the places for the penitents; in *my* time they were not allowed to come beyond the entrance."

Boodle lifted his eyebrows, and I saw that I had said something wrong again, so I resolved to be silent and watch the service. In the meantime we had been conducted to a red-cushioned seat and the door carefully shut upon us. I thought at first we were to be locked in, for fear we might wish to go away before the proper time, but I heard no sound of the key being turned upon us.

Preceded by the busy man in the short black gown and the stick in his hand a quiet gentleman arrayed in white ascended a short wooden tower and went down on his knees within it. The other Christians took no notice of him at all and might as well have been asleep for anything they seemed to care. In a little while he got up and muttered something and then began an address, "Dearly Beloved." I thought the dearly beloved objects of his affection seemed wondrous cold in their method of returning it, for though they arose from their seats they scarcely paid any attention to him or showed any animation whatever. When Boodle got into his seat he stood for a few seconds and stuck his nose into his hat.

This curious proceeding did not seem to excite any astonishment on the part of our neighbours. The ceremony to me had no meaning, and as the Blessed Cyril had always warned us never to do anything for the sake of mere form or without a meaning, I kept to my own practice and that of my fellow-worshippers in Holy Cross, and bowing low, reverently made the sign of the Cross. I heard the rustle of a silk dress evidently shaken with rage and disgust, and saw on my right an elderly lady whose face was suffused with anger. She edged off from me with a look of indignation, and whispered to her neighbour, "Puseyite!" What *could* she mean! I looked again, for I knew old ladies were often afraid of insects, and I thought perhaps some loathsome animal of that name might have been crawling on her muff.

"Shall I catch it for you, ma'am?" I whispered as politely as possible. The old lady shook herself again and immediately changed places with her companion. These English are strange people; what could I have done to offend her! I was grieved that I should have done so, and in my distress I very nearly turned into Irenaeus the Deacon, but on the whole thought I might complicate the situation still further by so doing. The service went on. There were singings, readings, prayers, but no Amens like claps of thunder, no responses like the roaring of the sea— such as *I* remember in Jerusalem and the churches where I had

476

the honour to minister.

The attitudes, too, of the worshippers astonished me. Boodle took it easy and sat through all the prayers, and many more followed his example. Some placed their knees upon high cushions, which conveniently hoisted their bodies up until midway they leant upon the red-cushioned seats. This was called kneeling, but it did not look to me like the attitude of the penitents in Holy Cross, in the year of grace, 348. I at first did as I was accustomed to do in the church of the Blessed Cyril, and stood upon my feet as we always did on the Lord's Day and on the Forty Days after the Resurrection Day, But seeing that this created astonishment, and being anxious in all things to avoid giving offence I went down upon my knees, declining the high cushion, which would have caused the action to become an unreality.

By degrees this sleepy hind of worship came to an end; though far be it from me to speak ill of any kind of Christian observance, I cannot help calling it sleepy, for none seemed the better or the worse for it, and not a muscle of any one's countenance changed. A gentle murmur was the utmost notice bestowed a any of the petitions presented to the throne in name, and the sentiments of sorrow, penitence, joy, and hope sung for them by a few voices near the magnificent instrument of music in the gallery, seemed to wake no answering echo in their hearts.

At the end of the church against the wall and covered with red was what looked to me an altar in spite of two red cushions at each end of it. We had no cushions to recline on in the church of the Holy Cross in the year 348 at Jerusalem. I had wondered all through the service when the Great Liturgy was going to begin, for of course the altar would not then stand useless. At last the gentleman arrayed in white went to one end of the altar, and placing his elbows on the cushion hoisted himself up to his knees on a short bench before him, whilst another gentleman likewise in white did exactly the same exactly opposite to him at the other end, and with their heads in their hands and their elbows on the altar they repeated something in a gentle and monotonous tone.

Whilst this was going on someone touched my shoulder in a manner which showed me it was no denizen of earth, and I saw above me the shade of the Rev. Edward Starch of Grubbington-in-the-Clay contemplating the scene with the most sublime satisfaction. "Ah!" he said to me, and spirit voices have the gift of not disturbing an earthly congregation, "this is the true spirit of Anglicanism, see how far removed from Popish superstition on the one hand and from Puritanical baldness on the other. Look at the bright example of Primitive Christianity!"

"Reading the Ten Commandments in front of a red altar with nothing on it?" said I, as one of the reverend gentlemen advanced to the rails in front of the altar. "It is not the least like what took place in *my* time!"

Now you must know that in the Holy Shades no religions animosities exist. Each ghost has his own peculiar liking, and generally continues attached to what he loved most during his sojourn on earth, but he never considers it necessary to use bad language to the other ghosts if they should be of a different way of thinking; and such terms as vulgar Protestant and superstitious Papist are never heard amongst us. We all hope there are many different ways of looking at the same truth. So I did not feel at all angry with the ghost of the Rev. Edward Starch, but calmly nodded to it as it floated above me.

I could not help imagining what would be the feelings of that old lady in the rustling silk if she only knew how close her dainty bonnet was to the peaceful shade; and worse still, should she ever discover that the quiet gentleman on her left was the Deacon Irenaeus of the year 348. After the Gospel and the Creed, one of the sleepy clergymen aforesaid ascended the steps of a high pulpit and began his sermon. "That is good," whispered the shade of the Rev. Edward Starch, "now you see the real primitive way of doing things."

"And where are the children?" said I, "I see none." The shade pointed to a gallery at the west end, over the music gallery. It was crowded with little faces, some full of mischief, most, heavy with sleep.

"Humph!" said I, "*we* used to place them close to the altar. The Blessed Cyril always said the children were worthiest to be near it. And where are the poor? I see none."

The shade pointed to the seats for the penitents as *I* thought, and I saw about a score of persons who looked as if they wished they were anywhere else.

"Ho, every one that thirsteth come ye to the waters, and he that hath no money, come ye, buy and eat; yea, come buy wine and milk, without money and without price."

I was startled; I thought it must be another ghost making a quotation in an ironical manner: but no, it was the text of the coming sermon, and the voice was very earthly.

Could anyone have a nobler theme? One to make the heart glow and the tongue utter words of fire, to rouse the whole man to animation. I could not help thinking what the holy Cyril would have made of it. But the sleepy preacher was, if possible, more sleepy than his congregation. He told them how thankful they ought to be that they lived in such a favoured land, where every one might hear the truth if he would listen, (here the deaf old people in the far-off free seats began to fidget); how thankful they ought to be that England was England, and not any other country; how thankful they ought to be for their pastors, meaning himself, no doubt, and the other gentleman in white, who was nodding his head in the most emphatic manner inside the altar rails, whether with sleep or with assent I could not quite make out; how thankful they ought to be that grace had been given them to do right; and, in short, how thankful they ought to be they were not as other men; and, having sent most of his congregation to sleep and very nearly himself also, he brought himself up with a jerk, and abruptly concluded before that catastrophe occurred. Then returning to the Holy Table, the offerings of the faithful were collected.

"Capital!" whispered in ghostly language the shade of the Rev, Edward Starch. "Capital! They have succeeded in carrying this point. This is the great Anglican battle-ground, the prayer for the Church Militant:" as the clergy resumed their former position at the north and south end.

After the prayer and whilst I was waiting for the Liturgy to proceed, to my astonishment and the great relief of the congregation the blessing was pronounced and the assembly broke up.

"Are we to go now?" said I to Boodle.

"Go? I should think so. What more do you want? Haven't you had enough?" Boodle yawned and looked about for his hat.

"But what does all this lead up to?" said I, "if not to the Bread of Life? and how can they all fast to this hour and then go away without the Celestial Food?"

Boodle looked at me in astonishment. "You don't mean to say you think these people have had no breakfast?"

"The Faithful at Holy Cross never ate until they had had the Holy Bread, and on Wednesdays and Fridays, the stations, you know, they took no food till three in the afternoon, for the services were not over till then."

"My goodness me!" said Boodle. "And where do you say is that remarkable place?"

"In Jerusalem," I replied.

"And does Bishop Gobat approve of these ritualistic proceedings?"

"I don't know," I replied. "I don't know anything about Bishop Gobat, This was a very long long time ago. In the year. . . ." Here I stopped, remembering I am a ghost and that Boodle did not know it.

"A very long time ago? I should rather think it was," said Boodle.

"Pardon me," I whispered, slightly irritated, "Have you any business to collect the alms of the faithful and not to give them the Bread of Life? It seems to me to be all take and no give."

"All take? I should think so. It's awful humbug *I* think; but it doesn't hurt *me* much, for I never put in more than a threepenny bit."

"No doubt you feel hurt at not receiving your due: bread upon the Day of Bread. No wonder your offering is small."

"Well, to tell you the truth, I have not had what you speak of for many a long year."

"What! are you excommunicate?" asked I in horror. Suppose I had been making friends with a profane person under the ban of the church.

"My dear fellow, what are you talking of? We don't do such things now-a-days."

As we went out I said to the busy man in black, who stood at the door—

"At what hour are the Holy Mysteries celebrated in this church?"

He looked at me from head to foot and said, "Mystery? Mystery? We doesn't have nothink of that 'ere sort here. We don't believe in no mysteries whatsomdever!"

"But surely, surely the Holy Sacrifice is offered some time or other?"

"Oh, you be one of the Red letter lot be you? *We* don't 'old to none of that ritualistic nonsense."

More puzzled than ever I went on with Boodle.

As we left the holy precincts, I said to him, "Have the majority of the faithful in that church never been within the sacred walls before?"

"Why should you think so?"

"Because in the opening address such great pains were taken to explain to those present what they had come for. It began if I remember right, 'Dearly beloved.'"

"Ha! ha! ha!" said Boodle, "that has been going on no end of a time. *Whenever, wherever*, you go to church, even if you go twice every day of your life, weekdays and Sundays, you will never be allowed to say your prayers until you have heard an explanation of why you came, and what you came for. For the last 300 years that has been going on with unintermitting perseverance."

"And the poor things have not learnt it yet; what a long time it takes to din an idea into an Englishman's bead. We certainly were not so long about it in *my* day. In fact we should 'not have gone to church at all until we were quite certain why we went."

"Come along," said Boodle, "we shall just be in time to hear the crack preacher at St. Timothy's Chapel."

CHAPTER 3
"THE POPULAR PREACHER"

There was a great crowd within St. Timothy's Church, and many stood in the centre passage and in the doorway. Except the mere fact of this standing crowd I could not see anything that the least reminded me of Holy Cross Church. At the end of the building, where in my day the altar would have stood, I saw a high wooden rostrum from which a grave, thin, yellow-looking person preached. He was clothed in a mourning garment of solemn black.

"Is he doing penance for the sins of the people?" said I to Boodle.

"What are you thinking of?" he answered, "the penance is, I should say, on the side of those who listen."

The faithful here were shut four or five together between very high walls, I supposed they were the wooden walls of Old England which I had heard of since I had been in London. Boodle told me the service began later at St. Timothy's than at St. Silas's, and that the sermon from the Rev. Ebenezer Growler was quite the thing to hear. The preacher was exciting himself in a manner which did my heart good to see, for I thought such earnestness could not fail to hit the mark.

"Listen!" said Boodle, "quite a burst of eloquence." And the preacher thumped the cushion in front of him, balanced himself on his toes, and shouted—

"Take heed, brethren, of superstition! above all of that new heresy called Ritualism! remember we have no priesthood, no sacrifice."

"Good heavens!" I whispered to Boodle, "does he not remember what the blessed Andrew said when taken before the Roman Prefect. . ."

"Blessed fiddlestick!" replied Boodle, "you don't suppose a

popular preacher has time to read anything, do you?"

I was amazed. I listened with shuddering frame to an elaborate disproof of what we at Holy Cross used to call the Catholic Faith. We were exhorted by Mr. Growler *not* to attend church except on the Sabbath; *not* to believe in absolution; *not* to believe in the priesthood; *not* to believe in times and seasons; *not* to esteem one day more than another; but above all to beware of certain, churches which he named in full.

As we came out, after three quarters of an hour of this wonderful performance, I said, "Are the objectionable churches tenanted by Gnostics?"

"By what?" said Boodle.

"By adherents of the Gnostic heresy?"

"I never heard of that heresy. We've plenty here, but none of that name, that I know of, at least."

"Tell me," I asked, "are these people superstitiously devoted to the priesthood? Do they throng to the churches to confess their sins before the whole congregation? Do they crowd inconveniently to the services so that their duties in the world are seriously hindered?"

"My dear fellow, it's all you can do to get them to come to church once a week."

"Then why did he preach to them as if they were never out of it?"

"Because that sort of thing goes down. The people haven't the slightest intention of honouring the priesthood, or of flocking to the churches, or of giving alms, or of beautifying God's House, and so the Rev. Ebenezer preaches up the holiness of ugliness and the filthiness of good works, and the people love to have it so, and he is asked to three dinners every night of the week."

"But he told them it was enough to keep the Sabbath, and yet they were keeping the Lord's Day. Now the primitive Christians kept both for a long time, but by degrees left off the Jewish Sabbath. His language was a little confused."

"Don't be alarmed," said Boodle, "we haven't the slightest

intention of keeping two Sundays a week, one is quite enough. When he said the Sabbath, he meant the Lord's Day."

"When he said Saturday, he meant Sunday. Very well, I shall know another time," I meekly remarked.

Just then I saw floating close to me the shade of the Rev. Edward Starch.

"Perfectly disgusting! was it not?" muttered the ghost,

"I am not sure it was more so than your pet service at St. Silas's," I replied.

"Why so," calmly inquired the ghost.

"Because *there* the preacher took certain truths for granted, but did not act on them. There was the appearance, but not the reality. He exhorted us to attend the Eucharist, and then sent us away without it. Now the preacher at St. Timothy's told us that there was nothing in anything, and gave us nothing. St. Cyril would be very much astonished at both of them."

"Humph!" said the ghost, and quietly floated away.

Now this dialogue being spoken in spirit language was utterly inaudible to my friend Boodle; he merely thought I was looking up to see if it were going to rain.

"But tell me," I continued, as we walked along the street, "what have the churches done which excited Mr. Growler's wrath to that enormous pitch?"

"St. Chad's and St. Thurstan's and St. Ethelbert's and the others? Oh nothing that *I* can understand. As far as *I* know they have kept exactly to the directions of the Book of Common Prayer, and when there were no directions they have tried to find out what was done at the time the Book was compiled."

"That does not sound so very had. But of course Mr. Growler is very particular in following the directions of some superior authority, as he is so anxious to make others take offence at the brethren."

"Not at all. He does the whole thing in his own way, taking what he pleases and leaving out what he pleases; but people don't mind it because he gives them very little trouble, and they come out pretty much the same as when they went in. Now the man at St. Chad's is always worrying about fasting and ; and confessing your sins and the like, and people get no peace of their lives with his bother."

"That sounds more like Holy Cross," thought I.

"He is such a nuisance that Growler has set two fellows to watch him to see if he does anything actionable; he might bend his knee half an inch too low or have too many things on the altar, and then Growler would have him up before the justices in a jiffy."

"Then the persecution here has not yet ended?" I said, my spirits rising at the prospect of something like primitive Christianity. "You still hear the pagan cry, 'To the lions with the Christians.'"

"Something like it; but the curious part of it is that instead of a Pagan cry, it is now a Christian cry, and instead of the lions, it is the lion and the unicorn. But come to me next Sunday and I will show you what goes on at St, Chad's."

The kindly Boodle turned the corner, waving his hand to me; and again I saw the shade of the Rev. Edward Starch.

"You won't like St. Chad's at all," said he, "I wouldn't go there if I were you. It's not in the least like anything Charles the First saw, or Laud, or Sancroft. It's not in the least like the interior of Bishop Andrews's Chapel, in the Hierurgia Anglicana. It's not in the least like St. George's Chapel, Windsor, or St. James's, Piccadilly."

"But my dear ghost," I replied, "you forget I have nothing to do with either. I go back far beyond two hundred or even *three* hundred years. I am looking for primitive Christianity, such as I remember it in the days of the blessed Cyril."

The ghost shook his head sadly. "If you're wise," said he, "you'll keep to the use of the last three hundred years."

"*My* 300 years are as good as *yours*," said I rather cantankerously, I must own, considering that I was a ghost of 1520 years standing.

Chapter 4
Sarum Use

St. Chad's was difficult to find. It was in a poor part of the enormous town; I mean it was in that part of the town which was tenanted by the poor. Hidden by a number of sordid and densely populated buildings, the exterior presented no very striking features, but when I reached the entrance I saw at once that some sort of affinity could be claimed with Holy Cross Church at Jerusalem. The area was grand and spacious, full of seats truly, but these seats were so unpretentious and low that they did not attract the eye like those of St. Silas. There were no locks and no bolts and no doors to them. Boodle, true to his appointment, had joined me at the door, looking as if he did not like it much, but that he considered himself bound to keep his engagement.

"Well, what do you think of it?" said he, "rum looking place, ain't it?"

"More like a church than anything I've seen yet. I am pleased beyond measure at seeing such a crowd of real worshippers. But tell me who are those evil looking persons to our left?"

"Oh, they are the spies."

"Spies? are they the persons who will carry the information to the Prefect?"

"Prefect, no. Privy Council."

"And how do they execute them here, by burning, crucifixion, or wild beasts?"

"We haven't got to that yet. It's a pleasure to come. Heavy fines are the great things now."

I had always heard England was a money loving country, so I supposed this was the greatest punishment the persecutors could inflict.

"And what will these persons do?"

"Oh, they will watch narrowly to see whether the incumbent of the church bows his knee in the middle of a certain prayer, and whether he holds the chalice and paten too high, and a lot of little things you and I should never notice. But what this people hate most, the people who employ the spies, I mean, are lights on the altar, above it, or around it."

"And why?"

"Because there is an old custom that two lights shall be set on the altar to show that Christ is the Light of the World."

"And do these people say He is not the Light of the World? What odd Christians they must be! What is the name of the society who employs these spies?"

"The Society for Promoting Christianity among the Jews—no, I don't mean that, I can't remember it exactly, I think it calls itself the Church Association,"

It was a grand service certainly. The music, the animation of the priests, the devotion of the people, the want of distinction between rich and poor, the prominent position of the altar, the evident subordination of all to the great Christian Sacrifice, was refreshing to one who, like myself, was anxious to see a revival of things as they were under the blessed Cyril. At a certain point of the service a servant of the Church walked quietly up to the altar and lit the candles. I saw, a self-satisfied smirk on the part of the spies, and heard the rustle of the paper on which they wrote down their remarks.

"That'll cost *him* £500," whispered Boodle to me, looking at the priest of St. Chad's,

"And serve him right," muttered the shade of the Rev. Edward Starch as it quietly floated by me, "I never lighted *my* candles at Grubbington-in-the-Clay. I considered they looked much better unlighted."

"They certainly were much more economical," I replied.

It did not matter the least when Starch and I talked in church, because as we only used ghost language we disturbed nobody. It was another thing when Boodle began, for his remarks were so loud I had serious thoughts of suddenly becoming invisible. I was ashamed of being in his company, for no wooden walls hid us as in the other churches. The main features of the service were grand, the sermon most interesting, and rousing, but there were various little affectations that puzzled me and made me still sigh for Holy Cross and its simple majesty; everything there seemed so thoroughly *natural*, whilst at S. Chad's people seemed to be wondering whether all they were doing was in proper order.

As we came out, and we did not come out until, as at Holy Cross, all was finished and an end made of the great Christian service of the Eucharist, Boodle turned to me and said, "Now I shall introduce you to that gentleman, and place you in better hands than mine. He will just suit you, for he understands all these things. Goodbye, I must be off home to dinner. Come and dine? no! well, never mind; see you another time." We passed into the little dark cloister leading out of the Church, and standing there I saw the individual in question, whom I recognised as one of the assistant priests with whose minute and rather nervous fussy ways I had been struck. He was a tall, lantern-jawed, cadaverous looking man, stiff as an iron rod and impracticable as a thunderbolt.

"The Rev. Octagon Fidgets," murmured Boodle to me, and I heard him whisper to the person in question something about—

"Red-hot Ritualist—just your sort, you know," meaning *me*. What he meant I could not imagine, no doubt it was something very appropriate.

The Rev. Octagon Fidgets bowed, and walking with me down the street, said in a hollow voice,

"*Miserable* service, wasn't it, Mr. ——I didn't quite catch your name."

"I should think you didn't, and you're not going to now," thought I to myself. Then in answer to his question, "Miserable service?" said I, "in what way pray, sir?"

"Why, in the first place, didn't you notice the frontal was all wrong?"

"What was the matter with it?"

"It was the colour of the Sunday, red. Now you know it ought to have been the colour of the saint whose day it was, that is— yellow, Sarum yellow—for St. Swithun, Bishop and Confessor.

It is true some people have a notion that Sundays of a certain class take precedence of the Saint's Day, but that is wrong, my dear sir, totally wrong;" and the Rev. Octagon struck his foot on the kerbstone with excitement. "I tell my respected incumbent over and over again about it, but he says he has little time for these things and he must stick to broad principles, but,—hallo—hallo—what is happening to you. . . ."

At this moment, forgetting all my caution, I subsided from the visible to the invisible, and became the shadow of the deacon Irennaus. The reason was the sudden appearance of the two Church Association spies, peeping round the corner. I was so horribly nervous at their self-satisfied leer that I felt I could not face them, and I was also afraid lest a natural infirmity of temper should invite me to wreak my bodily combative powers upon them. So all things considered, I judged it better to put such a course entirety out of my own power, and their utter incapability of appreciating the invisible prevented their perceiving that a spirit was near them.

The Rev. Octagon Fidgets had a considerable insight into the other world, so he did not entirely lose sight of me. In a few words I explained to him who and what I was, and he did not even seem He said he was only "too delighted to have the opportunity of making my acquaintance." But the martinet, fussy spirit was too strong in him to allow him to pass over his grievances, and he began again.

"*Don't* you think it a horrid shame to pass over St. Swithun?"

"When did he live?" said I.

"Somewhere about nine hundred and something,"

"All that is long after my time, you see I am not a fair judge."

"You don't know anything about the Sarum yellow then?" asked the reverend gentleman in a sepulchra tone.

"Not I."

"What did you cover your altar with at Holy Cross?"

"With the best we had, generally white embroidered with

black."

"Ah! the white linen cloth you mean, but did you have that embroidered?"

"Yes; why not?"

"The Privy Council would not allow that here, the white linen cloth must be perfectly plain,"

"*We* never allowed outsiders to interfere," said I indignantly.

"And what was your altar like?"

"Not so large as yours and not so high up. A marble table on four marble legs, the drapery hanging loosely over it, not stretched tight like yours."

"Humph," muttered the curate of St. Chad's

"And can you tell me," said I turning questioner in *my* turn, "why at St. Silas's the priest stood at the end of the altar, and also at St. Timothy's, whilst at St. Chad's he stood in front of it?"

"My dear sir, have you not heard that is the question upon which half of the clergy of England are ready to tear the other half in pieces? The whole Church in this country is up in arms about the position of the priest at the altar: whether he ought to stand with his back, or his right shoulder to the people; which way did you do it?"

"Neither," said I. "The priest stood behind the altar, facing the people. But then the altar was at the west end of the church. The priest faced east and the people west,"

"Humph!" said the curate again. "We seem to have departed from primitive practice in some things."

"Certainly," I replied. "For instance, it seemed to me very strange that the Epistoller and Gospeller should have read turning away from the people."

"That is old Sarum use," said the Rev. Octagon.

A very bad use, it struck me, "What is the use of reading so that people can't hear? When *we* read the gospel or the epistle we came out into the midst of the church and read with a load and distinct voice. Then" I remarked "there was no reservation."

"Ah!" said the curate, "it will be long before people have reverence enough to resort to the Blessed Sacrament for worship."

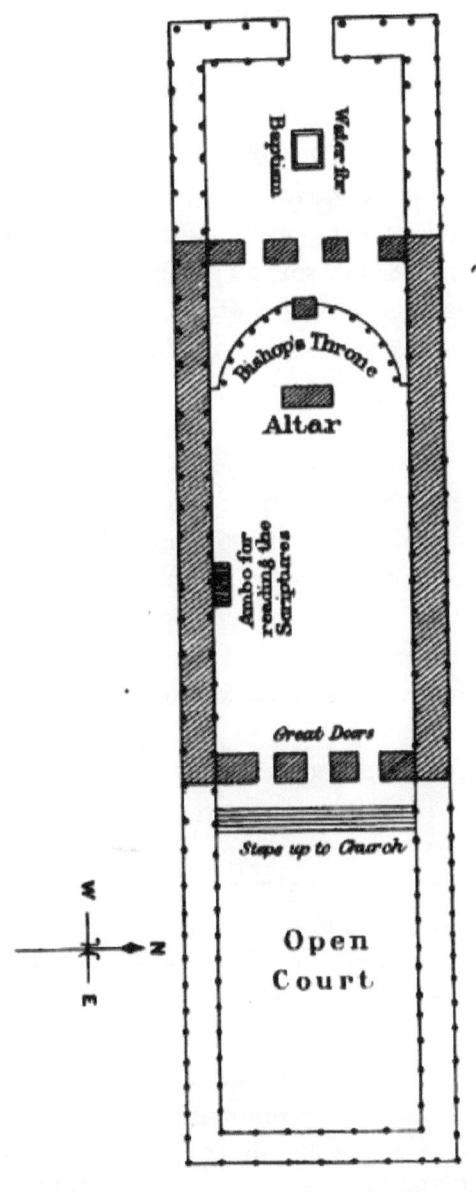

BASILICA OR CHURCH OF HOLY CROSS.

"I don't mean for worship," said I. "The reservation for purposes of worship was long after *my* time. We reserved for the sick and the absent, and sent it to them by the hands of the deacons. I was one of those happy persons who were messengers of the spiritual food—and very anxious were we that no one should be deprived of it."

"Humph!" said the Rev. Octagon again, "of course, as you were on the spot I cannot contradict you."

"Tell me too," said I, "why you shut the doors and allowed none to depart before the more solemn part of the services? I saw several most anxious to go away, and others fidgeting much."

"Because," replied the curate, "all should stay and worship. Those who depart show great irreverence towards that solemn service."

"But does it not show greater irreverence to detain the unwilling? In my time we bade all depart who were not prepared to communicate faithfully and devoutly, and diligent care was taken that there should be no irreverent gazers even in the vicinity of the holy place. No need of keeping people in by force, we were only too anxious to get rid of those who did not wish to remain. In *my* day it was esteemed too high a privilege to be forced upon anyone."

"But you would not send those away who have communicated earlier and wish to mingle their intercessions with the rest?"

"By no means. Let them stay and take their share in the priesthood of the people and in offering the holy sacrifice."

"But how?" said my friend; "you don't mean to deny that the consecration is effected by the words of Institution pronounced by the priest?"

"No; but I deny it is entirely and alone. We always esteemed it effected by three things. The pronunciation of the words Institution, the Prayer to the Holy Ghost, called the Invocation, which came after the Prayer of Consecration, and which I perceive you omit, and the Amen of the people. With *us* all three were necessary; and so you will see if you read the Liturgy of St.

James, which was used at Jerusalem."

"Oh dear me!" said the curate, "this is entirely a new light; and I thought if we went in for old Sarum we were sure to be alright."

"And I thought our Incomparable Liturgy was the model of all the primitive liturgies," said the shade of the Rev. Edward Starch as it floated down the Strand.

"No altar! No sacrifice! None of your Popery! Down with it all!" muttered the two spies, still skulking round a corner.

I was fairly puzzled as I thought over all the divisions of the most learned Church in the most religious country in the world. Certainly the blessed Cyril would have been lost in amazement, and as for me I could not find anything like the grandeur of Holy Cross Church in the year 347 or thereabouts.

One idea struck me as I prepared for flight, leaving the astonished Octagon standing on the pavement. As none of the examples I saw are exactly like what each professes to be, the image of primitive Christianity, would it not be better to leave off biting and devouring one another, and to work back by degrees to primitive models? I shall be most happy to come and show them my experiences of the same, but I do not for a moment suppose anybody will take my advice; for after all I am

ONLY A GHOST!

LEONAUR

ALSO FROM LEONAUR

AVAILABLE IN SOFTCOVER OR HARDCOVER WITH DUST JACKET

MR MUKERJI'S GHOSTS *by S. Mukerji*—Supernatural tales from the British Raj period by India's Ghost story collector.

KIPLINGS GHOSTS *by Rudyard Kipling*—Twelve stories of Ghosts, Hauntings, Curses, Werewolves & Magic.

THE COLLECTED SUPERNATURAL AND WEIRD FICTION OF WASHINGTON IRVING: VOLUME 1 *by Washington Irving*—Including one novel 'A History of New York', and nine short stories of the Strange and Unusual.

THE COLLECTED SUPERNATURAL AND WEIRD FICTION OF WASHINGTON IRVING: VOLUME 2 *by Washington Irving*—Including three novelettes 'The Legend of the Sleepy Hollow', 'Dolph Heyliger', 'The Adventure of the Black Fisherman' and thirty-two short stories of the Strange and Unusual.

THE COLLECTED SUPERNATURAL AND WEIRD FICTION OF JOHN KENDRICK BANGS: VOLUME 1 *by John Kendrick Bangs*—Including one novel 'Toppleton's Client or A Spirit in Exile', and ten short stories of the Strange and Unusual.

THE COLLECTED SUPERNATURAL AND WEIRD FICTION OF JOHN KENDRICK BANGS: VOLUME 2 *by John Kendrick Bangs*—Including four novellas 'A House-Boat on the Styx', 'The Pursuit of the House-Boat', 'The Enchanted Typewriter' and 'Mr. Munchausen' of the Strange and Unusual.

THE COLLECTED SUPERNATURAL AND WEIRD FICTION OF JOHN KENDRICK BANGS: VOLUME 3 *by John Kendrick Bangs*—Including twor novellas 'Olympian Nights','Roger Camerden:A Strange Story', and ten short stories of the Strange and Unusual.

THE COLLECTED SUPERNATURAL AND WEIRD FICTION OF MARY SHELLEY: VOLUME 1 *by Mary Shelley*—Including one novel 'Frankenstein or the Modern Prometheus', and fourteen short stories of the Strange and Unusual.

THE COLLECTED SUPERNATURAL AND WEIRD FICTION OF MARY SHELLEY: VOLUME 2 *by Mary Shelley*—Including one novel 'The Last Man', and three short stories of the Strange and Unusual.

THE COLLECTED SUPERNATURAL AND WEIRD FICTION OF AMELIA B. EDWARDS *by Amelia B. Edwards*—Contains two novelettes 'Monsieur Maurice', and 'The Discovery of the Treasure Isles', one ballad 'A Legend of Boisguilbert'and seventeen short stories to cill the blood.